… greatly enjoyed it'
NELSON DEMILLE

'Pike ranks right up there with Jason Bourne,
Jack Reacher and Jack Bauer'
JOHN LESCROART

'Logan is a tough, appealing hero you're sure to root for'
JOSEPH FINDER

'Fresh plot, great actions, and Taylor clearly knows
what he is writing about'
VINCE FLYNN

'Few authors write about espionage, terrorism,
and clandestine hit squads as well as Taylor does'
*HOUSTON PRESS*

'Taylor is one of today's premiere authors writing
about the world of special ops'
*ASSOCIATED PRESS*

'Mesmerizing . . . [Taylor] adds his trademark rapid-fire
pace and action scenes that rival the best
of Brad Thor and Vince Flynn'
*PROVIDENCE JOURNAL*

# AMERICAN TRAITOR

BRAD TAYLOR, Lieutenant Colonel (Ret.), is a twenty-one-year veteran of the U.S. Army Infantry and Special Forces, including eight years with the 1st Special Forces Operational Detachment—Delta, popularly known as Delta Force. Taylor retired in 2010 after serving more than two decades and participating in Operation Enduring Freedom and Operation Iraqi Freedom, as well as classified operations around the globe. His final military post was as assistant professor of military science at The Citadel.

**Also by Brad Taylor**

**The Taskforce Novels**

*One Rough Man*
*All Necessary Force*
*Enemy of Mine*
*The Widow's Strike*
*The Polaris Protocol*
*Days of Rage*
*No Fortunate Son*
*The Insider Threat*
*The Forgotten Soldier*
*Ghosts of War*
*Ring of Fire*
*Operator Down*
*Daughter of War*
*Hunter Killer*

**The Taskforce Novellas**

*The Callsign*
*Gut Instinct*
*Black Flag*
*The Dig*
*The Recruit*
*The Target*
*The Infiltrator*
*The Ruins*
*Exit Fee*

# AMERICAN TRAITOR

*An Aries Book*

First published in the UK in 2021 by Head of Zeus Ltd
This paperback edition first published in 2021 by Head of Zeus Ltd
An Aries book



9 7 5 3 1 2 4 6 8

A catalogue record for this book is available from
the British Library.

ISBN (PB): 9781838937775
ISBN (E): 9781838937782

Typeset by Divaddict Publishing Solutions Ltd

Printed and bound in Great Britain by
CPI Group (UK) Ltd, Croydon CR0 4YY

Head of Zeus Ltd
First Floor East
5–8 Hardwick Street
London EC1R 4RG

WWW.HEADOFZEUS.COM

*For the first responders during the initial trying times of COVID. From the medical workers to the person ringing up my groceries, this book would never have been finished without you.*

All warfare is based on deception. Hence, when we are able to attack, we must seem unable; when using our forces, we must appear inactive; when we are near, we must make the enemy believe we are far away; when far away, we must make him believe we are near.

—Sun Tzu, *The Art of War*

A lie will travel round the world while the truth is putting on its boots.

—C. H. Spurgeon

# 1

*April 9, 2019, Misawa, Japan*

Jake Shu saw the afterburners kick in, the flight of four F-35 Lightning II aircraft leave the gravity of earth and head into the night sky. It was but one of many flights leaving the airbase, a stream of lights bursting into the night one after the other, some headed out over the Pacific Ocean, others over the Sea of Japan, but this one was special. Special to him.

The cold began to seep in under his trousers, an unrelenting contact from the iron park bench he was sitting on, as if it was asking him to leave. But he could not. He had a mission here, and he would see it through.

The airbase in Misawa was about as far north in Japan as one could get on the main island, leaving him in the upper echelons of cold weather on the spit of land, but the April chill wasn't bad enough to drive him inside. He was too invested in a small bud in his ear.

Connected to a scanner tuned to the open-net air traffic control frequencies emanating from the tower behind him, he was listening intently. So much so he actually had a bead of sweat on his brow in the forty-degree air. Like a scientist conducting an experiment in a controlled environment, he was unable to alter the outcome once it was started, but he wanted to see the results. All that remained was to watch and wait. Or in his case, listen.

The initial contact from the aircraft sounded normal, which was not what he wanted to hear. He had a lot invested in this particular experiment, and if it didn't work, he would be the one paying the bill.

The F-35 jet, known as the "Lightning II," was the most advanced fighter aircraft ever envisioned. Capable of unimaginable things, from stealth penetration to combat control of synchronized drones, it was unstoppable. With construction on each airframe ongoing in more than twelve countries all over the world, it was the finest fighter aircraft ever to take to the skies. The ultimate killing machine, but it had an Achilles' heel.

Jake worked for a company called Gollum Solutions, a subcontractor of a subcontractor for BAE Systems—a common occurrence in the byzantine world of military procurement. You'd be hard pressed to find a military contractor who didn't take the profits first and then subcontract out, but in this case the subcontracting company's name had a double meaning.

It was derived from the riddle of the ring in J. R. R. Tolkien's novels. Built solely to gain the contract for the F-35, Gollum Solutions promised to solve the riddle through software, and in so doing make the F-35 invisible. Just as the ring could do. As enticingly clever as the name was, what the owners never realized was that there were two sides to the ring, and they would pay a price for it.

The ring in Tolkien's world was corrupting, with anyone who wore it turning against his nature to serve a different master, and the name Gollum would prove prophetic. Which is where Jake Shu came in. A Chinese American, he was well placed to create havoc for money. A Gollum in his own right, he had worn the proverbial ring, and had been corrupted.

Two months ago, he'd been detailed from his company in Australia to the F-35 final assembly plant in Japan—an unexpected advantage. Japan had the only such plant outside of the United States, with all other F-35s being built in Fort Worth, Texas, and because of it he had an opportunity.

He'd helped with the byzantine assembly process, his expertise being in software integration. He'd done the job he was asked—along with a bit more—and was now wondering if it had worked.

Sitting in the cold outside the control tower, now it was time to see if his inject actually mattered, because a human being was behind the controls. At the end of the day, he could alter the sensors of the plane, but the pilot was king. And yet that man only did what his sensors told him to do. At least that's what Jake hoped.

His inject was simple: Change what the pilot thought was correct. There was ample reason to believe that his alterations would work. Plenty of pilots crashed because they thought one thing and the unforgiving earth thought another. The difference in those cases was that they chose to disbelieve what their instruments were telling them.

What if the instruments themselves were telling the pilot something different?

The helmet of the F-35 was a monstrosity—a four-hundred-thousand-dollar piece of gear that offered the pilot innumerable feeds, showing him everything that was occurring within his airspace. He could read the world in real time, gaining an unrivaled capability to defeat anything that chose to fight. The pilot read all of those feeds and trusted them explicitly. And it was all software driven.

The pilot controlled cameras that could detail everything around the aircraft, allowing him a 360-degree view that would be impossible without the helmet. He had feeds telling him every threat near the aircraft within a hundred miles. He had sensors that detailed when to fire his weapons, only locking on when the computer told him it was correct, giving him an unparalleled ability to prevent collateral damage in modern warfare. He had more control over his destiny than any pilot in history.

But what if what he was seeing was wrong? If his actual experience wasn't what was happening? What if his helmet told him one thing, and reality was another?

Jake heard the control tower say, "Comet four-two, Comet four-two, go to thirty-one five. Inbound aircraft at thirty-seven."

He heard, "Yes. Understood."

He waited with bated breath, conflicted. If this worked, he was murdering a person he'd never met.

He heard, "Comet four-two, you just passed through twenty thousand feet. I instructed thirty-one five. Are you understanding?"

Most of the Japanese airbases used by the United States were manned and operated solely by Americans, a symbiotic relationship that Japan allowed because the country fell under the U.S. umbrella of protection. Misawa was different. It was the only combined airbase in the Pacific theater run jointly by both Japanese and U.S. personnel, and as such, had been chosen as the base for the first Japanese F-35s to showcase the partnership between the two countries. Jake knew that the men inside the control tower were Japanese, as was the man in the aircraft. They spoke English, because that was the air traffic control language the world over, but it was still a little surreal. Especially since he wasn't Japanese.

The pilot responded, a little miffed, "Yes. Knock it off."

Jake heard nothing for a pregnant second, and then the voice from the tower showed its first bit of urgency. "You've passed through fifteen thousand at five hundred knots. Acknowledge."

"I understand. I have it."

Nothing more. Then the voice from the tower became frantic. "You're at two thousand feet and going six hundred knots. Acknowledge. Acknowledge."

Jake waited, but heard nothing else. He knew the radar track ended at one thousand feet. He stood up, glanced left and right, and then saw the first indicator of his success—five men rushing out of the tower. He waited a beat, then sat back down, wanting to hear the tower's calls.

There was nothing else broadcast, the plane lost to radar intercept at one thousand feet. The recovery of the aircraft would take four months, the body of the pilot itself not found until a month after that, with the United States concerned that the Chinese would attempt to find the top-secret information lying on the ocean floor.

The final report was that the pilot had experienced spatial disorientation flying over the Pacific Ocean at night, where the horizon and the ocean joined seamlessly into one. There was a lot of chatter among the pundit class about the Chinese stealing the vaunted technology of the F-35 by submarine or other means, but they failed to realize that the Chinese had no intention of diving into the depths of the Pacific for technology that had been destroyed by a plane flying at six hundred knots straight into the ocean. Why should they?

Since Mao Tse-Tung, they had been the masters of

unconventional warfare, and this was just one more moment of their success. Why find an aircraft at the bottom of the ocean to learn its secrets when you can make every single one of them irrelevant?

Jake dialed a number on his cell phone and said, “It’s done. And I think it worked.”

# 2

*December 2019*

Amena spiked the ball and I dove for it, barely able to get it back into the air. A floater that I knew she was going to smash. She leapt up and hammered it again with a little bit of rage. I didn't even try, watching it bounce away. I looked at her and said, "Really?"

She gave me a little impish grin and said, "I thought your reflexes were quicker. Sorry."

We were in our small driveway on a narrow lane in Charleston, without even a net, and I knew she'd done it on purpose. All we were supposed to be doing was tapping the ball back and forth, like before a volleyball game, and she had decided to turn it into a contest. I wasn't sure if it was because she was mad about being forced to leave the house, or upset at herself for agreeing to the plan in the first place.

At thirteen years old, she was taller than most girls her age and was pretty athletic. I'd decided to get her interested in volleyball, because the school she was set to attend had a pretty good team. I'd paid for a couple of lessons, and in so doing had turned her into a monster.

A refugee from Syria, I'd collided with Amena on a mission in Europe after her family had been slaughtered by some very bad men. She'd ended up being pretty critical to saving a lot of lives, and after the loss of her family, she was all alone. So I'd brought her back to America after it was over. Okay, that sounds like I'd gone through the wickets with the U.S. Department of State to introduce a foreign refugee into America, but I hadn't. I'd basically smuggled her into the country using a covert aircraft belonging to the organization I worked with.

Called Project Prometheus in official top-secret traffic—but just the Taskforce to all of us minions—its sole mission was protecting the United States from attacks that others in the Department of Defense or the CIA couldn't prosecute, which is to say it operated outside of legal bounds. And therein lay the problem.

I'd basically turned an enormous covert infrastructure into my own personal coyote operation, but instead of bringing a load of Salvadorans across the Rio Grande in the back of a pickup, I'd flown Amena into the United States on a Gulfstream jet leased to my company. It was bad form all the way around, not the least because it could have exposed the entire organization, and with it our less than stellar following of the U.S. Code, but she was worth it. She had prevented a catastrophic attack at the United Nations headquarters in Geneva, Switzerland, and she'd deserved the rescue.

Of course, the higher-ups in the Taskforce hadn't taken that view. Called the Oversight Council, they supervised all Taskforce activity, approving each mission on a case-by-case basis. Except for this one. When they found out what I'd done, they tried to slip her back out of the country and introduce her into the refugee flow out of Syria, but I was having none of that. The odds of her ever showing back up in the United States were marginal at best, and she'd earned the right to be here, regardless of the less than legal means I'd used.

Amena ran into the bushes beside the driveway and grabbed the ball, knowing I wasn't going to chase it after that hit. She handed it to me and said, "If this isn't a honeymoon, why can't I go?"

I took the ball, knowing she was playing me. I said, "It's not a damn honeymoon. Quit saying that. You can't go because you have school. You've been begging to go to school for months, and today's the day."

"But that was before you taught Jennifer to SCUBA dive. Before you planned a trip to Australia. Before the choice was being stuck inside your house or going to school. Now it's going to Australia or going to school. I'd rather go to Australia. Unless this is a honeymoon for you two . . ."

In the end, me and the National Command Authority of the United States agreed to a compromise, which is a polite way of saying I took on the president of the United States over Amena's fate. It had been a little bit of a fight, but they'd agreed to wash her documents as having been sponsored by a global company that engaged in worldwide protection of antiquities. A company that was a do-gooder on the world stage, protecting what was honorable and just in the sands of history. My company, Grolier Recovery Services. It was a unique solution, because in truth, while my company did in fact run around the world saving old pottery shards, its sole purpose was to put a bad guy's head on a spike. But I'd agreed.

The sticking point was that the sponsor had to be something more than a company. It had to be a family unit, with actual names. Which is where Jennifer Cahill, my partner in crime, came in.

If I had a Facebook page, under relationships it would say, "It's complicated." Jennifer and I were business partners first and foremost, but we were definitely more than that, if either one of us had the courage to admit it. We'd danced around the commitment to our relationship for years, sometimes falling back onto just the business partner side of things, but always with the benefits side of the house, if you get my meaning.

My feelings had slipped out on occasion, as had hers, but we'd conveniently forgotten those instances, like an embarrassed family member who doesn't discuss what the drunk uncle blurted out at Thanksgiving.

The truth was I loved her and had just been too damaged to commit—and she had been the same way. Amena had short-circuited all of that angst, forcing us to face reality. Something I was happy about, but I wasn't so sure about Jennifer.

Because of the immediacy of her situation, Jennifer and I had actually tied the knot at the justice of the peace, becoming officially married, but Jennifer thought it had a veneer of corruption around it. When she'd said "I do," she'd expected a wedding, but there wasn't any time for that. We needed to be a family unit immediately—but she was still expecting a ceremony. Which is what Amena was talking about. We couldn't be taking a honeymoon when we hadn't had an official wedding ceremony.

I batted the ball to her, saying, "Stop that talk. You'll just get Jennifer wound up. You're going to school, and we're going to Australia. It's just a vacation."

The truth of the matter was we were leaving the country solely to make Amena rely on the boarding school she was attending. In effect, to take away her ability to call us every night or come running home for support. I was forcing some tough love, but I couldn't tell her that.

She hit the ball back, this time with a soft lob setup, and I leapt up and smashed it, driving it past her head and causing her to flinch, the volleyball bouncing into the street behind her. I hit the ground grinning and then heard, "What in the world was that? Are you crazy?"

Amena now sported her own grin, knowing I was going to have my ass handed to me. I turned around and saw Jennifer on the stoop of our Charleston single with a suitcase, looking like she wanted to gut me.

I said, "Hey, wait a minute. You didn't see what she did earlier. I was just acting like a front line on the court . . . She asked me to do it."

With a pious look, Amena said, "It's hard practicing with him. He is very mean."

My mouth fell open and Amena broke into a smile, chasing after the ball. She came back, stood next to me, and gave me a small hip bump, both of us looking at Jennifer, waiting on the pain. Jennifer shook her head and said, "I can't deal with two children. One is enough. Help me with the suitcase."

Amena lost her smile and said, "Why can't I come with you guys? If it's not a honeymoon?"

Digging into her purse for her car keys, Jennifer looked up in surprise and said, "Honeymoon? Who said that?"

She looked at me and I pointed to Amena, then picked up the suitcase, hustling to get out of the blast radius.

Jennifer said, "Amena, go inside and make sure you've got everything you need. You won't be able to come back here until we return in a couple of weeks."

Amena scowled, but unlike she would do with me, she listened to Jennifer and went back inside.

Jennifer came over to me and said, "What was that about?"

Cramming the last suitcase into the back of her little Mini Cooper, juggling the other bags, I said, "I'm getting that Jeep I saw online yesterday. I don't care how much they're charging. This is a clown car."

My ancient Jeep CJ-7 had been destroyed almost a year ago, and we still hadn't replaced it because I was a picky shopper and hadn't found one I liked, forcing both of us to use her little midget vehicle. But my attempt to deflect the question fell on deaf ears.

She repeated, "What's Amena talking about?"

I sighed, closed the hatchback, and said, "She thinks she can't go because I'm taking you on a honeymoon. That's it. She came up with it all on her own."

Jennifer snorted. "We're not having a honeymoon until we have a real wedding. You can't weasel out of that by taking me to Australia and then calling it a honeymoon after the fact."

I raised my hands and said, "That's not from me. That's from her. I didn't say a word. You know the only reason we're going is to get her settled at school. That's it."

Amena came out carrying a small satchel and Jennifer squinted at me. I lowered my voice and said, "Enough talk about why we're going."

Jennifer whispered, "If you think going to Australia and hanging out with some old Taskforce guys is my idea of a honeymoon, you've got another thing coming."

I grinned and said, "Hey, he's giving us a free place to stay. We're diving the reef. That was *your* idea."

Amena came up and asked, "So? Is it a honeymoon?"

Jennifer looked at me and I said, "No, it's not. We can't have that until after a proper ceremony."

"What's a proper ceremony? You guys go to Australia and I'll never see you again."

Jennifer laughed. "That's not going to happen."

I said, "What are you talking about? We'll be back in two weeks."

She became earnest. "Trouble follows you. It always has. You're going to get in trouble. And I'll be left alone."

I knelt down and said, "That's not going to happen, doodlebug. It's not."

She took my hands and said, "You promise?"

"I do. It's just a vacation. That's all."

She looked into my eyes and said, "Until the bad man shows up."

And I knew what she was telling me. She'd seen the bad man more than once, and was convinced it was the natural way of things. The bad man just always showed up.

I said, "Don't worry about that. You're in the United States. The bad man is gone."

I saw her eyes tear up and she said, "The bad man is always there. Even here. Don't leave me to him."

It broke my heart. I hugged her and said, "Hey, come on. There is nobody out to get you here. You're going to be in good hands. It's what you wanted."

She broke my embrace, looked into my eyes, and asked, "If the bad man finds you on vacation, you'll kill him, right? Come back to me?"

That took me aback. What kid thinks her parents are going to be attacked on vacation, and then wishes that the parents would kill the attackers? For the first time I realized that this was more than just a foster-parent relationship. We were never going to have a normal family, because we most decidedly weren't normal, as much as we wanted to be. She'd seen me operate—had seen me kill—but because of her love for me, she couldn't get it around her head that I was, in fact, worse than the evil she'd encountered. There was nothing on earth that would keep me from protecting her.

I looked at Jennifer and saw a tear in her eye. I hugged Amena and leaned into her ear, whispering, "I *am* the bad man. Remember that."

# 3

Yu-Feng "Paul" Kao didn't consider himself a bad man. When he looked in the mirror, he didn't see a trace of evil, but he was doing something bad now. And he knew it.

As an officer in the National Security Bureau of Taiwan—a combination of the United States' FBI and CIA—he had a duty to protect Taiwan. And sometimes that duty led to doing unpleasant things.

Tall and lithe, he had a shock of jet-black hair and an angular face full of sharp contours. His visage looked as if it were perpetually at stage three of a four-stage sketch, the drawing taken away before the artist was allowed to smooth over the rough edges.

He pulled into the tourist parking lot at the Shifen Falls, about an hour east of his headquarters in Taipei, dodging the engorged tour buses and the myriad of pedestrians wandering about like cattle. He found a spot away from the crowds and turned off the engine.

He turned to his passenger and said, "You ready to go?"

A young man with fear in his eyes, the person next to him said, "I guess so. What do I do if he attacks me?"

"He won't attack. He wants what you have. He wants to make some money. Just don't forget your cover story. Whatever you do, use the name Feng Main. Don't slip up and give him your true one. That'll be a deal breaker."

The kid nodded, seeming unsure. Paul patted his arm and said, "It'll be okay. Just don't forget to turn on the recorder. Get what he has to say, give him the money, and keep acting like you're a conduit from the PRC. He wants to believe. He wants the pipeline to continue. I'll wait right here."

The kid looked up sharply and said, "You'll wait here? Am I alone? Shouldn't we have more cops here? More people to help? Once I'm in the park, I'll be on my own."

"We already have people in there. If he tries anything, we'll be all over him. But don't force that. I need him to continue. I want to break open the entire network."

The kid nodded vaguely. Paul waited a moment, then leaned back and said, "What's your name?"

Hesitantly, the kid said, "Feng. My name is Feng Main."

"What do you do?"

With more courage, he continued, "I'm a university student. I'm a student."

"Who do you work for?"

Like a robot, devoid of fear, he said, "The People's Republic of China. The Ministry of State Security."

"Good. Stick to the truth and it'll be okay."

The kid opened the door, took one look back, and left, walking toward the bridge spanning the river by the Shifen Falls. Paul watched him go and prayed he'd make it back. Not just because of the case he was building, but because he honestly felt a little twinge of guilt for sending him in. There were no other operatives in the park. If something went wrong, the kid was on his own.

Feng Main was, in fact, a university student. A stupidly naïve Taiwanese native who had been approached by the People's Republic of China to foment insurrection inside Taiwan. The tradecraft had been sloppy and the payouts easy to find, so much so that it scared Paul. If the masters in Beijing from the Guoanbu—the Ministry of State Security—were this sloppy with Feng, it meant they just didn't care what he did. Which meant he was an afterthought, and Paul was missing the real penetration.

The PRC's MSS intelligence service was the largest in the world by far. It had tentacles that reached throughout the globe, and a history of successfully hiding what it did because it blended traditional trained operatives with people from the Chinese diaspora. It was impossible to tell whether someone was a real Chinese agent or just some immigrant with ties to the homeland whom they'd co-opted. And the MSS was very good at its mission.

Russia eliminating double agents with nuclear poison in London? Amateur stuff. North Korea killing the half brother of the leader with a nerve agent in Malaysia? Ridiculously overt. The MSS would never even have been mentioned. They were a controlled beast, without emotion, like a wall of water directed at a rock. They had no fear, no pity, and no sense of failure. Eventually, Paul knew, the rock would lose. His job was to turn off the water.

After the unrest in Hong Kong and the explicit indications that the MSS had been operating inside the city since before the riots, Paul had been directed to ferret out Taiwan's own hidden threat. In short order, he'd found Feng. And it hadn't been hard. Which made him question what he was missing. Clearly, the MSS hadn't put a lot of stock in the success of Feng. But they *had* recruited him to interface with the Bamboo Triad, and that would be enough to help.

The Bamboo Triad was a criminal gang not unlike the Cosa Nostra, an organized crime ring solely concerned with profit, running everything from prostitution to drugs in

Taiwan—with one exception: They also worked for the MSS to destabilize Taiwan.

Paul watched the kid disappear on the path and felt a pang of guilt. Maybe the MSS had been sloppy for a reason. Maybe they were trying to ferret out his own security service's reach. If that was the case, the kid was dead, but that alone would provide some help for Paul. He wouldn't be able to penetrate whatever plan the Triad had in play, but at least Feng's death would prove that the MSS had penetrated his own organization somehow.

It would be a small consolation to Feng, but sometimes bad things had to happen to protect the nation.

The kid reached the pedestrian bridge crossing the river and took one look back. Paul saw it, but ignored the fear spilling out. Feng disappeared, and Paul settled in to wait.

He would be waiting a long time.

# 4

Feng hesitantly walked across the footbridge, getting run over by kids and grandparents all marching to the falls. A light drizzle began to fall, coating him in a dusting of water. The other tourists began breaking out umbrellas, forcing him to dodge the spines. He slipped past one, hit another pedestrian with his back, apologized, and then was yelled at for stepping into a selfie picture attempt on the bridge. The encounters frazzled him.

He continued walking in a daze, wondering how his life had gone so wrong. He wasn't the only university student who had been approached by the PRC for help. They were brazen in their attempts, just as they were with the state-run television stations and every other aspect of Taiwanese life. The PRC was everywhere, and he still didn't understand how he'd been picked up when everyone else was doing it, and none of it was harmful as far as he could tell. Just small things, really.

He'd gotten money to spread stories accusing the incumbent government of corruption, or talking about how China had only helped Taiwan. Nothing but social media posts, and he was paid good money to do them. Then the PRC had asked him to do something more, and he'd agreed. More good money. It wasn't like it affected anything in Taiwan. He still heard his parents and grandparents bitching about Beijing, so it wasn't as if he were altering the balance of power, even with the presidential elections happening in January, three short months away.

And then he'd been put in touch with a man called the Snow Leopard. A leader inside the infamous Bamboo Triad. A completely criminal organization that was continually tracked by the police for drugs, prostitution, extortion, you name it. Only now they'd formed a political party, giving them protection for their political actions under the constitution of Taiwan while also giving them cover as being "persecuted" for their "political" beliefs. Called the Chinese Unification Promotion Party, it took all its direction from Beijing, and was a small but growing presence inside Taiwan, with a stated goal of allowing the PRC to absorb Taiwan.

Feng had put no thought into the Triad's control of CUPP because, honestly, politics bored him. Unlike his parents, who had had to practice air-raid drills as children, or his grandparents, who were convinced that every day was their last, he'd grown up in a democracy. It was unfathomable to him that a giant country like China would do anything against his little island. Which is why he took the money. It was all harmless.

Until it wasn't.

When Paul had first knocked on his door, a file of evidence on his misdeeds in hand, Feng's heart had dropped to his stomach. He was no master spy, and he'd immediately admitted everything he'd done, professing it was harmless. All he'd wanted was a little money, and nothing he'd done was that bad. It wasn't like he was selling state secrets. Just some social media stuff, which was allowed in Taiwan. What had he done that was criminal?

And then he'd been shown the last exchange, where he'd

actually transported money and dropped it off in a trash can. He'd protested, saying he had no idea where the money had come from or why he was delivering it. It was just another avenue for cash, and he'd done it. Paul had shown him how the money had ended up financing propaganda at a state-run television station, and Feng had become queasy, finally asking what Paul wanted him to do. He couldn't bring shame on his family, and he most certainly couldn't be outed as a Chinese spy. And now he was going to meet a member of the most brutal Triad on the island, ostensibly to get the man to commit to treason so Paul could rip the Triad apart.

It was a far cry from posting a couple of social media posts.

He reached the other side of the bridge, walked through the crowds surrounding various food stands. The rain began to pick up, but the children were still tromping about, riding metal horses and bench swings, running about through a mix of locals and foreign tourists.

He kept going, reaching the stairway to the lower viewing level, his breath starting to come in small gasps. He descended for what seemed like an hour, one switchback of stairs after another, all of them built into the rock face leading to the viewing platform. He reached the bottom and saw the giant granite wall to his front, the water spilling out like a miniature Niagara Falls. He glanced around and found that the metal stairs he had been using were grafted onto the old, ancient ones carved out of the stone, back when the miners came here for relaxation. They went right, behind the rocks to the river, but the new path led to the left, toward the viewing area.

He went that way, seeing the falls spilling out to his front. Ordinarily there would be a huge crowd fighting for selfies with the falls as a background, but the rain had put a damper on that. There was only a smattering of people in the overhang, and a single man sitting on a bench, ignoring the waterfall.

Feng hesitantly went forward, circling a family taking pictures, an umbrella blocking all of the shots from the falls. He approached and saw a man of about sixty, with salt-and-pepper hair, a thin mustache, and cruel eyes. It wasn't until he came close that he noticed a vicious scar circling his neck, like someone had tried to slit his throat and had missed.

The man looked up from his newspaper and said, "Feng?"

Feng nodded, and the man stood, saying, "Follow me."

As soon as his back was turned, Feng turned on the recording device, and then began to follow. They left the viewing area, going back the way Feng had come, but when the staircase began rising against the cliffs, the man took the old route. The one carved right into the rock. Feng looked around him, trying to spot the protection he had in the sparse people around, but saw no one who resembled a policeman. He wondered if they were hidden in the cliffs.

Feng continued following, and within minutes they were lost to the tourists, crossing over the rock wall and walking along the land next to the river, the expanse of stone blocking the view from the official tourist path. They descended into a small bowl, the waterfall lost from sight, and he saw two other men waiting, both of them squatting on their haunches like they were cooking dinner at a camp, a spilling of cigarette butts at their feet. They had been waiting awhile.

One had tattoos covering his face. The other had a narrow smile with gaps in his teeth that reminded Feng of a snake's jaw, but what drew Feng's eyes were his hands. They looked like they'd been dipped in acid, the skin misshapen as if melted wax had been poured over them. Feng felt the adrenaline rise, once again wondering about his police protection.

The man leading him felt the reticence and said, "I'm Chao Zheng. The Snow Leopard. Do not worry. Come."

Feng descended deeper into the bowl, shoved his hands in his pockets, and waited. The two men rose and circled him, until he was in a ring of them. The Leopard said, "You have the money?"

Feng shrugged a messenger bag off of his shoulder and lowered it to the ground, saying, "Yes, yes. But it must be used in a certain way."

The Leopard said, "I know. A very special way. But not the one you intended."

Feng said, "What?"

The Leopard pulled out a knife and said, "Not the way you intended. You claim to work for China, but you don't. I'll take the money, but it will be used for them, not what you wanted."

Feng said, "Wait, what? I'm here because you asked for me. I'm just the messenger. I'm a nobody."

"Take off your shirt."

And Feng knew he was dead. He didn't move. The tattooed man leapt forward and ripped his shirt upwards, exposing the recording device. Feng began to tremble, looking wildly around for a police presence that wasn't coming.

He said, "It's not me. I was captured. I was just doing what I was told."

The Snow Leopard leaned forward and said, "You're good at doing what you're told, yes?"

"Yes, yes, yes. I'll set them up for you, if you want. I'll do what you ask."

The tattooed man trapped his hands behind his back,

torqueing his arms up until he yelped. Feng said, "I'm not against you. I can help! I'm on the inside now. They think I'm with them. But I'm not."

The man with melted hands grabbed him by the hair, jerking him off balance to the water. He fell to his knees, looking up at the Snow Leopard, the river rushing by a foot in front of him. He said, "Please, I can help."

"I'm sure you can. I believe you. You'll do what I ask?"

"Yes, yes. I promise."

The Leopard nodded at the tattooed man and said, "I'm asking you to not hold your breath. This has to look like an accident, and it takes a lot longer if you do."

Feng sprang up, and was immediately shoved back onto his knees, the mud seeping through his clothes. He flailed his arms above his head, trying to break the hold on his neck, but failed. He shrieked, the sound lost in the rushing of river water. He felt his head being lowered, shouted, "No, no, no!" and then it went under the surface. He fought valiantly, then weakly, then his body went slack. The Leopard watched him struggle with the detachment of someone drowning a cat in a bag. When it was done, he pushed Feng's body into the current of the river, the carcass bobbing away from him.

He said, "So it's true. We've been penetrated somehow."

Acid hands said, "Maybe we should back off for a little bit."

The Snow Leopard picked up the satchel, opened it, then said, "Maybe we should ramp it up. Quit hiding. Take it to them for a change."

He turned to the tattooed man and said, "It's not like we don't have the support."

# 5

I saw Amena react to what I'd said about being the bad man, and realized I'd made a mistake. I really didn't want to give her any worries about being in the danger zone, like we were leaving her to the wolves, and my comment was not a way to start a new relationship—especially given her past.

It was a missed opportunity. Something I was famous for, at least in my own mind. But it didn't matter what I said. It only mattered what she thought. She leaned back from my hug and said, "You mean that? You'll take care of the bad man if he comes?"

Standing behind her, Jennifer said, "What? What was that? What did Pike say?"

I grinned and tried to cover up the comment. "Nobody is going to hurt you now. Ever. We're here for you. It's a new life."

She teared up again and said, "I want to go with you. For the honeymoon."

Jennifer knelt down next to me, giving Amena the full force of her love. She took her hands and said, "We're not going on a honeymoon. I don't know how you got that in your head."

Jennifer left her eyes and glared at me, saying, "We won't have a honeymoon until after a formal ceremony." She turned to Amena and said, "With you as a bridesmaid."

Amena's eyes widened, now broken from the previous

discussion, amazed at the invitation. She said, "Really? Like an American wedding?"

She looked at me, and I said, "Of course, doodlebug."

She turned to Jennifer for confirmation and Jennifer said, "I wouldn't want it any other way."

And that was enough.

Amena was one complicated young woman, not the least because she'd had her mother murdered in Syria, and then saw the rest of her family slaughtered in Europe by a group of assholes who deserved to be planted in the ground. At the time, I'd become a farmer of sorts, planting all of them with extreme prejudice, but what had stuck with me was Amena herself. And it wasn't misguided sympathy I saw in her, but her moral core.

I wouldn't go so far as to say she was a Mother Teresa, because she had a little pirate in her, but then again, that's what I truly loved about her. She wanted a family more than anything on earth, and we were trying hard to make it happen. At the end of the day, she was still raw, unsure of who to trust, which was why I was paying a fortune for a private boarding school.

Grolier Recovery Services was headquartered in Charleston, South Carolina, and our house was right off of East Bay Street, on the peninsula, a fixer-upper that had been paid for by our "real" contracts with GRS. Jennifer had come up with the initial idea to sponsor Amena at Ashley Hall, an all-girls school literally about a stone's throw away that had a boarding program for international students. Having been an institution of higher learning since Christ was a corporal, it had a plethora of foreign students—now mainly from China—and had readily agreed to allow Amena to attend, provided we sponsored her.

The school's motto was *Possunt Quae Volunt,* or PQV, which was Latin for "Girls who have the will have the ability." Something I really liked. But they'd never met Amena, and we were about to test whether her will would crush their ability to rein her in, because she was definitely a handful.

We loaded up the car and cut across the peninsula, dodging the tourist vehicles that couldn't find their way out of a wet paper bag, all of them confused by the byzantine one-way streets that made absolutely no sense. We finally turned onto Smith Street, right outside the school. In the rearview mirror I saw Amena grow a little wary when we parked in the fire lane. I turned to her and said, "Hey, this is what you wanted. I know it's a little scary, but it's for the best. You're in America now."

She said, "Would you have sent your daughter here?"

It was a profound question that hung in the air. My daughter was dead, and she knew the love I held for her. I said, "Yes. Cross my heart. Yes."

She said, "Okay, Pike. But only if I get to go on the honeymoon."

That brought a smile to Jennifer's face. She leaned over and brushed Amena's cheek, saying, "Okay, but you can't stay in our room."

Amena laughed and opened the door, right as my cell phone rang with a peculiar tone that Jennifer recognized. It was an encrypted call. Meaning it was from the Taskforce.

Before I got a word out, Jennifer said, "Come on, little one. Let's go check in. Pike can catch up."

They left, and I answered the phone with a little trepidation. Only the Taskforce could destroy everything I had planned.

"Hello?"

"So how's the little refugee hand grenade working out?"

I recognized the voice of George Wolffe, the deputy commander of the Taskforce, and then was forced to remember he was now the commander, as Kurt Hale—the original commander—had been blown up in my Jeep the year before. The emotion was a whipsaw, none of it reduced by the march of time.

I said, "Hey, sir, we just got here. She's checking in now. What's up with the call?"

He laughed at the angst in my voice and said, "Nothing, man. I'm really just checking in. The entire Council is worried about her. They just want to know the plan is going okay."

I breathed a sigh of relief and said, "That's good to hear, because it is. She's signing in right now and we're headed out to Australia, just like we talked about. What's up with the Taskforce?"

He knew what I was asking. It had been a rough year for our organization, and we'd been on hold since Kurt's death, with all the hand-wringers in the Oversight Council waiting on the shoe to drop that might expose our operations, but as far as I could tell, that hadn't happened. Mainly because I'd had a couple of Israelis tie off some loose ends outside of the Taskforce charter.

I heard him sigh, then say, "I wish Kurt were still here. I don't want this responsibility."

"What's going on?"

"China. China is going on. They're kicking our ass all over the place. Hong Kong is going nuts, they're taking over the South China Sea, they've infiltrated every university we have, stealing our technology, and they are locking up the Muslim Uyghur community into concentration camps."

I laughed and said, "Why does the Taskforce care about that? Sounds like a traditional intelligence community problem."

Because our unit was illegal from the jump point, Kurt Hale—our deceased commander—had developed strict limits to Project Prometheus, understanding the threat the unit could pose. Not wanting it to turn into an American Gestapo force, he had designed the Oversight Council and then dictated that we would only deal with substate terrorist threats. We wouldn't do state-on-state activities, like Wolffe was describing. Well, we had a few times in the past, but it was always the exception to the rule. Wolffe's tone told me the rule might be changing.

Wolffe said, "Yeah, you'd think so, but I'm headed into a National Security Council meeting as a backseater about selling F-35s to Taiwan. I'm supposed to just sit and listen, and nobody's told me why they demanded I be there, but you know they wouldn't ask me if they didn't want me to do something. What I'm hearing on the trap lines is that the established architecture can't penetrate what's going on in China. In 2010 the Chinese broke our covert communications and rolled up our entire network. The CIA is impotent now. They want something else."

And now the hairs really stood up on my neck. "Something like me? Like Grolier Recovery Services? Tell me that's not true. We don't even have a targeted threat. I don't do intel collection. I do the finish. Period."

"No, no. Nothing like that. At least I don't think so. I probably said too much. Get Amena situated and you're clear to head to Australia. Tell Dunkin I said hello."

I saw Amena come back out from the front of the school, looking at me. I said, "Will do, sir. Gotta go. But give me a call if you need me. I'll sort those fucks out."

He laughed and said, "You've never even been to China."

"I wasn't talking about the Chinese."

I heard nothing and said, "I gotta go. Good luck," and hung up the phone. Some things were more important than national security.

I exited the car, seeing Jennifer standing behind Amena with an administrator next to her, Jennifer's eyes wet. I walked to them and said, "So this is it, doodlebug. You make it through two weeks, and you can make it through anything."

I saw her lip quiver and squatted down, saying, "Hey, come on. I was teasing. You've been through much worse than this. Now all you have to do is make friends. I promise nobody here is going to try to hurt you."

The administrator, having no idea what Amena had been through in life, said, "That's true, honey. You'll love it here."

I wanted to smack her.

Amena said, "I want to come with you guys." And it broke my heart. But that was the whole point of leaving. She was very strong, and she'd be okay. I wrapped her in my arms and said, "Two weeks, doodlebug. We'll be back in two weeks."

She said, "Promise?"

"I promise. I'm pretty sure Jennifer will get us into more trouble than you'll find here."

She wiped her eyes and gave me a fake smile. I returned a fake one of my own, not realizing how true those words would become.

# 6

George Wolffe pulled into the checkpoint for the Eisenhower Executive Office Building, right across from the White House, and halfway hoped they'd turn him away. After all, he wasn't a member of the National Security Council, and as such, he didn't have an "all access" pass. All he had was a name, and he hoped the name wouldn't be enough to grant him access. He'd never been given a badge for the White House grounds, precisely to conceal the organization he worked for—Project Prometheus.

Badges had trails, and trails led to discovery.

He was ostensibly a GS-15 in the CIA, working as an analyst in the counterterrorism center. He had to be formally put on an access list each and every time he entered. He hoped this time it would fail.

It did not.

The guard handed him a badge with a giant "V" on it, meaning visitor, escort required, and waved him forward. He pulled into a spot and was met by some intern who looked to be about the age of the cheese in his refrigerator.

"George Wolffe?"

He exited the car and said, "Yeah. Who are you?"

With an attitude bestowed upon him by the perceived power he held, but belied by the pimples on his face, the man said, "I'm your escort. Follow my rules."

He turned and began walking. Wolffe rolled his eyes and fell in line behind him across the grounds to the building.

They walked up the stairs, passing through two more security checkpoints, then entered a conference room. The only man Wolffe recognized was the national security advisor, Alexander Palmer. The rest were strangers.

The guide said, "You sit in the back. The back row. Do not talk. You're just here to listen."

Palmer came over and the young man grew compliant, saying, "Sir, here's George Wolffe. Like you asked."

Palmer waved him away with a hand. "Yeah, yeah. Thanks."

The kid nodded, waiting, and Palmer said, "What do you want? An invitation to leave?"

Wolffe saw the disappointment on the kid's face and thought it wouldn't be his last. The kid wanted the trappings of power without actually sacrificing for them. He basked in being the chosen one but had never earned the right to be called such. Like just about every single politician in Washington, DC.

Wolffe shook Palmer's hand and said, "So why am I here?"

"This is a subcommittee meeting of the nonproliferation taskforce for Asian affairs."

"Yeah? No offense, but so what? Why did you ask me to be here? What does this have to do with the Taskforce?"

"Nothing . . . yet. I just want you to hear the debate. That's all. We're about to discuss the sale of F-35s to Taiwan."

Wolffe squinted his eyes and said, "What does the nonproliferation taskforce have to do with selling next-gen fighters to Taiwan? And beyond that, what the hell am I doing here? Come to think of it, what are *you* doing here? At a subcommittee meeting?"

His words caused a few people to look his way. Palmer raised his hands and said, "Hey, calm down. Lower it a notch."

Wolffe looked left and right, saw the interest, and said, "Yeah, okay. What do you want me to hear?"

Palmer glanced at the podium, where a man was about to start speaking, and said, "I work for the president of the United States. *He* wanted you to hear this. That's all I can say. You need to take your seat."

Palmer walked away, and Wolffe wondered what was happening. If President Hannister wanted him here, it was for a significant reason, but he'd heard no traction for China via the Taskforce. There were no terrorist threats coming from the country. He'd told Pike a story that he'd thought was just spitting in the wind, getting him prepared for the impossible, but now it looked like the impossible was coming true. But he was still the commander. The one who dictated Project Prometheus actions. He took his seat at the back of the room.

A man in a coat and tie brought the meeting to order, but he was clearly military by the fact that his suit looked like it had been purchased off the rack at JCPenney.

"So, let's cut to the chase on this. I don't want to spend a lot of time talking about extraneous stuff. We're here to decide whether the sale of F-35s to Taiwan is in the national interest. First on the order is that we don't have any to sell. Taiwan is begging for them, but we don't have them. But if we do in the future, do we recommend selling them to the ROC?"

Giving deference to Alexander Palmer, he said, "Sir, do you want to add anything here?"

Palmer went to the front of the room and said, "Okay, this is a big decision, not without consequences, which is why I'm here. Do we want to sell F-35s to Taiwan? If we do, it'll be a direct provocation to China. If we don't, we're signaling a loss of support to Taiwan. It's a no-win, but it's in front of us."

Since its creation in 1949, the Republic of China had been one of the most delicate balances in the entire portfolio of U.S. national security engagements, and like the shifting sands on a beach, it had gone through many changes with respect to the United States, from outright support in the early days, to Nixon's détente with China in the seventies, and then finally culminating with President Carter formally shifting diplomatic recognition of the country from Taiwan to the People's Republic of China in 1979, for the first time officially recognizing Beijing as the rightful power, and causing the abandonment of diplomatic relations with Taiwan.

Through it all, to this day, the United States had maintained a vague commitment of defense of Taiwan against Chinese encroachment—defined nebulously so as not to give Taiwan the courage to demand independence under the umbrella of American firepower, but still to give China a great enough pause that they wouldn't outright attack.

And that dilemma was driving the debate about selling the new F-35 Joint Strike Fighter to Taiwan.

A woman with a prim and proper blouse, looking like she should have been teaching English at a boarding school, said, "Not to be a minion of the fabled 'military-industrial complex,' but we just cut off Turkey from its purchase of F-35s for its acquisition of the Russian S-400 air defense system. That leaves a few F-35s in the wind. It's not like we're talking about ramping up production. We have them sitting around, and selling them to Taiwan is a hell of a lot better than selling them to Turkey. My opinion."

Sitting in the back, George Wolffe liked her opinion.

A man at the end of the table scoffed, then said, "So we just jerk those fighters away from Turkey and sell them to Taiwan? I understand we have an issue with Turkey right now, but taking their agreed purchase and selling it to Taiwan will be a mess of the first order. Turkey is a NATO partner. Taiwan is not. Why are we even talking about this?"

The woman gave him a laser gaze and said, "The weapons are already 'jerked' from Turkey. That's a done deal, by lawmakers. Not by you on this council. It's done. They bought a Russian air defense system against our expressed objections and lost the purchase."

Chastised, the man said, "It's not a done deal yet. We're still working on it."

Alexander Palmer, the arbitrator by his status alone, said, "Geoff, it's done. Turkey isn't getting the F-35. Let's focus on Taiwan."

Geoff glared at him, then flicked his eyes to the woman who'd called him out, but said nothing. Palmer said, "Can we continue?"

The man in the JCPenney suit said, "Yes, sir. I'll start with some background, if that's okay."

Palmer nodded, and the man flicked up a slide, saying, "The problem with China is that they work in the nether zone. The hybrid zone. They don't want to go to war with bullets. They want to win without a shot fired."

The first slide was about Africa, and China's inroads into that country. "This is what the PRC calls its 'Belt and Road' initiative, which is nothing more than a loan shark deal. They promise to help the country in question with infrastructure at low, low interest rates, and then when the country can't pay, they take over the infrastructure, basically owning the lifeblood of the country. Ports, airfields, oil wells, rare earth minerals, you name it, China's sinking its teeth into the globe."

He punched up another slide, showing a graph of technological innovation from 1980 until the present. He said, "Beyond that, China is flexing its muscle with technology. It's not hyperbole to say they are about to be the sole superpower of artificial intelligence. We don't seem to care about that, but China does. While Google and others fight our own Defense Department on some misguided attempt at personal salvation, they sell their skills to China in a torrent."

He flipped to another graph, saying, "And China is sucking it up in a superhuman way. It has developed the technology to a point that the entire country is a living, breathing surveillance state, and we've helped them to do it. And I mean we, as in the United States, have helped them to do it, not in an abstract way. Our companies sell them everything from facial recognition algorithms to biometric predictive software, creating the first full surveillance state from cradle to grave, which China is using on its own population. I'd like to say we could stop the tap on that, but if we don't sell it to them, they steal it in our universities."

He punched the slide deck and a graph showing Chinese economic espionage came up.

"This is what we know, but make no mistake, it's just the tip of the iceberg. The Chinese government has a huge ability to steal our technology, using what is known as the United Front Work Department, a division of the People's Liberation Army. A dedicated member of the Politburo, its sole function is to leverage the Chinese diaspora for its own ends. They do it through appeals to the homeland as a first step, then go all the way to outright blackmail or threatening of relatives. And it's very, very successful."

He flicked a slide and said, "Unlike China, we operate in a market capitalist system whereby each company operates independently. We don't band together and talk about our actions for a united front. What happens in the end is our companies tend to hide their exposure to China for fear of a market loss. Make no mistake, China doesn't operate that way. Every bit of data from the technology they sell here is going straight back to the PRC, from DJI drones to Huawei cell phone technology. They are kicking our ass even if we don't admit it."

# 7

Jennifer laid her head against my shoulder, and I had initially hated it, because now I couldn't move without waking her up. We had damn near fifteen hours of flight left, and she wouldn't let me booze it up like I wanted to. If the flight attendant came by, I'd have to use sign language to get a rum and Coke, because Jennifer's ears were tuned to the words "rum" and "Coke" even if she was sound asleep. But when I gazed at her face I knew why I let it happen. She snuggled in next to me, and honestly, I felt content. The booze cart came by and I let it go. The flight attendant looked at me, and I shook my head, letting Jennifer get her sleep.

Two movies and fourteen hours later, I sensed something pass by our row, waking me up. I opened my eyes feeling cranky. Which is how I always felt on long flights. All I wanted to do was get off the damn plane. How long could this thing stay in the air?

Jennifer was still sleeping on top of me, her head burrowed into my shoulder. Which aggravated me a little bit. How she could get a solid night's sleep on an airplane was a mystery to me, and I gave a split-second thought to waking her up. I did not, of course.

The sun had risen in between my groggy sleep and nonsleep, the light outside my airplane window growing brighter with every second. I saw the screen at my front was frozen, right in the middle of some year-old rom-com. I pulled out my phone and booted it up, logging on to the in-flight WiFi. I looked out the window and saw land below us. We'd reached the continent of Australia.

I sent Dunkin a message, saying we were about to land in Brisbane. We had to catch another flight to Adelaide, but we'd be at his place in less than four hours. I was sure he was on his way to work, but he'd see the message before he had to lock up his phone prior to going into his secure facility.

Dunkin's real name was Clifford Delmonty, and once upon a time he'd worked for the Taskforce as a network operations engineer, which was a polite way to say he was a hacker. A five-foot-seven-inch computer geek, at his hiring board for the Taskforce he'd made an impossible claim that he could dunk a basketball. He thought we were looking for some superhuman physical specimen and figured nobody would test him on his claim. Since we were looking for a guy who could work miracles with electronic devices, not play point guard, we hired him. Then made him put his money where his mouth was.

He'd failed miserably and figured he was fired on his first day. We kept him, but he now wore the callsign Dunkin as a reminder that it doesn't pay to exaggerate. The Taskforce needed the ground truth. No spin.

He'd worked for the Taskforce for several years and then was offered a very lucrative job by a start-up called Gollum Solutions, working on the artificial intelligence software for the new F-35 Joint Strike Fighter. They'd moved him to their headquarters in Australia, and he'd left an open invitation for anyone in the Taskforce to come visit. Because of Amena's situation, Jennifer and I had taken him up on the offer. Well,

Amena and the fact that Jennifer wanted to dive the Great Barrier Reef.

I thought about texting Amena, just to let her know we'd made it, but decided to wait. The whole point of leaving her alone was to get her operating on her own two feet. No reason to create a leash on our first outing, giving her the ability to text us at every moment.

The flight attendants came back down the row, handing out some godawful quiche for our breakfast, the mess looking like it had been scooped out of a koala's cage. I waved the offending meal away. She said, "Can I get you some coffee?"

I said, "I'll have a rum and Coke, if you don't mind."

Jennifer woke up, rubbed her eyes, and said, "What was that?"

The flight attendant started to hand me my order, and Jennifer said, "Are you getting a drink? It's six o'clock in the morning."

Chagrined, I said, "I guess I'll have a cup of coffee." The flight attendant gave it to me. I muttered, "It's five o'clock somewhere, damn it."

Jennifer smiled and laid her head back on my shoulder. In seconds, she was fast asleep. I waved at the flight attendant and mouthed, "Give me the rum and Coke."

# 8

From the back of the room, Wolffe saw a man at the end of the table raise his hand, a question on his face. Wolffe took one look at him and had an instant dislike. He could tell the man was a self-righteous prick who spent his life in books, learning the workings of the world without ever having felt the pain. Sure of his decisions despite never having to feel the brunt of what he decided, he'd probably left a university at the age of twenty-seven with a doctorate and had spent every other waking moment giving his advice to think tanks and the NSC.

The briefer said, "Yes?" The academic drew his hands underneath his chin, like he was pontificating to the world, and said, "Okay, okay, I get it. China is the boogeyman according to you, but selling F-35s to Taiwan is just asking to exacerbate the situation. What good will it do? Is there any proof that your dire predictions are occurring? It sounds like you're giving us a briefing on a foregone conclusion."

The briefer said, "I'm showing you the proof. It's on the screen, and these are only the penetrations we know of. If you want more proof, just look at Australia."

"What do you mean?"

Exasperated, the briefer said, "You're on the Asia counterproliferation subcommittee, right? Is that right? You're not just a visitor here today?"

Chagrined, the man said, "Yes, of course. I've been on this committee for over two years, and you didn't answer the question."

The briefer pursed his lips, as if he couldn't believe that someone that naïve was in the room. He said, "Australia is already compromised by China. If they aren't a lost cause yet, it's very close."

"How?"

"To keep from dragging this out, just two data points: One, China now owns the port of Darwin, the largest port in Australia with a gateway to China. That didn't just happen out of the blue. Two, there was a book written about the subversion of Australian politics by China, written by an Australian academic. China raised an objection, and the book wasn't allowed to be published because of some arcane law about national security. That's also not a coincidence. China raised an objection and the Australian government stopped publication. And why did they do that? Because of the economic threat China presents. The Australian government didn't want to upset the apple cart for profits. It's happening to them, and it will happen here. China wants to own the means of control, and they don't want to shoot to do it."

Alexander Palmer said, "What does this have to do with Taiwan and the F-35s?"

Relieved at the intrusion, the briefer flicked to the next slide and said, "Yes, sir, I was getting to that."

On the screen was a graph of the South China Sea, with nine dots outlining the sphere of influence China was asserting, well to the south of China's actual coastline.

He said, "China is also expanding on its own home front, claiming basically rocks in the ocean as their sovereign territory, which expands their reach. They get twelve nautical miles off their coast, like everyone else in the world. Find a rock at the thirteen-mile mark? They've just increased their sovereign territory by another twelve miles. They've taken over a bunch of islands in the Spratly chain—islands that are contested by a host of countries from Malaysia to Vietnam—and have now claimed those as their own, which will basically leave the entire South China Sea as the sovereign space of China. They call it the Nine-Dash Line."

The academic at the front of the table snorted and said, "And why do we care?"

Exasperated, the briefer said, "We care because if the world agrees to this, we have no right of passage in the South China Sea. Jesus Christ. Can you not see this? The ring is literally designed to prevent passage for every naval vessel on the high seas in one of the most trafficked sea lanes on earth. Do I need to spell it out for you?"

The academic said nothing. The room remained silent, so the briefer continued, "Look, once they set foot on the rocks they said they'd never militarize them. Now? They have missiles on them. They're literally bringing in sand to increase the size, building runways and infrastructure. They're building platforms for war."

The academic said, "Sounds like an Asian problem to me. What's that got to do with us?"

The briefer said, "Because everything they do is targeted at us. We have the largest economy in the world. They have the second largest. And they're dominating us. Are you guys aware that Disney released an animated movie last year called *Abominable,* and to get a sale in China they had a map in the movie depicting the expanse of Chinese sovereignty? The Nine-Dash Line? And when the NBA and ESPN went to China for a game they kowtowed to the same map? They're winning because we don't care. And we've done nothing to prevent it. Malaysia can't do it. Vietnam can't do it. And we don't do anything."

Calmly, juxtaposed against the earnestness of the man briefing, Palmer said, "Okay. What does this have to do with the sale of F-35s?"

The briefer took a breath and said, "Because the one thing China can't own is the Taiwan Strait. It's a sea lane that defeats all of their ambitions. They can take over and demand sovereignty with the rocks to the south, but if Taiwan exists, it's all irrelevant. It defeats all of that, because Taiwan is inside the range of their ambitions. You can't claim jurisdiction when you have an island that claims the same. China knows this. They want Taiwan. We see a lot on the news about Hong Kong, but that's a sideshow. At the end of the day, owning Hong Kong gives them nothing other than prestige. They need to own Taiwan, and they intend to. We need to prevent it. That's where the F-35s come in."

He pressed a button and the slide show went to a blank screen showing the NSC logo. He said, "Questions on what I've just shown you? There are background papers here on the table."

There was a brief moment of silence, then the room erupted in chatter, the members of the subcommittee all trying to compete with each other for airtime about their preferred opinion. Wolffe appreciated that they wanted to debate, but it struck him as all a waste of time. It was like watching a bunch of high schoolers at a mock UN convention. Eventually he grew bored with the discussion and rose to leave. Palmer waved at him, then met him at the door.

Wolffe said, "Not sure what this was all about. Good luck with the F-35 sale."

Palmer said, "It's about China. I wanted you to see the sausage making here, in this room."

"Yeah, it's sausage making all right. I'm not sure how I fit in, though."

Palmer glanced back into the room, making sure nobody could hear him, then said, "Because the president is thinking about targeting you guys against China. That's why."

Wolffe said, "We don't target states. That's sacrosanct. We do substate actions only. Terrorist organizations. It's in the charter."

Palmer said, "The charter might be changing. It's not like it's written in the Constitution."

Wolffe bristled and said, "You're changing the very nature of why we exist, and we aren't the tool for this. It's like telling a car mechanic to fix a refrigerator. In the end, the fridge gets fixed, but at a hell of a lot more pain. Have you learned nothing about the last twenty years of war, throwing SOF into the breach because it was the easiest solution?"

Palmer raised his hands and said, "I'm just telling you the president's thought process. Taiwan's election is coming up, and we expect the PRC will try some direct action to affect the outcome. He likes you guys. He thinks you can help."

Wolffe raised his voice. "We don't even have a target. No mission, no intelligence, no nothing. This is completely out of the blue. I don't need some lone wolf telling me what to do."

Several members of the subcommittee turned their heads at his voice. Palmer waited until they turned back around to their own conversations, then said, "Are you saying I'm a lone wolf on this? Do you forget who you work for?"

"At this point, I really don't know. Are you? You're a little young, but I'm old enough to remember Oliver North and Iran-Contra. I'm not doing that here."

Palmer bristled and said, "You've been doing it for years. Don't give me that crap. You work for me. For the Oversight Council."

"What the hell are you even saying? I'm your personal kill show?"

"No, no, of course not. Just get the men ready."

"We don't even have a target. That's what we do."

"You don't have a target *yet*. Get the men ready. Get off of Islam and start studying China. I want a team ready to go in the next week. Nothing big. Alpha exploration only. Any team but Pike's."

Wolffe said, "So now you're going to tell me the team to send? Kurt's dead, but his ethos is not. You assholes can't run roughshod over my organization. And it is *my* organization now."

Palmer opened the door and said, "Don't get aggravated. This is from the president."

Wolffe turned, "President Hannister said any team but Pike's?"

"Well, no. That's coming from me. You have plenty of teams to send, and Pike's a little hot right now dealing with the child."

Which was bullshit, and Wolffe knew it. Palmer just didn't like Pike because Pike never listened to him. But he always succeeded.

Palmer said, "We'll talk again tomorrow, with the Oversight Council."

Wolffe took the door handle and said, "Get one thing straight. I pick the team. You want one, you got it, but I pick them."

He was starting to leave when Palmer caught the door, saying, "What's that mean?"

Wolffe looked him in the eye and said, "Pike's on his way to Australia right now, with Jennifer. He thinks he's going on vacation, but I'm pretty sure you'll change that plan. There's your team. Reap what you sow."

Palmer said, "That's not going to fly."

"It'll fly if I say it will."

Palmer started to say something else and Wolffe cut him off. "Let me give you some advice. Kurt is dead. I'm his heir. Kurt didn't play politics because of who he was. I do. You want to go to the knives, I'll do so. And I'll win."

Palmer looked at him with his mouth slightly open, amazed at the brazenness.

Wolffe locked eyes with him and said, "It's sort of my specialty. Outside of using a knife for real."

# 9

Clifford Delmonty—AKA Dunkin—pulled into his designated parking spot and removed his smartphone from his pocket, intending to drop it into his center console like he did every single day he came to work. Due to the classified nature of his job, dealing with sensitive components of the F-35 Joint Strike Fighter's artificial intelligence engine, the entire office he worked within was designated as a SCIF—a sensitive compartmented information facility—meaning that no outside communications devices were allowed.

He opened the console, then saw a text alert from Pike Logan.

Despite himself, Dunkin was a little surprised.

Pike had talked about visiting for the last year, and then had said he was coming for real. They'd planned the trip to coincide with the Christmas holiday break, but Dunkin knew Pike's career, and had half expected him to say he had been delayed, without any reason why. In what seemed now a lifetime away, Dunkin had once worked for the Taskforce and understood that the Operator's life was not his own.

In truth, he was a little nostalgic for those times. The sense of mission. The sense of doing what was right for the world. Now he only worked for the almighty dollar, and while that had been very lucrative, he didn't have the same job satisfaction as he did before—even if his time in the Taskforce had meant Operators like Pike ripping him a new asshole on operations, asking for computer miracles about things they didn't fully understand.

He didn't want to admit it to himself, but he missed it.

The text told him Pike would be here in less than four hours. With the Christmas schedule, he could leave midday and make it home before Pike showed up. He typed out a quick message saying he wouldn't be able to text when Pike arrived because his phone would be in the car, but he was looking forward to the visit.

Pike had said something about diving the Great Barrier Reef, and Dunkin's girlfriend had been talking about that for a year, so it was the perfect opportunity to do so. Christmas break was coming up, and as it was the middle of summer in Australia, it would be perfect. Especially if he could get the Taskforce to pay for the trip.

Pike had said the entire thing was a vacation, but from past operations with him, Dunkin knew half of the time he was lying, doing some government business under the cover of his company. In the past, he'd been on the inside, knowing the lie. Now that he was on the outside, he wondered if he was being lied to for the support of some operation. But he honestly didn't care.

Pike had mentioned some wild story about an operation in Europe culminating with a Syrian refugee he'd brought back to America, with him wanting to make sure she was able to survive on her own and thus he was leaving her in Charleston, and the story was so crazy Dunkin knew it was a lie.

It sounded like a Taskforce operation. Who the hell would come to Australia because of a Syrian refugee? Pike himself used to make fun of some of the ridiculous cover stories they used, and this sounded just like one.

But if he could get his girlfriend on a dive trip that was paid for by the U.S. government, he'd be more than willing to open his small apartment for a night's stay with Pike and Jennifer. He just hoped his girlfriend didn't get jealous about Jennifer. And that Pike didn't mention his previous infatuation with her, which had almost caused Pike to pummel his ass.

Unlike his own girlfriend, Jennifer was a hammer in the looks department, but she was also quite possibly the most honest human he'd ever met. She was . . . well, just a good person. Different from Pike, she saw the hope in people, and always sought it out. Pike gave you one chance, and then just broke you in half when you failed to live up to his expectations.

And he liked that too. Pike was an apex predator, but he understood skill, especially when it was directed at the enemies of the United States. Something Dunkin had in spades in his own unique way, and it was a respect he missed in his current job.

He missed them both. Missed the life. Missed being respected for his skills. Missed it all. He shoved the phone into the glove compartment and exited, heading to the front gate of his company.

Located in what was known as the Edinburgh Defence Precinct—a squat, military-looking expanse of concrete buildings that spanned the size of a small town—it was adjacent to the RAAF Base Edinburgh and the Australian Defence Science and Technology center. With every compound surrounded by razor wire, and every building with a security entrance, the entire complex was made up of defense companies of all stripes, a veritable smorgasbord of military contractors. BAE, Raytheon, Lockheed Martin, Airbus, you name it—they all had offices here. And the security was commensurate with the stakes involved.

He walked up to the gate, showed his badge, and then leaned into a retinal scanner, a biometric device that would prove he was what his identification claimed. He pulled back and saw another employee approach. Jake Shu.

A short man with a wide waist from too much time behind a computer, Shu looked like an Asian Danny DeVito, complete with a balding head, ponytail, and a small gold hoop in his right ear.

Dunkin said, "Hey, Jake, I thought you were headed out on vacation today."

Jake smirked and said, "I was, but I'm apparently needed here more than there. I'll be leaving as soon as I can."

Jake put his eye to the scanner, and they were both let in, the walk down the long hallway awkward, with neither talking.

Dunkin had reported Jake two months earlier, after Jake returned from the ill-fated F-35 flight in Japan. The plane had slammed into the ocean at six hundred knots, and after the endless investigations, when Jake finally came home—the one person from their cell sent to help with the construction—he'd been noncommittal about the crash. It was quite possibly the biggest setback in F-35 operational capacity, with all of the various countries demanding to know what had occurred, and Jake had acted like it was expected.

Nobody in their company seemed to pay it any mind, but Dunkin did. He'd watched Jake on the floor and seen him do strange things. Nobody was allowed to have any separate media on the floor. All work had to be conducted on the terminals they had been assigned. Nothing was ever recorded or transferred from one computer to another—unless you had one of four accounts.

Jake was one of them. A genius at artificial intelligence, he'd been recruited from a start-up in Silicon Valley, and had the all-important gold badge. The one that let a person actually download information from a system and transport it to another.

The Department of Defense had realized early on that a thumb drive could be a recipe for disaster, and had forced all subcontractors to work through the problem within the systems themselves, over established secure lines, which was inefficient as all get out when dealing with similar problems across different platforms, but it prevented theft or hacking of the very information in play. That had lasted about a year before the contractors began screaming for a fix. And they came up with one—the golden badge.

Only select individuals would have the ability to transfer information outside the network of their specific program, and because of Jake's travel to oversee the software installation in Japan for the initial F-35s, he had that badge.

Dunkin had seen Jake do some quirky things prior to leaving, using his badge to access systems that had nothing to do with his work, but at the time he'd just thought Jake was a scientist. And scientists did quirky things, like Doc Brown in *Back to the Future*. There was no doubt Jake was a genius, with skills that eclipsed Dunkin's own.

And then the F-35 in Japan had gone down into the ocean, with Jake the sole representative of their company on site. The company that designed the artificial intelligence for the entire fleet of aircraft.

Dunkin followed the mantra of "If you see something, say something" and informed his superiors. They'd done a check of Jake's access and had determined that he was working within the parameters prescribed. Dunkin thought the security team was lax, intent on protecting their own fiefdom from embarrassment. So he'd held his tongue.

It hadn't taken long for the insular world inside the company to spring leaks about the attempted whistleblower. Dunkin's life had grown more difficult, with everyone assuming he was out to torpedo the company for a vendetta, while Jake had been allowed to roam free.

There was no love lost between them, even as they pretended nothing had happened. No official report had been filed, and no official reprimand had been administered, and thus, standing in the hallway, scanning their retinas to enter one of the most classified projects in U.S. Department of Defense history, they both just acted like the entire affair did not exist.

# 10

They reached the elevator together, and Jake pushed the button.

"Where you headed for your leave?" Dunkin asked.

"Cairns. I only have another year here and I haven't seen anything of the country. I'm taking the train from Sydney all the way up."

The elevator opened and Dunkin said, "I'm thinking about taking my leave up there too. I got a buddy coming into town today, and he's talking about diving the reef. You going to do that?"

Jake gave him a sideways glance and said, "No. I just have a relative that lives up there. A cousin from China."

"No shit? What are the odds of that?"

Jake chuckled and said, "I don't know. My parents moved to the United States, and his came to Australia. We've never met."

"Well, how'd you even know he was here?"

Jake gave him a look and said, "Family."

Dunkin took the hint and they rode the rest of the way in uncomfortable silence. When they exited on the third floor they had to badge in at yet another door, this one unmanned, and entered the beating heart of Gollum Solutions. Taking up the entire floor, it comprised nothing more than computer terminals in a cube farm, like one would see on

Wall Street or in a library, with the outer area ringed by offices.

Dunkin went to his cubicle and logged in, keeping his eye on Jake. That last look Jake had given him seemed almost like a threat telling him to back off, and he didn't like it. He was a computer geek, sure, but one with more than a little skill. He'd been through the direct support training course at the Taskforce, and had served in the military. While he wasn't an Operator, he was decidedly better than the average geek.

Most of the floor was empty, the majority of staff already having left for their Christmas break. In truth, Dunkin wouldn't have come in today at all, except his girlfriend had to work until three. He figured he could wrap a few things up and make a little money instead of just sitting around his apartment staring at the television. He did wonder why Jake was here, though. Dunkin knew that there was no rush for anything they were doing. The F-35 had been plagued with delays from the inception, and he knew it was a complete fabrication that management had "ordered" Jake in because he was indispensable for some problem. If that were the case, they'd all be in here working.

It crossed his mind that maybe it was because nobody else would be around.

He did his work, but occasionally scanned the floor, looking for Jake. He always saw him behind his own cubicle, banging away on some artificial intelligence code. Four hours into his shift he glanced up and saw Jake at a different terminal, doing something strange, and Dunkin knew he had no business at that terminal. Dunkin stood up, and Jake saw him, his eyes hooded like he'd been caught with his hand in the cookie jar.

At least that was what Dunkin thought.

Jake shut down the computer, and Dunkin saw him pocket

a portable hard drive. He went back to his own computer, logged out, and walked to the door, passing Dunkin. He said, "Done. Gotta catch my flight to Sydney. How much longer are you staying?"

The conversation raised Dunkin's hackles, because the two were most decidedly not friends. After the elevator ride, the question was odd, to say the least. That he might acknowledge Dunkin's existence with a head nod on the way out of the door would have been odd. Dunkin said, "I got a couple more hours until my buddy arrives. Might as well make some cash until then."

Jake nodded and said, "Enjoy your leave."

Dunkin smiled and said, "Same to you." He waited another twenty-five minutes, ensuring Jake was off the compound, before getting up and jogging to the security office in the corner.

Scott Mulroney, the chief in charge of cybersecurity for Gollum, was behind the desk, his appearance startling Dunkin.

Dunkin said, "Hey, what are you doing here today? Where's Paul?"

"He wanted an early leave. I took his shift."

Which wasn't good. Scott was the original person Dunkin had brought his suspicions to in the first place. And the one who had rejected them.

Scott said, "What's up?"

"Hey, I was just wondering why Jake still has a gold pass. He got it for that Japanese F-35 construction over seven months ago. Why does he still have it? Shouldn't we rescind it now?"

Scott rolled his eyes and said, "What is it with your hard-on for him?"

"Nothing, really. He was just in here today, and he was on both Kibler's and Larson's computers. No reason to be on them. They're working the artificial intelligence A2/AD for Taiwan. Not the F-35 program."

The anti-access/area denial program was the missile defense system that would prevent the landing of any Chinese forces on the island. Using artificial intelligence, Gollum Solutions was working to decrease the decision times prior to missile launch from minutes to seconds. It was the most highly compartmented program Gollum worked on—and another reason that Dunkin thought the company was a little shoddy in the security department. Why keep that on the open floor? Because you just trusted everyone to stay in their own cubicle? He remembered his work with the Taskforce and knew that the project should have been stovepiped somewhere else.

Scott put down the book he was reading and said, "He was doing work. That's what we pay him for. You heard the boss. The guy's a genius."

Dunkin knew Jake's history. Undergrad at Stanford, doctorate from MIT, blah, blah, blah. As far as Dunkin could tell, he'd done nothing but university research on artificial intelligence until Gollum had hired him.

Dunkin said, "I saw him with removable media, and both Kibler and Larson have nothing to do with the interface for visual simulations for the fourth-generation helmet. It's just odd. That's not what Jake does."

Scott turned to his computer and started tapping. Three minutes later, he turned and said, "No penetration or access to either system. They're locked down, last login yesterday."

*What?*

"Scott, I know what I saw."

"No, you *think* you know what you saw. You keep this

shit up and we'll be locked down. Lose the contract. Let it go, man."

Dunkin remained silent, and Scott said, "Unless you want me to take it to the boss, because you're accusing me of not knowing my job."

Dunkin shook his head, saying, "No, no. I don't need any more trouble. Sorry to bother you. I must have been confused."

Scott smiled and pointed at his screen. "Trust me, if he'd been rooting around like some Snowden clone, I would see it here. He didn't."

Dunkin nodded, thinking that having a beer in front of his television would be a better use of his time than continuing work here today. He said, "Yeah, okay. I'm headed out. Have a merry Christmas."

Scott brought his book back up with a wave of his hand. Dunkin badged out and exited the building, fuming over the lack of action. He reached his car, unlocked the door, and saw another car leaving the compound.

One that looked like Jake's. But he'd left over thirty minutes ago.

Hadn't he?

# 11

We landed in Brisbane after one of the longest hell-trip flights I'd ever experienced. We'd purchased the cheapest tickets we could because, at the end of the day, we really couldn't afford this vacation. I was now having a little bit of buyer's remorse, and not just because of the seats on the plane. Australia was way out of our budget. I'd broached going to California or something else closer, but Jennifer had talked about doing something really exotic. Something beyond just building a gap between us and Amena.

I'd wanted to tell her no, but I just couldn't. She'd mentioned the Great Barrier Reef in an offhand way, talking about diving and how that was stupid, because she didn't know how to dive. But I could see her eyes light up at the thought. That had been enough. I'd set up some SCUBA training with a buddy of mine, and she'd taken to it like a fish to water, to coin a phrase.

Now, eighteen hours later, exiting the aircraft, I was thinking going to Disney World in Orlando would have been a better bet. We had one more flight to catch, and all I wanted was to find a bed. But that was not to be.

We stumbled around the airport, getting our bags and clearing customs, then tried to find our next flight. We grew more and more frantic because the damn thing was boarding in forty minutes and the airport might as well have had

Chinese signs for all the good they did. Nothing was helping us to find our terminal. We saw a sign for domestic ticketing on the upper level and took the elevator, which led us nowhere. I began cursing, which is something I just do.

Jennifer said, "Calm down, Caveman. This can't be that hard. People on *The Amazing Race* do this all the time."

I bit back my response, and we reentered the elevator, this time with a guy who looked like a Crocodile Dundee reject, complete with cowboy boots and a leather hat. I had no time for him, and internally begged him not to say a word, because I was seriously getting pissed.

He said, "You guys Yanks?"

Jennifer, because she can't be friendly, said, "We're from America. Yes."

He nodded, like he knew what we were doing. He said, "I figured. You guys can't find your next flight, right?"

She said, "Actually, that's right. We're taking a flight to Adelaide and there is nothing in this terminal that tells us what to do."

He said, "Because you're in the wrong terminal, mate. That terminal is a mile away. Get back down and take the bus. You're literally at the wrong airport."

I began muttering under my breath, and Jennifer gave me a hip bump. The door opened on the ground floor. The man looked at me and said, "Gotta take some help once in a while. Even if she's the one asking."

I locked eyes with him, about to give him a little American justice, and saw the same pirate I was. "Yeah, you're probably right."

His crusty-ass self said, "I know I am."

He left the elevator, and we both stood there, looking at each other. I said, "What the hell was that?"

She grinned and said, "Maybe being an asshole all the time isn't the best solution. Let's go find the shuttle."

I chuckled, now back on an even keel, grabbed our bags, and said, "Okay, okay. Point noted. Let's go."

We exited the terminal, got on the first bus that arrived, and took a trip to the domestic terminal a mile away. Dumbest damn airport I've ever been in.

We made our flight, with Jennifer wide-eyed about being in Australia and me just wanting to get some sleep. Having been through a plethora of long-distance flights, I knew how the jet lag would hit. We would need at least a day to recuperate before we were normal.

We finally arrived at Adelaide, this time without drama. We found our rental car, I booted up our GPS and put in the address, and we left. I followed the signs out of the airport, getting into the suburbs of the city. Dunkin had given me an address about twenty minutes away, but you never knew with the GPS. It'll get you close, but by no means would it guarantee the solution. I'd learned that in another life while using GPS for "precision-guided munitions."

As we drove through the side streets, Jennifer said, "Looks pretty much like America."

I laughed and said, "Did you think crocodiles were going to attack the minute you exited the plane?"

She smiled, rubbed my arm, and said, "Yeah. Sort of, I guess."

We went up the coast, weaving along surface roads with Jennifer watching the GPS as my navigator. I felt my phone go off and pulled it out, saying, "Someone just texted."

"It's Dunkin. He's leaving work right now. He thinks we're still in the air."

"Tell him we're on the ground and rolling. ETA is . . ."

Jennifer looked at the GPS and said, "Twenty-two minutes."

She tapped on my phone and said, "He says we're going to beat him home. There's a key underneath the outdoor light. Unscrew it like you're changing the bulb and it'll fall out."

I laughed and said, "Looks like all that security training at the Taskforce didn't pay off. Tell him we'll see him there."

She did, and we continued up the coast, following every command from the GPS, trying to remember to stay on the left side of the road. Eventually, we turned onto a double-lane avenue called Semaphore, with a median of trees and a line of businesses on both sides. A little outside of downtown Adelaide, it looked like any small suburb in America. Except that they drove on the wrong side of the road.

Jennifer said, "Getting close. Slow down."

I did so and she said, "Here. Right here. On the left."

I looked and saw a two-story complex that was a little dilapidated, squeezed between a jewelry store and a Mexican restaurant. I had no idea how good that Mexican food was, but was fairly sure what I'd find in the complex. I'd lived in such places before.

I pulled into a parking spot outside the complex, saying, "Looks like he's saving a little money."

The building had two three-story towers, with a walkway between them and balconies at each level.

I said, "I don't think he's home yet. Let's go find his door."

Jennifer pulled out a GoPro camera and started filming, saying, "Here we are in Australia, first stop on our tour of the land down under. Say something for posterity, Pike."

I said, "Turn that shit off."

"What? Come on. Say something."

I put my hand over the camera and said, "Turn that off. Please."

She looked at me like I'd grown a third eye and said, "What the hell, Pike? You can't be on a video? It's our vacation."

I sank down into my seat, unsure of what I'd just done. Jennifer said, "Pike?"

I rolled my head back and said, "I'm sorry for that."

She said, "For what?"

I took a breath and said, "Heather always wanted to video us. I never let it happen because of my job. Everyone has a video of their child learning to walk or swim. I have nothing of Angie."

I turned to her and said, "I don't want to be on video celebrating life. I never celebrated hers."

She cupped my chin and said, "Pike . . ."

And that snapped me out of my pathetic melancholy, realizing I was destroying the very reason we were here. I put my hand over hers and said, "Sorry. I think leaving Amena took a little more out of me than I thought. You didn't deserve that."

She smiled and kissed my cheek, saying, "Well, you did that right. You should let it go." She opened the door, sprang out, and did a little dance. I grinned and she said, "Let's get this party started."

We exited the car and marched up to the second floor of Dunkin's apartment complex. We looked around a little bit, and Jennifer found the way. We walked down a dim balcony, the light muted by the overhangs, and ended up in a little cul-de-sac. Three apartments on the end, the biggest ones in the unit. Standing on a balcony were three Asian guys with maintenance uniforms on, but they didn't look like they belonged. I kept my eye on them for a moment, not wanting to go to work on the light fixture in full view of them.

It would look strange, to say the least.

# 12

Dunkin watched Jake's car disappear, feeling a little bit of unease at what he'd just asked the security manager. He fully believed that Jake was up to no good, but Jake could definitely affect his employment—especially if his employers sided with Jake over him. Jake was much smarter than Dunkin, with computer skills that were in another stratosphere. He decided to just let it drop. Enjoy the holidays without worrying about his job.

He got in his car, started it up, then pulled out his cell. He saw the text from Pike and texted back that he was headed home, knowing Pike wouldn't see the message until he landed. He was surprised to get an instant response. They were already on the ground.

He looked at his watch, realized they would beat him, and texted how to access his apartment.

He got back: Really? A key in the light fixture? Pike says the Taskforce training didn't take. We'll meet you there.

He smiled and realized yet again how much he missed the mission. The purpose.

He put the car into drive and left the parking lot. He hit the outside gate, waited on the bar to rise, and saw a pair of running lights turn on from a late-model Lexus. Unbidden, he thought about the surveillance training he'd been taught, about a "correlation of events." Leave a place and see someone stand up as you exit? Might be surveillance.

He smiled at the thought, swung by the car, and saw two Asians inside, one male, one female. He continued down the exit road, heading to the A9 thoroughfare, and a car swung in behind him. He looked in the rearview and saw another pair of Asians, this time young guys about thirty. Which was strange, but not unduly so. There were a lot of Chinese in Australia. It was just a fact of life, but two in a row made him think.

He wasn't paranoid—at least he'd tell you that—but he'd had enough training from Pike drilled into him that he lived by a simple mantra: If you think it's wrong, it probably is.

He entered the A9 with both cars behind him. He gently increased his speed, passing cars. The two vehicles behind him kept pace. He slowed back down to the speed limit, and they did the same.

He thought, *This is stupid. Probably getting off at the M2 for downtown.*

He continued in the traffic, not speeding or slowing down, and passed the exit for the main artery into Adelaide. They didn't exit.

The A9 would eventually run out, becoming Semaphore Road and leading right to his apartment complex, which was why he chose it for his job, but now he wanted to run a little bit of a surveillance detection route. If they were following him, they either didn't know where he was going or wanted to keep him in sight for some other reason, so they'd stick with him.

*If* he wasn't paranoid.

He exited early, before crossing the Port Adelaide River,

and saw both cars come with him. He began snaking through surface streets, making no obvious moves like he was trying to escape, and they stuck with him. After three turns his paranoia changed to true belief. They were following him. Why, he had no idea.

He entered Semaphore Road and continued straight, keeping his eyes glued to his rearview mirror. They were still behind him. He passed his apartment complex and kept going, pulling into a strip mall two blocks down, parking in front of a convenience store.

He waited. The two cars passed him, continuing down the block, then made a right. As soon as they were out of sight, he reversed, gunned the engine, and raced back the way he'd come, his mind spinning over his options.

Chen Ju-Long circled the block, moving rapidly so he could set up a box on the convenience store. He called the follow car and said, "Go long. I'll have the short." The car acknowledged, and he pulled back around, driving slowly, looking for a bumper position that would allow him to see the target leave the market, giving him the ability to trigger.

He pulled abreast of the convenience store and saw the car was gone. In the wind. He parked at the first spot he could find and said, "Target is unsighted. I say again, target is unsighted."

From the stationary team—the one that was supposed to take out the target—he heard, "We have a man and a woman at his apartment. Looking to get in."

"Who are they?"

"I have no idea."

"Stand by."

He called his other mobile unit and said, "Start concentric circles. Focus on the main highways. He went somewhere for a reason. See if you can find him."

He got an acknowledgment and called his contact, Jake, unsure of whether the man could be trusted. He had been recruited through the octopus tentacles of the United Front Work Department—a division of the People's Liberation Army that pressured the Chinese diaspora around the world—but the man could be setting them up. It had happened in the past, and would happen again. It couldn't be helped when you were recruiting someone of Chinese heritage who worked in a place like Silicon Valley. Sometimes it paid off, sometimes it didn't.

Jake had proven trustworthy in the past, executing the implant of the new F-35 jet fighter that had crashed, and he'd been well paid, but the PLA had also leveraged his extended family in China to gain compliance, putting them under the knife, so to speak.

It could have generated a need for revenge. The man could be trying to set them up as well.

Chen was well versed in the wilderness of mirrors inside the People's Republic of China. A staunch party member, he had worked his way up to the tip of the spear inside the Guoanbu, and was now the head of the PRC's Ministry of State Security's external kinetic branch. Meaning he executed what others had failed to do through less violent means. Given that, he knew the bounds of his playground. He was not a killer who wanted to kill. He was a killer who executed what was necessary. And he wasn't sure this one was necessary. Especially given what he'd already conducted inside Australia.

That killing had been necessary.

The phone rang forever, then Jake finally answered, saying, "Is it done?"

"No, it's not done. He didn't go home. He went to a store next to his apartment and we had to break off. When we reengaged, he was gone. I want to know why this is so important. Right now, we aren't in the surveillance footprint, but if we continue, we will be. Taking him at his home in a robbery leaves an easy answer for the police. Killing him somewhere else will invite an investigation because of the random nature. It's much riskier. They'll have to solve the crime and will use all means to do so."

"He knows what I'm doing. He saw me at the Taiwan desk. He suspects. I watched him talking to the security manager. If he lives, I'm not delivering what I have. I won't do it. It will seal my fate."

"What does it matter? You give up what you have, and it's done. So you lose your job."

"Lose my job? I'll be arrested as a damn spy! I did this because of my family. Now what do I do?"

"You did it for money. I ask you again, if we let him go, does that compromise the mission? I don't care about your fears. I only care about the mission. You'll be well taken care of inside China."

"I've never even been to China! I don't speak Chinese. I don't know anything about the country. You people said you'd take care of me."

"And we will. Answer the question. Will this compromise the mission?"

There was a pause, then, "Yes. Yes it will. If he gets back and tells them what I rooted through, they'll search the code. They'll see the penetration. They'll know what I took, and they'll patch it. I have what you want, but if he gets back and raises an alarm with the management, it will cause the mission to fail."

"I thought you could do this clean. No trace of penetration?"

"I can, from the machine's perspective, but not with Clifford's persistence. Nothing is one hundred percent. There may be a trace. I don't think there is, but there might be. I know we're clean from a cursory search, but I don't know about a complete forensics scan."

Chen considered the implications. What Jake said held a ring of truth, but Chen was seriously exposed in Australia at the moment, and thus so was the People's Republic of China. He'd just executed a man who had been bribed by the PRC—an act that had not gone unnoticed by the Australian authorities. A luxury car dealer in Melbourne named Nick Zhao, the man had been primed to run for Parliament—the first such deep penetration the PRC had ever managed—had become scared by the stakes and had approached the Australian intelligence agencies about his recruitment.

Which was how Chen came in.

Flat-faced and broad-shouldered, with muscles that came more from work than nature, Chen was the final solution for problems the Ministry of State Security could solve no other way, and he'd been called to resolve the issue of the errant parliamentary candidate.

Zhao had been found dead in a motel room, with the cause of death still under investigation. The entire press universe in Australia was breathlessly screaming that his killing was a Chinese operation to shut him up. Which of course it was. Chen wasn't eager to conduct another lethal operation in the land down under so soon. But this sounded like it was necessary.

He said, "You'd better have the data. If I do this, and you

don't, you won't have to worry about being arrested as a spy. You'll just have to worry about where you'll be buried. It won't be in China."

He heard breathing for a moment, like the man was hyperventilating, then, "I have the data. I'm headed to Cairns right now. Just like you asked."

"No aircraft. Trains only. Just like you were told."

"Yes, yes. I'll meet your man in Brisbane. He'll give me the meeting site in Cairns. Just like I was told. I have it all. Just get rid of that guy."

Chen said, "Give me his cell phone number."

"Why? I thought you had him. Have you lost him?"

His voice beginning to drip with menace, Chen said, "Ask me another question and I'll rip out your throat. The number."

Jake passed it, then said, "That's all I can do. This is your problem. Your skill set, not mine. I do the hacking. That's all."

Chen said, "You'll do what I ask, period," then hung up the phone. His female partner said, "So?"

He took a breath, looked at her, and said, "So it's going to be the hard way."

He got on the radio to the stationary team and said, "Capture the people at the door. We're headed your way. I want to interrogate them."

# 13

I waited for the workers to leave, and, of course, they didn't. In fact, they stared at me a little more intently than I would have liked.

Jennifer said, "Hey, let's just go back to the car. Wait on Dunkin. It's not like we're in a rush."

I glanced at them and said, "Yeah, I guess."

We turned to leave, and the lead maintenance guy advanced, saying, "Do you know the man who lives here?"

Turning to him, a little miffed, I said, "Why do you care?"

He pulled a small semiautomatic pistol out of his pocket, aimed it at my head, and said, "Because I do."

Jennifer's jaw dropped open. The other two men circled around behind us. One of them worked the door—whether he had a key or something else I couldn't see—and it swung open. The man with the gun said, "Inside."

*What the hell?*

It was surreal. I stood there for a moment, a little bit stunned, and he waved the pistol, saying again, "Get inside."

We entered, finding that Dunkin lived like every other bachelor on earth. It was a pigsty. Meaning it was also full of weapons for Jennifer to use.

I had no idea at all of why this was happening, but that was sort of irrelevant. The five-meter target was the men threatening me. The fifty-meter target was why. They'd learn the hard way that I was pretty damn good on a five-meter target.

We entered a den full of beer cans and pizza boxes, with a few choice implements lying around the room. Jennifer looked at a bottle opener with a corkscrew on the bottom, then at me. I nodded.

The lead "maintenance worker" said, "We don't want to hurt you. We only want to know where Clifford Delmonty is. That's all. Tell us and you can leave."

I raised my hands and tried my best to sound like a coward. "Hey, come on, what's going on here? We just came for a vacation. He gave us a room. I don't know anything about anything. Please."

The Asian pointed the pistol at my head and whispered, "You lie. You know where he is, and you're going to tell us where he's gone. Right now."

He flicked his eyes to the man behind Jennifer, who grabbed her around the waist. She shuffled forward, ostensibly in shock and trying to get out of his grasp, but moving inexorably toward the table with the corkscrew. The man jerked Jennifer's hair back and put a blade to her neck, halting her advance.

I screamed, "Stop! Stop! I don't know what you're talking about. Please, don't hurt us."

The lead man said, "We have no desire to harm you. Just tell us where Clifford Delmonty is."

I said, "I can't tell you what I don't know. Please. We're just here on vacation."

He nodded at the man holding Jennifer, who placed the blade of his knife under her breast. He turned to me and said, "We can do this a long time. The death will not come quickly."

And that was enough. He had sealed his fate. I'd toyed

with talking our way out of this, because we really didn't know anything, but the threat of them carving up Jennifer was something I just couldn't let stand.

I felt the beast stir, but needed to close the distance to the pistol in the man's hand. I baited him, still playing the role, saying, "Don't hurt her. Please. Please don't hurt her."

Like a fish sensing food, he took the bait, believing he was about to crack me. He advanced on me and placed the barrel against my forehead, saying, "Where is he?"

Jennifer was within arm's reach of the corkscrew, and the position of the knife the man held wasn't lethal—well, I was sure I'd hear about it later, but it wasn't a death thing.

I locked eyes with her for a split second, then turned to the man with the pistol, feeling the steel against my skull. I raised my hands in a gesture of surrender, getting them at eye level. At the level of the barrel.

I whimpered, "Okay, okay, anything. Anything."

"Where is Clifford?"

I said, "I told you—we don't know. We just got here from America. We were supposed to meet him here after he got off work."

He jammed the pistol harder into my head, leaning into my face and saying, "Do you really want to die?"

I saw his elbows bend, presenting me with what I wanted. I now just needed a little bit of momentary doubt. A hesitation.

I said, "Do you?"

The comment put him off balance, and the gun relaxed against my skull. I saw confusion in his eyes and slapped the pistol away from my head, trapping his wrist and rotating violently against the joint, whirling around in a tight circle, feeling his wristbone shatter as he flipped through the air.

I slammed him on his back, jerked the pistol out of his

hands, jammed it into his temple just like he had done with me, and pulled the trigger, exploding his brain out of the back of his skull.

I leapt up, seeing Jennifer's captor impaled with the corkscrew straight through his right eye, her arm working the weapon while the other one controlled the blade he had used against her. He screamed and began violently thrashing.

I shouted, "Off! Off!"

She bounced back and the man doubled over, grasping the corkscrew. I shot him in the head, dropping him to the floor. I turned to the third man, and he took a running leap to the door. I fired once, hitting him, but not a death shot. He bounced against the doorframe, and then went through it, running flat out.

I let him go.

Jennifer looked at me, hands on her knees and breathing heavily. I checked my newfound weapon, then took a breath myself. We stood for a pregnant second, saying nothing. Finally, she broke the silence, saying, "What the hell just happened?"

She was looking at me like it was my fault. I said, "What?"

"What was that? Don't give me a load of bull about how this was a surprise. Why are we down here? What did you do?"

Incredulous, I said, "Me? Are you serious? I didn't cause this. I should ask what you were doing on the internet during the flight down."

She took a deep breath, kicked the guy at her feet, and said, "You were going to let him cut me."

I smiled and said, "There's a shortage of perfect breasts in this world. It would be a pity to damage yours."

And the *Princess Bride* quote resonated, defusing the situation.

I bent down to search the guy I'd shot and she sighed, following suit with her target. She said, "What's this about?"

I found nothing worthwhile on the man at my feet, which in and of itself was important. I said, "I have no idea, but I know someone who does. We need to get the hell out of here."

She stood up, saying, "Not going to argue with that. This guy is clean. Not even a fast-food receipt."

Which meant this wasn't a simple break-in. I pulled out my phone and dialed a number, saying, "Let's go."

# 14

Chen Ju-Long had the apartment complex in sight when he saw a man come bursting out of the gate holding his hand to his thigh. Chen recognized him. He said, "What in the hell . . ." and whipped into the small parking space out front.

His female partner rolled down the window and said, "Get in."

The man spilled into the back of the car and they were gone, heading back the way they had come. The man in the back was panting, holding his leg. The woman leaned over and said, "Move your hand."

He did, and she said, "He's hit in the thigh. It's a gouge. It's deep, but not deadly."

Chen said, "What happened?"

The woman wrapped the man's thigh in a scarf, causing him to wince. He sat up and said, "We interdicted the couple as you asked. They were skilled."

"Skilled how?"

"They . . . took out the team."

"What do you mean?"

"They're dead."

Chen took that in, then said, "They were armed?"

"Ummm . . . no."

Chen looked in the rearview mirror and saw fear. He said, "What happened?" And the man told him. Chen couldn't believe it. He had not wanted to create another scene on the continent of Australia, and now he had. It would be a firestorm, all tied to one Clifford Delmonty. Now he had to find that man, if only to shut him up.

Chen said, "Who were they?"

"I don't know. They claimed they were just meeting Clifford for a vacation. Initially, they were compliant, shocked that we interdicted them, just like we thought would happen."

"And then?"

"And then they turned into something else. The man killed Li Kang with his own pistol, and the woman killed Bao with a corkscrew."

Chen was incredulous. "What? Bao was killed by a woman? With a corkscrew?"

"Well, not killed. Just stabbed in the eye. The man killed him with Li Kang's pistol."

Chen reached a stoplight and squeezed his eyes shut. It was a disaster. He said, "So this Clifford Delmonty is more than Jake says? Is that your read?"

The man hesitated, then said, "Possibly. It's hard to tell. The couple we interdicted were skilled for sure, but I can't say that Clifford is the same."

Chen shook his head and said, "You can't? Really? You pick up a couple outside of his door and they slaughter a trained team from the Guoanbu?"

His voice rising, he said, "To what would you attribute the action? Random chance? He's just a computer programmer who has friends who can kill on command? Or perhaps it was sloppy actions?"

The man sagged in the seat, not saying a word. Chen said, "Were the men clean?"

Now on firmer ground, the man said, "Yes. I had the cell

phone. Other than that, we had no pocket litter. They can't identify anyone short of using forensics in China. It will be a mystery."

Chen scoffed and said, "Except for where they were found." He pulled over and said, "Get out. Go clean up the mess you made. You are no longer of use."

The man snapped up and said, "What will I do? I'm shot. I can't go to the hospital. I don't even have a visa for Australia."

Chen said, "Get to the evacuation safe house. Call the number. There is a doctor on call. Get patched up, then get a cleanup crew to that apartment. Dispose of the bodies, then get the hell off of this continent. You've done enough damage."

"How will I get there?"

Chen turned around and said, "I honestly don't care, but if you fuck up your own exfiltration, cause a scene in any way, I will gut you. I promise."

The man left without another word. The woman said, "It may be time to call higher. Get that number in the system. Find its location."

Chen put the car in drive and said, "I really don't want to do that. So far, this is a local problem. If I call them, I'll have to penetrate the cell network here. It will raise questions. I'd prefer to handle it on my own."

"We don't know where he's run to, and no matter what Jake said before, we have to stop him now just to cauterize the wound we've created."

Chen glanced at her, wondering about her judgment. He understood her skill, but was still unsure about her. He knew her as Zhi Rou, but understood it was an alias. She'd been assigned to him as a honeypot for the mission against Nick Zhao, the man they were trying to infiltrate into the

Australian Parliament. Her sole mission was to get him to drop his willingness to testify about the PRC plan—to get him to reconsider talking about his recruitment, leaving China in the clear. Instead, he'd ended up dead.

She'd said that it was inevitable, that the man was going to press the case against the People's Republic of China, but Chen was doubtful. Maybe she'd just decided that killing him was the easiest solution. At any rate, she'd done it in such a manner that the authorities were still confused about how he'd died. Natural causes? Of course not, but so far homicide hadn't been mentioned.

A tall woman with a statuesque build, she had straight black hair and emerald eyes that belied a pure Chinese heritage, but her loyalty was unquestionable. She had killed for the PRC under his command, but he was still unsure about her judgment.

She saw him considering and said, "The longer we wait, the farther he gets away."

Chen pulled over. "Maybe you're right." He sighed and said, "Call up our contact at external branch. Get the Third Department active."

She pulled out her encrypted cell and began dialing the Third Department of the People's Liberation Army—the 3PLA, as it was known in the West, the direct mirror of the United States' National Security Agency.

She relayed the request, hung up the phone, and said, "It'll take some time. Maybe thirty minutes."

Chen shook his head and said, "Thirty minutes is too long. We'll have to readjust to a different city. He's on the run."

His cell rang, startling them both. The other car he'd sent on a reconnaissance—a fishing expedition, really—said, "We have him. We have him. He's headed north, back on the A9."

Chen said, "We're coming. Stay on him."

He put the car in drive and said, "About time we had some luck."

# 15

Paul Kao wound through the four-lane road that circled the massive concrete structures of the National Security Bureau on the outskirts of Taipei. Outside of the gate—which appeared respectable and official—the rest of the compound looked like a prison from the road, with drab concrete buildings and a sixteen-foot wall topped with concertina razor wire.

He slowed as he reached the main gate, really not wanting to enter. He knew what lay beyond. He had failed.

Separating from every other vehicle on the freeway, he took a left, rolling up to a soldier in an immaculate uniform complete with a ceremonial weapon and a white helmet. He showed his badge and was allowed access.

Unlike the other minions, who had to park across the freeway, he was allowed the small privilege of parking inside the compound. Not because of his position, but because of who he was meeting.

He pulled to the left, drove down the central road that ringed the buildings, and found a spot reserved for the chief of the Third Department of the NSB—the department chartered for the internal protection of Taiwan. The irony wasn't lost on him that his direct opponent was the Third Bureau of the PRC's Ministry of State Security—the bureau tasked with penetrating Hong Kong, Macau, and Taiwan.

He exited his car and entered a three-story concrete

building, walking up the stairs to the second floor. He went right, stopping at a door with flags of Taiwan standing left and right. He pressed the buzzer and heard a lock click open. He entered, saw a secretary at a desk, and said, "I have a meeting scheduled."

She pressed a buzzer, said something into an intercom on her desk, then waved him forward. From her look, Paul understood that she knew what the meeting was about. Maybe not the meat, but she knew he was here for bad reasons.

Paul walked into the office and saw a short, balding man of about sixty, with Coke-bottle glasses, a rumpled suit, and a bad comb-over. He would have been the comic relief in a cop movie if Paul didn't know his skills.

His name was Jiang "Charlie" Chan, and he was the man solely responsible for stopping the kraken tentacles of the People's Republic of China from overwhelming the nascent democracy that was Taiwan.

Most anyone under the age of sixty in Taiwan took on a Western name, if only to make it easier on business trips. Some chose the English version of a word that sounded close to a Chinese character in their real name. Others, like Paul, just picked one in primary school that was easy to repeat. Paul was sure that Jiang had chosen Charlie because of his last name. It was an irreverent comment on his job, and absolutely represented the man behind the desk.

Unassuming and underestimated by all who opposed him, both in the political realm of Taiwan and the intelligence arena in which he fought, he had been responsible for the protection of his country since he had been old enough to hold a job. His successes were legendary, and he was Paul's mentor, a man Paul highly respected.

Charlie looked up, his eyes magnified by his glasses. He

pointed to a chair, and then went back to reading something on his desk. Paul sat down and waited, not daring to fidget.

Eventually, Charlie closed a folder and said, "It was him. Fished out of the Shifen Falls. Apparently he fell in and drowned downriver."

Paul felt a little sick to his stomach, knowing he had caused the death. He said, "Are we sure?"

"Yes. We have a positive identification from the family. They are questioning why he was there. Of course, there is no answer forthcoming from this office. What happened?"

Paul told him all of the actions that had occurred up until he had watched Feng walk across the bridge, succinctly summarizing the intent and the mission. He had followed all protocols for dealing with a source, to include registration in the NSB cover database and informing his direct superior of his moves, gaining approval for the action, but as they say, success has a thousand fathers. Failure is an orphan.

"So, you had no backup?"

"No. It was too short notice, and honestly, you know as well as I do that nobody believes me. The Snow Leopard isn't just running drugs. He's subverting our democracy in conjunction with the CCP. They work hand in glove, and they're working to upset our elections. Nobody would believe I was using a college student to gain leverage against them."

Charlie fiddled with a pen on his desk, then said, "This looks bad. Bad all the way around. You did everything right in recruiting this source—which means there is a paper trail a mile long. It won't take long for that to hit the press, and in so doing you might have done more to hurt the election than anything the PCC has done on social media. We'll look like the police state we used to be."

Paul put his head in his hands, not wanting to reflect on

the fact that his hubris had led to the death of one of his sources. *He* was to blame for the loss. Nobody else. And the family would get no closure. None at all. Because of the Snow Leopard.

Which brought a thought to his brain, a trickle of hope. He rose up and said, "Did anyone see anything? Did the local police get anything? Maybe we can hang the Snow Leopard on a simple murder charge instead of espionage."

Charlie said, "Nobody saw anything. He drowned outside of the tourist area. Apparently he wanted to swim downstream."

"You surely don't think that is true."

"No, I don't, but it's irrelevant what I think. He's dead, and our penetration is done."

Paul stood up, turning in a circle, unsure of how to broach what he wanted to say.

Charlie said, "Quit being so melodramatic. Sometimes things don't work out. I don't blame you."

Paul stopped pacing and gathered his courage. "Sir, he's dead because we've been penetrated here. *Here*. Somehow, the CCP knew I was sending him in. They knew to alert the Bamboo Triad. They're ahead of us."

Charlie simply stared at him with his Mr. Magoo glasses, saying nothing. Paul continued, "Think about it, sir. There were a thousand different feeds on his case, from the first penetration to his recruitment. Somewhere in there, someone saw something and alerted the mainland. Alerted the MSS. We sent him in, and he was killed."

Charlie leaned back and said, "We?"

Paul clenched his fists and said, "Okay, okay, *I* did it. But I did everything right, and he was *still* killed. We have a mole here."

"Maybe he just did something stupid. Maybe it was on him."

"Maybe. But I don't think so. It doesn't smell right. His entire case was like a floater. It was easy to find him and easy to turn him. Like the MSS wanted us to find him. Like they didn't care."

Charlie said, "Paul, I think you should take a break. Take some time off."

Paul looked at him in shock, but pressed ahead. "Sir, it's not me. I'm not imagining things. It was like the breadcrumbs were laid out for us, precisely to see how we operated. Precisely to learn our methods of operating. I think it was a test case, and we have a mole. Me leaving isn't going to fix that."

Charlie looked at him for a moment, then said, "I think it will." Paul started to protest, and he raised his hand, saying, "I agree with you. I think you're right, but the mole is the least of our problems. I'll handle that. The bigger problem is the Chinese penetration of our electoral process and the Bamboo Triad. We need to pursue them, and I can't do it with the architecture here, precisely because it might be penetrated."

"What are you saying?"

"I'm going to relieve you of your duties for your 'reckless' actions. It'll be private, but I'll let the word out through the NSB. It'll get back to the mole, and he or she will report it as a victory to the PRC."

Paul let the words sink in, realizing the implications. "You're going to make me a Ronin? That's what you're going to do? So I'll never work in this world again?"

*Ronin* was a word from feudal Japan given to a Samurai without a master. Most of them turned into bandits, and the NSB had adopted the term to describe someone who had been expelled from the agency for cause. It held a double meaning—coming from Japan was the first insult; the second was the complete and total cutting of ties with the NSB. Once it happened, the person was excised from all who worked in Taiwan intelligence circles. When the word spread, nobody inside the organization would ever talk to a Ronin again.

"Yes. You'll become a Ronin, but only for a little while. I want you to go on the hunt, but you'll report only to me." He held up a folder and said, "There are other leads here. Others like Feng. See what you can do but report only to me. Nobody else. And not here. I'll set up a method of communication."

Paul nodded dumbly, astounded at the turn of events. Finally, he said, "Will I have any support?"

Charlie smiled and said, "You'll have me. That's it. You'll be on your own, like you were when we first met. Can you do that?"

The enormity of what Charlie was asking spinning in his head, Paul said, "Yes, I can. Thank you."

Charlie stood, letting him know the meeting was over. He handed him the folder and said, "No, thank you. Make no mistake, you will go through professional hell before this is over. To support this cover, I'm going to have to disavow you completely, but I believe the mainland is about to attempt something big, and I don't think we have a way to stop it. You might very well be our last hope."

# 16

Han Ming sat in the little office chair provided to him, the swivel seat broken to the point that if he leaned too far back, the entire thing would flop onto the ground. It was yet one more indignity heaped upon him, belying his stature in the larger hierarchy of the Ministry of State Security. As much as he would have liked to make the men around him pay for giving him the broken seat—he was sure it was an intentional slight—he could not, because they held his success in their hands.

He was the head of the ministry's Third Bureau. The commander of the branch that was responsible for reuniting not only Hong Kong and Macau—known internally as the easy—but also the gem: Taiwan.

He'd made the short drive from his headquarters near the Summer Palace on the outskirts of Beijing to the area known as Zhongguancun, the "Silicon Valley of China." Inside the sprawling neighborhood of internet start-ups and artificial intelligence research facilities resided the Twelfth Bureau of the MSS—the one dedicated to technology and cyber warfare, and the one he now needed.

He waited until the sycophant finished speaking about the ongoing efforts in Taiwan, then said, "So what's that give us in the end? A couple of bumps in a poll? What's the point? The current president is leading handily."

In truth, Ming had no tolerance for the new world of information operations. He didn't care one whit about social media campaigns and other manipulation. He was a dinosaur who didn't understand the new rules. He understood pain and death. That was the only way to succeed. Get someone under your thumb and leverage two things: pain or death, either to someone the target held dear, or to the target itself.

The man briefing cringed at his statement, thinking he'd failed. Yuan Bo, the leader of the Twelfth Bureau, said, "Han, I don't think you understand how this works. If we get the KMT man elected as president, we can begin building our takeover. We're looking at this in the long term, doing it without bullets. As the CCP wants. Nobody wants a war."

Han said, "I do get it, but your efforts won't matter. Hong Kong has short-circuited all of that. He won't win. We need to look at the problem set a different way."

"An invasion is not the way. Kinetic options are not something that will work on the world stage—especially, as you say, with Hong Kong. This way we begin to erode from the inside. If not this election, then the next."

His words struck a chord with Han. Erode from the inside. Han said, "Maybe you're right. Maybe there is a way, but not in the manner you envision."

"What do you mean?"

"You deal in information manipulation, correct?"

"Yes." Yuan waved a hand to the back of the room, where a westerner was working on a terminal, saying, "We have the best in the world here."

Not having noticed the man before, Han was startled. Yuan saw his look and said, "Don't worry, he doesn't speak Chinese."

"He's still seen me. And you, for that matter."

"He thinks we're an artificial intelligence research facility. That's all. Which, of course, we are. What were your thoughts?"

Han glanced back at the man, seeing him engrossed in some video. He said, "I have some assets working for me in Australia from the Fifth Bureau. Working on a penetration of Taiwan's anti-access/area denial systems."

Han saw Yuan's eyes grow wide at the mention of the Fifth Bureau—the one that dealt with the so-called illegals. The one that dealt with death. The Fifth Bureau was the element that was called when all else had failed and the project was deemed important enough that someone needed to be eliminated. Yuan worked for the MSS from behind a keyboard. He believed in his efforts, but he had never seen the sharp end of the spear. And he never wanted to.

Han continued, "Don't worry about them. You won't have to interface, but their actions could provide a lever for us to use. What I need from you is exactly what you said: Erode them from the inside."

"How?"

"Continue working the threads you have. Continue trying to get our man elected, but at the same time, let's explore attacking the current administration. Generate some angst within the population for their chosen leaders. If we do it right, it could cause a chain reaction that will give us a seam to exploit."

Yuan nodded, not understanding what was being asked. He said, "We're doing that. We've been attacking them on every available platform. It doesn't get any traction. They simply don't like China."

"Yes, yes, that's correct. And that's exactly what I want to use. What does the Taiwanese population most fear?"

"Our takeover."

"True, but that's not the fear I mean. What do they fear from their leaders?"

Yuan thought for a moment, then said, "Capitulation to us?"

"Exactly. Can you seed that fear into the fabric of their society? Make it seem as if the administration—while stridently hawking a hard line against the PRC—actually plans to begin increasing ties to us. It will generate unrest. Get people in the streets. Can you do that?"

"I can with some data points on the inside. Some leverage that I don't currently own."

Han nodded, saying, "Like what?"

"Videos of speakers, audio of them, images. Something I can manipulate. The more data, the better, to make it seem real. Fakes are easy to spot. Do you have anyone on the inside for that? Someone close to the administration? Can we use Leopard?"

Han said, "Leopard isn't any help. He's a damn criminal. Running the Bamboo Triad will help for the unrest, but not for what you want. Honestly, he's so hot right now I might have to eliminate him anyway."

Yuan's eyes widened at how casually Han made the statement. He remained silent. Han pulled his lip, thinking. Finally, he said, "We have a man on the inside. Code-named Ocelot. He's very highly placed, and we leverage him for information only. He can do it, but he'll have a short life span. If I use him, he's done."

Yuan said, "If your plan works, it won't matter."

# 17

Dunkin headed back the way he had come from work, his eyes glued to his rearview mirror. He entered the A9, driving north, and a car fell in behind him. He didn't recognize it as one of the two from before, but it still caused him angst. He thought about pulling the same stunt he had earlier, but instead just increased his speed. The car disappeared behind him, apparently minding its own business.

Dunkin exhaled, traveled another mile, and then exited the highway, turning onto a two-lane road divided by a median. His girlfriend's house was a little over a mile away. He saw traffic behind him but was no longer worried. It was a residential area, the avenue lined by houses on both sides. He crossed a creek, the bridge modern with a bike path to the right, the foliage on the sides of the road manicured. He began to relax.

He would be the first to admit his apartment complex was on the seedy side, but his girlfriend lived in an upscale area, all of the houses and duplexes fairly recent builds, complete with landscaping that extended beyond the yards of the residences. It gave him a blanket of security that was wholly undeserved.

He took a left off of the road, drove another quarter mile, and then pulled into his girlfriend's apartment complex, a modern three-story building with balconies at each level and a gate at the entry. He parked the car and sat for a minute, watching the ebb and flow of traffic. Nothing happened. He shook his head, now embarrassed at what he'd done, trying to come up with a story of why he had shown up three hours early.

He punched in the code to the gate, walked to a staircase that split the building in two, went up to the second floor, and found his girlfriend's door. He hesitated, wondering if maybe he shouldn't just go back home and meet Pike. Wondering if he wasn't going a little batty over Jake's actions.

He knocked. Nobody answered. He knocked again, and heard, "Hang on. I'm coming."

He strolled to the end of the walkway, thinking about what he would say. He put his hands on the railing and gazed into the parking lot outside. And saw the car that had been with him when he entered the A9, parked right next to his. He jumped back out of sight, the adrenaline from the last hour pouring back into him.

He crouched down and inched forward again, seeing another car approach. One he recognized as the model outside his office earlier in the day. An Asian man and woman exited, conferred with the other car, and then three doors opened, spilling out men. All Asian.

He felt his phone vibrate in his pocket, but ignored it, intently watching. One of the men pointed toward his floor, and the driver from the second car gave orders. He began panting, wondering what was coming. Behind him, he heard, "Dunkin? What are you doing?"

He turned around, seeing his girlfriend, Nicole Shoemaker, peeking out of the door with a towel on her head, wearing a bathrobe.

He sprang up and pushed her inside the door, saying, "Get some clothes on. Get dressed."

She shoved him back, saying, "What the hell are you doing?"

He ran to the window and looked out, then panicked. "Shit. Shit, shit, shit." He turned to her and said, "We have to go. Right now. Go get dressed. We have seconds."

She saw the sweat on his brow and smelled the fear. She said, "What's going on?"

"I don't have time to explain. Go get dressed!"

She nodded and ran into her room. Ten seconds later she was pulling on a sweatshirt over her bare breasts and hiking up jeans without panties. She shoved her feet into a set of flip-flops and said again, "What's going on?"

"No flip-flops. Put on shoes." He pulled the shade back again and said, "Jesus Christ! Do it now!"

She heard the urgency in his voice and ran back into her room. When she came back out, Dunkin was on the balcony at the back of the apartment, looking at the drop. She came to him and said, "What the hell is going on?"

"I don't have time to explain, but we need to leave right now. Right here."

"Over the damn balcony? Have you lost your mind?"

Dunkin cupped her chin in his hands and said, "You know when I talked about my past? Where I was some secret American commando?"

She hesitantly nodded, then said, "Yes?"

"Well, that was all bullshit. I worked for some commandos, but I wasn't one. Now someone's hunting me, and I don't know if I can keep us alive. I don't have the skill. We need to run. Run like hell."

"What are you talking about?"

He pushed her to the edge of the balcony and said, "You need to jump. I'll be right behind you. We need to do it now. We have seconds."

"Are you crazy? Jump? Why?"

"Because there are some men coming here who want to kill me! And they'll kill you! They're about five seconds away!"

He pushed her to the railing and said, "Hang over and drop. Please, dear God, don't fight anymore. They're coming."

She did as he asked, seeing the absolute terror on his face. She crawled over, hung for a moment, looked below her, then said, "I can't do this! Pull me up."

Instead, he pried her hands from the railing. She screamed, falling into the bushes below. He scrambled over and followed her, landing on his ass right next to her.

She stood up, incensed and confused, holding her hip. She punched him in the face, screaming, "You son of a bitch! I'm calling the police!" He took the hit, grabbed her hands, then held a finger to his lips, pointing to her balcony. She looked up and saw an Asian man exit. She said, "What—"

He cut her off, dragging her into the bushes underneath the balcony, out of sight. He said, "Where is your car?"

She pointed and he said, "You need to trust me. Let's go. We need to get the fuck out of here."

She said, "Are you nuts? I just fell twenty feet into some bushes. It's amazing I can even walk. I'm pretty sure I won't be walking tomorrow. What the hell is going on?"

"Nicole . . . Nicole . . . I can't explain right here. I just can't. We need to leave."

She took a breath, glanced upward toward her apartment, then nodded, saying, "Whatever you tell me had better be good."

The man went back inside, and they raced to the rear

parking lot, entered her car, and fled the area, saying not a word. When they were back on the A9, headed away from her apartment, Nicole said, "Okay, what the hell is going on? Who are you?"

Dunkin pulled out his phone and said, "I'm a nobody. I lied to you before. I'm not some secret agent man. I'm just a computer nerd. And I don't know why those guys were chasing me, but they were. They were trying to hurt me."

She said, "Wait, so you weren't in Special Forces?"

He saw a missed call from Pike Logan and breathed a sigh of relief. He turned to her and said, "No, I wasn't, but I have some friends who were. And they're a holy terror."

# 18

Chen entered the apartment with his pistol drawn, not wanting to make a mess of blood and gore, but willing to do so in order to cut off further disaster.

His team swiftly cleared the small area and found nothing. He saw the open balcony door, ran to it, looked over, and said, "They're in the wind."

His female partner, Zhi, said, "We need to find them. Kill them quickly. This is getting out of control."

He nodded and began giving orders, saying, "Find me anything that ties to this apartment. Find out who lives here."

Zhi said, "Let me recontact the 3PLA. That's the quickest way to locate him. They probably have the phone now. He needs to be put in the ground before this spreads like a virus."

Chen said, "I don't want to get them involved. We're on our own here. We've been given our orders, and they expect us to succeed."

She approached him and gently touched his arms. "You were willing to get them involved earlier."

"That was before we had a thread to him. We have one now."

"How? We have an apartment. And no bodies."

He said, "Did you kill the politician we'd recruited because you wanted to? Or because it was necessary?"

He saw the shock on her face, and the abrupt change

in demeanor. She dropped her hands and said, "Are you questioning my commitment?"

"No. Not at all. His death is proof of your commitment. I'm questioning your judgment."

She shifted yet again, closing on him and wrapping her hands around his neck, stroking his jugular with the middle nail of her right hand, saying, "You didn't question that judgment last night."

He felt the heat and pushed her away, seeing the crazy blossom in her eyes at his rejection.

He said, "Not here. Not now. Last night was a mistake. Get back into focus." She turned feral, looking like she wanted to use the nail for real.

They waited in silence, letting the men search. A cat jumped on a counter, allowing Zhi to pick it up. She scratched behind its ears as if she were rebuking Chen for his rejection of her. Eventually, one man came back with an assortment of bills and said, "These are all for a woman named Nicole Shoemaker. She's who lives here."

Chen took the bills and said, "Why did he come here? Who is she?"

"No idea. That's all we've found."

Zhi said, "You want to keep dancing around the issue? Or find the guy? We have his phone."

Chen saw her anger, and said, "Okay. Call the Third Department. Let's get them in play."

She gave him a smile, a dead thing that reminded him of teeth from a roadkill, and dialed the phone. He turned back to the men and said, "Get me an anchor here. Besides a name."

They went back to work, and he looked at Zhi. She hung up the phone and said, "Last contact was on the A9 headed north. His phone is now dead."

He slapped his hand on the counter. "That's perfect for this operation. We get them involved and they're no help. Just great."

Zhi said, "It's not all bad. They're tracking it now. The lead time is gone. If he turns it on again, they'll have a lock immediately."

Chen shook his head and said, "Yeah, but now the entire organization knows we're looking. We're illegals. We don't engage them without a reason, and usually that reason means someone has failed. In this case, me."

A man came out of a bedroom and said, "I have a lease for the place, but there's nothing else."

Zhi asked, "Is there a phone number on it?"

Chen looked at her and she said, "If his phone is off, hers might not be."

Which was pretty smart. He'd already alerted the hierarchy that he was in trouble here, so he might as well go all the way.

The man said, "No. It's just an address to the rental agency. It's in this building."

Chen said, "In this building? Where?"

"First floor. Right below us."

He looked at Zhi, and she nodded. He said, "Okay, we're going down there, but no killing. All we want is the phone number to the person in this apartment. Understood?"

# 19

Behind the wheel of his girlfriend's Hyundai, Dunkin raced out of the parking lot and away from the apartment complex. Nicole demanded to know what was happening, but he gave her no explanation. Mainly because he didn't have one. He handed her his phone and said, "Dial the last missed call. Put it on speaker."

She did, and Dunkin heard a woman answer, saying, "Dunkin? Is that you?"

He said, "Jennifer?"

"Yes. Yes, this is Jennifer. Where are you? We've been trying to call."

"Are you at my apartment?"

"Not anymore."

"But you were there?"

The phone went blank. Dunkin and Nicole heard a shuffling, like the handset had been dropped or they were listening to a butt-dial. From what sounded like a tunnel, Jennifer said, "Pike!" Then they heard someone snarl, "Is this Dunkin?"

Dunkin said, "Yes, it's me. Is this Pike?"

The tiny phone speaker did little to hide the venom coming out. "Yes, it's Pike, you dipshit. What the fuck is going on with you?"

"Pike, I'm headed out of town. I'm sorry. I know I said you could stay with me, but I've had an issue come up."

"No shit, asshole. I just killed two men at your apartment."

Nicole put a hand to her mouth. Dunkin wasn't sure if he'd heard correctly. "What did you just say?"

"I said I killed two men at your house. They were hunting you, and they found me. Tell me where you are. I'm on the road now."

Nicole said, "How did he kill two people? What's going on?"

Pike said, "Who is that? Who are you with?"

Now feeling real fear, Dunkin said, "It's my girlfriend. Pike, some men are chasing me. I don't know what to do."

"No shit. I'm pretty sure that's an accurate statement. Change your diaper and hang on."

The next voice he heard was Jennifer. "Pike says to get out of blast radius. He wants you gone from here."

"What about the police? Maybe I should go to them."

"Not yet. Maybe in the future, but if you go now, we're going to get wrapped up in a homicide investigation."

"What will waiting do? I mean, the people are dead. They aren't going to disappear. It'll just get worse, like I'm hiding something."

"Pike thinks this was done by professionals. He thinks they'll clean up the mess for us. The key thing now is to get you safe. Can you go somewhere?"

"Yes. We can go to Sydney. Nicole's sister has a place there. Is that far enough?"

"I don't know. How far is it?"

"About fifteen hours away. It's all the way on the eastern side of the continent."

He heard a muffled conversation, then, "Pike says that's

good. We're going to check out your apartment, then head there as well. He wants to know who the people who are tracking you." There was a scrambled bit of conversation, ending with, "No, I'm not going to ask him that."

Dunkin said, "I have no idea. I mean, I think I know why, but I can't believe it went from suspicion to killing people in the span of a few hours. I'm supposed to be on vacation."

He heard, "No, Pike, I'm not going to ask him that. Just drive the car."

"What's he want to know?"

He heard a sigh, then, "He wants to know how you could be so stupid as to set us up to be killed."

"I didn't do that on purpose! It just happened. I headed to my place and saw what I thought was surveillance, so I ditched them. I went to my girlfriend's place, and they showed up there as well. I was just running!" He muttered, "I'm not a Special Forces badass. This is insane."

Jennifer said, "They showed up at your girlfriend's place as well?"

"Yes! That's what I'm telling you."

"How did they know to go there?"

"I have no idea. It's not like it's on my employment application. They just did."

Dunkin heard some crosstalk, then Jennifer came back on, saying, "Does your girlfriend have a phone?"

He looked at Nicole, and she held up an iPhone 10. He said, "Yeah, she's got one. Why?"

"Pike says to turn off your phone and pull the battery. Make it dead. He thinks they're tracking your phone."

"Who? Who would do that?"

"Jesus, Dunkin, those are our questions. Just do it. Call Pike back on your girlfriend's phone."

# 20

Sitting in his car, Chen watched the front door of the rental agency, waiting on the man inside to leave. It was now past 6 P.M., and the storefront sign said it was closing time.

He had initially sent in Zhi, trying a bit of simple social engineering. She'd told the man that she'd been retained to watch over Nicole's cat while she was out of town, but that she hadn't left the required medical paperwork should the animal need to be taken to a veterinarian. Zhi only had her home phone number, having lost her cell number, and wondered if the man would give it to her?

The answer wasn't what they expected. Nicole hadn't put down a pet deposit and wasn't supposed to have a cat in the first place. The rental agent began to probe her connection to Nicole, asking Zhi how long she would be gone. He'd ended by pulling out a folder from the file cabinet, then dialing a number. He waited a beat, then hung up, saying, "It went to voice mail. I don't know how great a friend you are—since you don't even know her cell number—but you'll need to remove that cat or it'll cancel her lease."

She'd left, entered the car with Chen, and said, "He wouldn't give it to me, but I saw where the lease is stored. And I shimmed the door on the way out."

Chen said, "Good, good," and they'd begun to wait. At

twelve minutes past six, the realtor left the office. Chen called his team and said, "He's moving. Back lot. Get eyes on him."

Forty-five seconds later he heard, "He's in his car. Stand by," then, "He's rolling. He's gone."

A second man said, "I have eyes on the front door. You're clear."

Chen looked at Zhi and said, "Let's go."

They exited the car like they were just another resident at the apartment complex. No furtive looking around, no attempts to see if anyone was watching. Chen would leave that up to the team.

They went into an outside hallway, passing the first floor of rentals and stopping at the door of the leasing agency. It looked like a ground-floor apartment, the only indicator that it was not being a sign dictating hours of service.

Chen bent down and studied the lock, saying, "Bolt isn't engaged. Just the doorknob lock." Zhi reached into her jacket and pulled out a small device that looked like a miniature crowbar with a hook on the end. She bent down, found the shim she'd left in between the door and its frame, and slid it up until it contacted the lockset. She mated the tool to a receptacle for that purpose, then levered the device to the right, separating the door from the frame by about a quarter of an inch. Chen slipped another tool into the gap and popped the lock, the door swinging inward. He glanced back once, then entered. Zhi picked up the shim and followed, letting the door close again, locked.

Chen went to the window, glanced out, then called the team. "We're in. Status?"

"You're good. Nobody moving in the parking lot or on your floor."

He flicked his head to Zhi and she went straight to the filing cabinet. She went to work on the cheap lock, sprung it, then began flipping folders, looking for a name.

Chen's radio came alive. "Realtor is entering the parking lot. I say again, realtor is returning."

Zhi looked up at Chen, then redoubled her efforts. Chen said, "How long do we have?"

"A minute on the outside to him reaching you. Maybe fifteen seconds before he sees you leave."

He turned to Zhi. "Do you have it?"

Starting to frantically flip the folders, she said, "Not yet, not yet."

He called the team. "Can you interdict?"

"Not here in the parking lot. Not without a scene. He's got view of the door now. He's on the way."

Zhi held up a folder and said, "Got it!"

Chen said, "Give it to me." She did, taking a position on the left side of the door, away from the direction it opened. Chen wrote down the phone number, shoved it back into the filing cabinet, then said, "Back room."

The "office" was really just a converted single studio apartment, with a bedroom off the back that was now used as storage, complete with a television and a desk. They scrambled to it, closing the door just as they heard a key hit the lock out front.

The man entered, and Zhi flicked open her middle finger, like she was an American teenager insulting someone. The same finger she'd stroked his neck with earlier. The nail was longer than the others and trimmed to a point like a miniature dagger. She removed a plastic sheath, exposing a ceramic cap mated to the nail that had been sharpened as fine as a razor, giving her a half-inch weapon perfect for a carotid artery. Chen slowly shook his head, whispering, "No blood. No blood."

They heard shuffling out front, then a muttered "What the hell?"

They heard the file cabinet drawers opening and closing, then the tromping of footsteps to them. The door was flung open, and Chen came face-to-face with the realtor. He said, "Who the hell are you?" and Zhi snatched his head by the hair, bending his neck backward until he was off balance, forcing him to throw himself down to the ground to prevent his neck from breaking.

He landed on his back, his eyes wild, his hands thrashing left and right, trying to connect with the person over him. Zhi jammed his head into his chest, exposing the vertebrae of his neck in the back, then swung her mini-crowbar, smashing his spine just below the base of his skull.

The man went limp, then his body succumbed to the death, his bowels soiling his pants. She dropped his head, checked for a pulse, then said, "He's gone."

Chen said, "Get him off the carpet. Get him off the carpet before he stains it."

They rolled him onto the hardwood floor and Chen cursed, saying, "I told you no blood."

She looked honestly confused, saying, "There wasn't any blood."

He ran a hand through his hair. "I meant no *killing*."

Zhi took in the chastising, then said, "You should have been more precise. Do you have the number?"

A hand to his face, his fingers squeezing his temples, Chen said, "Yes."

"Then let's get it back under control."

Chen nodded and clicked his radio, saying, "We're going

to need a cleanup in here. Park as close as you can. We're bringing a body out."

The team acknowledged, and Chen said, "Go find some paper towels or something. Wipe up your mess."

She squinted her eyes and said, "Let me track the phone. Let them do the cleanup. I did the dirty work."

He looked at her for a moment, then said, "Okay. Find that handset."

She left him alone with the body. He crossed its legs and rolled the carcass onto its stomach, revolted at the stench. His men entered, and he stood, saying, "Figure out a way to get this guy out of here. If it means rolling him up in a carpet like an American gangster film, then so be it."

He went back into the den of the main office and saw Zhi hang up the phone. "Get anything?"

"Yes. They're on the main highway headed east. About a hundred miles away now, and growing."

"Where are they headed?"

"No idea, all they can tell me is that it's away from here. There are a hundred small towns and cities between us and the eastern coast. The biggest is Sydney."

"So we clean up here, get on the road, and wait for him to bed down."

"What about the men who helped him? The ones that killed Bao and Li Kang?"

"We deal with them when we have to. The main thing now is to eliminate Clifford. If I can do that without engaging the others, so be it. Chances are, they've already fled because of the men they've killed."

Zhi put the phone in her pocket, saw the men struggling to roll up the body in a throw rug, and said, "I think those men are like us. We forced them to kill, and they did so."

Chen watched the body leaving and said, "We might have forced them to kill, but they have never met anything like us. Now it's our turn."

Zhi said, "Don't underestimate them. I don't think they're going to quit because of a little blood."

# 21

The aircraft wheels hit the runway and I immediately turned on my phone, looking for a contact from Dunkin. I saw a text saying they were pulling over for a little rest. I didn't fault that, but it left him outside of my protective umbrella. Someone was trying to kill him, and he didn't have the skills to prevent it. I wanted him with me, here in Sydney, not sleeping on the side of a highway.

Jennifer said, "Did you get anything?"

I said, "Yeah, they've stopped. Still heading here, but they've stopped for some chow and a rest break."

We'd agreed that he wouldn't contact me over the cell network with a verbal call, because that would be recorded on the cell network. He'd only use his girlfriend's phone to contact me over iMessage—a feature of the iPhone that, when used over WiFi, was damn near impossible to trace. Something I'd learned tracking terrorists.

I texted him back, telling him we were on the ground in Sydney and to let me know when he showed up. The passengers started to stand up, waiting on the gate to open.

Jennifer said, "You think he's going to be okay?"

I stood up, opened the overhead bin, and said, "I hope so, but I honestly don't know. The people he's up against are professionals. I don't have any idea of the assets they're using to target him."

We'd never even made it to his girlfriend's apartment, having peeled off when he told us he was on the run. I'd circled back around and staked out his own place, watching to see what happened. I'd half expected to find a slew of cop cars with the lights going, but instead saw nothing. We'd waited for three hours, and then had seen two vans pull up with plumbing signs on their sides. They'd closed right up to his staircase and exited looking like they were about to fight Ebola, complete with matching jumpsuits and cotton masks. They'd marched through the gate like they were about to clean up the biggest turd in toilet history. Nobody paid them the least bit of attention.

I'd perked up at the arrival, and we'd watched them come and go, taking in rolls of opaque plastic sheeting like they were doing extensive renovations. Eventually, they'd come back out, carrying the sheeting with them, but now it took two men per roll. There were plenty of people coming and going, but once again, nobody seemed to care.

They were good, no doubt. They most certainly weren't some local thug force. There was some power behind them, and I was betting it wasn't from Australia. Not the least because every single one of them was Asian.

After seeing that, I'd decided that the best course of action was to get to Sydney for local protection of Dunkin until we could sort it out. Initially, I'd toyed with interdicting the plumbers, but without a team that was asking for trouble. These guys clearly had assets that I did not, and odds were they couldn't tell me anything that I couldn't find out from Dunkin. The most I'd get was a fight and a sullen asshole who'd rather die than talk.

Make no mistake, I had no illusions that they didn't know I existed—hell, they were pulling out bodies we'd left behind—but I didn't want them to know I was still on the hunt.

Instead of driving, we'd caught the last flight out of Adelaide before they shut down the airport at 11 P.M., getting the last two seats on a cheap commuter bird at 2220, and had hit the ground in Sydney right after midnight. Even with all of that, we'd beat Dunkin and his girlfriend using the roads. Which was okay because we still needed to find a place to stay. I wasn't going to ask to barge into his girlfriend's sister's house. Well, that had in fact crossed my mind, but it wasn't good operational security.

I handed Jennifer her bag from the overhead bin and she whispered, "You know those two are scared out of their minds. Maybe we should let them go to the cops, since we're in the clear now."

I glanced left and right, saw everyone concerned with their own exit from the aircraft, and leaned over, saying, "Yeah, maybe you're right. But we're not the ones that are going to call the cops. We'll let him do that. *After* I've talked to him."

I could tell she knew that was coming, and decided to poke her a little bit. "It's you. That's what it is."

She stood up and said, "Me? How is this my fault?"

"Amena said the bad man would come for you. And here we are, bad men and all."

The line started moving and she grinned, punching me in the arm. "It's not me. It's you. It always has been."

Which, really, was like a wife seeing a mess in the room and then asking the husband what had happened. It didn't matter what I said, I was to blame. And now I was actually married to prove it.

I started walking up the aisle and she said, "You going to call George on this, or just wing it?"

I looked at my watch and said, “It’s morning there, so I guess I should. But after we’re off the plane.”

When I finally dialed the phone, even I was astonished at what I heard.

George Wolffe paced the marble foyer of the Old Executive Office Building, waiting on his escort to take him to the second-level SCIF, barely registering the officer manning the checkpoint that kept him from venturing farther. He had more important things on his mind. Alexander Palmer had asked for a team to start exploring Chinese activities against the United States or its allies, and now he was supposed to present what was in the art of the possible. That was the easy part. What he wasn’t sure of was whether he should tell them that the art of the possible was now in motion.

This morning, his encrypted cell phone had gone off before he’d even left his house, the tone causing a Pavlovian response in his brain; something important had occurred.

With shaving cream still on his face, he’d snatched the phone off his nightstand to avoid waking his wife and then had padded into the kitchen, wondering who on earth would be calling so early. It couldn’t be good news.

And it wasn’t.

It was Pike Logan, and he had a story to tell. When he was done, George Wolffe had a hard time assimilating all of the information. He homed in on the most drastic.

“Are you telling me you killed two people in Australia? While you’re on vacation?”

“Yes, sir, but that’s not the point. They were targeting Dunkin, and they pulled a gun on me. It was self-defense. Did you hear what I said about Dunkin?”

"Pike, hold on a minute. Yes, I heard about Dunkin, and that you believe he's being targeted for something that you don't understand—but you killed two people? If you say it was self-defense, then it was self-defense, but that's not going to help with a police investigation. Have you thought about that? You need to get the hell out of Australia. Right now. We'll have to start burning your existence to the ground."

"That's exactly what I want. That's why I'm calling. Can you send the Rock Star bird down here to pick me up? I want to evacuate Dunkin with it. Get him out of the blast radius until we can figure out what's going on."

The "Rock Star" aircraft was a Gulfstream 650 that was ostensibly leased by Pike's company, Grolier Recovery Services, but in reality was owned completely by the Taskforce, which meant it would need release authority from Wolffe to fly to Australia.

While Wolffe thought over the ramifications, Pike continued, "Don't worry about a police response. I just want to get out of here without going through a commercial airport. I told you the guys were professionals. They cleaned up the mess they left behind. Nobody interceded. It's Dunkin's apartment, and he's not coming back. There will be no police response, unless it's in China."

And that got Wolffe's attention. "China? Why do you say that?"

"The people who are tracking Dunkin—including the two we killed—are Chinese. I'm sure of it."

"Why?"

"Because the entire team was Asian, and nobody else around this part of the neighborhood has the skills to do what they did. The Japanese could have done it, but they don't play that way, and it sure as shit wasn't a team out of Laos. It's the Chinese."

"What was Dunkin working on in Australia?"

"I have no idea. Something with artificial intelligence and the F-35."

*Holy shit.* Alexander Palmer was right. Even a blind pig finds an acorn every once in a while.

He said, "What's your status now?"

"I'm in Sydney. We're getting a hotel and crashing until Dunkin arrives. Can I get the plane?"

"Yeah. You got the Rock Star bird, but it's coming with your team. Don't evacuate. I have to brief the Oversight Council today. You just get your hands on Dunkin and hold fast."

# 22

Wolffe heard his name called and saw his escort coming down the stairs. The man held out a lanyard with the lowly "V" for visitor badge, and Wolffe put it around his neck. The man said, "Follow me," and turned without another word, walking back up the stairs. Wolffe fell in behind him, still wondering if he should broach the fact that he'd launched an entire team to Australia.

He'd been given the go-ahead to explore options, and his purpose today was to brief those options for a decision—only he'd already made one. But it was a little late for hand-wringing, because the briefing he'd sent earlier was in black and white. If anyone did any prereading, it was done.

His one saving grace was that it had been forced on him. He didn't ask the Chinese to attack Pike—hell, he was the one who said the Taskforce shouldn't be targeted against state systems. The Oversight Council set the ball in motion, not him.

Or so he told himself.

Before he knew it, he was outside a secure door. He saw no Secret Service men, which meant the president wasn't inside the room. That wasn't a good sign for Wolffe. President Hannister was one of the few who could look past the politics of an operation and deal solely with the costs and benefits.

The man said, "Electronics?" Wolffe put his cell phone in a cubby and said, "That's it. My briefing came over JWICS."

The man pressed a buzzer, and a red light came on over their heads. The door unlocked with an audible buzz, and Wolffe left his escort in the hallway, the man uncleared for what was happening behind the door.

Alexander Palmer greeted him, and Wolffe took a quick appraisal of the room: secretary of state, secretary of defense, director of the Central Intelligence Agency, chairman of the Senate Intelligence Committee, and a few private citizens who had been pressed into service to oversee the most volatile organization in the U.S. arsenal.

A fickle bunch, more often than not they'd fallen prey to the optics of an operation instead of the charter they'd been tasked with upholding. But after spending nearly three decades as a paramilitary officer in the CIA, Wolffe was well versed in politics. If Palmer thought he was going to run roughshod over him, he would learn the hard way.

Palmer met him at the door, saying, "So, you've developed some plans for China?"

Wolffe started walking to the front of the room, saying, "Yeah, I've done a little work. You told me to get a plan in motion. Remember that. This is on you."

He left Palmer with his mouth open and went to the computer system for his briefing. He booted it up, found the PowerPoint, and turned on the projector.

Without preamble, he said, "Thank you for having me here today. As you know, Project Prometheus actions are highly volatile. We don't use the project just because we can, and we shouldn't use it as a crutch when other systems fail to produce. Our charter is substate terrorist groups on the Department of State's sanctioned list."

He saw eye rolls and people looking at their watches, not wanting a lecture. He then plunged right in. "Having said that, I was asked to develop options for counteracting Chinese malign influence against our national interests, contradicting the Taskforce charter and—honestly—my own intuition. Before I could complete the analysis, though, a prior member of Prometheus was attacked in Australia by what I believe are Chinese assets. The man in question left us a year ago, and now works for a company that builds the artificial intelligence for the helmets used in the F-35. Because of the extraordinary confluence of events, I'm not here to brief you on options, but about an ongoing operation."

Nobody was nodding off now. Easton Beau Clute, the chairman of the powerful Senate Select Committee on Intelligence, said, "What do you mean?"

And Wolffe told him, succinctly summing up what Pike had stumbled across, ending with his order to send the rest of Pike's team to Australia under the cover of Grolier Recovery Services, Pike's company.

Alexander Palmer pinched the bridge of his nose, then said, "Wait, wait, wait. Pike conducted lethal operations in a Five Eyes state? Against China? Without any sanction whatsoever?"

The so-called Five Eyes was the intelligence collaboration of the English-speaking countries of the United Kingdom, Canada, New Zealand, Australia, and the United States. In addition to sharing intelligence with one another, each country had made a formal commitment not to conduct any spying operations inside the other member states. Wolffe knew that by invoking the nickname, Palmer was telling him this was bigger than a simple operation. It was tantamount to breaking an agreement that had been in place since the end of World War II.

Wolffe said, "Sir, we didn't initiate an operation. We simply reacted. Dunkin was in the crosshairs of a Chinese team, and Pike stepped in front of the bullet. That's basically what happened."

"Then why the team? Why send a team?"

"Because you told me to prepare a platform for operations against China."

"In *China,* damn it. Not Australia. And you've got that lunatic Pike involved. What are you going to do when he's arrested? Claim diplomatic immunity?"

"He won't get arrested. There is no crime scene." Wolffe walked them through what Pike had told him, saying it was one more indicator of a concerted effort from an intelligence organization with robust resources. Meaning China.

"In short, this isn't a JV team. You wanted me to explore options against the CCP, and I told you we had no thread. The Taskforce is a targeting organization, not an intelligence collection one. Well, now we have a target."

The secretary of state, Amanda Croft, said, "What is it you hope to do? Why did you send a team to reinforce Pike instead of an extraction team?"

"Honestly, the potential breach with the F-35 program was what energized this. Pike actually asked for an exfiltration platform. After he told me what he knew, I decided to reinforce him. I can pull them back, if the Council thinks that's the correct course of action, but Pike has a feeling for these things. Something's going on down there, and he's in the heart of it."

Palmer scoffed and said, "Pike creates his own messes. We're going to need the president to weigh in on this. We're talking about mucking around in the backyard of one of our staunchest allies."

Wolffe said, "Fine by me. I'm not freelancing here. You asked for a platform, and I'm giving you one. Brief the president, but make no mistake, as much as you might not like Pike, you can't argue with his track record. But get it done quickly."

Croft said, "Why? What's the rush on this?"

"Dunkin is on the run. Pike's going to protect him. That will happen no matter what the president says, and I'd really like some sanction here. I can't in good conscience tell Pike to back off with Dunkin's life in jeopardy."

Palmer said, "Which is precisely why I didn't want to use him. He doesn't listen to his higher command."

Wolffe shut off the computer and said, "He does listen. But what he's hearing is the protection of the nation, not our hand-wringing. He'll do what's right, and we owe him the support to accomplish the mission."

"Why? Why do we owe him anything? He went there on vacation, for God's sake. If the president says no, he's on his own."

Wolffe said, "You do that, and you'll regret it. You asked for this, and while I was against targeting Taskforce assets against a state threat—you were right. Something's going on in Australia, and it's bigger than your hatred of Pike."

# 23

Jake Shu found the correct platform, showed the conductor his ticket, then proceeded to drag his small carry-on into the train bound for Brisbane, wanting more than anything to just go to sleep. It had taken him an overnight hell trip just to reach Sydney, and now he had another train to Brisbane. Truth be told, he was growing tired of the effort. Initially, early on in his career, he'd enjoyed the thrill of doing something secret, but the travel for this one had become demanding. Why they wouldn't just use an airplane was beyond him. He knew how quickly someone's digital tracks could be found, and yes, being on a flight manifest would make things exponentially easier, but only if something went wrong.

If that happened, he'd increase his timeline by a couple of days, but that was about it. With his computer skills, he knew the incredible digital footprint each human emitted just carrying a phone, and because of that, he knew that in today's interconnected world, they'd find him no matter what he did. It never crossed his mind that the men he worked for had no thought of his protection. They only wanted to protect themselves, and two days would work for them.

Jake couldn't be faulted for that. After all, the United Front Work Department had been unfailingly helpful to him through the years. Their initial contact had been while he was an undergraduate at Stanford, eating ramen and running short of funds.

The scholarship he'd earned had paid for tuition and books, but he couldn't eat class schedules or lectures. A Chinese exchange student had introduced him to a man who could help—someone who helped all students of Chinese heritage out of pure goodwill. At first, the man had simply given him a monthly stipend—enough to get him through undergraduate school. By the time he was at MIT, he'd become dependent on the income. And then the first requests had come in, and Jake had leapt at the chance to prove his worth. He'd wanted to provide a little payback for all the help his Chinese friends had provided, and most of what they were asking for was going to be published anyway. It wasn't like it was a state secret.

And then the questions had become more aggressive, wanting information that wasn't published. Wanting to know what was happening inside the labs at MIT. He'd initially balked, and the United Front Work Department had backed off, but the money kept rolling in. Jake had continued to soak it up.

Then they'd made another request, this time addressing not only the money, but his extended family in China, for the first time showing him the help he could facilitate.

Or the harm.

In truth, he *wanted* to do the work. Wanted to repay them for his success, and it ended up being an easy justification in his mind. He'd support himself *and* his family in China, even if he'd never met them.

After graduation he'd taken his first job in Silicon Valley, and he'd continued the relationship, spilling little tidbits on the way. Like the proverbial frog in a pot with the heat slowly increased, he'd been drawn deeper and deeper until there was no way to get out, but even then, the information he'd provided was easy. In the past, the transfer of technology had been a simple affair, done in his own hometown.

This one had been decidedly harder.

The drive to the east coast had taken twelve hours straight, and he'd had to push it to make his train connection in Sydney because he'd hung around in Adelaide to ensure that the interloper Clifford Delmonty had been targeted. Another first.

He'd barely made the train. He shuffled down the aisle wanting nothing more than to find his seat and go to sleep. The trip up to Brisbane was another overnight, but at least now he didn't have to drive. He only hoped his seat would recline enough to give him a little rest. He didn't give a thought to the contact he was supposed to meet in Brisbane. That could wait. They acted like they controlled him, but they did not.

At least that's what he told himself.

# 24

I flipped the channel on the television, mindlessly cycling through the shows and slowly growing bored. Well, more like antsy. Jennifer was next to me in the bed, but she'd fallen asleep in her clothes. I'd managed about four hours, but the jet lag combined with the events from the last twenty-four hours had caused me to wake up and stare at the television. I wanted to poke Jennifer in the arm, because I was sick of being awake by myself, but I didn't. We were both waiting on Dunkin to wake up and tell us just what the hell he thought was going on, so it wasn't fair to cause Jennifer to lose sleep just because I couldn't rest.

At 4 A.M., Dunkin had called saying they were about an hour outside of Sydney. He'd given me his girlfriend's sister's address, and Jennifer had found a hotel that was close. I'd wanted to get right to it, meeting them at the apartment, but he'd said that his girlfriend was a little frazzled by the whole adventure and wasn't sure how her sister would take it if we all showed up. Jennifer thought it would be better if they got some rest first, and we'd agreed to let them sleep as long as he called as soon as they woke up.

That had been close to twelve hours ago, and I was not only sleepless, but getting a little hungry—not the least because the hotel Jennifer had found was some sort of hipster throwback from the sixties, complete with a single vegan restaurant on site. Nothing wrong with that, but man, I was craving some meat.

Called the Ovolo Woolloomooloo—yes, you read that correctly—it was built at the end of what once was a working wharf in a neighborhood called, of course, Woolloomooloo, but now all the old warehouses had been turned into restaurants, bars, and apartments. Apparently Russell Crowe, the actor, lived at the end of the wharf overlooking the water. At least that's what the bellboy told us when we checked in at the crack of dawn.

We'd put our bags in the room and had gone out for breakfast—trying to find some place that served actual bacon—and had ended up exploring the area. Along the back of the wharf was a stairwell that led to a huge expanse of grounds that turned out to be the Royal Botanic Garden Sydney, situated on a bluff. Adjacent to the bluff, facing our hotel and the water, was the apartment/condominium complex where Nicole's sister lived. She must have been doing pretty well, because she had a better view of the bay than Russell Crowe.

A two-story structure, it had entrances at the wharf side and walkways on the top that bridged a road and led straight to the garden, along with what looked like firepits and other amenities. During our walkabout, I'd been surprised to find it as close to our hotel as it was, and wanted to go up and knock on Dunkin's door, but he hadn't given me the actual door number, and the building stretched all the way down the wharf with a gated access, so I let it go.

We eventually found a small hotel serving breakfast. It was an ancient two-story brick and wooden building that looked like a saloon from the American Old West, complete with an upper wooden balcony surrounding it. Upon entering, we found the inside like an old saloon as well. It was a pub, and, as far as I could tell, not a real hotel at all. I learned that apparently every old pub in Sydney was called a hotel due to some obscure liquor law in the past about providing room and board as a "public house." This one might have had a room or two for a drunk to sleep it off, but nothing like a reception desk or room keys.

After a good carnivore breakfast, we'd returned to our hipster hotel, and Jennifer had finally talked me into calling Amena. It was a little after 9 A.M. here, and with the time difference, it would be 5 P.M. there, meaning she was out from school and living in her little dorm. I didn't want to, but maybe Jennifer had a point. We'd been gone for three days, and maybe she needed to hear our voices.

It was an odd feeling, honestly, because I'd lived just for myself for the longest time, and now I was afraid of what I'd find out. I didn't want to hear her life was a living hell in the dorm—even if I knew it wasn't. I had enough on my plate.

Jennifer had crawled onto the bed, put a pillow behind her head, and said, "You really think this is being a good father? Not calling? She needs to hear from us."

Which had really set me off. I said, "Father? Are you serious? We have a team trying to murder us here. You just killed a guy with a damn corkscrew. Don't give me that shit."

She pulled her legs up underneath her and said, "I know what I did. Don't remind me. You need to talk to your daughter."

Her eyes were so cold I was at a loss for words. I said, "Jennifer, we have something more important going on here."

She said, "There is nothing more important than Amena. Are you afraid to call?"

And she was right. I was afraid to call. I didn't want to hear her voice. Didn't want to hear that she was lost.

I said, "We can do that later. After we've gotten Dunkin on the plane and we're flying home."

She uncurled her legs, put her hands behind her head, and said, "We're not going home. You know it and I know it."

I looked at her, wondering where that was coming from. I said, "All we're doing is getting Dunkin out of here. That's it. We can talk to Amena when we get back to Charleston."

She leaned up on an elbow and said, "Then call her and tell her that. She's had one day of school. See how she's doing."

I played my last card, saying, "I can't right now. The school only has certain hours for calling the boarding students. We have to set that up in advance."

She squinted her eyes at me and said, "You don't think I saw you pass that cell phone? Seriously? It's not like you taught me or anything."

And I gave up, calling the drop phone I'd given my daughter.

She'd answered in a quiet voice, saying, "Is the bad man there?"

Taken aback, I said, "What? Amena?"

She said, "Yes. I have to whisper. I'm in my room."

I laughed and said, "No, the bad man isn't here. I just wanted to check in. How's it going?"

"It's okay. I miss you guys."

"But you have a room, and classes are going okay?"

"I have a room, but I'm staying with a Chinese exchange student. In fact, they're all Chinese."

"Is she nice?"

"Yeah, she's pretty cool. Her name is Flower Ju-Long. But I think she made up the name 'Flower.'"

"So you're going to live?"

She said, "Pike, I've lived through worse. When are you coming home?"

I felt the angst through the phone and regretted calling. I said, "Soon, but why does that matter?"

"Because . . . because I miss Jennifer. That's why."

And the answer tore at me. I knew she was lying. Well, mostly. I said, "We'll be home soon. Just focus on your studies. Can you do that?"

She sniffled and said, "That's easy. I can do that. There's nothing they've shown me here yet that I don't know. But I want you to come home."

I said, "I will be there soon, doodlebug. I promise."

She'd said, "I don't think so. Every time you go somewhere, you get in trouble."

I thought about what Jennifer had said earlier, and said, "That's true. But you'll be okay, right? If it takes a little longer?"

She said, "I'm okay. Just come home, whether it's a week or a day. Promise?"

"I promise."

I heard a door close and she said, "My roommate's back. I have to go. We're not supposed to have unregistered cell phones."

"Does she have one?"

"Of course she does. She calls her father, Chen, once a day. He's some bigwig in import/export, and he makes the time."

Which was a jab in the eye, but I let it go. I said, "Hang in there, doodlebug. I'm proud of you. I'm going to pass the phone to Jennifer."

"I can't talk anymore. My roommate's going to see. Tell Jennifer I love her."

I said, "What about me?" and she hung up.

It had hurt more than I wanted to admit. I dropped the phone on the bed and crawled in next to Jennifer. She smiled at me, rubbing my arms. She said, "That was a good thing."

And I promptly fell asleep. Six hours later, I was sitting in a room waiting on a guy I hadn't seen for damn near two years to call me because a bunch of Chinese assassins were trying to kill him.

*What am I doing with my life?*

When was enough going to be enough? Killing the bad man had been pretty cool when it was just me—when I believed I could separate my life from my family—but that had turned to charred ash the first time I'd tried to do it. Did I really want to try to do it again?

I looked at Jennifer sleeping on the bed and saw her legs begin to twitch, a dream penetrating her brain. I didn't want to know what the dream was. I'd had too many myself.

Killing a human being was a hard thing to do, and doing so with a corkscrew to the eye was about as bad as could be imagined. She put on a brave face, and honestly, she hadn't shown any regrets, but it made me worry.

Killing in combat, in and of itself, lends to more killing. It just does. The first time, you feel horrible, wondering if it was worth it. The next time, you feel a little less, happy to be alive. Eventually, you just feel nothing. Killing was what you were trained to do, and death was what you brought. If the guy on the other end was against you, then that's what he earned. You began to lose the difference between what was a justified killing and what was just making sure nobody on your side died. No matter what happened, you did it in the name of a greater purpose, and that gave you a blanket to cloak what you'd done.

Eventually, the system allowed you to end up killing

everyone under a justification of a greater good. As long as your men came home, it was cool. I didn't want Jennifer to enter that world. I'd done it once before, and not only in combat.

I remember a time when I was a child hunting rabbits with friends. My parents weren't exactly in control of me. They were gone most of the time, and we would go out hunting every day, killing upwards of two or three rabbits at each outing. We'd skin them at our camp, cook them up, and eat them. For some reason, the rabbits became an expression of our worth. Eventually, we'd taken to gutting the rabbits and putting their heads on a spike outside our camp in a macabre expression of our manhood.

My father had found me one day, sitting next to a fire with about twelve rabbit heads on sticks surrounding our camp, and had lost it. He couldn't believe, after all he'd done to instill values in me, the Lord of the Flies we'd become.

He and my mother were pure hippies, straight out of the sixties revolution, which is why my given name is Nephilim, but that didn't mean he was a wimp. He could live in the outdoors with nothing but a knife, and in his mind the animals we'd killed should have been prayed over for their sacrifice. They'd lost their lives to provide us food, and we'd shamed ourselves by turning that sacrifice into some macabre celebration.

And he had been right.

Looking back, I couldn't believe what we'd become either, until I entered the real world of combat for the first time. Killing just inured you to death, and it took strong convictions to let one kill and stay above the fray. Stay above becoming Lord of the Flies.

Watching Jennifer sleep made me worry. She was my moral

compass, and I didn't want her to be the kid that put rabbit heads on spikes. She never had before, but tonight she had been pretty even after sticking a corkscrew into someone's eye. Watching her twitch in her sleep made me wonder if she wasn't excising the badness of the whole thing. Becoming me.

My phone rang, startling me. It rang again and I knocked over the bedside clock trying to disconnect my phone from the charger and answer before it woke Jennifer.

I failed.

Jennifer sat up, knowing something was happening. I looked at her, clicked into the number, and said, "Dunkin?"

I heard, "They're here! They're outside my door!"

I bolted upright. "Who? Who's there?"

I heard slapping feet, something like a table being overturned, then, "We're running! Pike, we're running! I'm turning off this phone. They're tracking the phone."

I shouted, "Don't do that! Leave the phone on!"

He disconnected.

Jennifer leapt up, saying, "What's going on?"

"Get your shoes on. Dunkin is on the run."

# 25

Dunkin heard the doorbell downstairs and jerked upright, dazed. He checked the time, saw it was closing in on 7 P.M., and couldn't believe they'd slept that long. He poked Nicole's elbow and said, "Hey, wake up. Someone's here."

She slowly came around and the doorbell went off again. Dunkin said, "I thought your sister was gone for the week."

"She is. You heard me talk to her."

"Well, who's that? Did she say someone was coming by?"

"No. She said the place was empty. Nobody coming. No maintenance, nothing."

"We had to come through a desk guy. So these guys had to do the same thing, right?"

"I guess."

Dunkin peeked out the upstairs window and said, "I can't see the front door."

"What are you doing?"

"Nothing, honey. Nothing. Stay up here. And put some clothes on."

"Why?"

He snapped, "Just do it!" and went downstairs. He looked through the peephole and saw a bearded man in a maintenance uniform, shifting from foot to foot.

He opened the door. Before he could get a single word out the man was shoved into the room, falling on top of Dunkin.

Dunkin rolled over, looking through the open door and recognizing the same Asian man and woman who'd followed him from his workplace yesterday, the man with a pistol out, the barrel thick and long, like there was a piece of pipe screwed onto the end of the gun.

And his brain exploded in fear.

He sprang to his feet just as the maintenance man leapt up, waving his hands in the air and shouting. Dunkin shoved him like a blocking dummy, right back through the door. The man holding the pistol fired twice, and Dunkin felt the impact through the body of the man he was pushing. His blocking dummy staggered, colliding with the Asian guy, and Dunkin shoved, hard. They both fell back outside and the woman slipped through them, trying to come into the room. Dunkin saw another pistol in her hand and slammed the door right in her face, hammering her arm. The gun dropped to the floor and she screamed. He relaxed the door, her arm snaked back out, and he slammed it closed again.

He flipped the lock and shouted, "Nicole! We need to go! Right now!"

He took the stairs two at a time, hearing something bashing the front door. He reached the bedroom and found her bouncing on one leg, trying to put her shoes on. She said, "What's going on?"

"They're here! Where's your phone?"

She pointed to the bedside table and he snatched it up, saying, "Go out the roof exit. We can't leave from the front door."

She started moving and he dialed the phone, running right behind her. He reached the short stairwell to the roof access and heard Pike ask, "Dunkin?"

He shouted, "They're here! They're outside my door!"

He heard a shattering of glass, then the front door smash in. He pushed Nicole in front of him, urging her on. He heard, "Who? Who's there?"

He broke out behind Nicole on the roof and said, "We're running! Pike, we're running! I'm turning off this phone. They're tracking the phone."

He hung up, saw a shadow in the stairwell below, then a muzzle flash with no sharp bang. A suppressor.

He snapped back, catching Nicole silhouetted at the stop of the short stairwell. He dove on her, knocking her to the deck as another round split the night. He jerked her to her feet and screamed, "Run!"

She did so, straight across the bridge that led to the botanical gardens. He followed right behind her, breaking into a huge expanse of grass crisscrossed with roads and paths. They ran blindly for a hundred meters, then slowed, both gasping for air. Dunkin pulled Nicole behind a tree and peered back the way they had come.

Panting, she said, "Who are those people? Why are they shooting at us?"

"I don't know, but you need to turn off this cell." He handed her the phone, saying, "Take out the battery."

She said, "Why? We should be calling the police."

Looking fearfully behind him, he said, "Just do it! Please."

She did so, then said, "What now? These gardens close at eight. We can't be in here after that."

Dunkin said, "Getting caught after hours by the police is just fine by me. Do you know the area?"

"Yeah, sure. I've been here before."

In the darkening gloom, Dunkin saw a group of men exiting the roof of the apartment complex and said, "We need to go. Is there someplace to hide in here?"

"I don't know what you mean."

"We can't stay in this open area. We need bushes or buildings. Something. They're coming."

She nodded, grasping the urgency of the question. She grabbed his hand, leading him away and saying, "Deeper in. There's a clutch of little buildings and greenhouses. I used to play here as a kid."

She started speed-walking away and he glanced behind them, seeing the men from the apartment beginning to fan out. He said, "We need to get to people. We need to find a crowd. This place is a killing zone."

"We can run straight through to the highway on the left. We get to the buildings I was talking about and we can exit right onto the street."

Dunkin pushed her back and said, "Go, go."

They ran up a path, threading through the bushes and passing multiple signs describing the foliage to the left and right. Eventually, they reached a small creek, and Nicole said, "This way. To the left. There are a bunch of greenhouses."

Dunkin nodded in the fading twilight, pushing her forward. They reached a collection of buildings, one after the other, and Nicole left the path, walking forward through the trees. Dunkin saw a solid twelve-foot fence made of metal, and she said, "Right over that. The expressway is on the other side."

He looked behind him, saw nothing, and darted forward, saying, "Let's get out of here."

He reached the fence, studied it, and found it had crossbeams every four feet, like a ready-made ladder leading up. He scampered up the side, reached the top, and looked over. He saw the expressway right next to the fence, cars steadily driving by.

He heard a screeching of brakes and whipped his head to see a vehicle bouncing over the curb. It stopped half on the sidewalk next to the compound of buildings they'd gone around. Five men spilled out and began climbing the fence to get into the park.

*Holy shit.*

He dropped back down and said, "We can't go this way. We need another way."

"What? The park is closed. Nobody can get in."

He grabbed her shoulders and hissed, "They're coming in right now! A car just came here and let off at least five! He's parked on the street below the fence!"

Her mouth opened but no words came out. He heard a thrashing in the vegetation and said, "We have to go. Now."

He took her hand and led her back through the foliage, trying to remain quiet. They reached the path and he heard a pounding of feet. He jerked her forward, running to the first structure he saw. They entered an enclosed area full of giant ferns and ducked down, leaving the path and hiding in the vegetation. He whispered, "Where can we go from here? How do we get out?"

Her eyes wide, she said, "Maybe we should talk to them. Maybe there's been a misunderstanding."

"Are you crazy? Nicole, there is no misunderstanding. My buddy killed two of them. They're not our friends."

"Maybe your friend is crazy."

Dunkin heard someone enter and held a finger to his lips. Two men passed in front of them, both looking left and right and both holding pistols. Nicole's eyes widened at the sight of them. They passed by, going deeper into the enclosure, and she whispered, "To the left. We need to cross the path and get inside that shed. From there we can get back into the park without using the paths. We need to run straight north. Straight to the harbor."

"What will that get us?"

"The opera house. It'll be full of people. It's right on the ferry terminal, and it'll be jam-packed. We just need to keep running. All paths to the north eventually lead there."

Dunkin nodded, listened, then said, "Let's go."

They scampered across the stone path, sidling into a wooden maintenance facility, and Dunkin slowed, the darkness of the interior making it hard to find his way. He walked forward in the gloom, crouched over with his hands outstretched, and accidentally kicked a bucket, the thing falling over in a racket. He jerked upright, breathing with an open mouth, and heard the men in the fern park running toward the sound.

He grabbed her hand and they began moving faster than the darkness allowed, bumping into metal shelves and knocking over planters. He reached a door, turned the knob, and found it locked. He backed up, then ran at it, slamming his shoulder into the frame. It didn't budge.

A man rounded the corner of the shelves and Dunkin leapt on him, throwing him into a rack of tools. They fell to the ground and Dunkin attacked like a wild man, windmilling his arms over and over like Ralphy in *A Christmas Story*, smashing the man's head into the concrete until he ceased moving.

Nicole shouted, "Dunkin!"

He jerked his head at her shout, and saw the twilight spilling through the open door. He jumped up and ran toward her, saying, "How'd you do that?"

She said, "We're on the inside, dummy. I turned the lock."

Dunkin felt like an idiot. He smiled, then heard another man floundering in the back just like they had. There was a stab of light, the beam sweeping back and forth, and they both sprinted through the door.

Stumbling back into the park, they ran until they reached a tangle of paths like spaghetti. Dunkin said, "Which way? Which way do we go?"

Nicole took off down a path to the left, shouting, "This way!"

Dunkin followed her, hearing the slapping of feet behind him. They crossed the creek again and she took a branch to the right, him right on her heels. He jerked her up short, hiding behind a tree.

The men kept going on the other path. He patted her arm and said, "Let's go, but not as fast. Just fast enough to get there. I need to hear."

They did so, and eight minutes later Dunkin saw the harbor, then the iconic Sydney Opera House. Four minutes after that they were through the gate and in a plaza at the back of the giant structure, dodging tourists wandering around trying to get a nighttime selfie. Dunkin glanced behind him at the gardens and saw nothing. He breathed a sigh of relief.

Nicole led him around to the front, and they entered a swirling mass of people on a promenade next to the Circular Quay of Sydney Harbour, the Sydney Harbour Bridge framed like a postcard across the water. They disappeared into the crowd, and she said, "What now?"

He said, "We need to put some distance between us and them. I don't want to stay here. Do you know of any other place where we can sit and think? One that's full of people close to here?"

She thought a minute, then said, "Yeah, I do. The oldest pub in Sydney. It'll be packed tonight."

# 26

When she heard my words on the phone with Dunkin, Jennifer leapt out of bed and began slapping kit into her pockets, saying, "Where are they? Which way did they go?"

I shoved the suppressed pistol I'd taken from the man in Adelaide into my waistband and said, "I have no idea. All he yelled was that they were there. We need to get to the apartment. Maybe he's holding them off."

We exited our room and ran down the indoor balcony overlooking what was once a working dock, but was now full of tourists and others living in the apartment complex that flowed out from the hotel. I'd have liked to see Russell Crowe eating some vegan appetizer as I went by, but that wasn't going to happen.

We ignored the elevator, taking the stairs of the old wharf, bouncing down them two at a time and bursting out into the lobby. The front desk person and concierge looked at us like we were insane, but as far as I could tell, we were the normal ones, the desk clerk having dreadlocks and painted nails on his hands and the concierge pink hair and two rings through her nose. *Crazy is as crazy does.*

We hit the pavement outside and stayed on the wharf side, not going to the stairs that led to the upper level with the roads, but instead running next to the water toward the apartment complex. We came within fifty meters and I put a hand on Jennifer's arm, slowing her.

Her eyes scanning the building, she said, "We never got his room."

"Yeah, I know, but it's a single stretch of building, one condo after another. They're all two-story, and they all face the water. If he's still there, we'll see activity."

She said, "There! On the end! Two from the end!"

I saw three Asian men come running out of a condo and jump the wall that was supposed to keep people out. The wall that was designed to force you to the front gate where you proved you belonged.

They raced around the back of the complex to the road that separated the building from the bluff of the botanical garden. I saw a pair of headlights stab the darkening twilight, and then heard tires squealing. The illumination from the headlights disappeared.

I said, "They're not in the apartment anymore. Either those guys are going to stash a body, or Dunkin got out."

Jennifer pulled my shirt and started jogging to the stairs that led up to the gardens, saying, "Well, they didn't get out the front, or those guys wouldn't have run to a car. They'd have been chasing Dunkin. If he escaped, they went out across the roof. We need to get to the gardens. If they're on the run, that's where they are."

We ran to the stairs that we'd found earlier in the day and took them two at a time, reaching the top and cutting back the way we'd gone before.

We crossed a road and I said, "The park is closed now. Remember the big iron gate?"

She pointed in the twilight and said, "Gate's still open."

I saw a jogger exit and realized "park closed" probably

meant nothing more than a sign to ward off people. I glanced around, didn't see anyone looking to stop entrance, and fast-walked through it, entering the gardens proper. I stopped at a large tourist map on a post and said, "This place is huge. It runs all the way to the opera house. We'll never find them here."

She had her phone out, calling someone and pointing at me to continue on down the path. I did so, my head on a swivel. I heard her say, "Creed, hey, it's Jennifer. I need a lock on a phone."

And smiled. She was finally breaking the rules, all because she liked Dunkin. I *was* rubbing off on her.

The feeling was short-lived, because she handed me the phone, saying, "I'm getting stonewalled about 'sanctions' and 'mission set.'"

Bartholomew Creedwater was also one of our "network engineers," meaning he was a hacker just like Dunkin. He'd worked with Dunkin in the Taskforce and was a friend, but tracking a civilian phone in a foreign country using Taskforce assets was making him skittish. He wanted an official order from the command to do it. Or an ass-chewing from me.

Which is what he got.

"Creed, damn it, I need that phone lock right now. Dunkin's on the run from some Chinese assassins. They're going to kill him and you're going to let them."

Creed had been hired when he'd been caught hacking government systems as a lark while he was in grad school. Not our systems, but NSA and DIA. We'd noticed the arrest, and had intervened surreptitiously, offering him a way out. Work for us and don't go to jail. The point being, I knew he didn't really care about breaking the law. He just wanted to make sure it was worth it.

And Dunkin's life was worth it.

He said, "Pike, with all the shit that's gone on after Kurt's death, I'm not sure about this. There's a new sheriff in town. He might not be as amenable to your tendency to leave the reservation. I don't want to get caught in the back blast."

I reached the small bridge that led to the apartment complex over the road the other car had escaped from, saw nothing, and squeezed the handset like I was choking out a competitor in MMA. I said, "Get me that lock, or I swear to God I'm coming back and kicking your ass. He's in here somewhere, and he's on his own. I'm his only chance."

I read out the number to the girlfriend's phone and waited. Jennifer kept looking at our six, checking the area. She grabbed my arm and said, "There's a team. Two guys. They're locking down the edges."

I looked where she indicated and said, "That's them. And they're still working. Which means Dunkin's still on the loose."

I returned to the phone and said, "Creed, I need it now. I'm running out of time. These guys are ahead of me. They have the lock, and I don't."

He came back and said, "Pike, there isn't a lock. His phone is off. It's dead."

*Shit.*

"Are you sure?"

"I'm sure that number you gave me is turned off. No signal."

I said, "Okay. Stay alert. I'm going to call you back with a new number."

I hung up and Jennifer said, "What was that about?"

I looked north and saw the two men were gone. I started walking down the path toward the last known sighting, saying, "We don't have any idea where Dunkin is in this maze, but those fucks do."

"So?"

"So let's get some answers."

# 27

Dunkin followed Nicole down the concrete path, threading his way through tables and stools full of tourists out enjoying the harbor night. He half thought about staying there due to the size of the crowds, but the entrance to the Sydney Opera House from the park was a choke point. Short of swimming in the harbor, this was the only way they could have left the park. Staying here was asking to get found.

They jogged up the path next to the water, moving around the street performers and panhandlers out front of the Circular Quay ferry terminals, and Dunkin stopped, saying, "Where do these ferries go?"

Nicole said, "All over the harbor. Come on. We need to get to George Street."

"Wait. We should take one of these. Get all the way across the bay. They won't know where we are after that."

"Dunkin, I don't know this city *that* well. I have no idea what ferry to take or where to go once it lands."

Unconvinced, Dunkin said, "That may not matter. There's probably a hotel at the far end of one of these. I think we should take one of them."

"That's fine, but let's figure it out first. We can do that after we talk. I know they go to the Heads and the zoo, but not much else. No reason to run off on the first ferry."

He nodded, realizing she was thinking more clearly than

he was. All he wanted to do was run, but maybe taking a breath and coming up with a plan was a better idea. They kept moving, dodging the mass of people coming and going from the ferry terminals. She led him across a small park and up some stairs, reaching the first major road, George Street. She said, "This is what's known as The Rocks—the first place inhabited by the original Western settlers of Australia."

He said, "You mean the criminals?"

She smiled and said, "Yeah, them too, but that's a little bit of a myth. They were here, but we had a lot of just plain old settlers all scrabbling for a living on the rocks of the wharf. It wasn't pretty. This place was nothing but whorehouses and gambling dens for the sailors."

She glanced at him and said, "Given what's just happened, you'd have probably fit in."

He grinned and said, "Not unless they had computer terminals."

She shook her head. "It wasn't a computer terminal that was shooting at me."

He let that slide, saying, "Let's get to the pub. I'll tell you what I know and we can figure out a plan."

They crossed George Street, jogging through the traffic, then passed restaurants and bars until they saw an awning proclaiming "Fortune of War—Since 1828." As they came closer, Dunkin heard music spilling out. He began to relax. Nicole was right. This place was perfect.

They showed identification to a bouncer, and then entered pandemonium. There was a man with a guitar blaring American music from the seventies, rugby on multiple television screens, and a raucous crowd either attempting to sing along or shout over the noise. She pulled him to the back, finding a two-person high-top table and taking a seat.

Dunkin looked around, noting a back room and a stairwell leading up. He said, "Well, it looks like you found a crowded place."

"I told you. Nobody's going to try anything in here. No way."

He leaned in and kissed her, saying, "Thank you for trusting me. Sorry this happened."

She pulled back and said, "Okay, so what *is* happening? What's going on?"

He felt the last twenty-four hours sap the will out of his body. He said, "I'm honestly not sure. Can we get a beer?"

She said, "Are you kidding me? No, I want to talk. Not drink. No more stonewalling like you did on the drive up here. I want to talk. Now."

He slid off his stool and said, "I will, I will. Let me get a beer and we'll talk."

He stood up, not waiting on a reply, fighting his way through the crowd to the bar and going over what he would tell her. How he could explain what had just happened. In his own mind, he didn't understand it. How was he on the run from trained Chinese killers? What had he done to get attacked? He'd already thought about every mission he'd run with the Taskforce, and knew that wasn't it. He'd drifted to his current work, but nothing he'd done would warrant such extreme measures.

It had to be Jake. He hadn't imagined seeing him when he left work for vacation. And he hadn't imagined him doing something nefarious. Jake had done something bad, and had known that Dunkin would figure it out—and so Dunkin had been marked for assassination. Now he had to find a way out of this. They'd ditched the Chinese in the short run, but whatever Jake had done had been worthy enough to dedicate the team in the first place, and Dunkin was sure it had the blessing of the Chinese government. With those resources behind them, he was sure they'd find him again.

The first thing was to break Nicole away. Get her out of the line of fire. Staying with him would only put her in danger. Although she might *already* be in danger just by her association with him. Along with her sister now.

He put his head in his hands, overwhelmed by the odds against him and the stakes involved. He needed some help. And then he remembered Pike Logan. He jerked his head up like he'd stuck his finger in a light socket, just as the bartender came to him.

"Whoa, mate. I'm here. What'll you have?"

"What?"

"You want a beer? Or are you just here to think?"

"Yeah. I'll have two Four X. Draft."

He took them, paid the tab, and fought his way back to the table, seeing Nicole on her phone. He leapt forward, spilling the beer on the high-top and causing her to jump. He said, "What are you doing?"

"Googling the ferry schedule. You said you wanted to get away from here. What is with you?"

He tried to grab the phone and she turned away from him, saying, "Quit it! It's still loading."

"Turn that damn phone off! Right now!"

Truculent, she did so, saying, "So how do you plan to see the ferry schedule? Brain waves? What has gotten into you?"

He set the beers on the table and said, "I'm sorry. It's just not safe to use that phone."

She stood up, putting the phone in her pocket and saying, "Yeah, yeah, yeah. I got it. I have to use the loo. Watch my purse. And you'd better have some answers when I get back."

He said, "Don't turn it on in the bathroom."

She walked away without a word, heading to the stairs to the upper level, causing Dunkin to feel like an ass. He sipped his beer, thinking about how he was going to contact Pike. He couldn't do it with any phone they owned. Well, maybe he could. He could use her phone for a split second—or even his—set up a meeting spot, then turn the damn thing off.

He nodded his head, then started to develop a plan about what he was going to tell Nicole. He couldn't tell her any classified information, but he had to give her enough to make her believe him. Lost in thought, he took a few more sips of his beer, and then realized that Nicole had been gone a long time. He glanced up the stairwell, waiting to see her come back down. She did not. He looked at his watch, startled that it had been over ten minutes. Maybe fifteen. He began to grow concerned, wondering if she'd just left him here in the bar.

He saw her purse across the table and realized that wasn't the case. Something was wrong.

# 28

Jennifer caught up to me in the park and said, "Whoa, whoa, what do you mean, 'Get some answers'? What are you looking to do?"

We entered crisscrossing paths, the foliage increasing on both sides. I said, "It means the least we can do is take out some of the opposition. The most is we use these guys to find Dunkin."

A jogger came by us, the sun finally dropping past the horizon. She said, "I'm not sure we can do that here. It's still crowded."

I started moving with a purpose, looking left and right, trying to find the guys who had been searching the park. If they were gone, it was bad news. It meant they were no longer needed.

I said, "Guess we should be discreet, then."

We snaked through displays of exotic vegetation, the growing darkness making it hard to see people on the trails. We crossed a little creek, a sign pointing the way to the Sydney Opera House, and Jennifer grabbed my arm.

To our front was some sort of fern greenhouse, but that wasn't why she stopped me. Outside the greenhouse was a group of seven men and a woman, deep in conversation. All of them Asian. They talked for about five seconds, and then split up like a flash-bang had gone off in the center, the man and woman running down a trail, four others racing back up the path to the freeway, and a single man running back by us, toward the rear of the park.

I watched him go by us, and said, "That's our man."

She said, "What are we going to do?"

"Take him down. He's rear security. They're sending him just to watch the backtrail to the apartment. And wherever Dunkin is, that guy's in touch with the others hunting him. If we can't find him, they will."

She started to say something and I cut her off. "Stop. We're doing it. And I need your help. Right now."

I watched her deliberate for a half-second. She looked left and right, saw no one, and said, "If it's going to work, we need to hit him quickly. Before someone else shows up."

I grinned and said, "Get ready to catch this guy's attention, because he's going down."

We followed behind him until he was back at the pedestrian bridge to the roof of Dunkin's apartment. He pulled up against the metal rail, lit a cigarette, and just stood there.

I said, "Get him back into the garden. Away from the bridge. I can't take him there."

She said, "How? What do you want me to do?"

"Figure it out," I pointed to her left and said, "but get him next to that patch of bushes. I'll be inside."

She gave me her disapproving teacher stare, but I saw she was willing. She leaned in and pecked me on the cheek. "You'd better take him down quickly if you want anything more than that. No letting him get a knife on me, like last time."

I smiled and said, "Won't happen."

"Promise?"

"I promise. Now go."

She went down the trail and I sidled over next to some Southeast Asian shrub that was apparently the cat's meow, according to the plaque in front. All I cared about was it could hide me in its leaves while still allowing me to strike.

I watched her walk to the railing next to the bridge, then engage the guy in conversation. She talked to him for a minute, and he became agitated. He pushed her away, and I knew that she wasn't going to get him to follow her. I started to consider my options, and she leaned into his ear, whispering. His mouth dropped open, the cigarette falling out, and she literally kicked him straight in the ass.

He swung at her and she took off running right at me. He pulled out a suppressed pistol and took a shot, the snap of the round causing her to flinch.

*Jesus Christ. Bad call.*

She passed me and he followed like an Olympic sprinter right behind her. She shouted, "Pike! He's shooting!"

He came abreast and my mind began snapping through courses of action like a neon strobe. Originally, I'd planned on a movie-type stalk where I appeared behind him like the alien tracking Sigourney Weaver, taking him down while he was stationary, but that was out of the question now.

He passed right to my front, and I made my decision. I dug my heels into the earth and sprang up, slamming into him like a linebacker and hammering him to the ground with my full weight. I felt the air whoosh out of his lungs, but he still brought the pistol to bear. I slapped it aside and punched him in the throat, crushing his trachea. His eyes went comically wide and he started gasping for air, his lungs wheezing like he was breathing through a straw. His arms and legs started flailing around like a turtle turned over, his breath coming in rasps. I knocked the pistol out of his hands and dragged him deeper into the brush, away from the view of any stray joggers. I rolled him over, now sitting on top of him, working through the damage I'd caused trying to save his damn life.

Jennifer had forced me to react instinctively in self-defense, but I needed what was in his head. He struggled for air, his throat swelling with the injury I'd inflicted, and then his eyes rolled back into his skull. He passed out.

He was breathing now, and I didn't know if he'd die later from the blow I'd given him, but I sure as shit lost him for any information.

Jennifer reached me, saw the damage, and said, "What happened?"

I started searching his body, saying, "What happened? *What happened?* You caused him to start shooting, *that's* what happened. What happened with you?"

She heard my tone and looked like she'd been slapped. She bent down and started helping me with the search, saying, "He wouldn't come with me. He had no interest. I had to get him to you."

I pulled out a passport, pocketed it, and said, "So how'd you do that?"

"I told him I was Dunkin's girlfriend, and then kicked him in the ass."

I stopped what I was doing and said, "You did what?"

She said, "What?"

I shook my head. "Maybe we should talk more before I send you out."

She kept searching his jacket pockets, not looking at me, and said, "Maybe you shouldn't let a guy put a knife to my breast."

I grinned. "Okay, touché. Find a phone?"

She caught my eye and grinned back, saying, "Nope." Then, "Wait . . . Got something."

She pulled out a small radio, the transmitter spitting out Chinese. She tossed it to me and I heard chatter like a military operation, only in a language I couldn't understand. I said, "Get Creed back on the line. We need this translated."

She did so, and Creed started his usual bullshit. I took the phone and said, "I need something translated from Chinese."

I held my phone up to the speaker of the radio, let the chatter go on for a second, then put it back to my ear. He said, "Pike, what the fuck? I don't speak Chinese. I can't work miracles."

I said, "Oh, bullshit. Get the translation software going, right now. Slave it to your phone. I'm going to do it again, and you'd better be ready."

He dropped the phone and I heard a bunch of shuffling going on, then he came back, now sounding like he was speaking through a tube. He said, "Okay, Pike, go."

I put the phone back to the speaker of the radio, but nobody was talking. I waited, then heard Creed through the phone saying, "Pike? I said okay."

I put it back to my ear and said, "Nobody's talking. Just wait."

I replaced it, and then there was the singsong chatter of Chinese. I let it go for thirty seconds, and then it quit. I brought the phone to my ear and said, "What about that?"

"Pike, the translation is really pathetic. All I got is something about a place called the rocks and something about the fortune of war."

"What? What does that mean? Didn't you get the transmission?"

"I did . . . Pike, I'm telling you, all it says is that they're in 'the rocks' and they're tracking the 'fortunes of war.' Most of the words came in garbled. The software isn't designed to go from radio to phone to me."

I looked up at Jennifer and said, "We are truly screwed. He's not getting anything. All he's getting is something about rocks and the fortune of war."

"Rocks? As in *the* rocks?"

Surprised, I said, "Yeah, why?"

"That's a section of Sydney. The oldest in the city. What else?"

I was amazed. I should have let her do the talking. She always did research before we went anywhere, and she'd clearly done it for Sydney before we flew. I said, "Something about fortunes of war. Does that mean anything to you?"

She said, "No, but let me look." She started working her phone, and the one in my hand blurted, "Pike, there's something else. Something about back alleys. Wherever they are, it's got back alleys."

Which sounded like the oldest section of any city, so Jennifer was tracking. She looked up from her phone and said, "The Fortune of War is a pub in Sydney. It's in The Rocks."

My face split into a smile. Into the phone, I said, "You're a genius, Creed! Owe you."

He said, "Wait, what? What did I do?"

I hung up and stood, saying, "You're the real genius. How do we get there?"

She smiled, liking the compliment after my chastising about the insanity she'd just pulled, saying, "Quickest way is through the park, right next to the opera house. What about this guy?"

I scooped up his pistol, handed it to her, and glanced back at the bridge to Dunkin's condo. I said, "Leave him for the maintenance crew in the morning. One more Chinese mystery."

# 29

Dunkin grabbed Nicole's purse and went up the stairs, glancing backward as he did so. Nobody followed him. He reached the top and found another bar area, but this one much smaller, with several chipped tables and plastic chairs full of people staring at two flat-screen televisions showing rugby. He paused, getting his bearings, and was bumped by patrons trying to go back down the stairs to the bar below. He apologized, then asked for the bathrooms and was pointed to a hallway, another stairwell beyond going down to a different area.

He went toward it and saw the Chinese man who'd stormed her sister's house exit the hallway. He ducked back into the bar area, peeked out, and saw Nicole being pushed forward by the Asian woman who'd been with him at the house. The one whose arm he'd slammed in the door. He shouted, "Nicole!" The woman pushing her forward turned, and a bar patron tried to enter the hallway for the bathroom. She shoved him aside, focused on Dunkin, and the patron knocked her arms away, clearly drunk. She grabbed him by the hair at the back of his head, exposed his neck, and flicked a finger against the jugular, then held him away from her body, ducking her head.

The hallway turned into a fountain of blood, his neck jetting gore and coating the walls. Dunkin couldn't believe the amount of bodily fluids spraying out. It was like a garden hose that had been split, blood shooting all over the place. She dropped the man at her feet and the outer edge of the crowd in the upstairs bar reverberated, jerking upright, sure something had happened, but unable to assimilate just what, like a beehive that had been hit on the outer edge. None of them could understand the bloodbath right in front of them.

The man in front of Nicole turned, saw Dunkin, then the carnage his partner had wrought. Dunkin saw his face contort in anger at her action, but he still drew a pistol. He aimed and the barrel spit fire.

Dunkin dove to the ground and the upper bar devolved into pandemonium. He leapt up, saw the Chinese woman shoving Nicole down the far stairwell and the man advancing on him. He turned and began shoving people out of the way in a panic, trying to get back to the first stairwell. Trying to get through the mass of people who were all intent on their own survival. The gun belched twice more, hitting a man to his front. The body dropped, clearing the way for him.

Dunkin jumped over him, leaping into the stairwell. He lost his footing and tumbled down, spilling onto the floor of the downstairs bar.

Several patrons laughed at him, assuming he was drunk, one hoisting him to his feet. Dunkin looked behind him, saw the Chinese man aim, and leapt backward. The bullet impacted the man who'd helped him up, and the bar patrons near him stood slack-jawed and confused, trying to understand what was happening.

The killer reached the bottom of the stairs and took aim again. Dunkin threw a high-top table behind him, tossing two pint glasses in the air and causing the Chinese man to dodge back.

The drunks in the bar started yelling and Dunkin began bulling his way to the front door, causing a ripple as he passed. He reached the entrance, turned to look behind him, and saw the Chinese man sprinting back up the stairs.

The music stopped, the entire bar now confused, but knowing something wasn't right. The bouncer entered, tried to trap him, and Dunkin ducked under his arms, hitting the street at a sprint. He turned right, saw two Asians with a look of shock at his exit, and went left, running up George Street through the crowds, the men giving chase.

He passed a tunnel in the wall of buildings and skidded to a stop like a cartoon character, then darted inside. He ran thirty feet and slowed, hugging the shadows of the tunnel and staring back at the light spilling in from the avenue. He saw the men run by, continuing up George Street.

He heaved a sigh of relief, then remembered Nicole, snapping him back to the threat. He might be relatively safe now, but she was not. He knew they had taken her for a reason. They were after him and would use whatever leverage they could find to get to him. Which meant hurting her, and he had no way to get her back.

Nothing.

He felt a debilitating rage erupt, causing him to turn and slam a fist against the wall. He sank down to the ground, curled his arms around his legs, and rocked back and forth, thinking.

They had her. Those assholes had her, and it was because of him. His mind began to ricochet with fantasies of what he could do, and he found himself returning to the world of the Taskforce, when living or dying had been just a bad decision away. When things mattered beyond money.

When he worked with men who had felt like he did.

He began panting, the adrenaline coursing through him. He stood up and began walking, reaching the end of the tunnel, seeing a small alley, a sign proclaiming something called the "Nurses Walk" and the "Surgeons Court." He advanced slowly, seeing a familiar emblem to his left. A Starbucks coffee shop, something that was now more ubiquitous than the reviled golden arches of McDonald's.

He breathed a sigh of relief, and then had a thought. Something he should have realized in Fortune of War. He could use his own phone there to contact Pike. Leave it on airplane mode and use the WiFi with iMessage or FaceTime. There was no way to track that.

He just hoped Pike hadn't simply returned to the United States. He couldn't blame him if he had. He understood the sanctity of the mission. He'd screwed up whatever Pike was doing in a big way, and now he was quite possibly on his own.

He glanced back down the tunnel, seeing a couple walking forward and laughing, snuggling together. He leaned against the wall, letting them pass. He exhaled and followed behind them, figuring he'd at least try to contact Pike.

He rounded the corner, saw an outdoor patio with tables scattered about, the area teeming with people drinking coffee and using the free WiFi. He started to walk to the door and a single table penetrated his brain. One with Asians.

He thought he was becoming paranoid, because there were plenty of Asians in Australia, but he glanced back just the same.

They were all males, and they were all staring at him. He opened the door and went inside, getting in line to order while looking to his rear.

When he reached the front he said, "I'll have a grande latte and, is there a back way out of here?"

"What?"

"I'll have a grande latte. And *is there a back way out of here?*"

He said the last part louder than he meant to. He realized he was sweating profusely. He wiped his brow. The woman looked at him like he was a lunatic, glanced back at her manager, and said, "No. Just the bathroom. No back way."

She hesitated again, then said, "What's your name?"

Looking back the way he'd come, Dunkin said, "Huh?"

"For the order? The name?"

He paid and said, "Nicole. Her name is Nicole Shoemaker. Remember that when the police come."

She said, "What?"

And he left her, not going to the receiving end of the line, but back out the front. He exited, walking fast, and saw the Asian table react. He took off running and heard a shout behind him.

He glanced back and saw the Asians barreling through the crowd, pushing people aside in order to get a shot at him.

# 30

We reached the back of the opera house and were forced to slow down because of the crowds. I said, "He's probably eight minutes ahead of us, which means those assholes have had eight minutes to set up for a kill."

Dunkin's girlfriend's phone had finally pinged, with Creed giving us a geolocation. I'd immediately tried to call it, but it went straight to voice mail. It had turned on for a single minute, then dropped off again.

Speed-walking next to me, dodging the drinkers at the tables beside the harbor, Jennifer said, "Let's hope your training counted for something. If he's smart, that pub is packed with people. Hopefully full of redneck Aussies to protect him."

I grinned and said, "So I'm a redneck?"

She looked at me and said, "I didn't call you that. But apparently that's the first thing that popped into your head."

We hit the turn toward the ferry terminals, seeing magicians and other street performers, and I said, "Nothing wrong with being a redneck. As long as you can fight."

She dodged a man in front of her and laughed, saying, "I guess that makes me a redneck, too."

"Keep that in mind, because we're probably both going to be rednecks here soon."

We reached the end of the quay, seeing a rack of stairs, and I said, "Where to, Jedi? Which way?"

She looked at her phone and said, "Straight up. That's George Street. It's a hundred meters down the road."

I stopped and said, "Okay, here's the play, and it's pretty simple. I'm sure they're boxing that place and waiting on him to leave. Don't worry about identifying the threat. Let's just go in like we want a beer, find him, and get him out. Any Chinese killers are going to stand out in a rugby bar, so I seriously doubt they're sitting inside. We get in, get him out to George Street. From there, we walk him away."

She was looking at her phone, and said, "This place actually has more than one establishment. There's a hotel and another bar on the other side, both connected by an upper level. One with a back exit away from George Street. We can actually get him out without leaving through the front door."

I kept walking and said, "Sounds good to me. We locate him, I provide close-in security, and you conduct a recce. You come back to us and lead us out. Okay?"

She nodded and we hit the stairs at a run, turned onto George Street, and saw a crowd spilling out of a place with an awning proclaiming "Fortune of War." I said, "Shit. Something's happened."

We raced to the front, found a drunk staggering outside, and said, "Hey, what's going on?"

"Somebody came in and started shooting the place up. Bunch of bullets flying and Chinks running around. It was out of a movie. I think they killed two people."

"Chinks? What do you mean?"

"Goddamned Chinese. But it was a Yank doing the killing. I saw him running."

A woman to his left said, "Bullshit. It was the Chinese

doing the shooting. I saw them. The Yank was running from them. He ran right out the door."

Jennifer said, "Which way did he go?"

She pointed up the street, and we left, jogging for speed, but feeling the panic of losing the thread. We went two blocks and saw nothing. No crowds, no police, no nothing. If he'd gone this way with a pack of assassins chasing him, there would be some wake left behind, like a boat churning up the water. We slowed to a walk and I said, "Where could he have gone? He didn't come this way. Not with a bunch of gunslinging assassins after him."

She looked at her map and said, "Remember when I said a back exit? Maybe he's one street up. A walking path called the Nurses Walk."

"How do we get there?"

"There's an arcade entrance ahead. It cuts into it."

We speed-walked forward, took a left, and continued, passing tourists shopping for souvenirs. We left the arcade behind, entering an open ramp. We reached the top and saw a group of men standing in a circle, with Dunkin in the center.

I jerked Jennifer to the side and said, "That's him. Shit. They've got five guys around him."

She said, "What do you want to do? Maybe we should get the police."

"No time. They'll kill him or extract him before we can leverage that." I thought for a second, then said, "It's us. Sorry, but it's us."

She saw the scrum and said, "Okay, okay, but no one-on-one here. We work together."

And that caused me to relax. Even with the odds, it made me feel comfortable. I'd trained Jennifer and knew what she was capable of, but training only went so far. Fortunately, I'd seen Jennifer go Beast Mode once before, and when it came to kill or be killed, *she* was the one left standing. But I needed that same commitment from her here. The will I knew she had, and she had just given it to me.

I said, "I can do that. You set them up, and I'll take them down. Just watch for a blade or a gun. That's the first target. You ready?"

She nodded and I saw her vibrating with the adrenaline and said, "Easy. Act like we're drunk. On a date. We need to get close to them. Can you do that?"

"Act like I'm on a date with you? Yeah, that's easy. Because it's always an act."

I chuckled and said, "Okay, redneck. Get ready to fight."

# 31

Dunkin began sprinting up the alley away from the Starbucks, chanting a mantra in his head. *Give them a reason to quit. Give them a reason to quit.*

Before he'd learned he had a genius for computers, a long time ago, in a land far, far away, Dunkin had once been a member of a Long Range Surveillance Unit in the U.S. Army. Established to drop deep behind enemy lines, with no hope of support, they'd had the hangman's noose of compromise on their heads for every mission. If it happened, they were well outside of any help and pretty much on their own. They'd developed a method after compromise to get the people hunting them to quit: Just make it too hard to follow.

When given the choice between chasing a team up the side of a mountain, or across a river full of crocodiles, the theory was that the average grunt—no matter the country—would choose to slow down or stop, providing the team another day of survival. And the theory had proven correct on more than one instance. But those had all been training missions. Dunkin had never dropped behind enemy lines for real, and he wasn't sure it would work here, running on the streets of Sydney. There was nothing he could use to get them to rethink. No mountains or snake-infested rivers, and so he resorted to straight-up speed and endurance. If he could outlast them, they'd eventually quit. And he had an edge in that department, because, unlike other computer nerds, he was an endurance runner.

In that endeavor, he might have eventually won, but he failed to realize that the ones behind him weren't the only ones chasing him—and he couldn't be faster than the speed of light of a radio call.

He sprinted up the narrow alley called the Nurses Walk, looking for a way out. He saw a sign for something called the "Mission Stairs" and an alley for an arcade leading back to George Street. He opted for the narrow brick staircase leading to open sky above. He darted onto the stairs, thinking any effort on his part would enhance his distance to the men behind him. Give them a reason to quit.

He had almost reached the top when two men appeared, coming back down toward him, both with snarls on their faces.

He turned around, bounding back down the stairs toward the arcade tunnel. He hit the ground and ran right into the group from Starbucks. One man grabbed his collar and he whirled to the left, spinning out of his grasp. He hit the ground on his knees, sprang up, saw the arcade tunnel, and was clocked in the head by another man, knocking him back down.

He rolled over and crabbed on his back, scuttling toward the tunnel. One of them circled around him and kicked his hands out from under him, leaving him flat on the ground. Another aimed a pistol at his head, saying, "Get up. Now."

He said, "Fuck you. Where is Nicole?"

He was encircled by them and knew he was done. He saw the man glance behind him and had a thread of hope. They were worried about someone witnessing this. Especially after the actions in Fortune of War. If he could stay here long enough, even on the ground, they'd be forced to leave.

The man crushed that notion. He jammed the barrel right into his forehead and said, "Get up now or I'll kill you right here. And your friend will get the same."

He looked for a way out, begging for someone to come by and see what was happening. Anything. Anybody to help.

Nobody appeared.

He raised his hands and stood, trying for bravado, saying, "You'd better not hurt her."

The man punched him in the stomach and said, "You should be more worried about what we're going to do to you."

Dunkin doubled over in pain, knowing he was dead, but not wanting to go out on his knees. He stood up, prepared to take the bullet, and said, "Fuck you. Shoot me here, asshole."

The man raised his fist and another tapped him. They crowded together, the man jabbing the pistol into his ribs, saying, "Not a word. Let them pass."

A woman and a man holding hands came out of the arcade tunnel, laughing and kissing. He desperately wanted to shout at them, but after what he'd seen, he held no illusions that the man with the pistol wouldn't kill them both.

The two came abreast of the group, entering the light and heading for the stairs. Dunkin watched them pass, and the streetlight hit the girl full enough so he could see her face. A blonde, with an athletic build and a surfer look. *Almost like . . .*

And Dunkin's mouth fell open just as the girl's date ripped the man with the pistol off of his feet, slamming him to the ground.

The four others reacted, assaulting the threat, but it was like children trying to stop a bear attack. And that was without the woman joining the fight. Dunkin stood in shock as they systematically destroyed the group, working in unison, the woman setting up one for the man to shatter a knee, the man setting up another for the woman to snap an elbow into his face as she threw him over her back, one body after another flipping through the air and slamming into the ground.

In eight seconds, it was over, five men on the ground groaning and bleeding, unable to continue the fight.

Dunkin simply stood, his mouth still agape.

Pike Logan stood up from hammering the temple of the last man and said, "You too big of a pussy to give us a hand?"

He said, "I . . . I . . ."

Jennifer said, "We need to leave. Right now."

Pike grabbed his arm and said, "Follow us."

They took off running to the Mission Stairs and Dunkin finally got his voice back. He said, "Pike, we can't leave. We need to go back."

"No way. We need to leave here. Right now."

He stopped climbing the stairs, and Pike realized he wasn't following. Jennifer turned around and Pike said, "What the hell are you doing?"

"They have Nicole. They took her. They're going to kill her because of me."

# 32

Jake Shu dragged himself off the train in Brisbane, tired beyond belief. This was getting to be the worst idea he'd ever had, no matter the price they were paying. He exited the Roma Street train station and waved down a cab.

He gave the address to his hotel, and the cabby, trying to be friendly, said, "Stamford Plaza? That's a pretty nice place. You here on business?"

Jake honestly had no idea what the hotel was like. He'd purchased a room simply because it was near the meeting location, and he really had no patience with the questions.

"No. I'm sorry. I'm really tired. I'm on my way to Cairns for vacation."

The cabby tried again. "Where you from?"

"I live in Adelaide. I'm just going on vacation."

The cabby gave him a strange look and said, "You don't sound like it."

"I'm from the United States, but I work in Adelaide. Look, I'm really tired."

Now interested, the cabby said, "Why didn't you just fly to Cairns? Paying for all of these trains is just as expensive and takes three times as long. No wonder you're tired. You know there's an airport up there, right?"

Jake snapped, "Yes, I do. I'm not an idiot. I just wanted to stretch out the trip. See the sights. It's why I'm here right now."

The cabby nodded, not saying another word. Four minutes later he pulled into a circular drive for a hotel that was way out of Jake's league.

He said, "Here we are."

Jake took one look at the hotel and thought, *My contact is not going to be happy with me staying here*. He knew the hotel would ask for his passport and reason for staying, and that was something the Chinese hated.

But screw them. He was taking the risk. Not them.

Playing the ignorant American, he tipped the cabby to get him off of asking any more questions and went inside. He checked in, watching his passport get scanned and answering pleasant-seeming questions about why he was only in the hotel for a single night. He answered them, went straight to his room, and flopped on the bed, checking his watch. He had about thirty minutes before the meeting. He was cutting it too close.

He went to the TV stand and found a local tourist map. He had been given very specific instructions on what to do and wanted to make sure he executed perfectly. He pulled out his phone, playing with an app that encrypted and hid notes from prying eyes, then read through the instructions one more time, tracing his finger on the map along a walkway/bike path that ran down a riverfront. He marked his first stop, a parking garage, and memorized the location. It looked like he could step right out of the back of the hotel and be there in less than five minutes.

He glanced at his watch, saw the meeting was in a little under twenty minutes, and sighed. Not enough time for a nap. He decided to get closer so as not to screw up anything.

Jake took one last look at the tourist map, folded it up and placed it in his pocket, then left the hotel through a bar and grill in the back. He gained his bearings on the river and began walking on an attractive path set right next to the water, the walkway full of pedestrians. He entered a tunnel, and within seconds he was almost run over by a bicyclist, the man cursing as he veered out of the way before slamming into a wall. The cyclist righted his bike, shouting, "Can't you see the bike path markings? Idiot."

People stopped to look, and the near collision set Jake's teeth on edge. He scurried farther into the tunnel, then took a seat on a bench, checking the time. Still ten minutes to go. He took a couple of deep breaths, watching the patrons come and go, now recognizing a special lane for the bikes on the other side of the tunnel. An Asian man came into the tunnel and, instead of passing, took a seat next to him. Right next to him. He was big. Bigger than the average Asian, and the invasion of Jake's personal space amped up his angst yet again. He stood up.

The man did too.

He began walking, and the man followed. He quickened his pace, and the man did the same. He reached the turn to the parking garage and took it, glancing behind him. The man was right there.

In a panic, he opened the door to the parking garage and was immediately thrown forward into a wall by another man. He was swiftly searched, then the large Asian spoke in Chinese, and the man holding him nodded. Pinning Jake's neck into the wall, in English, he said, "Apparently, you are a buffoon who cannot follow instructions."

Jake stammered, "Wh-what?"

"You were given a specific time to be here, and specific instructions of what to do. You did none of them."

"I just wanted—"

The man cut him off, forcing the sharp edge of his forearm into Jake's throat, saying, "I don't care what you want. Listen to me closely, because if you screw this up, we won't be so nice. Leave here, continue traveling down the path. You will see a beer garden to your left. You will go to that beer garden and then to the outside patio. You will see a man with a newspaper drinking coffee. If he is reading the paper, you will walk to his table. If he is not, and the newspaper is folded on the table, you will leave. Is that understood?"

Jake nodded, wondering what he'd gotten himself into. The man continued, "If he is reading the paper, you will ask, 'Mind if I take a seat?' If the man says, 'Go ahead,' you will sit down. If he says, 'Yes, I do mind,' you will leave and wait for future contact. Is that understood?"

"What? No, I don't. This is all I know. Future contact? I don't have any further instructions."

The man pinning him to the wall looked at the other, and the larger one said, "Room 347 of the Stamford Plaza hotel. Train ticket to Cairns tomorrow at seven A.M."

The knowledge they had of Jake's movements made a bead of sweat form on his brow. The man said, "Do you understand?"

Jake nodded, and the man released him, straightening his clothes and saying, "This is all for your protection. Do not screw it up."

Jake said, "I never had to do any of this before. And I've worked for you for a long time."

The large man pushed him toward the door. "You've never worked for us. Trust me."

Jake entered the tunnel again, now sweating profusely and wishing he'd never agreed to this transfer. The United Front

Work Department had always been unfailingly polite. These men were a different story.

He exited the tunnel into the sunlight, wanting to glance behind him, but not having the courage. He continued straight ahead, passing pedestrians all out enjoying the day, and wondered if he looked like he had a disease with the sweat pouring off of his brow. He wiped his face, then saw the beer garden, a huge establishment with six-foot-long pine tables scattered about. He walked up the stairs, saw the hostess, and said, "I'm just looking around. Is that okay?"

She said it was, and he exited onto the back deck overlooking the water. He glanced around and saw a wizened old man reading a newspaper, looking like an Asian Yoda.

*That can't be him.*

They didn't say what to do if there were two people reading papers.

But this was the only man on the deck, and instead of beer, he was drinking coffee. Jake approached, feeling ridiculous with all the empty tables around him, and said, "Can I sit down?"

The man looked at him, then nodded. Jake took a seat on the bench across from him and fidgeted under his gaze. The man did look Chinese, but was clearly closing in on the end of his life, with a thin mustache whose ends drooped past his chin.

The man said, "What were your instructions, idiot?"

Taken aback, Jake said, "To come here and ask for a seat."

"No. It was to come here and say, 'Mind if I take a seat?' Not, 'Can I sit down?' You have an issue with attention to detail."

Jake said nothing. The man folded up the paper with precision, then said, "If that continues, you will be cut free."

"What does that mean?"

"You do not want to find out. Do you have the data?"

"Yes. It's on a hard drive."

"Encrypted?"

Now on familiar ground, Jake scoffed and said, "Of course it's encrypted. Unbreakable, without me."

The man passed across a small envelope and said, "This is your contact information in Cairns. You will follow the instructions to the letter, to include the encryption scheme. Now, what do you have?"

The abrupt change in tone caught Jake off guard. He said, "Wait a minute, I don't like how this is going. I've already passed the F-35 data. I don't even know who you are."

The man leaned forward and said, "Do you intend to check out of your hotel tonight, before your train trip tomorrow?"

Once again adrift, Jake said, "No . . ."

"Good. Because I don't like hunting people. It's easier to just find them where they say they'll be. Now, what do you have?"

His eyes piercing into Jake's soul, Jake gave up. "I now have the data on the A2/AD systems for Taiwan. The one they're using to decrease their alert using artificial intelligence."

The old man took a sip of coffee and said, "How will that help us?"

Jake took a breath. "I have no idea. You guys asked for it. I got it. I'm not a missile engineer. I work on artificial intelligence."

"Can it be manipulated? Like you did with the helmet?"

"Yeah, I suppose. I didn't do it, but it can be, with the right people."

"So we can make the system think something's happening when it's not?"

“Yes. Of course. With the right people working it.”

“Good. We have the right people. Leave me now.” The old man returned to his paper. Jake hesitated, wanting to ask something else, and the man glanced over his news, saying, “Do you have an issue hearing?”

“No. No, I don’t.”

“Then leave me. Before I lose my patience.”

# 33

Paul Kao sipped his tea and kept an eye on the door of the massage parlor at the end of the street, doing what he did best: waiting. If he were honest with himself, he'd felt mixed emotions after having been cut free from the National Security Bureau. Elation for the trust Charlie Chan had in him, but disappointment because he didn't have any inroads into what Charlie really wanted.

He knew the threat was real and was glad Charlie believed the same, but he wasn't nearly as good of an operative as Charlie seemed to think. He relied on cultivating assets to accomplish his work, and after the death of his last contact, and his firing, none of his other contacts would talk to him. He had no thread at all. Which left the one lead he did have—the Snow Leopard.

He'd gone to the fabled Huaxi Street market, a seedy underbelly in one of the oldest sections of Taipei. Once the legal area for brothels, it was otherwise known as Snake Alley because of its history of restaurants that served up fresh-killed cobras after a snake show.

Those times were long gone, and the market no longer held any exotic charm. A desolate area, it now consisted mainly of "massage parlors" built onto the skeletons of the brothels of the past, with ancient masseuses standing outside trying to entice a dwindling clientele, along with newfound fortune-tellers intent on taking over the decrepit space and resurrecting its glory.

None of that mattered to Paul. He'd worked inside the city for decades, infiltrating everything from corrupt individuals infatuated with the new money surrounding the needle skyscraper known as Taipei 101 to the men and women clawing for survival in the slums within the heart of the city, all of his efforts dedicated to one thing: saving Taiwan from the communist threat. Others could deal with the rich stealing money through corruption or the poor dealing in drugs. That wasn't his calling, and never would be. There was a greater threat in the wind, and he'd dedicated his life to preventing it.

He'd worked inside the underbelly for a long, long time, and had learned that this area had been a bastion of the Bamboo Triad for decades, from the height of Snake Alley to the end of the brothels. He knew that the Snow Leopard ran his network here from a specific massage parlor, and so Paul set up surveillance.

He was on day two of his efforts without seeing the man, and was thinking about changing tactics. Maybe the Leopard had left this area. Maybe he didn't own this parlor anymore. Maybe he'd left the city entirely, feeling the heat after killing Paul's contact.

Paul wanted to believe that, but knew the Leopard wasn't that sophisticated. Or that smart. He was here. It would just require some time and patience.

At least that was what he told himself. Wanting to prove Charlie Chan's investment in him had been correct.

After his second cup of coffee, on the second day of surveillance, he'd seen a person enter the parlor who seemed out of place. One who was decidedly not of the local clientele. A tall man in a suit, he was something different. Paul perked up, taking note of his appearance, cataloging him for future surveillance: patrician face, crisp mustache, slicked-back hair cut short, and a suit that didn't fit. Like it had spent years in the closet before he had donned it again.

He wasn't Bamboo Triad, that was for sure.

Paul watched him glance furtively around and then enter, telegraphing his history without even wanting to. He was from power, and he didn't want to be seen here in the lower depths of Taipei.

In 1992 it would have been normal. He might have been an average man who would visit this seedy neighborhood, like all the other foreign visitors—but even then, it would have been after the sun had set. Not now, at noon.

No, this man was different. And because of it, Paul continued to watch.

Three coffees later, he saw the man leave, never having identified the Snow Leopard. He wondered if he should wait. After all, the guy could have just come in for a handjob and a latte.

He surreptitiously took multiple pictures from his phone as the man walked by him down the market alley. He went through the tunnel-like entrance and Paul sat for a second, wondering if he should call for advice, and then remembered he would get no advice. He was persona non grata at the NSB. There was no one he could call. All Charlie Chan had left him was remote access to NSB databases for research, but nothing real-time in the way of support. So it was up to him and his instincts.

And his instincts told him to follow. Forget about the Snow Leopard.

He watched the man leave the market and continue on down Huaxi Street, dodging the traffic across Guilin Road.

He began to lose his target in the crowd, took one more glance down toward the massage parlor, hoping the Snow Leopard would make an appearance. He did not, and Paul made his decision.

He stood up and gave chase.

He kept the man in sight on the crowded sidewalk, staying far enough away that he wouldn't be able to see a brush pass or other contact, but close enough that he could build a pattern of life. Who was this guy? Why was he in the Bamboo Triad area? And did any of this mean a damn thing?

The man took a left on Guangzhou Street a block ahead, and Paul sprinted to catch up. He reached the corner and didn't see him. He walked forward, the front of the famous Lungshan Temple to his left and the Mengxia Park to his right, glancing all around to determine where the man had gone. There was a metro station under the park, and multiple alleys leading away, which meant he'd lost him. If the man had chosen any of those directions, he was gone.

Which left the temple. If he were there, Paul could find him. It wasn't a conscious decision, as it was the least likely place—but it was the only one that made sense to search, given his choices. And so he did.

He entered the temple using the right door, still remembering the religious training of his youth, trying to confuse the demons chasing him. To his right was a waterfall with tourists around it, taking pictures. To his left was a small garden. His target wasn't in sight.

He left the courtyard and went into the temple proper, once again using the right door. He let his eyes adjust to the dim lighting and saw patrons tossing stones to his left, a ritual intended to give them an answer to their questions. He wandered about for a bit, circling the crowds and smelling the incense, and then recognized the man in the suit at the rear of the temple, moving toward the worshipers throwing the stones.

Paul darted to the side, hiding in the crowds and watching. The target waited a bit for others to finish, then collected a pair of stones, tossing them on the ground. He didn't spend any time in reflection, not even caring how they turned up, tossing them two more times and then moving to a rack of drawers that looked like an old-school Dewey Decimal System library card catalog. He pulled out the drawer two from the top, retrieved a roll of paper, and Paul knew it wasn't for his fortune.

The ritual for retrieving such scrolls was intricate, involving multiple throws of the stones, then shaking a batch of sticks in a drum to tell one which drawer to pull for his fate, all reflecting the religion of the temple. The man had done none of that, which meant he was faking the throw just to get to the drawer. Because something was in it that he needed, and he wanted to camouflage why he was opening it.

And it became clear. *Someone's passing information through the temple.*

The suit left, and Paul ran over to the rack of drawers, elbowing people out of the way to get to the one he'd seen the target use. He opened it, sifted through the papers, and saw nothing but the usual mystical answers to the prayers given—none of them really providing any insight without paying a mystic at the back of the temple to interpret. Just a collection of phrases that one could find salvation within, like a scrap of paper broken from a fortune cookie—and in fact the temple ritual was the genesis of that pastime.

Paul stood back, ashamed of his aggressive actions, the people around him glaring. He turned to leave, and recognized the Snow Leopard across the courtyard of the temple. He backed up, unsure if he was mistaken, staring hard. It was him. Chao Zheng, the Snow Leopard, in front of a Tao deity, bowing as if in prayer.

The recognition shook Paul to his core. The man was here for a reason. That area was exactly where the suit had been.

He was torn between following the unknown or staying on the Snow Leopard. He hesitated for a moment, saw the Leopard move to a different cubicle with a different deity and begin praying again. Paul wavered a minute, then left the temple at a trot, trying to find the suit.

He ran up the street, seeing nothing, and was aggravated that he'd left the one link he had, thinking about going back to the temple. He didn't. He kept walking, moving rapidly. He stopped at a crossing and was amazed to find the suit at the same stop. Waiting on the light along with thirty other people.

*Why would a man like that still be walking? Why not Uber or a taxi?*

He faded back, and then followed him for another ten blocks, the man continuing to walk in the heat. They passed the giant memorial park for Chiang Kai-Shek, skirting the memorial itself, and entered the government section of Taipei.

*Why walk this far?*

And it became clear—the man didn't want a record of his actions. Nothing that said he had been picked up at the temple—much less the snake market—and dropped off here.

Paul was now sure he was on to something, but had no idea of what. He followed the man past the parks and gardens surrounding the memorial, toward the presidential palace. He stayed far enough behind to keep from being spotted, his anxiety growing greater, and saw him leave the street, bounding up the steps of one of the ubiquitous government buildings in the area.

Paul watched the man disappear inside and saw a sign for the Ministry of Foreign Affairs.

*This is it. That man is the link.*

But he had no idea what that link meant or who the man was.

# 34

Chao Zheng—the Snow Leopard—watched his new contact leave the Lungshan Temple, darting through the crowd like he was escaping a police cordon. It made him smile. The man was clearly not used to dealing with the likes of the Snow Leopard, but that was the truth for about ninety percent of the people Chao extorted. The life of the PRC elite was not the same as his life, even as they used him for their own ends.

They hadn't even cared about his existence until he'd proven useful. Proven he could affect the views of the local population in Taiwan. Then they took notice. They looked at him as a lever to jam into the crack of Taiwan society, breaking open the schism of the old world versus the new, and he was more than willing to be that tool. As long as he was paid in the end.

He knew they wanted to sow discord in Taiwan, but even as a Taiwanese national he didn't care. His world was singular in its goals: money. Pure and simple. He wasn't driven one whit by the politics of China or Taiwan. He cared about money, and he'd found a way to make it.

The People's Republic of China wanted more than anything to infiltrate the island nation of Taiwan with its propaganda and other active measures, and he'd proven he could do that. He'd worked for more than two years inside a political party he had created, leveraging Taiwan's nascent democracy to use every bit of the PRC's assets against Taiwan, and in so doing had become intertwined in the success of the endeavor, so much so that he was now vested in the outcome. Even as he didn't know what that outcome ultimately would be.

Pretending to pray alongside the others in the temple, he waited until his contact had been gone for ten minutes, and then left, walking back to his little fiefdom of Snake Alley. He entered through the intricate arch of the market, seeing the people go out of their way to ignore him. Wherever he looked, women sweeping, men pushing dollies, they all glanced away, not wanting to incur his wrath.

As the leader of the Bamboo Triad, he owned this section of Taiwan, and they knew it. If you aggravated him, you might find the rent doubled because you had to pay to ensure your establishment didn't burn to the ground. Or worse.

He went to the end of the market, took a right down an alley so narrow he had to move sideways to get past trash bins, then entered a nondescript doorway with a camera the size of a lipstick tube affixed to the jamb. Inside a small anteroom was the same man who had helped drown the informant at the falls, his face hard to read because of the tattoos covering it. He sat behind a chipped wooden desk, a Pentium desktop computer on top old enough to have a slot for a Zip drive. Leaning against the wall were two women both past their prime, heavy makeup on their faces and dressed in what might have been charitably called sultry in 1980. Now it just looked sad and worn out.

The women jumped to attention at Chao's arrival. The man smiled, but knew better than to ask how the meeting had gone in front of a couple of whores.

Chao asked, "Is the WiFi working?"

The man nodded and Chao waved his hand, saying, "Leave me. All of you."

When the small room had cleared out Chao pulled up his smartphone, turned on airplane mode, then connected to the WiFi network of his office. Once he was online, he opened an app called Telegram and dialed a contact. He waited until someone answered, then read off a series of four emojis: "Monkey, tent, pile of shit, smiley face."

The man who answered said, "Same. Stand by."

Telegram was an end-to-end encrypted messaging application used the world over for journalists with confidential sources and resistance groups in totalitarian countries—along with other, not so savory individuals with something to hide, like the Snow Leopard.

The emoji on his screen ensured his call was encrypted end-to-end. If the four emojis on his phone were the same as those for the person answering, he was secure. And as he'd turned off all cell activity from the phone, working solely through his WiFi network, he was essentially invisible, even if someone knew where to look.

He waited a few seconds, then heard a new voice say, "This is Lion. Is this Leopard?"

Chao enjoyed the fact that every single code name for this operation had come from the nickname he'd earned on the streets of Taipei. He had no idea who "Lion" was, but knew he was very high in the PRC of mainland China. He said, "Yes. Meeting is done."

"Do you have it?"

"Yes. I got two on my phone right now."

"Are they good?"

"One is. It's a speech the president gave to the members of the Mainland Affairs Council, so it was openly filmed.

High-quality production. The other is not. It's from a different, private meeting of the MAC, and Ocelot is petrified of being compromised. You can see the minister's face, but he kept the camera on his phone low. It looks like a drunk took it."

"That's fine. Makes it look clandestine instead of staged. Is the audio clear on both?"

"Very clear."

"How long did they talk? We need something to work with."

"The minister is thirty minutes, with the audio very clear. The video, not so much. It moves up and down, like the idiot was jerking off while she spoke. The president's speech is less time, but it's much cleaner, because it was staged."

"Did anyone else say anything in the meetings?"

"Not for the president. That was a canned speech, but the minister got some questions. A couple of people talked, but they aren't on the screen. She just recognizes them to speak, and then answers the questions."

"Perfect. You said Ocelot had some issues?"

"Yeah. He's petrified. He knows if you use the MAC video he'll be done. For the minister's discussion there weren't that many people in the room. It won't be hard to find out who filmed it. On the other hand, he's actually *in* the presidential video. You can see him, so it's clearly not him filming."

"Yeah, but that means there's a record of that video. Something they can compare against. That makes the minister's video more important. It looks like the truth by the way it was taken. The president's video can be refuted by all of the other copies out there. Ocelot is still needed, though. You need to massage him. Make sure he knows we'll take care of him."

"I don't know if I can do that. I'm not, shall we say, at his level of society. He doesn't trust me at all. And the candidate you wanted me to prop up is doing well. The social media campaign is working. He's rising in the polls like a rocket. We may not need Ocelot."

"He *was* rising in the polls, but the protests in Hong Kong are forcing us to lock down, and that's going to work against us in Taiwan. We need him."

Chao scrunched his eyes, unsure of what that meant, his small world now crashing into a bigger one. He said, "Hong Kong? What's that got to do with our candidate? He's winning."

"He's winning *now,* but he probably won't succeed because of Hong Kong. Us clamping down inside that state will impact the election in Taiwan, no matter what his message is. That's not my concern, though. I don't care if he loses."

Chao sat up and said, "Then what am I doing all of this for if not him winning? Isn't that the point?"

"It *was* the point. It's not anymore. Now we're going to use that candidate to cause the strife we need."

"What's that mean?"

"It means send me the video through Telegram. You keep Ocelot on a leash. That's all it means."

Chao thought through the implications, and his own small world in it, and said, "But you'll keep me in mind, yes?"

"Of course. We always take care of our own."

# 35

Sitting inside the less than impressive headquarters of the Twelfth Bureau, Han Ming hung up the phone and looked to the commander, saying, "It's working, but we're losing control."

"What do you mean?"

"That asshole in Taiwan is not with us. The Leopard is not a patriot. He only wants money. He is not to be trusted. We need to put a plan in place to eliminate him. He knows too much."

Yuan glanced at him, then said, "That's your department, not mine."

"Yes. True. I'll deal with it. He's sending the videos. You'll need to be careful in the alteration. I don't want to bludgeon the people, just seed doubt. Both need to say that if the administration wins another turn, they're going to engage China. Make it subtle."

"Who's on them?"

"One is the president herself. The other is the president's handpicked minister for the Mainland Affairs Council. The cabinet position that's supposedly coordinating all business relationships with us. If she is released talking about giving in to us, it will cause immediate repercussions."

"Like what?"

"Riots. Other unrest. Something else to exploit."

"Exploit how?"

"That is not your concern. Stick with the digital world. I'll make you a script for the video. You can do this, correct? Here in the Twelfth Bureau?"

Yuan Bo remained quiet for a moment, then said, "Yes. I have the assets here, but they aren't all Chinese."

"Who?"

"The American contractor. The one working with our commercial artificial intelligence cell."

Han scoffed and said, "That's insane. Get someone else."

"If it's as important as you say, it'll have to be him. We just don't have the expertise in this. It's what he does. It's how he's made his name."

"What do you mean?"

"He's an expert at facial recognition. He's the man who's helped design all of our systems. Remember when we couldn't get our false positive rates down? How the system was untrustworthy when we deployed it?"

"No. I had nothing to do with that. Get to the point."

Yuan nodded and said, "Okay, okay. He started a company called BackRub when he was still in college. He had an idea about using digital traces for advertising in stores, where the consumer would enter a shopping area and his or her phone would start sending ads based on the phone's digital trace. On the side, as a lark, he started manipulating videos using the algorithms he designed. 'Deep fakes,' he calls them. He just did it for fun, but both of those efforts needed massive amounts of data for the AI engines to work through. The more data, the more accurate the rendition, be it video or cell phone tracking. And his company had invested in a way to achieve it."

Han walked to the window in the office, seeing the

American typing away on a computer keyboard in the next room. He said, "Why can't *we* do it?"

"Because in order to develop an algorithm that does what his does—that does what we want—we needed that data."

Han turned back and said, "Where'd *he* get the data? We have more people here in China than he does in the United States—and more cameras."

"Yes, we do, but we're much more homogeneous than the United States. In order to perfect the system, we need black faces, white faces, brown faces, faces of all nationalities. We were stymied because we have primarily Chinese faces. He invested in a company called Link, which is touted as a modern-day phone booth. Basically, it's a network of kiosks in New York City that anyone can use to connect to WiFi or make an internet call, like phone booths in the old days. They're scattered throughout the city."

Satisfied that he'd explained the problem, Yuan Bo said, "That's why he has the data, and it's why he's become the best at what you want done."

Aggravated, Han said, "You talk in riddles. Kiosks? Why does that matter?"

Yuan held up his hands and said, "Because the Link kiosks aren't a public service. It's designed to make money, and that money is through targeting everyone who walks by them with ads. Every single kiosk has a continuous Bluetooth connection to slave to the phones, which we don't care about, but each also has a camera to provide security. That camera is recording twenty-four/seven. Collecting faces from the most diverse location on the planet. Every minute of every day each of those kiosks is taking pictures of the people passing by. *That's* the data we used to decrease our false-positive rate on our own surveillance systems. And it's the same data that's made his manipulation algorithm the best in the world."

"Can't we just take his program? How hard is that to do?"

"We could, I suppose, but he's really the best at it. If you want it to look real—to sound like something someone can't crack as fake within twenty minutes, he's the guy we need to use."

"Can he be trusted?"

"Yes. Not because I trust him, but because he's already corrupted. If he doesn't work with us it will spell his doom. Like all of them we co-opt, we started small, dangling money for results. Now we own him. If the United States knew he was conducting a massive surveillance operation in New York City to benefit the facial recognition and surveillance programs of the People's Republic of China, he'd be destroyed."

Han looked back through the window and nodded, saying, "Okay, but he doesn't leave here. No contact with anyone in the United States. Once he's given the mission, he stays here until it's done."

Yuan looked like he'd swallowed sour milk. Han said, "What?"

"We can't do that. BackRub isn't huge, but it's rich. He's the CEO. He can't just drop off the planet. He's going to have to act like a CEO, talking to his people in the United States."

Han nodded, saying, "Okay, but implant all his devices. I want to know what he says, and I mean whether that's a text message through a computer or a voice call."

Yuan nodded and said, "That's already done. He's under full-scope surveillance right now. So far, he has done nothing untoward."

Han tapped his fingers on the sill, thinking. He said, "Okay.

But if he's as good as you say he is, he's probably got a way to communicate we haven't found. Be on the lookout for that."

Yuan nodded and said, "What's next?"

"I'll get you the script. I want it done soon. A day at the latest. Other things are in motion. Ocelot is going to have to implant what Bobcat took from Australia. He can't be burned until then, because we need his access."

"Bobcat is okay? I thought there was trouble with that."

"There is, but he's clear. The Fifth Bureau is on it. He's meeting a man to transfer the data as we speak."

Not liking talking about the assassins of the Fifth Bureau, but overcome by curiosity, Yuan asked, "So they eliminated the Americans? The ones interfering with the Bobcat mission?"

Han went to the door without answering, saying, "Make sure the videos are perfect. Within a day."

Yuan nodded, and Han opened the door. He turned back and said, "Don't ask so many questions. Do your job and let the Fifth Bureau do theirs."

# 36

Chen Ju-Long watched Zhi Rou feed their captive with a spoon, her hands handcuffed to the arms of a wheelchair they'd decided to use as her restraint device. Zhi was surprisingly gentle, without a trace of the animosity or rage he'd seen the night before.

The woman—Nicole—was frightened out of her mind, constantly weeping and begging them to release her. Chen took no joy from her display of emotion, and made sure she was treated with dignity, but releasing her wasn't going to happen. They'd failed to kill Clifford Delmonty, the man who suspected what Jake—Bobcat—was up to, but they had at least gained some leverage with the girl.

Nicole was the one connection they had to Clifford, and in his mind, the only way they could negate the potential leak he presented. They had been on the defensive since the initial contact because they hadn't known the man had help. They'd made a mistake in attacking here in Sydney without a complete assessment, believing they were the hunters, but it hadn't turned out that way. He had been arrogant in his blind supremacy, but he wouldn't make that same mistake twice. Whoever they were, they didn't have the technical capabilities he had, or the lethal team he owned, of that he was sure. The man had simply gotten lucky.

Clifford Delmonty wasn't in bed with a U.S. government

agency and had no contacts in the intelligence field they could find. They had his entire work history through nothing more than hacking his LinkedIn account, and short of a brief six-year stint in the U.S. Army as an infantryman, he'd worked solely in the private sector as a computer engineer.

In addition to LinkedIn, they'd cracked his personal Gmail account and discovered email exchanges with a man called Pike Logan—apparently an old Army buddy from years ago—wanting to visit for a vacation. *He* was the one who'd upset their plans. A coincidence they couldn't have predicted, but one that was easy to deal with, once they knew what they were up against. Logan was a hard man, no doubt, but he was no match for the skill of Chen's team.

Except for the woman. Chen couldn't explain her. *How did she manage to kill my man with a corkscrew?*

Maybe the idiot reporting the incident was lying. Or maybe he'd missed what had actually happened. Either way, *Chen* had the upper hand now. He had the girl, Nicole.

Chen watched Zhi spill a little bit of orange juice on Nicole's lips and grow embarrassed, almost like she was ashamed at her skill at feeding. Gently, as if she were wiping a child's face, she cleaned up her mess, cooing soft nothings as she did so. Completely different from the way she'd acted last night, when they were attempting to remove Nicole from the bar.

Chen had seen her get bumped by the drunk in the hallway, which should have been an easy fix. The captive girl was between them, and the drunk was just trying to get to the bathroom. Everything was still in the box. And then Zhi had pulled off the plastic from her ceramic nail and slit the man's throat from ear to ear, her face glowing in an ethereal light. Soaking up the spouting blood. Soaking up her power to create death. Reveling in her ability to kill like she was a child burning ants with a magnifying glass.

It had nearly led to disaster. They'd managed to get the girl out the back and away from the carnage, but the disturbance had led to the target escaping, not the least because he'd lucked into finding his friend again.

Zhi finished cleaning Nicole's face, put away the utensils, and then wheeled her to the bedroom at the rear of the house.

She came back out and said, "She won't tolerate much more of this. She's breaking down from the strain."

He picked up his phone, willing it to ring. Wanting his team to tell him they'd found the Americans. He said, "Nothing we can do about that. She'll last as long as we need her to. A day. Maybe more. Then we're done with her."

"Do you intend to kill her?"

He glanced up and said, "Of course."

"We can't do that. She isn't worthy of killing. We should let her go."

"What are you talking about?"

"She doesn't deserve to die."

He set down the phone and said, "And the man last night did?"

She brushed a strand of hair out of her eyes and said, "He stood between us and getting her out of the bar. So yes."

"He was nothing. He was a drunk. Your actions may well have destroyed this entire operation. And now you want to spare the girl? That will do the same."

"She doesn't deserve this. The drunk did."

He stood up and advanced on her, the fury growing. He backed her up with his rage alone, until she was against the wall. He said, "You harm anyone else without my permission, and I will kill you. I *will*. Do you understand?"

She glared at him, and he placed his hand on her throat, loosely. He said, "Do not test me. You want to try, raise that hand. Show me the nail. I'll break your neck before you can bring it to bear."

She rolled her eyes theatrically, then giggled, saying, "So does this mean we're no longer lovers? Or is this our first fight?"

He dropped his hand and shook his head, saying, "Don't test me. I need you here, but I mean it. The mission is more important, and that girl is going to die. Understand?"

She nodded, and the phone on the table finally rang.

He went to it and answered, hearing, "It's the same. Different restaurant, but same area. Maybe a block over from the last time we checked."

"So they're not in the hotel we thought?"

"Might be, but if so, they don't turn the phone on inside it. Only outside."

Chen knew that wasn't the case, because the phone had been tracked by the Third Department since it had miraculously come back to life. It hadn't been turned off in the last twenty-four hours.

He had hoped to learn where the Americans were sleeping by tracking the phone, and thereby conduct a clandestine assault to eliminate them, but when they'd first targeted the geolocation, it had been inside a restaurant on the busy Argyle Street in the heart of The Rocks entertainment district. They'd pulled back and waited on it to move. When it did, they'd closed in again, and now he was learning it had just shifted restaurants, which was a problem, because he was running out of time.

Jake, the man his superiors insisted on calling Bobcat, was on an overnight train to Cairns, with a meeting in two days.

Chen needed to leave here to ensure that went according to plan. *That* was the mission. This was a cleanup that would only matter if Jake did something stupid. And after the report from the meeting in Brisbane, Chen wasn't too impressed with him so far.

"How did that phone not go to a bed-down location in the last cycle of darkness? It stayed in the same place?"

"Apparently so. So far, it hasn't moved more than a hundred meters. It's stayed in heavily populated areas."

*They're smarter than I thought. They're waiting on a call.*

"So we need to go to plan B. We need to leverage the girl. Come back here. We need to devise a trap using her. I'm going to initiate contact to prepare them. We need to control this from every angle."

# 37

Dunkin and I rolled into the central market on Argyle Street, a grouping of conventional streets interspersed with lanes only allowing foot traffic, the pedestrian areas lined with cafés and booths selling handcrafted wares.

Dunkin was agitated and had been since we'd left the Nurses Walk the night before, which I understood, but I'd convinced him to wait and let it play out. We had no lead on where they'd taken Nicole, and I knew they hadn't snatched her because she was a fount of information. They'd taken her because of Dunkin—which made her a lead I was hoping to leverage.

I'd made him turn on his phone, knowing that they'd track it, but also knowing it was the only number they had, if they wanted to contact us. Which I'm sure they did.

I wasn't stupid, though. We didn't sit around a hotel room with it turned on, waiting for a call, because I'd used that technique more times than I could count to turn the cell phone into a GPS beacon telling me where to hit. Something I fully intended to do when they made contact with me through that very phone.

My team had found a restaurant in a large food court area right off Argyle Street, surrounded by people out enjoying the bars, and had sat there all night. Now it was my turn to babysit the phone.

I dialed an encrypted number, saying, "We're here. Where are you?"

I heard, "I'm with the jarhead. Where do you think he'd go? Look for the first beer garden you can find next to the street. Munich House or something. Right on the corner."

I laughed and said, "I know it. Be there in five."

Dunkin said, "Who are we meeting?"

My intent was to keep that phone in a populated area for as long as it took, and with just three of us—me, Jenn, and Dunkin—that would have been hard, but my team had landed in the middle of the night, giving me extra bodies.

Jennifer had picked them up, and at four in the morning I'd put them to work, babysitting the phone while I went back to the hotel to get some shut-eye. Dunkin had awakened me at eight in the morning, aggravating the hell out of me, but I'd agreed to take him with me, against my better judgment. He was the one person the people hunting could recognize on sight.

Jennifer was at the hotel coordinating with the Taskforce to track whatever phone contacted Dunkin's, and we were in standby mode, just switching out bodies to wait on a call. If it ever came.

I saw the beer garden across the street, just now opening at 9 A.M. It was Saturday, and the roads were starting to bustle with the weekend markets, awnings and pop-up tents erected for the tourists and locals to come buy handcrafted artwork and knickknacks.

The beer garden had a slew of pine tables out front, just like you'd find in a similar spot in Germany, but all were empty except for one. In the back corner was a six-foot-tall man with long black hair, a ratty T-shirt from some band nobody had ever heard of, and a puka shell necklace, like he had washed ashore last night from a shipwreck and hadn't bothered to change. Across from him was a black man built like a fireplug. Short, and all muscle, he was wearing a long-sleeved shirt and cargo shorts with Solomon hikers on his feet, looking more like an outback tour guide than a tourist.

Dunkin saw them from across the street and said, "Is that who I think it is?"

I crossed, saying, "Yeah. It is. Don't say anything stupid about Nicole. They didn't come here for that."

We went through the entrance and to the table. The castaway said, "I can't believe I flew all the way here to sit watching a phone."

I grinned and said, "Trust me, when it rings, you're getting some high adventure. But if we sit here all day we'll be too drunk to execute."

He pointed at the black man and said, "Blame Brett. He picked the place."

Brett held up his hands and said, "It's not like there were a lot of choices. Other than the park bench we spent the night on. Knuckles wanted to stay where we were. I wanted breakfast."

Brett was my designated medic. A former Force Recon Marine, he had spent the last decade as a paramilitary officer in the CIA. Knuckles was my second in command, and a Navy SEAL. I didn't hold their previous employers against them, being Army and all, because they were some of the best men I'd ever operated with—even if Knuckles dressed like he was trying to audition for *Bachelor in Paradise*.

Actually, he'd never have to do that, because he continually had women auditioning to be in his private version of the show. It sort of sickened me.

Knuckles said, "Since you let Veep go to sleep last night, I figured it was okay to get some breakfast on your dime."

I ignored the jibe and said, "You guys remember Dunkin from back in the day?"

They looked at him, trying to place the face, and then the recognition dawned. Brett said, "Oh, yeah. I remember. The guy could dunk a basketball better than me. Is that right?"

Dunkin went red in the face and Knuckles said, "Take a seat."

Brett scooted over for Dunkin and I sat next to Knuckles. Changing the subject away from his callsign, Dunkin said, "Who's Veep? Someone new on the team?"

I said, "Remember that op in Europe? The last one you did before you left the Taskforce? The kidnapping?"

"Yeah, of course. With the vice president's son?"

"Yep. That's Veep."

Nicholas Seacrest—Veep—was the millennial on my team. An Air Force Special Operations Combat Controller, he got his callsign because his father had been the vice president of the United States, the same man who was now the U.S. president. For security reasons, Veep went by his mother's maiden name. Getting him on my team had taken a little bit of arm-twisting, but Veep had wanted to come over, and I liked the skills he'd shown during the operation. Since I'd pretty much saved the day by rescuing him and several other prominent politicians' kids from certain death, I had a few blue chips available to help it along.

Dunkin said, "Wait, Seacrest's father isn't the vice president anymore."

I said, "I know."

Incredulous, he said, "You have the president of the United States' son on a Taskforce team?"

Knuckles said, "Not just any team. *Our* team. Sort of helps in the chain of command department."

Dunkin nodded, taking that in, then said, "So why did you guys come over here? What's your real mission? I knew Pike was bullshitting about a vacation."

I could see he was about to explode because of Nicole, but was taking my earlier proscription about not mentioning her to heart. He wanted the help, and trusted me, so he was fishing for information without giving anything away.

Knuckles said, "I don't really have any idea why I'm here. Wolffe told us that Pike was on the trail of some badass Chinese secret agent men. That's the extent of my knowledge."

Dunkin looked at me, and I told him the truth. "I really came here on vacation. You getting hit sort of changed that. They're here because of you. Why don't you tell us what this is all about?"

Dunkin looked around the table, then came back to me, stuttering out, "I . . . I don't know. I really don't."

Brett said, "Oh, bullshit. You know something."

He put his head in his hands and said, "All I know is that Jake Shu was doing something hinky, and then I was attacked."

I said, "You mean *I* was attacked. What was hinky?"

"Look, my job is classified. I could get fired for talking about it."

All of us just sat there and looked at him. He said, "I'll get *fired*."

We continued staring.

# 38

Dunkin felt our glares and said, "Okay, okay. There's this guy named Jake Shu. He's in my department, and we work on the F-35 program, specifically the artificial intelligence used in the synchronization of the helmet to the sensors around the plane. He's always acted a little strange, digging into programs that didn't concern him and asking questions that made no sense for his specific project. I didn't think anything of it until a few months ago. You remember that F-35 that went down in the Sea of Japan?"

I said, "Yeah. Everyone was worried about the Chinese stealing the tech. But it crashed by pilot error."

"That's what everyone believes, but the last guy to work on its assembly was Jake Shu. Outside of Fort Worth, Texas, there was only one final fabrication facility in the world, and that was in Japan. We sent Jake to help them, and then that plane crashed. He came home like it was no big deal. Japan thought it was big enough to stop final fabrication at their plant."

Knuckles leaned forward and said, "So the Chinese set out to kill you because of this? Doesn't make any sense. Sorry."

"No. That's not the only thing. I reported him early on and my company did a sham investigation, finding nothing, but he kept doing his strange shit. The last day at work—the day Pike showed up—he was on the A2/AD systems outside of our entire F-35 program, and he saw me watching. He still had the golden key and he—"

Knuckles cut him off. "Slow down. What the hell is a 'golden key'?"

"Because all of our stuff is classified, there is no transfer between terminals. Only people with a certain authorization—what we called the golden key—could do it. Because Jake went to Japan, he had the key, so he could access whatever he needed to remotely. Anyway, he was accessing the A2/AD system—"

Now it was Brett cutting him off. "What's the 'A2/AD system'?"

Dunkin glanced at me, looking like he thought we were idiots. I said, "Well, I don't recognize that acronym either. Go ahead and explain."

"A2/AD is anti-access/area denial. It's the systems countries use to prevent encroachment on their terrain. Surely you guys have heard of it, right?"

He got blank stares and said, "Okay, you guys have been doing the counterterrorism thing too long. The Department of Defense has shifted focus to what they call 'great power competition,' meaning they're looking at major wars. Every country on earth has taken the lessons from both Gulf Wars in Iraq, which is if you let America build up combat power, you will lose, so the name of the game now is A2/AD. If you prevent us from getting in, you win the war. Really, I'm sort of surprised you haven't heard of it."

Brett said, "Yeah, well, we've been a little busy saving the U.S. from real threats instead of theoretical ones. I haven't had the time to read the latest dispatches from the RAND Corporation. How does this matter?"

Dunkin looked to see if Brett was kidding, saw he was

not, and said, "We're the main contractor for A2/AD artificial intelligence for the Republic of Taiwan. We're the ones developing the systems for them. The theory works for Taiwan against China just like it works for China against the United States. If Taiwan can prevent the Chinese from entering, then they can win the war, but unlike China—which can monitor U.S. naval deployments and other indicators that measure in weeks—Taiwan needs to do it in hours. That's all the time they have."

I was beginning to see the utility of the data Jake might have had access to. I said, "So you think Jake has the ability to delay this time for the Chinese?"

"No. That's not it. That's not it at all."

"Then what? What's the big deal?"

He sighed, then said, "Okay, I can't give you a big class here, but artificial intelligence relies on two things: computing power and data. That's it. We have the computing power to make stuff work. What it needs is data. There's a computer program from IBM called Deep Blue, which was designed to play chess. The first time it played, it only had the rules, and was defeated by a human. A thousand times later, after playing game after game, it defeated the best grandmaster in the world. It needed data. That's the threat."

"What do you mean?"

"The Taiwanese want to tighten the circle for decision, so they asked us to develop AI that could ascertain what was happening throughout their unified field of sensors and develop a plan of attack. In essence, tell the master that something was happening that deserved attention faster than the master could do on his own. But we haven't developed the data for that yet. It's vulnerable to manipulation."

I said, "So you think this system could be used to cloak an

attack? The Chinese could manipulate it so that when they begin the big invasion, the Taiwanese won't know it?"

"Yeah, maybe, in the future, but not today. It's only a test system right now. It won't be integrated into the actual defense for at least two more years. Even if China attacked, and Jake could trick the system into not alerting, the legacy stuff would see it."

Brett said, "So why do we care? We've got two years to figure out what he did to the system. I don't see the threat."

Dunkin took a drink of water and said, "I didn't either, but I've been thinking about it. Jake took that data for a reason, and I think it's the opposite. Jake could give the Chinese the ability to manipulate the information so that in essence they could cause the Taiwanese to believe an attack is occurring when it's not. It's a whole different problem set—and one that could succeed, given our work with them."

We sat there for a second, and Knuckles said, "You mean Jake could cause something like that movie *War Games*? From the eighties? Some dumbass computer projecting an attack when one isn't happening?"

Dunkin lit up, saying, "Exactly! It's like the WOPR! Remember when the computer played tic-tac-toe until it exploded? That's a machine learning through data. That movie was really sort of prescient. But we haven't refined the data, so it can't learn what's right or wrong. It'll just say it's bad stuff coming."

Brett said, "Prescient. Great. I'd rather be fighting in the eighties than this crap. At least I could see the target."

I said, "So you think Jake has some AI stuff that will affect the ability of Taiwan to defend itself? That's what this is about?"

"Yes. I think Jake has data that will cause Taiwan to

defend itself when there isn't a threat. I think they're going to manipulate that program to do what they want."

Knuckles said, "Well, that sounds like the Chinese special agent shit I was looking for. So what's the next step? Where's this Jake Shu? Let's go wring his ass out. I didn't come here to surf."

Dunkin looked at me, begging me with his eyes to tell them this wasn't about Jake Shu but about Nicole, worried that he'd lost his ability to control his destiny because he'd given up what he knew. Worried that he would be tossed aside like the drunk in the bar last night in the name of great power competition.

I winked at him and turned to the team, saying, "Jake's going to have to wait. We have a more immediate problem here."

Knuckles rolled his eyes and said, "I knew it. Nothing is ever simple with you. What's the 'immediate problem'?"

Before I could answer, Dunkin's phone rang. We stared at it for a beat, and then I picked it up, showing it to Dunkin.

He said, "That's Nicole's number."

I signaled Brett to contact Jennifer, letting the Taskforce know we were in action, and then hit the button.

"Hello?"

# 39

Chen heard someone answer the phone and said, “Is this Clifford Delmonty?”

“No. It’s a friend of his. Who is this?”

Chen smiled, glanced at Zhi, and said, “The friend from last night?”

“Yes. Is this the asshole from last night?”

Chen let that go, saying, “Let me speak to Clifford.”

“Let me speak to Nicole, asshole.”

Chen felt a spasm of rage at the arrogance, but bit it back, remembering the mission. He said, “If Clifford Delmonty is not on this phone in the next five seconds, I’ll have my friend cut her throat just like the man last night. This isn’t hard. Put him on the phone. We both want the same thing.”

“We do, I agree. It’s why I haven’t gone to the police and screamed about a kidnapping. It’s why we didn’t go back to the bar and tell everyone what we know about the assault there. Don’t toy with me. Clifford isn’t here. I’m sitting at a restaurant in The Rocks. But I’m sure you know that, because you haven’t tried to attack this phone location right now. So, what do you want? We want the girl. What do you want?”

Chen hesitated. This man wasn’t some old friend of Clifford’s. He was someone in the game. He hadn’t gone to the police because he didn’t want to become involved any more than Chen did, and he *knew* Chen would call. He *knew* Chen wanted something. And he knew Chen could track Clifford's phone. He was not just an Army buddy. He was something else. Which explained the woman who could kill. It caused Chen to reevaluate his entire plan. In the span of seconds, he came up with a new one.

"I want the thumb drive Clifford has," Chen said. "The one with the data from our company. The data he stole. I will tell you where the transfer will happen soon."

"How are you going to do that? Launch a bat signal in the sky? Surely you don't expect me to leave this phone operational and carry it around with me, do you? I'm not that stupid."

Chen smiled in spite of himself. That's *exactly* what he was hoping. He said, "Turn it back on at seven P.M. tonight. In the same place, if you want. I don't care. I'll give you instructions for the delivery of Clifford's drive. It will be him, and him alone, bringing it. If I see any help, I will kill the girl. And as you know, I will have help. Do you understand?"

"Yes. Yes, I understand. I'll tell him. Don't hurt her. We'll comply."

"Good. Because I *will* hurt her."

And then Chen heard something else come through the phone. Something from outside even the pain he understood he could inflict. A whisper pregnant with menace floated into his ear.

"Listen to me closely. Do *not* hurt her. You don't want to do that. I promise. Leave her out of this, or I'll make you pay in ways you can't fathom."

It wasn't the words themselves. It was the tone . . . or the cadence . . . or something, like the man was reaching through the phone with his voice, imparting a vision that would come true.

Rattled, Chen said, "Just stand by that phone," and hung up.

Zhi said, "What was that about?"

Chen stood silently, thinking about the man on the other end. *Feeling* his skill.

Zhi said again, "Hey, what was that about?"

Chen shook his head and said, "What?"

"That stuff about a thumb drive? What was that?"

He put the phone on the table, saying "We need to get the American, Clifford Delmonty. I couldn't very well tell him that in order for his girlfriend to live he had to sacrifice himself. I have no idea what his code of ethics is. He could just flee."

"So what was that about a drive? He doesn't have one."

"You know that, and I know that, but he doesn't know what we know. As far as he knows, we *believe* he has a thumb drive. It gives him a reason to show up. If he thinks all he has to do is provide us with a drive instead of his life, he'll do so."

"What? He's not that smart."

"The man with him is. They won't know what we're talking about, but that man will create conditions to fake it. Trust me, I heard him. He's in the game. He'll create a thumb drive to get the girl back. All we need to do is give him some specifics. Something to prove it's 'the drive' we want. He'll create a dummy, convinced he's tricked us, and he'll send Clifford to deliver it. He's smart, and I'll use that to cause him to outsmart himself."

Huang Min, the leader of the assault team under his command, entered the house, saying, "I didn't get close enough to see the people around the phone, but from my work last night, it was Clifford's friend. Pike Logan. I'm sure it's still him. They're too afraid to go home with the handset on, and too afraid to turn it off."

Chen nodded and said, "After last night, how many men do we have that can still fight?"

"Not counting us, four for fighting. Two for surveillance, but only one of those is ambulatory. The other one needs a cane to get around, so he's good for a stationary trigger, but he can't follow."

Chen looked at the bandage on Huang's face and said, "So six that are clean, or do they look like you?"

Huang glanced down, then said, "They all have damage in one way or another. Things that stick out. But it's the best we can do unless you want to pull from the north."

Chen nodded, thinking. He said, "I can't do that. We've had too many issues already with this operation, and that one in Cairns is the entire reason we are here. All you need to do is kill two men. Can you do that?"

"Yes, sir. How hard could it be?"

Chen scoffed and said, "Apparently, pretty damn hard."

Huang smiled and said, "Yes, this has been a little more difficult than we expected, but now that we know the threat, we can mitigate it."

"If we were to plan an assault, where would you want to do that? It has to be something in the open. I've demanded he bring something to the meeting, and that's what he thinks he's going to do, so he won't agree to some back alley at night or coming here. So it's got to be a public area where he feels safe."

Without hesitation, Huang said, "The botanical garden. There are plenty of places to meet there where we can control the area and eliminate him."

Chen shook his head, saying, "No way. We chased him through that entire area. He knows it's a killing ground now because we tried to kill him there. He won't set foot in that place."

Huang thought a moment, then said, "The Taronga Zoo. It's open, public, but it has plenty of space to do what we want."

"You sure?"

"Yes. He'll want to do it at a pub or mall, but the zoo will give him complacency. And it has plenty of trails around to leave the body."

"Good. Take a man and conduct a reconnaissance. Figure out a plan of attack. I have to go meet our control."

Zhi said, "You want me to go with you?"

"No. Stay here with the girl. With the ferry ride, I'll be gone for a couple of hours."

"Good luck with the meeting."

"Yeah. I don't think it's going to be very pleasant."

# 40

Walking back to the hotel, the Sydney Opera House behind us, we entered the Royal Botanic Garden just as I finished my call with Jennifer, getting the track to the phone that had contacted us.

I hung up and Knuckles said, "Well?"

"She's got a location. Some place called Manly, which is just a little bit funny."

"Where is it? Near here?"

"Don't know. She's working with Creed at the Taskforce, necking down all the pertinent information. She'll have a target package by the time we get back."

Dunkin said, "So you guys are going to hit it, right? Rescue her?"

I didn't answer, angry over what I'd been told on the phone call earlier. Truthfully, I wanted to smack him, but that could wait until we got out of the area.

We'd left the beer house right after the call, me turning off Dunkin's phone and each of us exiting one by one every two minutes out of the back of the restaurant, spilling into an alley that led to the food court we'd initially staged within the night before. An open courtyard with tables surrounded by various restaurants, it had a walled archway that led back to Argyle Street. Once we were together, we'd crossed over to the Nurses Walk and begun our route home using nothing but back alleys and cut-throughs that allowed us to check our backtrail for anyone behind us.

It wasn't the best countersurveillance plan. If they had a full-on team against us, it would more than likely fail, as they could just use stationary elements and radios to keep us pinpointed, but I was pretty sure that I'd put a little dent in their ability to mount a full-scale surveillance effort when I'd rescued Dunkin.

Still walking, my rage growing, I turned to Dunkin and said, "I'm not doing a damn thing for Nicole until I know what the hell is going on here."

He looked like I'd slapped him. "What do you mean? I told you what I thought was going on. I don't know anything else."

Knuckles said, "Who the hell is Nicole?"

I held up a finger, cutting Knuckles off, saying to Dunkin, "The man on the phone said he wants a thumb drive of data that you stole. That's what he's after. He's not after *your* ass, which explains why those guys were outside of your apartment and attacked me. They didn't want *you*. They thought *I* could get them the data."

Dunkin's face went slack, processing what I said. He was either a world-class actor, or he really didn't know what I was talking about. He said, "Thumb drive? I have no idea what that means. What does that mean?"

I stopped right outside the exit gate and put my finger in his chest. "It means *they* know more than *I* do. That's what it means. If you want to save Nicole, you need to come clean. I don't give a shit if you're doing something illegal. I want to *know*."

Dunkin said, "Pike, I'm telling the truth! I've never done anything illegal . . . well, except when I was working for you.

I just had a computer engineering job with Gollum Solutions and I saw Jake doing some flaky stuff. That's it. Maybe . . . maybe he's on the run and they think I took whatever he has. Maybe that's it. Maybe they're just confused."

I started walking again, beginning to believe he was telling the truth. I said, "Well, that's not going to help us too much. But maybe it won't even matter."

We crossed down to the wharf heading to the hotel and Knuckles asked again, "Who the hell is Nicole?"

I told him what had happened, from the moment we'd set foot into Australia to the actions last night, only pausing when we went through the hotel lobby to prevent the freak show manning the desk and bell stand from hearing. Once we were up on the balcony headed to my room, I finished with, "Jake Shu is the hundred-meter target, but all we know is that he was supposed to go vacation in Cairns. He could be anywhere. Nicole is the five-meter target, and we're going to get her ass out of the fire. While doing that, we're going to exploit her target site to see what we can find."

I unlocked my hotel door, finding Jennifer staring at a laptop, Veep standing behind her.

Knuckles took in what I'd told him about a potential operation. He said, "You got any sanction for an Omega action on Australian soil?"

"No. I've got Alpha only. But I'm going to use the imminent threat clause for that. We go explore the house under Alpha, find Nicole in duress, and then save the day."

All Taskforce operations had to be approved by the Oversight Council, and they ranged from Alpha—introduction of forces to explore a potential problem, which is where we were now—to Omega, authorization to take down a known danger using kinetic means. Built into that was the ability to flex based on the circumstances of an imminent threat. If I had Alpha, and in my "exploration" I discovered a life in danger, I could operate on my own authority. Left unsaid was that I *knew* there was a life in danger before I even started Alpha.

Brett rolled his eyes and said, "Won't be the first time we've done this shit."

Jennifer saw us enter and I said, "Hey, Veep. Hope you got some rest while all of us were working."

He smiled, no longer the new guy and used to the ribbing. He said, "I'm available for the recce."

I said, "Where are we talking about?"

Jennifer said, "It's Manly, a place at the North Head right across the harbor. I've got the house necked down, but the satellite imagery isn't that good. It's in the woods on a cliff near the shore, right in front of some national park. It doesn't look like a place that's going to be easy to hit. They picked it for a reason."

I bent down to her computer screen and saw a cove of water, then a steep climb of foliage with houses jutting out from the green. I said, "Which one is the target?"

She pointed to an icon on the screen, but all I could see were roofs covered by the trees. She said, "That's it. Satellite is no help."

"Where is it?"

She scrolled the map back, bringing the bay into view. "It's known as the North Head. At the end of the harbor." She tapped the screen and said, "That's the southern one. It's what made this harbor perfect for the settlers back in the day. The heads protect everything."

The screen showed Sydney Harbour enclosed by two juts

of land, one north, one south, like the claws of a crab, the one to the north holding the target icon.

I said, "How do we get there?"

She said, "There are a number of ferries that go all over the harbor, which for the recce is probably the best bet. You could drive, but that's a long, roundabout trip."

I nodded and said, "Okay, Veep and I are going to check it out. Jennifer, keep working the target with Creed. Anything you can find, neighborhood architecture, WiFi service, whatever. Knuckles, you and Brett get some rack time. I'm not sure when this is going live and I need everyone on their toes."

Knuckles said, "You planning on hitting this with that little bit of intelligence?"

"No. I don't even know if Nicole's there. We'll take a look and see what we can find. We'll decide later. Go get a couple hours of sleep. I'll plan the recce."

He nodded, leaned over, and gave Jennifer a kiss on the cheek saying, "Hey, Koko, good to see you. I don't even get a hug?"

She smiled and stood up, giving him a quick embrace. "Glad you showed up. I can't keep him in the box by myself."

She hugged Brett as well, saying, "Glad to see *both* of you. We need the help."

Brett laughed and said, "You got that right. Anytime he's on the loose, you need help."

I scowled, they left, and Dunkin said, "I should go with you."

"That ain't going to happen."

"No, Pike, I mean it. You mentioned WiFi. I can penetrate that. You're just talking about a walkaround, right? I can do a pen-test outside the house. I might be able to find out something you can't."

Pen-test stood for penetration testing, meaning he might be able to penetrate the WiFi of the house and gain access to cameras, door alarms, or whatever else. Which was something we might need.

I said, "You got a kit for that?"

He shuffled foot to foot, then said, "Yeah, but it's in Nicole's sister's place. Across the quay."

*Shit.*

"Okay, Veep, you're up. Dunkin, take him to the townhouse and pinpoint, but don't go in. Tell Veep what he's looking for and where it is. That place is going to be a crime scene from the dead body you left, so no pushing the envelope. Veep, if you can get in, then get in, either from the roof or the ground floor. If you can't—if there is any police presence besides some crime scene tape—then back off. If that's the case, Dunkin stays here with Jennifer and you and I conduct the recce. Whatever you do, *don't* get compromised."

Veep nodded and said, "Easy day. We'll be back here in an hour, one way or the other."

They started walking toward the door and I tugged Veep's shirt. He turned back and I said, "No hero shit here. I'm trusting you not to push it."

He said, "You're telling *me* not to push it?"

He saw my eyes and said, "I got it, Pike. I got it. That was a joke. No high adventure. Trust me for once."

I nodded and said, "I *do* trust you. That's why I'm sending you. I'll give you the high adventure if you can get back without compromise."

He smiled at my affirmation and said, "I have no doubt."

They left and I turned to Jennifer, saying, "You got

anything else at all on the target? We're really working on nothing here."

"That passport we took off of the guy in the park came up in a Taskforce database search. He works for a Chinese import/export company. A nobody, as far as that goes, but the company is tied to the People's Liberation Army. I've been talking to the Taskforce about it, and on the surface that wouldn't seem to be much, because the PLA is inside every damn company from China, but these guys are deeper than most. The Taskforce says they don't do a lot of import/export work, which means they're probably a cover instead of a company."

I nodded and she said, "If it's solely a cover, it's pretty good. They have a webpage, Twitter account, all of it. I printed out their org chart from the 'about us' page. There aren't any pictures, but there are names."

I saw the president at the top, Chen Ju-Long, and the name registered with me, but I couldn't figure out why. I said, "You recognize that name?"

"No, should I?"

"No. I guess not. But I've heard it before."

It tickled my brain, like a piece of meat between my teeth, my tongue worrying it over and over trying to break it free.

# 41

Chen Ju-Long exited the ferry at Darling Harbour next to the Sydney Aquarium and began walking inland, checking his watch. He didn't have far to go, but he most certainly didn't want to be late. He was sure he was about to be excoriated for Bobcat's idiocy, and yet he was just the cleanup crew. He didn't run Bobcat. He just policed the mess.

And the mess was big indeed.

He walked swiftly through Sydney's business district, ignoring the professionals out and about, cutting into the mall inside the Queen Victoria Building. He'd planned enough time to identify surveillance targeted against him, and used the building to do so.

He went to the second floor, bought a coffee at a local stand, and took a seat, watching the escalators that led to his level.

He didn't see anything that spiked. He waited a few more minutes, then went back down the escalator, exiting the building on the southern side, not where he'd entered.

He continued up George Street, not paying any particular attention to his backtrail, and reached Hay Street. He walked straight north, crossing Hay Street and going under the ornate paifang arch of Sydney's Chinatown. He went a block and stopped outside of a karaoke bar called Destiny. He checked his watch, saw he was within the window, and entered.

The venue was closed at this time, but that didn't matter to him. He ignored the velvet rope blocking access to a stairwell and went up, exiting into a garish bar area, full of neon, mirrors, and chrome, with a large stage to the left, microphones empty and televisions off, the lighting muted and dark. An Asian woman was behind the bar, cleaning glasses. She saw him and left, going into the kitchen in the back.

He went right, down a hallway to the private rooms, and saw a fit man in a business suit standing outside a door. The man nodded at him, opened the door, and said something. Chen waited, and then was waved forward.

He entered, finding the small room ringed with a couch that wound its way around the walls to a television screen and a microphone stand. Interspersed at intervals were cocktail tables. Behind one table in the rear was his control, a wizened older man with a drooping white mustache. The man pointed to the cushion on his right, saying, "Have a seat."

Chen did so, waiting. Control said, "So I understand there have been complications."

"Yes, sir. More than I expected."

"Your earlier report mentioned a possible compromise, but you had it under control. Now you say that it is *not* under control?"

"Not yet. I still believe my original estimate that he's just a computer engineer, but we've had a confluence of events. The same day we attempted to eliminate him, a friend of his showed up here for vacation. That man is more dangerous, but still within the scope of our capabilities. I intend to have this settled by tomorrow on favorable terms to us."

The old man nodded, then said, "You will kill them both?"

"That is my hope, but the primary problem is Clifford,

not the other one. If we eliminate him, the other man will know something has happened, but he really can't affect our operation. Even if he went to the police—which he seems disinclined to do right now—he will not have any concrete evidence to break our operations."

"He has concrete evidence to break open your company. Didn't you say the man in the park lost his passport? Which is directly tied to your cover company?"

"Yes, but that company was made for this mission. If we have to burn it, we do so. We'll all be off this continent by then, and the friend won't be able to break open the actual operation."

"Can your men accomplish the mission here without you?"

Taken by surprise, Chen said, "Possibly. Why?"

"I met this Jake Shu—Bobcat—in Brisbane. He might be a genius with computers, but he's an idiot when it comes to tradecraft. A walking barrel of mistakes. I would like you to take over the northern portion of the operation to ensure there are no mistakes. Deal with any unforeseen problems that might occur, like you did here."

Chen was genuinely surprised. He had assumed he was to be chastised for the way things had escalated here, not praised.

"Yes, sir, I can do that. Can I bring Zhi with me?"

"Is it necessary?"

"I might need a female touch. It gives me options. Options that aren't needed here anymore."

Left unsaid was Chen's worry that if she remained behind, she might do something catastrophic during tomorrow's operations, like she had the night before—or, worst case, she might convince the team here to let the girl, Nicole, go.

"So be it."

They sat in silence for a moment, then Chen said, "When would you like me to leave?"

"Immediately."

"As in flying?"

"No. Trains only. I don't want your name tainted on a manifest to Cairns if you fail to kill both men."

Chen stood, saying, "Then I'd better leave. I need to ensure the plan is in place before I go."

His control nodded and said, "Don't let me down."

"I won't, sir. They have managed to screw up a simple transfer through luck, not skill. They are about to see the difference."

# 42

We boarded the ferry with our tickets, nobody saying a word in the line to the gangway, not wanting the people in front and behind to hear anything. Once inside, we went to the small upper deck at the front of the boat, standing near the rails, away from the larger seating inside, and Dunkin began whining again about the timeline.

"Pike, you should have brought your weapons. If we get there and see it's only guarded by one guy, we could hit it today. With any luck, it'll be easy."

Knuckles said, "We don't deal in luck. We deal in skill. Please, before I punch you in the mouth or throw you off of this boat, shut the hell up. I'm sick of hearing it."

He cowered and sat down. Brett sat next to him and said, "Actually, I deal in lead, friend."

When Dunkin just looked at him stupidly, Brett turned to us and said, "Do none of you recognize a good movie quote when you hear it?"

I chuckled and said, "Dunkin, trust us. Nicole is coming home. Don't push anything. Just like in the Taskforce, your skill is here to enhance ours. And we *do* deal in lead."

He nodded and we rode the rest of the way in silence, Dunkin occasionally glancing at Veep for support, as they'd bonded a little bit on their separate mission.

Veep had surprised me, because I was sure that townhouse

was radioactive, but it turned out the police had vacated, leaving nothing but tape behind, and Veep had managed to penetrate the house through the roof access using a key provided by Dunkin. He hadn't even had to pick the lock. He was in and out in thirty seconds, finding the small pen-test kit that apparently all computer geeks carried around.

Not thinking they'd be successful when I said Dunkin could come on the recce, I'd almost changed my mind, but decided to bring him along because he might prove useful. Now, with his constant whining, I wasn't so sure. This was reconnaissance only, no matter how dire he thought the situation.

The boat made two stops down the harbor and finally docked at Manly, on the North Head. We exited the ferry terminal, went up top, and saw a quaint little downtown square lined with shops, ice cream parlors, and bars. Veep said, "Wow. This looks like Key West."

Knuckles said, "Or downtown Coronado, if you went to a real dive school."

Dunkin said, "Can you guys quit kidding around? This is serious."

They both looked at him, realizing he misunderstood the levity, but said nothing, letting me answer as the team leader.

I said, "Dunkin, we aren't here to find the next McP's Pub. Give us some slack here and let us do our work. Brett, where are we headed?"

Brett pulled out a tablet and brought up a software program that looked like Google Maps, Jennifer's marker highlighted.

He traced his finger on a lane that snaked along the coast of the head, sandwiched between the hills and the ocean. "We go up the shore path, hit a beach cove, and it's right there."

We studied it for a moment, and I said, "Okay, then, let's start marching. How do we get to the path?"

He pointed and said, "Through the town. We hit the beach on the far side of the square here, and the path is right there. It's used by tourists and locals, so there's no bother about blending in. Once we get there, though, it's a little bit of a guess."

I said, "We'll deal with the pinpoint later. Let's go."

We crossed through the square, passing the usual T-shirt shops and tourist bars, then hit the Manly Beach. Brett said, "Not sure why they call this beach 'Manly.' Looks like every beach in the U.S., just with more Speedos."

I chuckled and pointed, saying, "Is that the path?"

Off to our right was a pedestrian way that wound up the coast against the cliff, houses above it jutting out for the view. He said, "Yep. We go until we hit a cove called Shelly Beach. The target is up the hill from that."

"How far from here?"

"Maybe a half mile. Maybe less."

We started walking, leaving the sandy beach and entering the bike/pedestrian path. I kept an eye on the houses up the hill to my right, going through my mind how I would take one down. Before I knew it, the path ended in a cove with a large stretch of sand full of people out enjoying the sunshine, a bar and grill called the Boathouse to my right.

We stopped next to a row of benches and Brett said, "See that staircase?"

He pointed, and I saw a set of concrete stairs with a pipe handrail snaking up into the trees, lost from sight. I said, "Yeah?"

"That thing goes right by the target on the left side. Take a look."

We gathered around the tablet and I saw Jennifer's icon on top of the trees about a hundred meters away, straight up the hill. The stairwell from the overhead disappeared just like it did in real life. I circled a finger around the top of the ridge, following the roads and finding another staircase farther down the beach.

I said, "Okay. Brett and Veep take the stairwell going up. Knuckles, you get the cool job. Take a seat in that outside courtyard of the pub. Get some atmospherics on foot traffic, police patrols, and anything else. Dunkin and I are headed the long way around. We'll circle and come down the staircase. Brett and Veep do the opposite. Goal is to pinpoint the target and get enough close target reconnaissance to assault. Look for breach points, avenues of approach, and any danger areas."

I got a nod and said, "Dunkin, on me."

We broke from the group and continued down the footpath past the pub until we reached a short staircase leading to a parking lot above us. We took the road out, heading higher and higher, and Dunkin said, "Is this how you usually do things?"

Looking at my phone, seeing the target location going by us as we went higher, I said, "What do you mean?"

"I just thought there was some sort of secret to this work. All you did was tell people to walk by the house. Is that all you do? I mean, being a top-secret Operator and all?"

I laughed and said, "It's not black magic. It's experience and skill. Now you know why nobody wanted to hit this place cold when you said so. We have no idea what we're walking into. Yet."

He nodded, not convinced that what we did was worth the accolades we got, and I could feel his pain. I mean, ordinarily I'd have an entire ISR package of drones and real-time reach-back to the Taskforce, but when I'm going off the reservation, like I was doing here for Nicole, I had to execute without the high-speed tools.

I saw several blacktop lanes snaking down the hill from the main road at regular intervals and said, "One of those is ours."

We kept climbing and saw a park to our right, full of swingsets, monkey bars, and kids playing. Deep on the other side, down the slope, I saw Brett come out of the tree line.

I said, "That's it," and crossed into the park. We met in the middle, I'm sure causing some parents to wonder if we were drug dealers or pedophiles, and he said, "It's right down the hill. A three-story house built into the side of the ridge. It's got a fence around it next to the stairs, but it's literally about six feet away from the path."

"Thoughts?"

"It'll be easy in, but hard to clear."

He pulled out his tablet and said, "Veep, shoot me what you've got."

Veep airdropped the pictures he'd taken, and Brett pulled them up one at a time, saying, "There's no yard. It's right in the woods looking out over the ocean. No way to set up any prior surveillance, so we'll be hitting it cold, and it looks like a tangled mess inside because of the slope."

I studied the photos for a few seconds, then said, "Okay. Head on around and see if you can pinpoint which driveway is theirs. Go down it as far as you can, but don't get compromised. See if you can get another take on the far side. I'm taking Dunkin with me. We'll meet at the pub."

He nodded and we split up, Dunkin and I heading down into the trees until we found the concrete staircase. We walked down it, the light dwindling as we entered into the foliage.

Dunkin started walking slower, like he was sneaking up on a lizard on the ground. I realized he wasn't behind me, turned around and said, "Get your ass down here. A CTR is supposed to look natural. Not like we're slinking around like burglars."

He bounded down the stairs to me and said, "What's a CTR?"

"Close Target Reconnaissance. It's what we're doing now. Jesus. Just act natural. I'll do the work."

We kept walking, the stairs dropping through the trees, passing houses on the left, but none on the right. Fifty feet down the slope, we reached the target. It was a modern-day build right into the side of the slope, but one that was going to seed. A rental.

It looked to have been constructed in the nineties, but hadn't had a whole lot of maintenance, with the fence next to it falling down in places, and the few landscaping plants growing out of control. I kept walking, looking for breach points and finding a few.

It had large windows facing the view of the ocean, now clogged by vegetation, and at least one door leading to a path that ran to the stairs. One that we could use for a mechanical breach. The hard part was the damn building just spilled down the slope, not giving me any indication of how many levels it had or how many rooms. If we wanted to rescue Nicole, we needed to know more.

I slowed a bit, evening my pace while using a GoPro on my belt to record everything I saw. Dunkin said, "Is that it? Is that the place?"

We were alone on the trail, but I still glared at him, saying, "Yeah, that's it. Shut up and keep moving."

He said, "What about my pen-test? Let me help."

And I pulled up short, remembering why he was here. "Can you do something here?"

He looked left and right, like he was about to pick someone's pocket, and said, "I can try."

"Jesus. You're killing me. Do it. We have probably a minute before someone shows up."

He rotated his backpack around and pulled out what looked like a mini-iPad with two antennas. He booted it up, saying, "This will take a second."

I saw a ton of information scrolling down his screen, all of it a foreign language to me. I waited, growing impatient, then said, "Well?"

"I'm in. It's a rental. Stand by. There are a ton of things on this network. They don't have tight security because they have to pass the access from one guy to the next."

"And?"

For the first time, Dunkin looked at me with confidence, saying, "And they have a Roomba."

# 43

Paul Kao watched the unknown subject he called Fly Boy park his car in a makeshift garage, the attendant waving him closer and closer to the wall, sandwiching the car between two others on the outskirts of Jiufen, a small, compact mountain town an hour northeast of Taipei.

A mining settlement that blossomed during World War II, Jiufen came to life not unlike the gold rush towns in the United States. Originally a Wild West of settlers digging for precious metal in the mountains, it eventually became a city, albeit one that was based on an ephemeral economy. When the gold ran out and the Japanese were defeated, it became a mountain highland backwater—until it found tourism.

Now Jiufen's main livelihood was catering to people from around the world who wanted to traverse the so-called Old Street, a market spanning a narrow maze of alleys that used to be the heart of the town. And still was, because it was the primary reason tourists came to visit.

Why Fly Boy was here was a mystery.

The day before, Paul had sat outside of the office building next to the presidential palace for five hours, not wanting to leave the one anchor he had to what he was convinced was a growing conspiracy, and his waiting had paid off.

The man he'd followed from the temple had finally exited, now wearing the uniform of a colonel in the Republic of

China Air Force, which explained why his suit earlier didn't fit well on his body. He wasn't used to wearing one.

Paul had been shocked at the sight, straining his eyes through a set of small binoculars to ensure he wasn't wrong. But he hadn't been. It was the same man who'd met the Snow Leopard. He could *not* be an agent of China. The rigors of a background investigation for his position were just too hard to overcome. The Snow Leopard an agent of China? Yeah, sure. He was a crime lord. An Air Force colonel? No way.

*Right?*

Paul had taken some long-range photos, hoping to get the man's nametag in one of them, then followed the officer to his car, tracking him to a nice little house in the hills on the outskirts of New Taipei. He'd waited for the man to settle in for the night, and then had approached the car, affixing a small GPS beacon to it.

He'd then set up stationary surveillance outside the neighborhood, waiting yet again. In between, he'd used his remote cloud access to the cutout only he and Charlie Chan knew about, dumping the photos and everything he knew about the man for Charlie to identify. Charlie would wash it of Paul's fingerprints, determine the identity, then use a digital drop box to report back to Paul.

The following morning the GPS had alerted that it was moving, and Paul had positioned himself to see the car exit, to ensure his target was inside. Fly Boy had driven by him, now wearing a short-sleeved civilian shirt. Paul followed the GPS trace to Jiufen, staying close but not right behind Fly Boy's vehicle, and had watched the target park, then begin walking up the hill toward the center of town. Paul did not want to believe that he was watching a traitor in action. There had to be some other explanation—perhaps even that the colonel was running his own operation against the Snow Leopard.

At least that's what he hoped.

Paul illegally parked his own car down the street and raced to catch up, running up the avenue next to the mountain, passing by an ornate temple and entering the cloistered concrete buildings of the town. He saw Fly Boy walking toward the Old Street, a small knapsack over his shoulder, and fell in behind him, keeping a crowd of tourists between him and the target.

Fly Boy entered the narrow walls of the street, the crowd swallowing him, and Paul moved forward to keep him in sight. The market itself was more like a tunnel, with food shops, trinket stores, youth hostels, and teahouses. It was a mass of humanity, with people eating samples and tourists from all over the world taking pictures.

The lane was so narrow that two men with their arms outstretched could touch either side, the crowds constantly interrupted by minibikes transporting supplies. It was chaotic and claustrophobic, and the worst place for a singleton surveillance effort, but Paul had no other choice.

He kept Fly Boy in sight, threading through the crowds, wondering if the man was simply out shopping. He saw his target dip into a souvenir shop that sold ceramic figurines and walked by, glancing as he did so. Fly Boy was meeting with a man whose face was covered in tattoos. Not a tourist. In fact, not a normal civilian. He looked like a killer, and his tattoos marked him as a Triad member.

They exited, now behind Paul but walking in the same direction. Paul ducked left, going into a noodle shop to let them pass. Once they were gone, he reentered the flow of traffic, staying far enough behind them to remain clean. They took a turn down a narrow stairwell that dropped down to a plaza clogged with people, walking toward a large building ringed with red lanterns. Paul recognized it as the Amei Teahouse, one of the oldest continually operating businesses in Jiufen.

A three-story structure made mostly of wood, it towered over the square of the town of Jiufen like a grand old lady, regally distinct against the drab concrete buildings to the left and right. Paul looked for a way to enter without being seen and saw a lower level with a small footpath. He went down it and was immediately confronted by a busboy, who said the entrance was above.

Paul held up his camera and said, "I just want some pictures."

The busboy left, and Paul snaked his way underneath the restaurant, threading through the kitchen and cleaning areas, the staff doing nothing more than looking at him oddly. He stumbled into the hallway that led to the bathrooms, saw a stairwell going up, and took it, walking slowly.

He reached the top, peeked around the corner, and saw Fly Boy sitting with the Snow Leopard at a large table, the tattooed man now absent. Around him sat a ring of young men, ranging in age from eighteen to twenty-five. All in rapt attention. The Snow Leopard said something, and Fly Boy opened his knapsack, passing out sheets of paper. They eagerly took them. One of the kids asked something, and the Snow Leopard reached underneath the table, pulling out bundles of cash. He looked left and right, then spread them out like he was fanning a deck of cards. He said something, and the kids nodded, quickly stuffing the cash into their pockets. He said something else, and they laughed. Through it all, the colonel sat silently, taking it in.

Paul went back down the stairs and exited the back of the restaurant on a small spit of concrete that led away from the plaza, wondering about his next move. First, he needed the man's identity. Next, he needed concrete proof—pictures and innuendo at this point would mean nothing—but that was a mission he could accomplish while Charlie Chan completed his investigation. If he had concrete proof, and they then had the name, Charlie Chan could bury him—*if* he was in fact a traitor.

And, in truth, Paul wasn't sure.

He walked down the path, seeing an old mining tunnel in front of him. One of the many penetrant alleys that threaded through the streets. Once used to extract gold, it was completely covered in graffiti from tourists and locals and led underneath houses and restaurants to another section of the town. Paul had no idea where, but it would be better than showing himself back on the main old town road.

He stooped low and entered, walking forward, still lost in thought, planning his next steps. Moving in a crouch, he rounded a corner, walking past wooden support beams, the graffiti now hard to read in the harsh light provided by a single strand of incandescent bulbs. He saw a shape in front of him, coming forward. The shape entered the light, and Paul recognized the tattooed man.

He felt an electric shock, but showed no emotion, thinking he could pass without the man even knowing who he was. Plenty of tourists used this tunnel, and he would pretend to be just one more.

The man tilted his head, looked behind him to be sure he was clear, then spread his arms, saying, "Just you and me."

Paul drew up short, still trying to bluff his way through. He said, "What? What's that mean?"

He could turn and run, but the bend in the tunnel told him he wouldn't make it out before the man reached him, and there was probably someone behind Paul as well. Somehow, he'd been made.

The man pulled a balisong butterfly knife out of his pocket, theatrically flicked it open and closed twice, then seated the blade. He attacked, supreme in his confidence.

Paul danced back, keeping his eyes on the knife, ignoring everything else. When it went by him in a sweeping slash, he trapped the arm, locked up the wrist, and leveraged the elbow, swinging the man with his own momentum into the rock wall.

The man slammed into it and bounced back. Paul reversed, holding the arm and ducking under it until the joints were wound as tight as a piano wire. He rotated down and flipped the man in the air, the tendons in the joints tearing as he did so, the shoulder separating from the socket.

The man slammed into the ground with a scream, the knife bouncing away. Paul controlled the arm and searched his body. He pulled out a bundle of papers, seeing the same ones that Fly Boy had passed around.

Paul said, "You want to live? Who are you?"

The man started to fight back and Paul torqued his elbow again, the broken shoulder joint feeling like a sock full of rocks grinding together, and the man screamed again. Paul said, "Why are you here? Why is the Snow Leopard here?"

The man said, "You're too late to stop this. Nothing you do will stop it now."

"Stop what? What am I too late to stop?"

The man glanced at the knife on the ground, then looked Paul in the eye, saying, "Stop the tide of war. You have no commitment. Unlike me."

The man swept out his free hand, scraping the ground for the knife. Paul saw the danger and ripped the arm back against the shoulder, but not before his hand closed on the blade.

The man shrieked like a child from the pain and whipped his good arm across his body, stabbing over his shattered shoulder blindly. Paul dropped the destroyed arm and danced back, dodging the jab, then leapt forward, slamming both hands on the wrist holding the blade and trapping the arm against the man's body, the knife edge ending up against his neck.

Surprised, having only acted out of the instinct of self-preservation, Paul seized the opening presented, slapping one hand against the back of the blade and using his other to jerk the arm down. The edge sawed into the neck, the skin splitting open like a pierced drumhead, exposing muscle, and then the blade crossed the carotid artery.

A jet of blood shot out across the tunnel and Paul leapt back, watching his victim roll over, his eyes wide in shock at the carnage spilling into his lap. The man dropped the knife, clamped his hand on the wound, and began to writhe around, looking like an earthworm on hot pavement, his other, useless arm flopping around obscenely. Eventually, his movements slowed, then stopped completely.

Paul backed up, then turned, looking behind him for a threat. He saw none, and took off running.

# 44

The morning sun was low enough in the sky that the breeze still had a slight chill coming off the water, which worked in our favor in that we didn't look out of place wearing light jackets to cover our weapons and other kit. What couldn't be concealed on our bodies was stored in a small backpack each of us had at our feet.

Sitting on benches waiting on the next ferry to Manly, the Operators made small talk, calm about the coming mission. Dunkin was the only one acting a little itchy.

I sat next to him and said, "Don't worry about anything. We'll get her back. All you need to do is play your role."

The last twelve hours had been a little chaotic, but it had been Dunkin who had come through in the end. Each man on the recce had come back and drawn a sketch of what they'd seen, and we'd put them all together until we had a pretty clear picture of the outside of the building, but with the structure built on a slope, I was still concerned about the floor plan inside. Usually, an unknown floor plan would be no problem—it was something we expected—but this house was so unique I wanted to know where to focus, which is where Dunkin's skill proved invaluable.

It turned out the rental agency had a Roomba cleaning robot on each floor, designed to vacuum at designated intervals. The key Dunkin had found was that the robot had to learn what it was being called to do, using artificial intelligence to teach itself where to go. The first time it cleaned, it bumped into everything in the house. The next time, about half that. By the fortieth cleaning, it had mapped what was in the house, and it stored those maps in the cloud.

Impressing the hell out of me, Dunkin had penetrated the rental WiFi through the washing machine in the house. Connected to the WiFi node for some idiotic reason that no rental person would use, it had no security at all. Dunkin had cracked into that seam, and then explored the WiFi network, finding the Roomba. From there, he'd cracked the robot's footprint for cleaning, and we'd ended up with a pretty good map of each floor of the house, to include furniture, doorways, and closets. It wasn't perfect—it didn't have a detailed description with things like "table" or "kitchen island"—but it did have each floor detailed in simple squares, some shaded and some not, specific enough to show us exactly what we were up against. It was what we called a golden egg. While we trained to clear a house with an unknown floor plan, with all tactics designed for the unexpected, we *always* wanted the golden egg of what it actually looked like.

And now we had it.

Eventually I'd had to leave the team, letting them complete the planning, forced to travel back to the beer hall to take the 7 P.M. call from the asshole who held Nicole. The call had come in, and after talking to them, I was convinced that they believed Dunkin had stolen something from them. The man was too real on the phone. Too visceral. He wanted that thumb drive, and he wanted it in a bad way.

I'd promised to have Dunkin bring it, and then had demanded to hear Nicole's voice. He'd done so, letting me talk to her for all of five seconds—and it was heartbreaking.

I'd asked her a question only she and Dunkin would know, and in between sobs, she'd answered correctly. I so wanted to tell her that I was bringing vengeance to the men who held her, but I couldn't, knowing they were listening.

She had ended by saying, "Tell Dunkin I don't blame him. Tell him not to grieve for me."

And I understood she thought she was dead. In situations like this, be it a captive in a cave in Afghanistan or a house in Australia, given enough pressure, people just resigned themselves to their death, waiting on the hammer. Nicole had reached that stage of resignation. Truthfully, most of the time that was an accurate assessment of a situation like this.

This time it was not.

I'd told the man on the phone again not to hurt her, and he'd agreed, saying he only cared about the drive, and that it had better be real. I had no idea what the hell he was talking about, and neither did Dunkin, but after I came back, he'd spent three hours building up a fake thumb drive that would fool even the CIA.

When I returned, I could hear the team still spitballing ideas about how to breach and which way to clear, and I wanted to join them, but I had one other headache to take care of, and that was the Oversight Council. Since I'd been jerked off of my vacation and activated for an Alpha mission, I'd sent the required Project Prometheus situation reports—leaving out the Nicole rescue—but George Wolffe had sent back that he wanted an actual SITREP via our VPN. I had no idea why, and really didn't want to do it, because Wolffe had a sixth sense when it came to me going off the reservation, and seeing him face-to-face might be a giveaway.

I went upstairs to our bedroom, looked over the balcony at them plotting, and thought about making Jennifer take the call. But she was down there planning right in the middle of them. Sometimes it sucked to be the leader.

I dialed up the VPN, waited for it to connect, and then saw Creed's face on the screen. He said, "Pike, you got me?"

I said, "Yeah. Where was that last trace? The one from thirty minutes ago?"

"Same spot. Called from the same location. Stand by."

Which was good news. I waited, and then saw George Wolffe's bushy gray mustache take over the screen. He sat down, pulling back from the camera until I could see his whole face. He said, "Hey, Pike. Got the last SITREP. How's it going?"

"Going well, sir. No police trace to us, Dunkin is free and clear, and I'm tracking the men who attacked him. Still no real clear view of why it happened, but my report details what Dunkin thinks. You got any track on this Jake Shu?"

"We have a data dump on him now, and looking at it in hindsight, he *has* had some significant interactions with Chinese nationals. Given his job, it wasn't enough to spike, but put together with what you found, there's plenty of smoke."

"Perfect. Where's he now? I'm sure you've looked at phone data, credit card statements, that sort of thing."

"We got one hit in Brisbane at a hotel. He paid cash, but they took his passport. After that, he's a ghost. No known phone, no use of credit cards. If he's got that stuff, it was provided for him. Probably bank cards loaded for use at ATMs and a burner phone. You're going to have to find him for us."

That took me aback. I usually leveraged the Taskforce for leads, not the other way around. I solved the problem they provided. I didn't find the problem. I did the fix and the finish.

But I made a mistake in my answer, because George assumed my mission in Sydney was precisely to find Jake Shu, not realizing the two sets were related but distinct missions.

I said, "How am I supposed to find him? Dunkin said he was heading to Cairns for a vacation, but that's probably bullshit. What am I going to do?"

He narrowed his eyes and said, "Do? You're going to explore that phone we've been tracking. By the SITREP, you said, you had a target house to explore. Go explore it."

I couldn't tell him that everyone in that house was going to be dead, and the exploration would end with the barrel of my gun. I backpedaled, saying, "We're taking a look at it tomorrow morning. We'll conduct a CTR and see what we can find. Use Dunkin to explore the systems in the house, maybe find another lead, but it's pretty weak."

He said, "It's always weak until it isn't. You'll find a link to continue. Look, this is getting more serious. We're receiving a lot of intel from multiple agencies and sources saying the Chinese are going to attempt to upset the Taiwan elections. They've already gotten their preferred candidate neck and neck with the incumbent, which is insane. With the intel you've picked up, we think it's bigger than the election. The Chinese are going to try to erode the actual defense of Taiwan, and if that candidate wins, he'll help them do it. We can't do much about the election, but we can stymie their attempts to degrade the defense posture. We concur that Jake Shu may be the key. Find him."

I told him I would and disconnected, wondering what the hell I was going to do. I'd been given a critical mission by the national command authority of the United States, but to execute it, I'd have to kill Nicole. I couldn't make this hit a capture mission. Maybe we'd get someone, but odds were, with our limited force, we'd have to kill them all just to rescue her. Maybe we'd find something inside, but I wasn't counting on it. These guys were professionals. They wouldn't be leaving another golden egg on the dining room table.

So I could completely rearrange this mission, focusing on capturing one of the men or penetrating the house surreptitiously for information, which would take three or more days of work, or I could rescue Nicole. There wasn't a way to do both. In fact, letting her die would probably be the catalyst to break open Jake's location, because it would cause the team to move, most likely linking back up with Jake Shu.

I'd gone back downstairs and the team had briefed me on several courses of action. I'd settled on one, but Jennifer could see I was distracted. We'd sent the men off to their own rooms and then gone to bed. Once the lights were out, she'd said, "What's going on?"

I said, "Nothing. Just ignoring the national command authority of the United States. That's all."

She turned the light back on and said, "What's that mean?"

I told her about the call, and that something bigger than Nicole's life was in play, and I was about to screw all of that up by this assault. We'd win tomorrow, of that I had no doubt, but we'd lose the bigger mission. And it didn't sit well with me. It was an impossible choice.

She looked at me, seeing the conflict, and said, "There isn't a choice here. It's a duty. I know I'm not in command, and it's not my decision, but if I get a vote, you made the right one."

"Have I? I mean, sometimes we have to do bad things for the good things to happen." I touched her neck, where a circle of gold like a thick washer hung on a necklace, the Bible verse Romans 3:8 engraved upon it. I said, "Sometimes we do evil that good may come. This time I'm doing good to let evil roam free."

She leaned in and kissed me, saying, "You don't know what tomorrow will bring. You don't know what you may find. You can't predict the future by letting this girl die."

I leaned back and said, "It's not that simple."

She rolled over, snuggling into my shoulder, and said, "It *is* that simple. It really is. You alone have taught me that. Let's get Nicole and worry about the rest later."

I exhaled and she said, "Not that it's the right time to bring this up, but Amena wanted to talk tonight. I got a message through your burner phone. I told her we couldn't, but we need to talk to her sooner or later. Let her know we might not be home on time."

And like lightning leaping from point to point, I made the connection to the name Chen Ju-Long. I bolted upright in the bed and said, "That's where I've heard that name before."

"What are you talking about?"

"Amena's roommate's dad is named Chen Ju-Long. She said that on the phone."

"Yeah? So what?"

"The only people who go as exchange students to that school from China are bigwigs. And this guy in charge of the fake import/export company here, buried in the heart of the Ministry of State Security, has the same name. He's running the entire ring of assholes chasing us, and from your research his name is Chen Ju-Long. He's a bigwig."

"Okay, okay, you can't think it's the same guy. For all we know the name is like 'John Smith.' Let's worry about that tomorrow. Can we do that?"

I settled down, realizing she was probably right. I said, "You think I'm nuts with that?"

She snuggled into me and said, "No. Not nuts. I've seen you pull more rabbits out of the hat than are possible. But we need to get some sleep. Big day tomorrow, and one step at a time."

# 45

The ferry arrived, the deckhand pulling in the boarding ramp. We stood in line and entered with a host of other tourists, the team instinctively settling into the back corner, away from the other passengers. The boat broke free of the dock, and once we were under way, the tension increased exponentially. We were about to execute a hit, and there was no way to hide that kind of adrenaline.

The phone call had dictated that Dunkin meet his contact at the entrance to the Taronga Zoo at 12 P.M., right outside the cable car station that led to the top.

We'd debated back and forth about whether to let him go as if he wasn't even in the room, and I'd finally decided to launch him because I was sure they'd put more than one guy on the mission—maybe up to four—and the more people we got out of the house, the better. The argument against putting him in danger was that the meeting was set, so those guys would be gone regardless, but I'd decided to hedge my bets. If he didn't show, I didn't want a bunch of calls going back to the house when we were preparing to breach—or, worse, if they had a private boat or some other means to get back in a hurry, interfering with our assault. We would be solely focused on the inside of the house. I didn't want to worry about something coming from the outside behind us.

The meeting spot itself helped me decide. There was no

way they'd kill him at the entrance to the zoo. They'd take the thumb drive and he'd be gone.

I'd given him his part of the mission, but he wouldn't be going in alone. Jennifer was going to follow him and provide protection. If they tried anything, she'd stop them, either with a bullet or something tamer. Either way, he was in good hands.

His mission was to drag out the meeting, then pass the thumb drive, telling them that it was encrypted, and he'd give the key once he had Nicole. Of course, there was no key, and with any luck, we'd have Nicole long before the men he was meeting could relay the request.

The ferry continued bouncing across the choppy water of the harbor, the target location getting inexorably closer, and Dunkin leaned over, saying, "Are you sure this is going to work?"

I said, "What part? Yours, or mine?"

He thought a minute, then said, "Well, both, I guess."

"Mine's going to be flawless. Yours is up to you. But you have Jennifer. If something isn't right, if you feel your life is in danger, just say the word. She'll interdict. They might try to extort you with words, but you'll be at the front of the zoo. They won't do anything there. Whatever you do, just drag it out and don't go anywhere else with them."

"What if you haven't called saying you've got Nicole? What then? What if the meeting is about to end or they ask me to go somewhere else in the park? Should I do it?"

"If it's just a walk in the zoo, then yeah, that would be okay. Don't get on a boat with them or in a car. Use your own instincts."

I saw he was scared and said, "Look, they're killers. There's no doubt about that, but they're also professionals. They aren't gangbangers from Compton. They want that drive, and they may try to scare you to give them the encryption with death threats against Nicole—but we both know there's nothing on the drive, so just pass it and stall, tell them to call us at the predetermined time, and get out of there. Don't worry about them freaking out and killing Nicole. That will be over. I promise."

"What if they don't let me leave? What if they want to take me hostage?"

I looked at Jennifer, and she said, "I'll be right there, and we're connected in real time by radio. You give me the word, and I'll drop them. But don't do it in a panic. We're going to be at the entrance of one of the biggest tourist attractions in Sydney, with the only escape a scheduled ferry. They aren't going to harm you right there."

He nodded, taking solace in her words. He said, "Are you sure you can get Nicole out of there? I mean, if I do all of this, and you fail, she's definitely dead."

Knuckles leaned in and said, "Trust me, there is no fail here. Your Roomba thing prevented that. We know exactly how we're getting in, and exactly where we're going. With you doing this mission, we'll have maybe only five guys to deal with, and they haven't seen anything like what we're going to bring. It'll be over in minutes."

The ferry captain announced the stop for the zoo, the boat slowing down to slide into the dock, with multiple people standing up for their day of fun in the sun. Dunkin stood as well, looking a little green.

I said, "Hey, just stall them for as long as you can. That's all. You bullshit your way through this like you did through our interview, when you said you could dunk a basketball. This meeting isn't going to be near as bad as that hiring board. I promise."

He smiled, relaxing at the memory, saying, "Yeah, you got that right. Worst pressure of my life."

I fist bumped him and said, "Stand by the radio. The next time this ferry shows up, you get on it. When you do, Nicole will be on board."

He nodded and walked to the exit. Jennifer turned to follow and I caught her arm.

"Don't let him do anything stupid. He's scared shitless. If the meeting looks bad, then break away. We'll deal with the repercussions of radio alerts or anything else."

She said, "I got this end. Don't *you* do anything stupid. When the ferry comes back, I want you on it."

Brett said, "Stupid is as stupid does. We're about to conduct an unsanctioned slaughter of Chinese nationals in a Five Eyes country. Can't get much more stupid than that."

She smiled and said, "If Nicole's on the boat when I get back, that won't be stupid."

He nodded and said, "I know. Take care of Mr. Basketball there."

"I will."

I watched her walk off the ferry, then kept my eye on her even as we pulled away, feeling a sense of foreboding. Knuckles snapped me out of it, saying, "Okay, let's go over the plan one more time."

# 46

Charlie Chan forged a contact statement from a confidential source, cleansing Paul's message traffic as if it had come from a routine report inside the department. He stamped it with a compartmented security clearance that would guarantee nobody would see the results but him, his assistant, and the people who conducted the analysis.

While his primary concern was protecting Paul's status as still being active inside the NSB, he had others that were just as important. Paul was quite literally the most highly classified project Charlie Chan had ever run, with extremely sensitive repercussions, but the Air Force uniform concerned him. With the elections coming up in Taiwan, tension was everywhere, with citizens seeing Chinese PRC around every corner, and if word got out that there might be an inside threat high up in the Taiwanese defense forces, it would generate chaos and a lack of confidence.

It might also be lynching a man who didn't deserve it.

He pressed a button on his desk and said, "Mouse. Come in here. I have a special task for you."

The speaker said, "Yes, sir. On the way."

The door opened, revealing a short man of about forty, wearing thick glasses and a rumpled suit. He had been Charlie's assistant for more than eight years, and had a habit of moving at all times like he was about to jump from some threat. Charlie said it reminded him of a mouse nervously sniffing a bit of cheese in a trap, and had taken to calling him "Mouse" because of it. He was Charlie's trusted right hand, but even he wasn't privy to what Paul was doing.

"Yes?" he said, coming forward.

Charlie slid the folder across and said, "I need to know who this man is, but it is extremely close hold. I want you to hand-walk it to the L Directorate and have them do a compartmented search. Facial recognition, target association, organizational connections based on historical movement, and whatever else they have. You stay for the duration. When it's done, and they have a dossier, you bring it straight back to me."

Mouse nodded, pulling the folder off of the desk. He said, "Where did it come from?"

"Compartmented source, but that's irrelevant. It's the information that's explosive."

Mouse said, "Which one? Which project did it come from? It might help me work with L Directorate on the analysis."

Because of his position, Mouse was read on to every program Charlie ran at his level, and had access to all of those below.

Charlie leaned back in his chair and said, "I told you it's compartmented. A single use. It's not a program you're aware of."

Mouse did his nervous shuffle, taking the implicit reprimand about asking questions without another word.

He turned to leave and Charlie said, "Remember my orders. Your hands only, and you stay until it's done, even if that means you spend the night."

Mouse said, "Yes, sir," and walked back down the hall to his office. He placed the folder on his desk, then flipped it open. He took one look at the photo on top and knew he had a problem.

He stood up and locked his door, then opened the bottom drawer of his desk, kneeling down and reaching inside, shoving his hand upward until it connected with the drawer above it. By feel alone, he flicked a switch on a compartment affixed to the steel, then pulled out a cell phone.

He hit a speed dial number, waited for it to connect, then said, "I have a Dragon Alert on Ocelot."

Waiting on an update for his deep fake video inside the Twelfth Bureau, Han Ming listened to the report on the phone, rubbing his forehead. What was once a clean, pristine intelligence operation was slowly but surely unraveling.

First, Bobcat was proving to be an idiot, and the Fifth Bureau men were proving to be little better, with a breach of Bobcat's operation still running loose on the Australian continent.

Now his highest mole inside the National Security Bureau of Taiwan was reporting that the commander of the unit itself was focused on Ocelot. Which would be devastating.

He didn't mind sacrificing Ocelot, because even that outcome would pay untold publicity dividends, but he needed him for the endgame. Ocelot had to be protected.

He said, "Who is working the issue? Can we tic off the knot?"

"You mean eliminate the source? No. I have no idea who it is. It's stovepiped, even from me."

"I thought you were read on to all programs."

"I did too, but this one, according to Charlie Chan, is a one-off. A one-time mission for a one-time target. And somehow he's focused on Ocelot. It's not like that college student I fed you—the poor nobody that one of Charlie's men turned. It's much more compartmented."

Han thought a minute, then heard the door open, seeing the Twelfth Bureau commander, Yuan Bo, enter with a smile on his face. Han snapped his fingers and pointed to the door. Yuan exited with a scowl.

Into the phone, Han said, "So this is so highly secret that the only person who knows about it is Charlie Chan himself?"

"I believe so."

In his position of commander of the directorate responsible for the takeover of Taiwan, Han was well versed on Charlie Chan. He was a nemesis who had been a thorn in Han's side for close to a decade. A consummate professional who had thwarted many penetrations Han had conceived, and, in truth, because of this, Han respected him. Respected his dedication and his skill. But Han had a mission, and he wasn't going to let respect get in the way of succeeding. He'd considered this option many, many times, but had never followed through because of the implications, but now it seemed he was given no choice.

"You believe Charlie Chan is running this operation at his level? Nobody else is involved?"

"As far as I can tell, yes, here at headquarters. Somebody in the field had to feed him the information, but I have no idea who that would be. He told me to walk it through personally. And I'm the sole man outside of him who's read on to every operation the NSB conducts. Why?"

Han thought of the quote from Sun Tzu, speaking from the past. *Secret operations are essential in war; upon them the army relies to make its every move.*

He said, "Because I'm going to tie off the knot. Don't take that package anywhere for analysis and stay by the phone."

# 47

Jennifer exited the ferry, leaving a family between her and Dunkin. Once on the dock, she whispered, "Dunkin, Dunkin, you copy?"

She heard, "Yes. I got you. How about me?"

She continued up a winding staircase, seeing the crowds start to disperse left and right, the ones to the right having chosen to walk up the hill into the zoo. The ones to the left had paid extra to ride the cable car to the top and walk down, saving themselves the trek both ways.

She said, "I got you. Linkup is to the left, outside the cable car. I'm going to hang back. You see the ticket counter?"

"Yeah. I see it."

"That's where you'll go in. Show them the ticket, then go to the left. When the guy makes contact, just say, 'I have what you want.' Do you understand?"

"Yes. Yes. I get it. Jennifer, I can't do this. What if he puts a knife to my chest?"

She heard herself from years ago, when she had first started operating, when *she* was the one saying the same thing to Pike. Now she was the protector, and Dunkin was the protected. It actually brought a smile to her face, because she had grown comfortable in her skills.

"Dunkin, they aren't going to threaten you in front of the cable car entrance. It's surrounded by tourists. Just do what they want. The mission is to extend the timeline. That's it. Whatever it takes. Pike is about to dock at Manly, and he'll handle what we both want. You just need to make the meeting."

Dunkin said, "Okay, okay." There was a pause, and then she heard a muffled command. Then, through Dunkin's radio, "Yes, that's me. I'm here for Nicole."

She raced up the stairs, reached the path to the cable car entrance, and saw a line of people waiting to board, the cars rolling in every five seconds in an inexorable tide. She scanned left and right, and found Dunkin talking to a man right outside the entrance.

She said, "I've got you. I've got you. You're secure."

She heard, "I have the drive you want, but I'm not giving it to you unless I get proof Nicole is alive."

There was a response that she couldn't hear, and then Dunkin said, "I'm not leaving this zoo. Take the drive. It's encrypted, though. If you want the results in it, you need to release Nicole. That's the deal."

Jennifer went higher on the path, standing on the curb to see over the crowds. She saw Dunkin talking to an Asian man, his hand outstretched holding the thumb drive. She said, "Be cool. It's working. Be cool."

She heard something else garbled from the man, and then Dunkin saying, "Why can't we do this here? I have the drive."

And she felt her first bit of panic. She said, "Dunkin, don't listen to him. He's lying to you. Do *not* leave this area."

She heard "Yeah, I can go into the park, but I'm not leaving it. Understand that. If you want the thumb drive, I'm not leaving the park. Where do you want to go?"

Some more mumbling came through the radio, and Dunkin

said, "I will do that, but no games. If you want the encryption, you need me."

Jennifer saw them enter the line for the cable car. *Oh no.*

"Dunkin, Dunkin, don't get in the car with him. Don't do it!"

She watched him enter the line and darted forward.

"Dunkin! Don't get in that car!"

She heard him whisper, his face away from the man he was with, "This is the way to save Nicole. It's a five-minute ride. I reach the top and pass the drive."

He entered the car, just him and the man with him.

She knew she'd lost. She said, "Dunkin, watch his hands. Watch his hands."

She joined the line, able to cut forward as a singleton, just like a lift at a ski resort. She entered the car directly behind him, joining a family of three.

I crawled up the slope to the target house, pulled out a scope, and took a long look at the front of the house from the woods. Into the radio, I said, "Same story. We're good. No activity. No outside security."

I scrambled back down the hill, hitting the concrete stairwell that the tourists used, seeing my team in a security position, all of them covering 360 degrees without appearing to be doing anything other than standing around.

I said, "Okay, this is it. Everyone in here is hostile. If it's not Nicole, it's dead."

They nodded at me, and we went up the concrete stairs to the outside of the gate that led to the house. I took a breath, and then Veep flagged me.

A couple of kids were coming down the stairwell, laughing and talking. I said, "Keep moving. Look natural."

We resumed walking up the staircase, and they spilled past us without even registering we existed.

On the net, I said, "Parents? Where are the parents?"

We kept walking, and Knuckles said, "I guess this isn't the U.S. No parents."

I said, "Reverse. Breach now. Follow the plan."

The floor schematics from the Roomba had shown us that the majority of the living space was on the final, bottom floor—the one that overlooked the ocean. In between was a second level with a kitchen and laundry area, with the top area being a couple of extra rooms that had no view of anything. Which is where we'd determined Nicole was being held. But it wasn't where we were going to focus our efforts.

We knew that these assholes had a lot of manpower behind them. The fight Jennifer and I had in the alley attested to that. I figured the team was at most ten strong, but had hoped that at least four of them were out hunting Dunkin, which left six for us. The only way we would win was with what we called relative superiority. It sounded like some counterterrorist commando secret, but it actually came from Clausewitz. As in Carl von Clausewitz.

Back in the day when we were fighting with pikes—no pun intended—he had determined an immutable truth: *Where an absolute superiority is not attainable, one could produce a relative superiority at the decisive point by making skillful use of what one has.*

And that was the secret of what we were about to do. We would hit them with overwhelming force, using speed, surprise, and violence of action. We were only four men, something they could easily overcome by their numbers—if they knew we were coming. But that wouldn't happen. When we entered, we'd take them on as a team, attacking each threat with relative superiority. And we would win.

It might seem counterintuitive, but we weren't initially focused on the hostage—we were focused on the threat. If we could eliminate it, then we could take our time with Nicole. We figured she was at the top of the house, in one of the small rooms, which meant the men were in the lower level. So we were going to flow in at the middle level, with three going down and one going up.

Three on six wasn't good odds, and some on the team wanted to stick with four, but, while we believed Nicole was most likely chained to a bed by herself, we couldn't guarantee that one guy wasn't up there guarding her. Which meant one person had to go up and clear all by himself.

Veep had volunteered, and I'd let him take that mission. If he found her secure, he would immediately join the fight. If he didn't, he'd clear the room of threats and still join the fight, so the loss of manpower was measured in seconds.

Knuckles cracked the gate next to the concrete stairs, an old, worn-out section of fencing with a rusty latch, and we flowed down the small walkway to the house. We stacked on the door, Knuckles pulling security with a pistol while all of us dropped our bags and started withdrawing folding-stock Sig Sauer MCX Rattler rifles.

Designed for close-quarters combat, chambered in 300 Blackout, they were short-barreled and integrally suppressed—meaning with our subsonic ammunition, they were quiet, along with being incredibly reliable, the system having endured a grueling life in combat with special operations to prove its worth.

Knuckles turned the doorknob, gave me a shake of his

head, and I nodded. He dropped his bag, withdrew a small steel battering ram that looked like a cut-off telephone pole, cinching his hands into the handles on top. We called it the Bam-Bam, for obvious reasons.

He looked at me, knowing this was the endgame, and I rotated to the door, putting my barrel on the window.

I turned behind me, seeing my men spread out in security positions, protecting against all threats.

Into the radio, I whispered, "I have control. Stand by."

The barrels of all weapons rotated to the door, the team closing into a stack.

"Five . . . Four . . . Three . . . Two . . . One . . . Execute, execute, execute."

# 48

Jennifer let the cable car door close, then took a seat across from the family of three—a man and a woman and a small child of about six.

She ignored them, turning to the window at the front of the car. The mother asked, "Where are you from?"

Not looking away, she said, "The United States."

The father said, "Really? So are we. Whereabouts?"

She heard Dunkin say, "I'm not doing shit until you prove Nicole is alive."

Torn between the mission and compromising herself with the family she was with, wanting them to just shut up, she turned back around and said, "I'm from South Carolina."

On the radio, she heard, "Hey, hey, there's no reason to pull a gun here. You won't get the information on this thumb drive unless I give you the password."

Jennifer pressed herself against the glass, wanting to jump between the cars, knowing what was coming. She heard the Asian through Dunkin's radio, delivering the damage. "You still don't get it. *You* are the password. And now I'll cut it off."

The mother said, "South Carolina? We're from Florida. We've been to South Carolina. Small world."

And Jennifer heard the bark of a pistol.

***

My mind now in assault mode, everything happened in slow motion. I saw Knuckles wind up, then hit the lock with the Bam-Bam, splintering it. The door bounced off of its jamb, and Knuckles ripped it open. I exploded inside, the first man in, and immediately went to the stairs I knew were there, hearing the team behind me. I entered the second level and found a man making a sandwich in the kitchen, wondering what the noise was about. I put two rounds into his head and kept going, racing down to the lower level, trying to find the ant pile of enemy.

I reached the family room at the lower level and saw two men leaping up from a couch. One of them raised a weapon, and I hit him with a double tap, then saw the second one spill over backwards from someone else's rounds.

I kept clearing, reaching a door, then heard, "Jackpot. I say again, Jackpot."

I entered a small storage area, bounced back, and found Knuckles with me.

He began racing down the hallway, and I followed, Brett right behind me, all of us thinking the same thing: speed. Clear every room. Eliminate the threat.

A man popped out of a room in front of us, saw the devil, and dove back inside. Knuckles kicked the door in, entering and shooting. I saw him go left, saw a body on the floor and went right, finding the room empty. We flowed back out, hitting room after room, but the rest of the house was empty.

Two minutes later, we were done. The house was clear, and Nicole was secure.

We'd killed five men, including one in the room with Nicole that Veep had dealt with.

He'd brought her downstairs, and she was almost catatonic. She had no idea what was happening, blubbering like she thought *we* were going to kill her. Brett, our designated medic, started working on her, checking her for wounds and monitoring her vital signs.

To the others, I said, “Start SSE. Find me something for Jake Shu.”

Knuckles and Veep started digging into the house like they’d just killed Osama bin Laden, and I turned to the girl, saying, “Hey, are you okay?”

She continued crying, not answering me. Brett said, “She’s stable. No wounds, and she can walk.”

I knelt down in front of her and took her hands, getting her attention. “Hey, it’s over. It’s all over.”

Her breath hitched, and then began to drop into a steady rhythm. I said again, “It’s okay. It’s okay.”

She said, “Dunkin? Where is Dunkin?”

“You’ll meet him soon. I promise.”

She nodded for the first time, and I turned to Brett, saying, “Okay. Get her out of here. It’s a long trek back to the ferry, and we can’t afford to miss the next one.”

# 49

Hearing the gunshot explode over her radio, Jennifer leaned forward into the glass, trying to see what had occurred in the car in front of her. The woman behind her said, "What part of South Carolina are you from?"

Jennifer didn't respond, watching the cable car skirt the roof of a two-story animal enclosure, giraffes roaming around the ground outside. She saw the door open, and a man appear. He climbed out, hung for a moment, then dropped out of the car onto the roof, rolling over and scurrying to the wall. Inside the car she could see a body slumped over.

*Dunkin.*

She saw the killer slide over the side, hang for a moment, then drop out of sight. He appeared again, running across a small corral. He leapt over a moat, climbed a chain-link fence, flopped to the other side, and began sauntering back down the hill in the regular pedestrian path. Nobody seemed to have noticed the escape. No one pointing, no one chasing him, no nothing. Not even in her own cable car.

The mother said again, "What part of South Carolina? We're from Naples."

The edge of Jennifer's car crested the building, the roof about a ten-foot drop away. She turned around and the mother recoiled at the expression on her face, pulling her child into her body. The husband stood up and said, "What's wrong?"

Jennifer said, "I'm sorry. I have to go."

"What?"

She jerked the emergency handle at the roof of the small car and the door slid open robotically. The mother screamed and the father advanced on Jennifer. She turned around and said, "Back off. I'm not going to harm you unless you try to stop me."

He saw the same look the mother had, held up his hands in surrender, and sat down, protecting his family with his body. She nodded and swung out of the car, holding the railing on the outside of the door. She lowered herself to the bottom of the chassis, reached underneath, latching on to another rail with one hand and letting go with the other. Now hanging underneath the car, she looked below her, seeing the roof passing by, and let go, absorbing the fall with her legs and rolling over.

She stood up, seeing the husband glancing out the door as the car traveled on, a look of amazement on his face. She sprinted to the wall the killer had used and studied what was below her, not wanting to drop into a pen of lions. The corral was empty.

She slid over the side, grabbed a drainage spout, and began sliding down it as fast as one of the monkeys in the zoo. She jogged to the edge of the moat, judged the distance, then backed up, returning at a sprint. She launched herself into the air and cleared the far side, rolling again. She sprang to her feet and leapt up to the fence, clinging to the chain link like a lizard, scampered higher, then flung herself over the side, landing in a patch of bushes. She exited onto the walking path of the zoo, and just like the killer, nobody noticed her antics.

She began jogging down the path in his last known direction, scanning left and right, not really thinking through what she was going to do when she found him. Not wanting to dwell on Dunkin's fate.

On her failure.

She rounded a corner and saw the man talking to two others. The security for the hit. She hadn't spotted them earlier, but she'd known they were in the area.

The man mimicked shooting someone with his hand, his index finger extended, and the others laughed, bringing an unbridled rage from the depths of her soul. She had experienced such a fury only one other time in her life, and it was for the same reason. Someone had taken a friend of hers.

She wanted to kill all three, in cold blood.

She thought about calling Pike and asking him for direction, but she knew she couldn't do that while he was in the middle of his own operation. And in truth, she didn't want to put the decision on him. He would tell her what she already knew, and she might fight that decision if it came from him. Killing them now wasn't right. It wasn't allowed in a civilized world, ruled by laws. It was against her moral code.

The men began walking down the path to an enclosure next to a sign advertising penguins, and she put her hand on the butt of her weapon, thinking. Torn between her primal instincts and her conscience—what she wanted to do and what she should do. She should flee the area, protecting her cover from the inevitable investigation. Nothing she did now would bring Dunkin back. It would only jeopardize the ability of her team to solve why it happened.

They disappeared into a tunnel made of fake stone, underneath a body of water above, and she followed.

She entered behind them, finding both walls lined with

plexiglass windows, small penguins racing by under the water, the light inside wavering like a lava lamp.

She moved forward, passing a family, and then saw the three men ahead of her, all pressed against the glass watching the birds.

She came abreast of them, glanced the way she'd come, and saw that a family that had been in the enclosure had left. She closed on them and one turned, seeing no threat. She smiled at him and he nodded, then poked his friend, saying something in Chinese.

The man glanced back at her, the three of them beginning to move farther down the tunnel, heading toward a sign that read "Ferry Exit."

She said, "Leaving the zoo so soon? You just got here."

The killer turned to her with narrowed eyes. She glanced down the tunnel, seeing nobody. He said, "What was that?"

She drew her pistol, put it right between his eyes, and pulled the trigger.

The back of his skull exploded, spraying the plexiglass windows with brain matter. The man to his left looked on in shock. The man on the right reacted.

Jennifer's brain retreated from any consideration of what was right or what was wrong. She thought only of who would live and who would die. Like a computer, she analyzed the reaction and thought one thing: Threat.

He drew a gun from a holster at his back, and she swiveled her barrel to his chest. In the game of speed, she was light-years ahead. She lined up the holosight on his chest and fired a controlled pair, punching holes in his heart and lungs.

She turned to the man on the left, but he didn't even attempt to draw a weapon, even as she knew he had one. He held up his hands and said, "No, no. I did nothing."

Lost in primal rage, she said, "You did enough."

His face pleading, for the first time she noticed a white scar tracking through his eyebrow and into his cheek, giving him a sinister appearance belied by the fear on his visage. He said, "Please, please don't."

She tightened her finger on the trigger, taking up the slack, one foot-pound away from releasing the sear, and stopped.

She said, "Get the fuck out of here."

He turned and ran the way they had entered. She followed him with her barrel until he disappeared into the sunlight. She looked at the bodies on the ground, then began sprinting down the tunnel to the ferry, trying to outrun the images in her head.

# 50

The sun long gone, with twilight turning into darkness, Charlie Chan closed and locked his office, still without any word from his assistant about the mysterious man that Paul had found. He did, however, have another problem besides Paul. Before Mouse had left on his mission, he'd come in with an urgent request from another operative in the NSB, one who was working to disrupt the burgeoning drug trade with the Triads. Because the agent was in deep cover, he couldn't return to NSB headquarters and had requested a meeting through their covert communications system.

Apparently he had something to talk about that he couldn't put into a standard situation report, and it was volatile enough that he wanted to talk to the director. It was unusual, but not unduly so. The NSB dealt with crime at all levels, as did the Triads. Maybe he'd found something outside of drugs—something like what Paul was working.

Either way, it was worth a look. He told Mouse he'd make the meeting, but admonished him to stay until he had an identification from Paul's dossier.

He went to his car in his rumpled suit, his eyes burning from lack of sleep. The upcoming election was taking its toll on him. China was going to do anything it could to disrupt Taiwan's way of life, and nobody here seemed to really care or believe it was happening.

Only a few understood the threat. Many lived in blissful ignorance.

He started his vehicle, winding down the mountain road, replacing the forest of trees for one of concrete as he entered the downtown section of Taipei. He parked in a garage near the Jiantan MRT metro station. He shut off the car, then sagged in his seat, wanting more than anything to just go to sleep. He shook his head like a driver who had nodded off at the wheel, trying to wake up.

He knew the Chinese were watching him all the time. Not 24/7, but enough that this meeting wasn't without danger. If he wanted to keep his man alive, he would have to conduct an intricate dance, and he wasn't sure he had the energy. But one slip could mean a man's death.

He crossed over the main highway and walked down Jihe Road, heading toward the chaos of the Shilin Night Market, a bustling rat maze of alleys selling all manner of food and continually packed with both locals and tourists. A good place to meet a contact because it was so hard to control.

He pushed through the crowds, the throngs so great it was like slogging against the flow of a river, people boxing him in and bouncing him left and right.

He entered a long warehouse-like building, the outside proclaiming "Shilin Market" in garish neon, threading through the upper level, seeing families fishing for shrimp in outsized tanks, and several stalls lined with games of skill, including one with what looked like automatic weapons.

Charlie knew the weapons were Airsoft guns that fired a pellet. Pop a balloon, and you win a prize. Laid out on the table were all manner of weapons seen in every action movie on earth, from SCAR to suppressed Glocks.

What he didn't know was that this stall was owned by the

Bamboo Triad and cloaked a deeper purpose. It was nearly impossible to obtain a gun in Taiwan, but easy to set up stalls like this, and the difference in the weapons could only be ascertained by picking them up and working the action. They looked exactly like a real one, which is why everyone wanted to shoot them.

He kept walking, failing to notice a man who had broken from the crowds at the doorway when he entered. The man was tall and skinny, with narrow teeth, and his hands looked as if they'd been boiled, the skin pockmarked and deformed. He kept Charlie's pace, blending in with the flow of patrons who swirled about. Known as the Tracker, he was a counterintuitive choice for the mission because of the distinctive nature of his hands, but he was good at his job, having proven it when he'd doomed Feng Main's mission at the falls.

After Charlie passed the Airsoft stall, the Tracker approached, picking up a weapon and ignoring the kids shooting at the balloons. The woman working the stall said, "You want to try your luck? See if you can pop some balloons?"

He said, "Yes. I think I will."

"What do you want to shoot? We have them all. MP5? HK416? That's what the Special Forces use."

"I want a Glock. A Snow Leopard Glock."

The attendant went white and said, "What?"

"I want to shoot a suppressed Glock. A Snow Leopard Special."

She nodded, saying, "Yes, yes. I have to get that from the back."

"Do so. I'll bring it back to you in under an hour."

She disappeared, and he watched the children shooting

at the balloons, some hitting, others not. One child glanced at him, saw the hands, and quickly turned away. Nothing new. He was used to such a reaction, and had been since his arms and lower body were burned in a meth lab fire eight years ago.

The attendant returned, holding a box. She said, "I am responsible for this. You must bring it back, or I will have to pay."

"Of course. I know how this works. And you will put it back where you found it. Right next to the other fake Glocks."

She nodded, a bead of sweat appearing on her face. He took the weapon and continued on, nobody at the stall noticing the exchange, more focused on their own shooting prowess.

He knew that Charlie would be conducting a surveillance detection route, but that was irrelevant, because he was the one who had set up the meeting through a man he knew as Mouse. He enjoyed the futility of it all, the great Charlie Chan working his fabled tradecraft skills for no reason at all, so much so that he wanted to get a glimpse of it.

He knew he shouldn't, but he couldn't help himself. He followed Charlie Chan's path down to the lower food court, entering a narrow stairwell. At the bottom, he exited into an enormous warehouse-like space overwhelmed by the smell of exotic spices, the pop of frying and steam dominating the area. The place was jammed with stalls in which all manner of food was being cooked, the vendors so close together that it was hard to tell one from another, the cooks harried as hundreds of people shouted orders, received their meals, or attempted to find a seat at one of the plastic tables crammed together like the mess hall of a ship at sea.

He walked down the stalls, passing menu after menu extolling the virtues of the cuisine, then saw his target to the front, sitting on a stool facing a wall with a board nailed into it, the makeshift shelf holding a bowl of noodles.

He didn't go any deeper into the food court because he didn't want to be remembered, and he had a healthy appreciation for Charlie Chan's skills. He went back up, regretting his decision to gloat over the useless SDR.

He'd wanted to kill Charlie Chan for years for the pain he had caused to the Bamboo Triad, and now he had the chance. This was no time to glean petty enjoyment. Having proven his commitment by the drowning of the student at the falls, the Snow Leopard had told him he wanted to see his skill. It was a no-fail mission from the highest levels—which he knew meant the People's Republic of China—and if he succeeded, he would be promoted.

He jogged up the stairwell, leaving the food court behind and reentering the crowded outside streets. He threaded through the throngs of people, snaking down one alley after another, passing stall owners making dumplings with handheld propane tanks, like they were cooking with a flamethrower, and others shouting out the sweetness of their desserts, the crowd individually fighting to walk this way or that, bumping together like electrons in a particle accelerator.

He reached a bar called Funky Fresh, although calling it a "bar" might have been an overstatement. In reality, it was another stall that was about thirty feet wide, with enough stools and tables to hold maybe ten people. It was empty except for a single table with a man and woman, either European expats or American tourists.

He passed by them, taking the last of four stools at the plywood bar counter, waiting and watching.

The interior was dark, the only lighting coming from neon

beer signs scattered about, the back of the bar decorated with an eclectic mix of mannequin heads and fake skulls. He ordered a drink and waited, watching the street.

He accidentally caught the eye of the expat sitting with the girl, and the man seemed to think it was an invitation. He stood up, swaying a little bit from the alcohol, and approached. Within thirty seconds, the Tracker learned that the man was an English teacher from the United States, and was completely arrogant, believing his own superiority by virtue of his heritage. Dressed like something out of a yoga school in Tibet, with long hair, sandals, and a makeshift coarse-wool hoodie, he droned on and on until he saw the Tracker's arms in the light of the neon.

He leaned closer, saying, "Whoa. What happened to your hands?"

The Tracker scowled, saying his first words. "Get the fuck away from me."

The man staggered back, saying, "Just trying to be friendly."

The woman at the table stood up and scurried over, saying, "Sorry about that."

And then she saw his hands as well, giving him the blank look of someone pretending not to notice. Fueling his rage.

"Leave me be."

She grabbed the arm of the drunk and took him back to the table, looking over her shoulder at him as she did so. It was a potential problem.

He waited, glanced at his watch, and saw that the meeting time had come and gone. He wondered if he'd been made because of his ill-advised penetration of the food market, growing afraid for what he would tell the Snow Leopard if Charlie Chan failed to show.

As he was going through the options in his mind, debating

on whether to attempt to find his target once again in the food court, Charlie Chan appeared, scanning the tiny stall.

The Tracker swiveled around and stared into the mirror behind the bar, seeing Chan take a seat at a small high-top table six feet away from him.

He felt his breathing increase, waited on Chan to order a drink, then slipped off of his stool. He drew his weapon, keeping the barrel low on his leg, the suppressor making it harder to conceal. He stood directly behind the one man dedicated to wiping out the Bamboo Triad. He should have just pulled the trigger, but once again couldn't help himself.

He sat down at the high-top table and said, "You are waiting on someone, yes?"

Charlie's eyes squinted, then began darting left and right, looking for additional threats. He saw only the drunk expat. He said, "You have me confused with someone else."

"I don't think so."

The Tracker pointed the pistol underneath the table, out of view of Charlie. "We finally meet."

Charlie said, "What?" and the Tracker pulled the trigger, sending a bullet right into Charlie's spine, the muted spit still loud enough to sound like a hard clap.

Charlie jerked upright, then leaned across the table, clawing at the Tracker's face as if he wanted to peel off the skin. He pulled the trigger one more time.

Charlie slumped over the table, then slid off of his stool. It was an unsatisfying end, Charlie showing no recognition of how he'd been defeated.

Behind him, the drunk stood up at the noise from the pistol, then saw the body. He said, "Hey, is he okay?"

The Tracker said, "What do you do again?"

"I teach English. Here in Taiwan."

"English? Why do we need to learn English?"

"Uhhh . . . so you can compete with China? I help you guys compete with China."

The woman went to Charlie's dead body and said, "This man is bleeding!"

The Tracker ignored her, saying, "So *you* are responsible for the death coming."

Confused, the man said, "Death? What are you talking about?"

The Tracker raised the pistol and the drunk's muddled brain failed to understand what was happening, but the woman did. She shrieked, and he whipped his gun toward her. The pistol barked again, cutting off the scream like someone had flipped a radio switch.

The man stumbled backwards at the death of his girlfriend, and the Tracker swung the pistol to him.

# 51

Unlike my former boss, Kurt Hale, George Wolffe listened to my report without any verbal explosions, only raising an eyebrow at some of the more serious results. I was impressed, because if it had been me on the other end, I would have wanted to fly to Australia and kick my own ass.

I'd sent a short SITREP earlier, but with the time difference, I knew it wouldn't make it to Wolffe's desk until he arrived, and I hadn't wanted him to read it without me being able to explain, so I had requested another VTC. At 6 A.M. his time—10 P.M. mine in Australia—I was told he was available. I'd dialed up and given him the damage. When I finished, he exhaled and said, "So you know for sure Dunkin is dead?"

"Yes. It was reported on the news tonight, along with the other bodies. The entire zoo operation was a shitshow."

He leaned back and said, "Why? What went wrong?"

"Sir, it was honestly my mistake. The Chinese suckered me with the thumb drive red herring. I thought they really wanted it, but I now think they simply wanted Dunkin and knew just asking him to show up was a nonstarter. Even so, we had it covered. Dunkin failed to follow instructions. We don't know why. He was given explicit parameters, one of which was not to enter any conveyance alone with the target. He did so. He left his security and entered a cable car by himself. There was nothing we could do at that point."

"And the others that died? Why was there a shootout? Why didn't the security just leave? Are you blown? Did they target you? It concerns me."

"No, sir. We aren't blown. Jennifer followed the men who killed him, looking for a link for further exploration. It wasn't wise, but they didn't know who she was. They didn't target her, she targeted them."

I struggled to maintain my composure at this point, the pain of Dunkin's loss biting deep, because I had been the one to send him to his death. I made it seem like a clinical report, but I really, really wanted to find the man who had ordered the hit and skin him alive.

We'd rescued Nicole and taken a sizable toll against the enemy ourselves, but we hadn't found the owner of the so-called import/export company or his girlfriend. Mr. Chen Ju-Long. That man was at the root of both the mission and Dunkin's death, and while I'd wanted to protect U.S. national interests before, now I wanted to make him pay personally.

And that was something I was good at.

Wolffe said, "What about the girl? Nicole? She's a breach."

"Yes, sir, she's a *potential* breach, but I think we can contain it. She has no idea who we are."

"How did she get involved in this?"

I started to stretch the truth a little. "When we'd originally interdicted the men against Dunkin, he'd been separated from his girlfriend, and he'd lost contact with her. We just assumed she'd gone back home, but upon conducting the Alpha mission against the target house, we learned that they'd taken her, holding her hostage as leverage against Dunkin. They forced our hand. Instead of a controlled exploitation of the target house, we had to conduct an in-extremis Omega mission."

He squinted his eyes and said, "How did you not know she was being held? Did Dunkin not try to call her? What was the leverage if they never told him they had her?"

I felt the heat through the video connection. I said, "Sir, I can't explain what they were planning. I can only tell you what I found. Maybe we short-circuited the plan, I don't know."

He said, "This is going to be a hard sell today. Especially since you got nothing out of the house, and lost Dunkin in the process."

And that set me off, causing me to lose my composure. "You can tell those fucks on the Oversight Council they can kiss my ass. I didn't 'lose' Dunkin, like he wandered away in a store. He's dead. Gone. That's all that matters here."

I shook my head and said, "Jesus, if they get mad because we saved a girl's life but didn't get something they can use against China in the process, then tell them they can get on a plane and put their own asses in the breach."

He said, "Okay, okay, calm down. I agree. I'll handle it. You think extracting her to the U.S. is the way to go?"

In my written SITREP I'd requested an exfiltration flight for Nicole, just like we would do if we'd captured a terrorist, only she'd get to ride up front drinking champagne, instead of in the back, tied up with a hood on. Right now, she was in our hotel, getting babysat by Veep with the television off.

I said, "Yes, sir, extraction isn't perfect, but it's the best course of action. I didn't tell her about Dunkin. She's overwhelmed as it is, and only knows she was rescued by some American force. I told her she's now privy to a secret operation that Dunkin is working, and needs to cooperate for her own protection. She's agreed. Getting her out of here until this is over is the best way to plug the breach. We can deal with the fallout later. I know it won't be pretty, but it's the best solution right now."

"Okay, I'll divert a Taskforce bird from Indonesia. It's doing nothing but wasting per diem on the beach anyway supporting Johnny's team. It'll be there before dawn. What about the threat? Did you get any more leads? Tell me you have something."

I stretched the truth again, saying, "We have nothing on Jake Shu, other than he was supposed to go to Cairns. We might have something on Chen Ju-Long, but I won't know for a couple of hours."

"Jake Shu is still a ghost from our end. No digital trace. What do you have on Chen?"

"Nothing yet. The team's sifting through what we got from the house."

Which was true, but our sensitive site exploitation of the target house had delivered absolutely nothing. The place was clean, their tradecraft pristine. We might get something from biometrics from the men we'd killed, but I doubted it would go further than Chen's import/export "company."

He looked at his watch and said, "Keep working it. Let me know before you go off half-cocked again."

I said, "Sir—" and he cut me off, saying, "Yeah, yeah. You had no idea the girl was there. Look, I'm sorry about Dunkin. I truly am, but don't let it affect your ability to operate. China is the threat, not the assholes they're using. Get me a lead, not a bunch of dead bodies."

And I realized he knew I was stretching the truth, but also that he was good with it. He was reminding me not to go off on a killing spree, like I had last year in Brazil after Kurt Hale had been killed. The problem was it wasn't me this time.

I'd disconnected and then gone upstairs to our bedroom,

finding Jennifer lying on the bed mindlessly flipping through television channels.

She glanced at me, and I could see she hadn't been focused on the television. She said, "How'd it go?"

"Okay. He didn't believe my bullshit, but he let it slide. He's sending an aircraft for Nicole."

"When are you going to tell her?"

"I don't think I am. Right now she believes that we already evac'd Dunkin and we were only staying because we needed to rescue her. It made her appreciative of our efforts. More compliant to the plan. She won't get on the plane if she doesn't think Dunkin's at the end of it."

She sat up, saying, "*That's* what's important now? Her compliance?"

I sat next to her and said, "I know that sounds cold, but what's important is finding and punishing Dunkin's killer, Chen Ju-Long. And we can't operate if she goes running to the police talking about Chinese assassins and Dunkin's murder."

She lay back down, staring at the ceiling, saying, "Because I killed those men at the zoo. It went from a single murder of Dunkin to a mass shooting event over two different areas. The man I shot will be on the surveillance systems getting into the cable car with Dunkin, which means the police will ascertain that it wasn't one killer running amok at the zoo, but some type of conspiracy."

She was right about the repercussions, and I didn't want to make her feel worse, but it might be as bad as "some type of conspiracy involving a blonde woman," because she was sure to be on the camera boarding the next car. I didn't think that would happen—at least not soon—because the news reports had nothing like that yet, instead focusing on the background of Dunkin and the dead Chinese.

She continued, "And they're going to question Nicole's sister about the maintenance worker who was killed there. Another link."

I said, "Which is why we need to get her out of here. Nicole told Veep that her sister didn't even know she was going there. It happened too fast. Nicole just knew that the condo was empty because her sister was out of town on business, and she had a key. Her sister isn't even coming back from overseas for two more weeks. That's a dead end."

"They're going to make a link to the import/export company, just like we did. And when they do, they're going to make another link to the house you assaulted. There has to be some kind of rental records. The zoo and that house are going to be tied together."

I said, "I know. In fact, I'm counting on it. If they find nothing but Chinese guys all over the place, the focus will go against Chen Ju-Long and the PRC. The Aussies are already on high alert because of the rampant spying China does here. If it puts pressure on his ass, that's fine by me. It'll take the heat off of us."

She nodded vacantly, then turned to me and said, "I shouldn't have killed those men."

And I realized she wasn't really concerned about screwing up the mission. She was wrestling about whether she was a murderer.

I said, "Scoot over." She did and I lay down next to her, taking her hand and saying, "You made a call. It's not a moral decision. It's a military one."

"I didn't have to kill them. I could have simply left the zoo."

"You didn't kill the one that was surrendering. You let him go."

"Yeah, that was probably a screwup too. He knows what I look like. I mean, not only did I kill those other two, but I let the last one flee. If I'm going to do wrong, I should have gone all the way."

I chuckled and she let go of my hand, saying, "It's not funny."

I knew it wasn't humorous, not the least because I had a smoldering rage at Dunkin's death, and absolutely no regret for what Jennifer had done. I couldn't let it out in front of her, because it would just prove she was right, given her moral compass, but the men who had killed Dunkin would *all* be planted in the ground. I would ensure that was the case before this was done. I couldn't tell her that—or the team—because of how I'd acted in the past when things became personal. I'd gotten pretty good at hiding the beast inside me in front of the team, but I was going to let it out before this was done.

They were dead men walking. Period.

I said, "Well, yeah, it is a little funny. You're the only Operator I know who can beat herself up *both* ways on a decision."

"Tell me I'm wrong, then."

"Okay, you're wrong. What were you going to do? Make a citizen's arrest? This is combat. I sure as shit didn't start screaming 'freeze' as I cleared that house looking for Nicolc."

"That's different. Nicole's life was on the line. Dunkin's was already gone."

And her eyes began to water. I sat up and said, "That's not fair. Dunkin's death is *not* your fault. You don't get to shoulder the blame for him disobeying instructions. The Chinese were ahead of us with the thumb drive ruse, and *I'm* the one that sent him."

"Okay, okay. It still sucks, though. And I still didn't need to murder those men."

"Stop it. It wasn't murder. It was combat. *They're* the murderers. The first one was the man who killed Dunkin. The second drew a weapon on you. He was a threat. The third surrendered. And you let him go."

She nodded and said, "I know, I know. I think what bothers me most is that I'm not as bothered as I should be by doing it. I've been waiting to feel guilty or dirty or something—especially after killing that guy with a corkscrew."

"It'll come, trust me, but it's just a natural reaction. It doesn't mean you're guilty or dirty."

She took my hand again and said, "I came close to killing that guy with his hands up, though. Really close."

"Close doesn't count. Lord knows I've come close to doing plenty of stuff that would make you mad."

She scrunched her eyes and said, "Like what?"

"Like killing that damn cat of ours. But I haven't."

She finally chuckled and said, "What now?"

I said, "Now comes a little Pike magic."

I picked up my phone and she asked, "Who are you going to call?"

"Amena."

# 52

As was usual, Amena was running behind trying to make it to breakfast. If she had it her way, she'd have just slept in and shown up to the morning meeting with the rest of the students at Ashley Hall. But that wasn't to be for the small selection of boarding students.

Living across the street from the school in a renovated three-story Charlestonian mansion, she shared a room with her Chinese roommate, Flower, with the other Chinese exchange students sprinkled throughout the house. To ensure they made it to class on time and deal with any other problems, they had a live-in couple who came around checking to make sure they were awake each morning.

Which meant she couldn't sleep in even if she wanted to.

She sat on her bed brushing her hair, waiting her turn in the shared bathroom. There wasn't a formal structure to its use, but they'd fallen into a rhythm. The room across the hall started, then she let Flower go. She went last before trekking across the road to breakfast.

She was startled by a buzzing in her desk drawer, then realized what it was: her Batphone.

She ripped open the drawer, saw it was Pike, and answered, saying, "Pike, this is the absolute *worst* time to call. We're all getting ready for breakfast."

"Why's that the worst?"

She hissed, "Because I'm not supposed to have an unregistered cell phone! It's why you snuck this one in to me!"

"So is your roommate going to turn you in? You said she had one."

She said, "Hang on. Don't hang up, but hang on."

She stuck the phone into the waistband of her skirt, went down the hall past the bathroom, pausing and saying, "Flower, I don't think I'm going to breakfast. I didn't finish my essay last night, and I think I'm going to work on it now."

Flower turned from the mirror and said, "I can help, if you want. I finished mine."

"That's okay. I know what I want to say, I just didn't finish last night. Just bring me a banana from the cafeteria, and thanks."

Flower smiled, and Amena continued down the hall, exiting onto the long second-floor balcony. She closed the door, pulled out the phone, and said, "Okay, Pike. I can talk now."

"Well, good. How are you doing, doodlebug?"

She put on a brave face, but truthfully, hearing Pike's voice almost made her cry. She said, "I'm fine. When are you coming home?"

"Soon, doodlebug, soon. Looking forward to it. How are classes going?"

"It's harder than I thought it would be, but nothing I can't handle. Algebra is easy for me, English not so much. They want us to talk all the time, discussing books. I hate it. Luckily, most of the girls here my age haven't traveled that much, so when I talk, they think it's like genius-level stuff, when it's just how the world works. Sort of helps since we spend so much time speaking in class."

She heard Pike snicker, then, "And your roommate? How is she?"

"She's shy, but really nice. Actually, I'm sort of the outcast here because everyone else is Chinese. I think they all knew each other before they came. They don't do it on purpose, but I'm sort of the bug in the jar in the house, which in itself is another jar full of bugs in the school. All of us get treated weird, and then when I get back here, I'm treated differently yet again."

"But it sounds like you're doing okay."

"I am if you'd come home. If you're not, then I'm going to start acting out. Stealing stuff. Causing trouble."

She said it as a plea. She'd never really do that, but she wanted Pike and Jennifer back in Charleston. Enough of that vacation in Australia. Pike's answer left her speechless.

"That's good, because I have something I want you to steal."

She scrunched her eyes, saying nothing, sure she'd misheard. He came back, saying, "You still there?"

"Uhh . . . yeah?"

"You said your roommate's father is named Chen Ju-Long, right? What's he do?"

"He's some bigwig import/export guy in China. All of the girls here are either daughters of millionaires or work for the government. I have to lie about you all the time."

He laughed and said, "Just so I'm sure, his name is Chen Ju-Long and he's an import/export guy?"

Aggravated, she said, "Yeah, Pike, that's what I said. You want to talk to her instead of me? She's about to go to breakfast, which I'm missing because I'm talking to you."

She heard his voice grow serious, saying, "No, doodlebug, I have a favor to ask. A little mission for you."

She said nothing, confused. He said, "You still there?"

"Yes, but what?"

"Look, I don't have time to explain. I need you to trust me on this. I need you to get her burner phone and find the number for her father."

"What are you talking about?"

"Amena, I need it for a work thing. He's involved with something over here. If it doesn't pan out, it doesn't pan out. But just do it for me."

Her head spinning, remembering her past, she felt a rash of sweat break out. She said, "Involved in what? You're on vacation. Right? Was that a lie?"

"No! It wasn't a lie. Look, this is no different than when we met. I ended up in a situation, and I think your roommate can help me. That's all it is."

She closed her eyes and said, "The bad man found you. I knew it would happen. You're not coming home."

He said, "Oh, no. I'm coming home. Make no mistake about that, but I've run into a spot of trouble over here, and I think your roommate's father is involved."

She felt a blast of fear, saying, "What trouble? Where's Jennifer?"

"Whoa, whoa, she's right here. Don't panic. I'll put her on the phone when we're done, but I need the father's cell phone number. He's carrying that with him for her, or he wouldn't have given her the phone. It's separated from everything else I can find. Look, she's probably a lovely girl, and this may be nothing, but I need to check."

She exhaled in relief and said, "What happened?"

"I'll tell you when I get back—if it even pans out."

She went through what he was asking, then said, "Pike, I

can't get to her phone. She keeps it in a desk drawer with a lock. I don't have the key."

And she heard a laugh that infused her with calm. Not condescending at all, it was more like he was amused at her lack of confidence, and they were sharing an inside joke.

"Amena, it's a desk drawer. You've picked the pockets of people all over Europe. You broke into an aquarium from an outside window over a cliff. You can't get into a desk drawer?"

She smiled and said, "Yeah, I can do it. I've already done it on my own drawer. It's not much of a lock."

"Why did you pick your own drawer?"

"I was bored."

And she heard his infectious laugh again. He said, "That's what I want to hear. Hang on, Jennifer wants to talk to you."

She saw the Chinese girls walking down the hall, all headed to breakfast, and said, "Pike, I can't talk to her right now. They're leaving for breakfast. If you want the phone, this is my only shot at it."

She heard a pause, then, "Okay, but Jennifer's going to be mad at me. This one is on you. Don't blame me when it's over."

She felt another grin leak out, liking being wanted, and said, "I'm coming on the honeymoon."

He started to reply, and she saw the caretaker husband through the window. She cut him off, saying, "Gotta go," and hung up.

She shoved the phone into her skirt, left the balcony, and went back toward her room, running into the husband on the way.

He said, "Hey, aren't you going to breakfast? Most important meal of the day, or so they say."

She said, "I know, but I have to finish an essay. Flower's bringing me a banana. I'll be okay."

He was a kind man, but given her past, and her previous independence, she'd grown to find him a little overbearing. As if he was failing if she didn't make every meal.

He nodded, saying, "If you need help on that sort of thing, you need to bring it up. There's no reason to miss a meal because of homework."

She came close to saying, *Can I miss a meal to sleep in?* But didn't.

She nodded and went back to her room. She wanted to close the door, but knew that would look suspicious, or would make him come knock. She left it open, sitting on her bed, breathing shallowly with an open mouth to allow her to hear the house.

There was a creak of stairs, and then a door closing down below. She was alone. She darted over to Flower's desk, turned on a lamp, and snatched a paper clip, bending it into a large U shape. She glanced at the door, then bent another one into a straight pick. She shoved both of them into the lock face, torqueing the U-shaped one to apply tension to the lockset, then using the other to pop the pins.

She knew the lock itself was juvenile, and had cracked many, many like it in the past when she'd had to steal for survival, but now she wondered what she was doing. Betraying a roommate who'd only been kind to her? For what?

But she trusted Pike and Jennifer more than anyone left on earth. If Pike said it was needed—if it was to find someone who'd tried to harm Pike—she'd do it.

She worked the paper clips, glancing down the hall, and

felt the lock spring free. She reached inside, sliding her hand back and forth, finding the phone. She pulled it out, an old iPhone 6, and pressed the home button. As she feared, it was locked.

She flicked her hand on the screen, pulling down notifications, and saw two missed calls from the same number. She had no idea who it was, but it was all she could get. If Pike wanted more, it would be a little bit longer to figure out.

She heard a creak from the stairs and shoved the phone deep inside, then closed the drawer, hearing it lock automatically. She turned off the lamp and sprang back, scrambling to her bed. The house manager appeared in the doorway, saying, "Why are you here in the dark?"

She said, "I . . . I was trying to think about my essay."

He smiled and said, "Or trying to go back to sleep? Amena, I know it's hard being at a new school, and trying to make friends, but hiding isn't the way to solve the problem. I promise."

She sat up, playing an act she'd learned deep in the heart of her worst years, before she'd met Pike, when she'd been caught red-handed doing something wrong. She sniffled, then said, "You may be right. I'm sorry. I'll try. I really will."

He flicked the lights on and said, "That's what I want to hear. It's never as bad as you think."

He studied her for a minute, then left the room.

She thought, *It's* always *as bad as you think.*

She pulled her phone out of her skirt and texted Pike, saying, This had better not be for nothing. Flower is a good person.

She heard footsteps on the stairs and stopped, hiding the phone. Flower returned, giving her a banana and saying, "Did you finish the essay?"

Feeling like a traitor, Amena said, "I did. Thank you for this."

Flower said, "That's what friends are for. My father has always told me that family is what matters."

She left the room and Amena texted Pike the number.

Because family is what matters.

# 53

Jake Shu exited the rail station in Cairns almost giddy from lack of sleep. None of the trains offered sleeping cars, and he'd been operating under a crushing amount of anxiety. After meeting the man in Brisbane he was convinced he was being watched 24/7. Every person who passed him caused paranoid thoughts. So much so that he'd made a little bit of an ass of himself on the train ride up, snapping at a man who'd simply asked if he could sit next to him.

The rest of the train passengers had looked at him like he was a lunatic, and he'd backed down, apologizing, but the incident had done nothing to throttle the sweat flowing out of his body.

He took his small carry-on off the train and walked across a street to a mall, entering a food court. He saw a McDonald's and immediately gravitated toward it, buying lunch and taking a seat, wondering what the hell he'd gotten himself into.

He stroked the top of his thigh where he'd strapped the hard drive containing the information he'd stolen. Terabytes of data that could be manipulated to give all sorts of mischief.

He had begun to believe the money wasn't worth it. Wasn't worth *this*.

He devoured his hamburger, then pulled out his phone and googled the place where he was supposed to stay. Apparently one that didn't register passports and took cash. He had a feeling it wouldn't be as nice as his hotel in Brisbane.

He memorized the blue line on Google Maps and exited the mall, walking through the suburban sprawl on the outskirts of Cairns, dragging his carry-on behind him.

Ten minutes later, the sun beating down on him, he found himself sweating outside a less than spectacular backpacker hostel called Asylum. Unlike the ones in the heart of downtown Cairns, competing for the college crowd with beer nights and swimming pools, this one catered to transient workers. People who were here only for a short spell and needed cheap lodging.

He walked inside, finding a lobby with chipped furniture and a reception counter made of plywood. He checked in, the woman saying, "Oh, you have a private room. We don't get too many of those."

He smiled, saying, "I'm a big spender."

The woman laughed, and he paid cash, twenty-eight dollars a day, the woman not asking for any identification. Two minutes later he was in a closet-sized space with a single bed, next to it a metal locker and a floor lamp. No sink, no bathroom, no nothing.

He threw his bag on the floor, unbuckled his pants, and ripped off the tape holding the hard drive on his thigh. He held it in his hands, staring at it. The bane of his existence. He set it on the table and texted his contact, saying, I'm here. And this place sucks. You need to get here soon, or I'm leaving.

Surprising him, his phone showed bubbles, a response coming immediately. He waited, and then read, Stay where you are. Do not leave until told to do so. I will be there soon.

Piqued, he sent back, I'm not staying in this shithole for days. Tell me where to go. I'm done with this.

He watched the bubbles on his phone, and when they appeared, he wished he'd never told these people he'd arrived:

You leave that place and it will be the last thing you do.

He didn't respond. He sat on the bed and put his head in his hands, wondering how his two-week vacation had come to this.

Paul rolled out of bed and immediately checked his COVCOM—covert communication—connection with Charlie Chan, a hidden application in his laptop that was encrypted end-to-end and impossible to find even if the computer was forensically autopsied.

There was nothing, disappointing him. He wanted to know what the NSB had gleaned about the Air Force officer. Wanted to stop the evil he believed that man was doing.

He sat back down on his bed and wondered what that meant. Surely with the information he'd sent it wouldn't be that hard to identify the man. How many Air Force colonels had access to the Foreign Affairs building?

Since sending the message, he'd discarded any notion that he might be mistaken about the colonel. The flyers he'd taken off of the man he'd killed in Jiufen—the same ones the colonel had passed around the table—told him that.

Apparently the Snow Leopard was paying people—students—to conduct massive protests, just like what was happening in Hong Kong, only this time instead of a spontaneous uprising protesting the PRC, it would be funded by them. Something that would cause a debilitating police response and follow-on ensuing chaos where the law enforcement personnel were the enemy. Something so great it would reverberate throughout the country, creating a seam for the PRC to exploit.

The flyer hadn't dictated a timeline. It simply said there would be a "trigger," and when they saw it, they were to take to the streets "just like the brave people of Hong Kong."

He knew if he'd interdicted that one instruction in a backwater like Jiufen, there were many others. Meetings and cash exchanging hands all over Taiwan in preparation for a massive response. The PRC was infiltrating at the root level, and the implications made him sweat.

Paul didn't know what exactly the trigger would be, but the information was so explosive it was something Charlie Chan should see, because there was most definitely a traitor in the mix. Someone who was doing much more than just buying Facebook posts like his student asset who had been killed. Someone who was planning actual violence. The traitor was going kinetic, and Charlie Chan needed to identify him.

He reread the flyer, then turned back to his computer to analyze the data, trying to make a connection on his own. His generic homepage blared a headline: "NSB chief dead."

Incredulous, he read the headline again, not wanting to believe it, then pulled up the news article. It was true. Someone had killed Charlie Chan.

He had no idea if this had something to do with his current tasking, or if it was something else entirely, but one thing was for sure: Whether intentional or not, it had effectively cut him off from all support. He now had no contact inside the NSB.

He had been portrayed as an outcast, ostensibly thrown to the wolves because of "incompetence," with Charlie Chan leveraging that to allow him freedom of action. And now he had none.

He looked at the flyer again, feeling rage. It was the mole, he was sure. The same one who had set up his student asset at the falls. The same one that Charlie had been worried about, causing him to send Paul into the wilderness, now forever known as a Ronin to everyone at the National Security Bureau.

But unlike Chan, he was still alive. And he had a target.

He began planning for surveillance of the unknown Air Force colonel, mapping his house location and the Foreign Affairs building, seeking vengeance for the death of his mentor.

Becoming a Ronin for real.

# 54

Han entered the twelve-story technology building in Beijing's Zhongguancun district, wading through the crowd of engineers, each convinced they were the next sure thing in the world of technology. All of them showing absolute disdain for the Communist Party of China in this new entrepreneurial wave. It disgusted him, but he took some private consolation in that every bit of the technology they worked on would only help the PRC obtain dominance, both inside and outside of the country.

He showed his badge at the counter and took the elevator to the second floor, passing through yet another security gate, but this one much more stringent, because it was the entrance to the Twelfth Bureau's laboratory.

Yuan met him in the lobby, saying, "You have a call on the secure line. I don't know how they knew you'd be here, but they're calling."

Han said, "I told them I'd be here. Who is it?"

"They didn't say. Just that they wanted to talk to you."

He nodded and followed Yuan down a hallway, stopping at a small closet with a digital phone affixed to the wall, the keypad replaced by a screen showing Chinese characters. He entered, closed the door, and picked up the receiver, saying, "This is Lion."

"This is the Tiger element. We are on the way to Cairns as instructed. There have been some issues."

Han closed his eyes and said, "What?"

"We interdicted the American. He is dead. There will be no leak from that end. Bobcat is secure and I'm headed to his location now, but there was a problem."

"What problem?"

"The team that interdicted the American was attacked. We don't know by whom, but it was total. They eliminated everyone in our safe house and killed two more men at the interdiction site for the leak. Someone is hunting us, and they are very, very good."

"Better than you?"

"No. They let one of my men go. They should have killed him outright at the interdiction site, but didn't. If they had, I wouldn't have any of this information. They are not immune from mistakes, but they remain a threat."

"How do you know Bobcat is secure? Do they know where he is?"

"No. No way. He's been gone for a day. If he was the target, they wouldn't have wasted so much time on the American. If I were to guess, they were solely focused on Clifford Delmonty. Now that he's gone, they'll leave. I don't think this had anything to do with Bobcat."

"And yet they had a team that could kill all of your men? Nobody does that without government backing. And no government does that backing without significant fear of something else. A government doesn't care about the individual. They care about the state."

"In our world. Not in theirs. I think this was a coincidence of us falling into an old Army friend of Clifford's. They ended up having skill that we didn't account for, to include a woman as deadly as Zhi Rhou, but I believe they're done. Their mission was Clifford, and he's dead now."

"I need to know we are contained. The next phase of this is critical. I cannot have them interfering."

"We are contained. I promise. I'm on a train headed to Cairns. Bobcat is in Cairns. I have already made contact with him. I just need to know what you want me to do with him. Take the device and dispose of him? Bring him with me? What?"

"Bring him with the device. I don't want to kill him only to find out we don't know how to use the data. This is too critical to try to figure out what he has. He knows. Can you get him out through nontraditional means?"

He heard a pause, then said, "I think I can, but it will take significant assets. I'd rather leave him with a bullet in the head."

"Start planning the extraction. But keep a bullet in your gun for him."

"Will do. We're reaching the station. I have to go."

Han disconnected and exited the secure room, saying, "Where's Yuan?"

A man scurried to the back and brought him out. Yuan said, "Is everything okay?"

"Everything is fine. Where do we stand with the videos?"

"They're done. And they're good. The American outdid himself."

"I want to see them. And him."

"You want to see the American?"

"Yes. Right now."

Yuan left and came back with a skinny man wearing rumpled jeans and a stained shirt, sporting a four-day growth of beard, reminding Han of a drug addict. He didn't believe that was true, but he definitely saw someone who lacked self-discipline.

Yuan said, "This is Jerry Tribble, the American helping us with our facial recognition efforts."

Han shook his hand and said, "I understand you've helped us with something else as well."

Jerry glanced nervously at Yuan and said, "Just a little side thing I did as a favor. A birthday joke for a friend, right?"

Speaking in Chinese, Yuan said, "I told him it was a gift for the head of the AI unit here. A gag gift for his birthday."

Han studied Jerry, then replied in Chinese, "Did he take the money?"

"Yes."

"Did it go through his corporate contract?"

"No. Straight to him."

"He is not naïve. He wants to give himself some plausible deniability if his work is discovered. Can it be?"

"What do you mean?"

"If you study the video at the micro level, forensically, can you identify his fingerprints on it?"

"Not really. Well, you can identify some of the code as being very similar to what he has done in the past, but that's about it."

"And he knows that, yes?"

"Oh, yes. Of course. It's why he's making excuses about birthdays."

Han thought, *Time to drop the hammer.*

He switched to English and turned to Jerry, saying, "Did you recognize the people in the videos?"

Jerry glanced at Yuan and said, "Yes. Well, one of them. It's the president of Taiwan. I don't know the other one."

"And you think it's a birthday gag?"

"Uh . . . I guess . . . I mean, isn't it?"

"How much did you ask to be paid for this gag?"

"I didn't ask anything. Yuan offered."

"How much?"

Jerry rubbed his face and said, "Twenty-five thousand U.S. dollars."

"Paid directly to you, correct?"

Now looking a little sick, Jerry nodded.

"Do you think we'd spend twenty-five thousand dollars, all hidden from oversight by going directly to you, for a birthday gag? Does that sound reasonable?"

Rocking from foot to foot, Jerry said nothing.

Han said, "You work for us now. Continue as you have and it will be very lucrative. Payments just like the one you received."

Jerry swallowed and nodded again.

Han said, "Of course, you can leave at any time, if that is what you wish. We can send you back to the United States with this gag birthday gift hanging around your neck, along with the previous help you have provided from scraping pictures of people in New York City."

# 55

Chen and Zhi arrived at the small safe house, paying the driver and exiting the cab. It had taken longer than he would have wanted to get here, but with the proscription on flying, it was what it was.

They walked up to the front door, Chen taking a look at the surrounding area and liking what he saw.

A house on a street corner in the outskirts of Cairns, it was a two-story structure built of clapboard and bricks, with a side yard that gave it distance from the next house over. All good. What he liked best was that the back of the house butted up to a road that had a canal behind it, with a small bridge leading to a running path. The only downside was that the chosen location happened to be on the second floor of a duplex, with someone else living below.

Given the multiple escape routes, he still liked it. He didn't believe that would ever prove necessary, but he liked the thought process.

Zhi said, "Looks like the men here aren't as bad as the ones in Sydney."

Chen smiled and said, "No mention of Sydney. We were as much at fault as they were."

She flashed her eyes, and he said, "Don't. No talk of Sydney."

He walked up the outside stairwell, rang the bell, and waited, staring into the camera above the doorjamb.

The door opened to a trim, handsome Asian in a T-shirt, ropy muscles flowing out of his sleeves. Of average height, he was as lean as a cheetah, causing Zhi to stare in admiration.

She said, “Hello. We are from Control.”

He slid his eyes up and down her body and said, “I'm Bear. And I'm the control here. This is my operation.”

Chen pushed past him, not wanting a fight, but knowing one was coming. Bear was the team leader for the endgame operation in Cairns. A good man, but apparently not as trusted as Chen, or Control wouldn't have sent him up here, leaving the Sydney mission to collapse.

He leaned his bag against the wall, turned to Bear, and said, “I'm now in charge here. That's the end of it. Understand?”

Incensed, Bear said, “No, I don't understand. I was told you were coming, but not why.”

Zhi said, “It's not personal. It's from Control. Just execute.”

Angered at the statement, he turned to confront her, and then saw her eyes. He hesitated, and Chen said, “I *am* in charge here. It's not an insult to your team. It's because I have a better understanding of the mission. We've already executed actions in Sydney, and this mission has become more prominent than it should have been.”

Bear squinted, wanting to say something else, but did not.

Chen said, “Good. Let's do this together, because it's a no-fail event.”

Bear said, “Like Sydney?”

When Chen didn't answer, he said, “Yes, we've all heard about the mess in Sydney. You don't need to be on a Fifth Bureau COVCOM to see it. You just need an Australian news station.”

Chen realized that it was time to put the command question to rest. He advanced on Bear, snapped up his hand, and slammed it into Bear's throat, pushing him into the wall. He said, "We need to work *together* now. I do not want to fight."

Implicit in the question was the fact that he would, in fact, fight. And he would win. A man appeared from the back of the house, and Zhi drew a pistol, pointing it at him. He disappeared.

Bear dropped his arms and said, "No fight. No fight. I didn't mean to imply it was your fault."

Chen pulled his hand away and said, "Good. Very good. Trust me, I know what I did wrong in Sydney. I underestimated. I don't intend to do that again. And I appreciate the strategic nature of the safe house you have. Your skill is not in question here."

Bear nodded and Zhi hid her pistol.

Chen walked into the kitchen, took a seat, and said, "Who's below us?"

"A couple. We've met them, but they stick to themselves. They provide us a little buffer should someone want to assault."

Chen nodded, realizing the arrangement could have prevented what had happened in Sydney. The couple below them wasn't a downside at all. It was protection against an assault force that wanted to remain as invisible as they did.

He said, "What do you have for the exfiltration?"

Bear took a seat across from him, saying, "I think this whole thing is insane, but I have the assets lined up. We can get him offshore, and we can then transfer him to a plane, but it's been really, really hard to set up. Why can't we just get on an aircraft here?"

"There's a reason Sydney was a mess. There are others who might be chasing Bobcat, and they have the stink of a state. I can't afford to put him on a plane in Australia. He'll get snatched. I have to get him out of here by other means. I'm sure it was painful, but I appreciate the effort."

"Who are the others? Australia? The United States? Who?"

"I don't know. Honestly, I think the team that hit us in Sydney wasn't a team. I think they were just friends of the American whom we targeted, and they had more skill than we knew. We were taken by surprise, but I don't want that to happen a second time. I'm taking no more chances."

Bear nodded. "Okay. I certainly don't want this to end up like Sydney. We're with you. What do you want us to do?"

Chen relaxed, saying, "Bobcat is secure in the hostel we rented. I want to bring him to me and make sure he has the data, but I don't want to taint this house. I'm going to set up a meeting with him, ensure he's clean, and then get him here under our control."

Bear nodded, saying, "And then?"

"And then we get him out of here, the long way."

# 56

As he had hundreds of times before, George Wolffe entered the Old Executive Office Building for an update to the Oversight Council, only this time he was the acting commander instead of sitting in the back row.

Hollywood movies made such gatherings ominous, with a drumbeat of music detailing the pressure that was to come, but in reality the meetings were mundane, even given the stakes involved. They debated the nuances of life-or-death missions like they were evaluating the purchase of a stock. In truth, Wolffe had always hated these things, but he had no choice now. Since Kurt Hale had been killed, he had become the face of the Taskforce.

He reached the door to the conference room, saw no Secret Service personnel, and entered, finding Alexander Palmer waiting on him, the rest of the Council in their seats. He said, "Where's the president? This is worthy of his attention."

Palmer was terse, saying, "He had competing interests. Just give us what you know."

Wolffe heard the tone, but knew better than to ratchet up the tension. There was no love lost between the two, but Wolffe understood he needed to get approval for an Omega operation, and antagonizing Palmer in the absence of the president was unwise.

Wolffe thought Palmer was a political toad, more

concerned with the latest popularity index than what was necessary for security, and Palmer thought Wolffe was a cowboy willing to use the Taskforce at the slightest provocation. It wasn't the best match for deciding the fate of the country's national security direction, but Wolffe could live with the politics as long as they didn't overshadow real strategic problems.

He stifled what he wanted to blurt out, instead saying, "What I *know* is that we're about to be in a war defending Taiwan. Or we're about to lose Taiwan by our inaction. Is that enough for the president's attention? He should really be here."

Palmer said, "Oh, come on. You guys always say the world is ending. Brief the Council on what's happening, and then let us decide."

Wolffe said, "Fine by me. I'm not the one who said go chase China, but I'm a believer now."

Palmer said nothing, allowing Wolffe to move to the front of the room.

He reached the head of the table, turned on the laptop, and brought up the Project Prometheus logo. The room went quiet, the buzz of conversation falling away.

He said, "First, thank you for taking the time out of your day to do this meeting. I know it's painful, given your real jobs, but it's necessary. We deal in a world of gray, and we have to make black-and-white decisions. I'm going to ask you to make one today."

He flipped the slide, showing a graphic of Taiwan, then said, "This is the national security flashpoint of the world. We talk about great power competition and how we're focusing on China, but we're missing the actual battle. It's not going to be a full-scale war. It's going to be a slow bleed."

Alexander Palmer interjected, saying, "I'm sorry, but I thought you were here to brief us on Taskforce actions. Not give us a class on geopolitics."

Wolffe bit back his initial response. He said, "Yes, sir. I am talking about Taskforce actions."

He paused, looked around the room, then set the remote on the table, ignoring the briefing slide.

He said, "Look, here's the deal. Russia took over Crimea with nothing but a social media campaign and a few Spetsnaz soldiers. They won because we stood by. I believe that same thing could potentially happen in Taiwan. We didn't really give a damn about the Crimean Peninsula, letting Russia walk right in, but we'd better damn well care about Taiwan, because if we lose that, we're ceding the entire Pacific Ocean to China. This isn't like the domino theory from Vietnam. This *is* the domino. And Pike is on that threat."

Amanda Croft, the secretary of state, said, "Are you seriously saying that China is going to invade Taiwan?"

"Yes and no. From what Pike got from Dunkin, Jake Shu stole not only information related to our F-35 program, but also data from an artificial intelligence program for the defense of Taiwan. On the surface, that's just more espionage, but looking at Crimea as an example, they may be planning on a hybrid war."

Palmer said, "What's that mean?"

"It means they aren't going to do it like we've been wargaming for the last three decades. They aren't going to conduct a cold-start invasion. They're going to foment chaos inside the country, stirring it into a frenzy, much like we see happening in Hong Kong. Once they've got everything boiling, they're going to have Taiwan initiate the action, allowing them to claim self-defense."

Easton Beau Clute, the chair of the Senate Select Committee on Intelligence, said, "How are they going to initiate chaos? What would cause the catalyst? It's not like they can tell the people of Taiwan to riot. They hate China."

"I don't know the catalyst, but they didn't tell Hong Kong to riot either. They just did."

Unconvinced, Clute asked, "Where are you getting this from? We've seen nothing to indicate anything like this."

Wolffe said, "Honestly, I'm extrapolating from intelligence Pike has gleaned from Dunkin, and it's by no means ironclad, but he has a target we need to interdict."

Palmer said, "What target? The last thing we were talking about was a breach of the F-35 artificial intelligence systems. Now you're extrapolating that it's a full-scale takeover of the entire country of Taiwan?"

"Yes, but I'm not saying we need to launch a carrier group to the Taiwan Strait—although that might be wise—only that there are potential repercussions in play beyond simply trying to alter our F-35 program. And Pike is on that thread."

Amanda Croft gave him a suspicious look, and Wolffe knew if he was losing her, he was losing them all. She said, "Give us the background."

He did, walking them through everything he knew, detailing Dunkin's killing and the rescue of Nicole, to include her coming to U.S. soil. In between, he expanded on Dunkin's theory about the AI systems for the defense of Taiwan.

When he was done, he said, "I can't vouch for the intelligence as solid, but the target is the same: Jake Shu. Even if Pike is wrong on the overarching threat, Jake Shu needs to be interdicted for the F-35 program alone. We need to know what he knows."

He looked at the Council members and saw slack-jawed

amazement at his statements, completely ignoring his request for action.

Amanda Croft said, "There's a dead American in Australia? And Pike killed a team of Chinese because of this? How is it you didn't lead with this information? You act like it's just business as usual. Jesus Christ, what are you thinking?"

Before Wolffe could answer, Palmer waved his hand, raising his voice. "Wait a minute. Besides the damn killing, did you just say you brought an Australian national back to United States soil from a Taskforce action?"

Calmly, Wolffe said, "Yes, to both of you. Dunkin is dead. Pike killed a team of Chinese, and he also saved Dunkin's girlfriend. She is now on the way to the United States, where the Taskforce will sequester her in a hotel until this is complete. All of that is irrelevant now. Pike has a thread, he's clean, and I'm asking for Omega."

Palmer blurted, "Have you lost your mind?"

Easton Clute held up his hand, cutting him off. He asked, "What is this thread?"

There was no way Wolffe was going to let slip that the thread came from a thirteen-year-old Syrian refugee who'd recorded it from a Chinese exchange student at a boarding school in Charleston, South Carolina.

He said, "I'm not going to talk about sources and methods. Suffice to say that Pike has gleaned what he believes is the cell phone number for the Ministry of State Security agent controlling all operations in Australia. He believes that the number will lead to Jake Shu."

Palmer leaned back and said, "I don't care what he believes. This is over. There is no way I'm giving Omega authority to Pike after what you just said. We'll be lucky to keep this under wraps from the Australians. Bring him home."

The red light over the secure entrance came on, telling the Council that the door was about to be opened and the room was no longer secure.

Exasperated, Palmer said, "What the hell? Keep that door closed. Whoever is behind it can stay behind it."

He turned back to Wolffe and said, "We don't give Omega on Pike's say-so. You've done enough damage in Australia."

The door opened and Palmer said, "Shut that damn thing! This is a closed hearing."

A Secret Service agent appeared and said, "President Hannister is coming in." He didn't say it like he was asking permission.

The room stood, and President Hannister appeared in the doorway, saying, "Take your seats. Please."

Wolffe remained standing, waiting on the questions and not wanting to repeat everything he'd already said.

Hannister took a seat next to Palmer and said, "So we're here for an Omega operation? This Jake Shu guy? Is that it?"

Palmer said, "Yes, sir. At least it was before I heard what George Wolffe briefed. He thinks it's pretty serious. More than just the F-35 program."

Hannister nodded, looking at his watch and ignoring Palmer's words. He said, "Cut to the chase. I don't have a lot of time."

Wolffe said, "Yes, sir. Interdicting Jake Shu will potentially disrupt an operation targeted at Taiwan, and time is of the essence there as well. If we wait, we may lose Jake Shu for good."

"So if we give you Omega for Jake Shu, you either save the world, or you just uncover some espionage to the F-35 program?"

Wolffe wanted to smile, but didn't. President Hannister

had just reduced the issue like he was making soup stock. All that was left was the problem, without the hand-wringing.

He said, "That's correct, sir."

Palmer said, "Sir, it's not that simple. You haven't heard what's been briefed. There is a significant signature from our operations in Australia, and I'm not sure it's worth—"

President Hannister cut him off, saying, "I don't see the issue here. Have we met the parameters for an Omega operation?"

Amanda Croft said, "Yes, sir. I think we have."

Palmer gave her a glare, and she gave it back.

Easton Clute said, "When it's boiled down like you just said, I agree. It's a single target, regardless of what we believe about the stakes. He's bad either way. I say get him off the board."

Palmer said, "Has anyone thought about the ramifications here? What about what George just briefed? Even without that, it's outside of the Taskforce charter. We don't use the Taskforce for state-on-state actions. We're talking about attacking China in a Five Eyes–allied state."

Wolffe couldn't believe the words had come out of his mouth. Palmer was the one who'd started this whole adventure. He wanted to slap the man, but he was beaten to the punch by the president.

Hannister said, "I don't care about the political implications. I care about the results. Put it to a vote."

Technically, President Hannister had no more say over Taskforce operations than anyone else at the table, the Oversight Council having been designed precisely so he'd be just one more vote, but there was no doubt his opinion held sway.

Palmer said, "Sir, you didn't hear the briefing. It's Pike

Logan that we're talking about. He's already killed people in Australia, leaving us exposed."

President Hannister turned to Wolffe and said, "This is coming from Pike Logan?"

Hesitating a little bit, afraid of what Hannister thought of Pike, Wolffe answered, "Yes, sir. He's on the thread, and he thinks it's real."

Hannister glanced around the room, then settled his eyes on Alexander Palmer. "Then it probably is. Put it to a vote."

# 57

Jake Shu saw the train approach and was surprised at its antique appearance. A modern locomotive up front, the rest of the train was car after car of small cabins with wooden bench seating and open windows. He supposed he should have known it would be more of a Disneyland ride than the type of train he'd used coming to Cairns, given the nineteenth-century train station he'd had to locate to board it.

Called Freshwater Station, it was full of antique train pieces splayed about the grounds in between dioramas and pictures from the construction of the railroad. It was more of a museum than a train station.

He sat inside a small veranda next to the tracks along with seventy or so other tourists, all headed to Kuranda. When the announcement of the arrival came, most of them stood to see the retro train arrive, then began to file out to the platform. He followed, looking for the number of his car and wondering, not for the first time, if what he was doing was smart.

He'd been snapped out of a nightmare this morning by his phone bleating. He'd sat up in his lumpy mattress, disoriented, then had remembered where he was. The nightmare hadn't ended by waking up.

He'd rubbed his face, picked up the burner phone, and saw a message to call a number. He'd done so, and had received very specific instructions to leave his threadbare hostel and take a train from a station about twenty minutes outside of Cairns to Kuranda, a town high in the rainforest.

Once an outpost for the railroad and logging concerns in the nineteenth century, it had transitioned to a reclusive hideaway for the counterculture and artists in the twentieth century, and was now a small enclave catering to tourists, filled with markets, restaurants, and a few animal enclosures for visitors to see indigenous creatures like koalas and kangaroos.

As he'd received in Brisbane, the instructions were very specific, designed, he was told, to ensure his own safety, but he began to suspect it was the opposite—to ensure theirs. They wanted his data, but not to the point where they risked being arrested as soon as they met.

He took a seat at the back of his car, the single assistant inside asking him to place his backpack under the wooden bench. He did so, and found himself facing an Asian man and woman on the bench opposite. They said nothing to him, spending the time talking in Chinese with each other, apparently excited for the journey.

The train left the station and began crawling up into the mountains, the tracks threading through tunnels and incredible switchbacks so tight he could see the tail of the cars behind him like the coil of a snake. He glanced at the Chinese couple and saw the woman stroke the man's neck with a finger, its nail longer than the others, making him wonder if she was a cokehead. The man next to her didn't do anything to counter that image, as he had a scar that tracked through his eyebrow into his cheek, giving him a sinister look no matter how much he smiled.

They continued winding through the rainforest, the tourists in the train craning their heads out of the windows, cameras and phones snapping pictures. Eventually they pulled into an old station called Barron Falls, nothing more than a concrete platform. The conductor gave a short speech about the significance of the area, then said they were taking a ten-minute stop to view the scenery.

The tourists on the train began to exit. Jake intended to remain behind, having no interest in seeing the falls and being much more concerned with protecting his hard drive. The train car emptied, and the Chinese woman across from him stood up, speaking to him in English.

"Are you going to see the view?"

Surprised, he said, "Uh . . . no. I think I'm going to just wait until we leave again."

She leaned forward, saying, "You should really get out and go to the viewing platform. It's gorgeous."

He said, "I'm just on here to get to Kuranda. I don't care about the view."

She traced her long fingernail against his cheek, and he felt it, much thicker than an ordinary nail. She said, "Get off the fucking train. Go to the viewing platform."

She turned, took the hand of her partner, and left the car. He sat dumbstruck for a moment, then exited as well, seeing a gorge spilling away from him, a huge rock face across the chasm with a spit of water running down it for hundreds of feet. Caught in the swirl of tourists all jostling cameras and selfie sticks, he stood for a moment, looking for the viewing platform. He saw a stairwell to his right disappearing into the jungle, a steady stream of people going up the stairs.

He followed them, reaching a wooden boardwalk that snaked through the trees. He continued, finding another set of stairs. He went up and entered a large deck hanging over the side of the chasm, the foliage cut away to allow a view. At the railing were the two Asians, pretending to look out over the gorge. He approached, and the man said, "Keep going. You're not getting back on the train. You'll cross a footbridge over the train tracks and find a parking lot. We'll stay here to see if anyone follows."

Jake nodded and continued on the path, sweat now breaking out on his neck, the fear bringing out an animal odor underneath his shirt. He wasn't a trained spy, but even he could see the extent of the preparations. They'd thought it through thoroughly.

They'd picked a single source of travel—the train—and then had broken that source by pulling him off prior to reaching the final station at Kuranda. Anyone following him would be immediately identified because *nobody* left the train at the falls. Why would they? They'd paid for the trip to Kuranda. If there was anyone on him, he'd be blamed. And possibly killed because of it.

He crossed the bridge spanning the tracks and found a stairwell leading down to a small parking lot. Descending warily, he saw a man at the base of the stairs. Another Asian. He debated whether he should approach or just walk by like he was headed to a car. He decided on the latter, shouldering his backpack and stomping down the stairs like he belonged.

He reached the bottom and saw only two vehicles in the lot, both occupied. He passed the man and heard, "Go to the vehicle on the left."

He stopped and turned to the man, about to ask a question, and the man said, "Keep walking, idiot. Get in the car."

He picked up his pace, now sweating freely from both the heat and the fear. A man exited the vehicle and opened the rear door, not saying a word.

Jake slid inside.

★★★

Jennifer pulled off the Kennedy Highway and into Kuranda Village, driving through a traffic circle in search of the central parking area. She found it, slid into a space, turned off the vehicle, and said, "Any movement?"

In the second row of seats, Veep flicked a tablet, zooming in, and said, "Yeah. It's now in a hotel." He rotated the screen, stared at an image, then said, "The Barron Falls Hotel. That could be trouble. The technology doesn't give a granular enough geolocation to pinpoint a room. If he's staying there, it's going to be some work."

I looked at Jennifer and she smiled. Veep said, "What?"

I said, "I'm betting it's not a hotel. It's a pub."

Knuckles googled, and sure enough, it was a restaurant/pub with a gaming room in the back.

He said, "That's a good thing, but we're still going to need to identify Jake Shu, and we don't even have a description. All we have is this phone, which isn't his."

Brett laughed and said, "That's what you think the weak link is? Not that we're chasing a geo-trace gleaned from a kid in Charleston, South Carolina?"

I said, "Hey, it panned out, didn't it?"

The night before, Amena had texted me the number, and I'd immediately sent it to Creed in the Taskforce, asking for a geolocation of the handset. Of course, he'd initially refused, needing to know the provenance, because we weren't allowed to target phones willy-nilly just because we wanted to. Even as top secret as we were, we had built-in checks and balances to keep Project Prometheus from turning into a secret police state. I knew he'd do it if I pushed, but that wasn't fair. I'd told him to get George Wolffe back on the phone.

He came on, and while I could stretch the truth for a mission if I believed it was in the greater good, I wasn't going to outright lie. It would have been easy to tell him I'd found the number from the SSE of the hostage house, making a story of how we'd discovered it in our exploitation, but that was a bridge too far. It was so tenuous that I wouldn't be able to explain if the number Amena found was for a handset in San Francisco—and it wouldn't be fair to put that person in the crosshairs as being involved in a Chinese Ministry of State Security operation when it could have just been Amena's roommate's cousin. Even I had some limits.

I told him everything, just laying it out. He was incredulous. I said, "Hey, sir, I'm just asking for a poke. I'm not looking to finger the handset for future exploration if it's not anywhere near my target deck."

"Pike, I can't turn on the intelligence systems of the United States of America based on what your little refugee found in her roommate's phone. Are you insane?"

"Not as much as you'd think. I did some digging, and the only people who come over to the U.S. as exchange students at the grade school and high school level are bigwigs from industry or the government—which, given that the People's Liberation Army owns most of the industry in the country, means it's all from the Communist Party. And it's the same name as the guy we're chasing."

"Same name? Out of a country of a billion people? Seriously?"

I exhaled and said, "Yeah, I know it's weak, sir, but do the poke. It's all I have. If it's in Australia, I'll explore. If it's anywhere else, just bury it and I'll try something else. Remember, you said you wanted some Pike magic. And here it is."

He muttered something, then said, "This isn't magic. It's lunacy."

But he'd done it, and an hour later he'd called back, now beginning to believe. The phone had pinged halfway between Sydney and Cairns. Further pings saw it inching along the same path, on what we surmised was a train or a car. We'd boarded the Rock Star bird for the short flight up, and by the time we'd landed, it had moved again, this time to a small village called Kuranda in the mountains.

Which made no sense, but I was betting the jump to Kuranda was for a specific reason. It was a tourist town with absolutely nothing to offer except for a single thing: It could be controlled relatively easily.

One, it was small. Two, it was isolated high in the mountains. Three, it had limited methods of egress: the road we had used, and two other, more eclectic methods—an old rail line back down the mountain, or a very long gondola system called the Sky Rail. I was betting that the location was because of Jake.

Knuckles showed me the "hotel" website, and I said, "Okay, there's a pub, an eatery, and a back room for gaming. We split up. Veep and Brett, you got the restaurant. Knuckles and Jennifer, you get the pub and gaming room. I'm going to stage outside watching the entrance. Mission is to identify Jake Shu. If we can't do that, at least identify the man with the phone—Chen Ju-Long. Secondary mission is to get a tracking beacon on the group, if possible. Knuckles, what do you have as assets?"

"I've got a Copperhead and a DragonTooth, depending on what you want."

Both of them were micro beacons that would give us a geolocation of whoever was wearing them, but like everything in life, there were trade-offs. The Copperhead worked off of the cell network, meaning it could transmit a location as long as it was within cell range of a tower, and would do so continuously, while the DragonTooth worked off of transmitting to a satellite at scheduled bursts, which meant it would lose signal if it was in a building or under a bridge just like satellite radio. The difference was the DragonTooth could transmit for a week, while the Copperhead only lasted for a day, maybe a day and a half.

I said, "Use the Copperhead. They'll be at a bed-down before dark, and that's all we need."

Knuckles nodded and everyone started working through their kit. He paused and asked, "What about a target of opportunity? You got Omega for Shu, right?"

"I don't want to push it here. Let's develop the situation. Even getting a beacon on them might be a bridge too far."

"But if it presents itself, we should be ready."

I thought for a second, nodded, then said, "Not going to argue with that. What do you have in mind?"

"ABS. If we ID him and can get some ABS on him, one of us could stage in the toilet. He'd separate from the majority of Chinese and be ours."

ABS stood for Atomic Blow Shits. It had a more official name—something like XB 948—but we called it ABS because of what it did. It was a chemical compound in a lipstick tube that, when rubbed on the skin, caused the person to have explosive diarrhea in seconds, so much so that he was pretty much ineffective and unable to resist.

Used to debilitate an opponent without him knowing what had happened, its only downside was the mess you had to deal with afterward as you helpfully took him for "medical attention." It worked well to camouflage a hit in the middle of a crowd, but had its downside—namely, if the guy wasn't wearing a diaper, you'd be in deep shit. Literally.

I said, "Okay. Sounds good to me—but only if the conditions are absolutely right. I don't want to have to exfil from here with a guy shitting his pants. They're liable to call an ambulance. Worst case, we're fighting through a bunch of Chinese assassins protecting Jake."

# 58

Jake Shu's vehicle stopped outside a low-slung single-story building with a tin roof, the outside surrounded by bushes and trees. He remained quiet, waiting on instructions.

The driver said, "Get out and go inside. Look for an Asian man wearing a leather outback hat. Go to him and take a seat. He'll tell you the next instructions."

Jake nodded and did as he was asked, sliding out of the car. Once outside he said, "You'll watch my pack?"

The driver lowered his sunglasses and said, "No, you buffoon. Take the backpack with you."

Jake nodded rapidly, opened the door again, and pulled out his backpack. The car moved away without another word, and he turned back to the building, seeing a long sign proclaiming "Barron Falls Hotel."

He went up the wooden steps and paused on the porch, looking left and right for the man in the outback hat. He saw no one.

He entered the pub, seeing a bistro to the left and a deeper area to the right. He went that way. He passed by a cheap grill serving hamburgers and fries and entered a larger area with gaming machines and tables spilled about, a long bar at the far side taking up the entire wall.

He stood in the doorway a moment, surveying the room. The entire place was taken over by college kids in backpacks and fathers wanting to get a beer, their children dancing about. At the back of the room, he saw a burly Asian, his shirt looking too small for the muscles underneath. On his head was a leather outback hat. The same one sold at every tourist shop in Australia, it looked incongruous on his head. Seated next to him were two hard-looking men.

Jake hesitatingly advanced to the table, glancing left and right for the boogeyman. The man looked up, saw him, and pointed at a seat. Jake took it, waiting.

The man said, "You must be the infamous Jake Shu. The one with all the information."

Jake nodded, unsure of what to say, and the man continued, leaning forward. "The same boy who was such a screwup he caused the death of my people in Sydney."

Jake's mouth opened without speaking. The man said, "My name is Chen Ju-Long, and that wasn't a question."

Glancing at the killers left and right, he remained mute. The one on the left leaned over to Chen and whispered in his ear. The sweat broke anew on Jake's forehead. He wiped it away with a napkin and Chen said, "Feeling guilty?"

Jake finally spoke, trying to sound confident, but failing. He said, "I have done nothing wrong. I've worked with you people for years, always producing. I have no idea what you mean about dead people. All I did was tell you that there was a leak. That's all I did."

The woman and man from the train appeared, taking the empty chairs to his left and right. He stiffened, and the woman leaned in, stroking his cheek with the heavy nail, saying, "You have been a very bad boy."

He didn't know what to say, not wanting to antagonize them. Chen said, "Do you have the data?"

He nodded rapidly and put his backpack on the table, pulling out the hard drive. He said, "This is it. It's the algorithms for PRAYING MANTIS, the experimental artificial intelligence systems for the defense of Taiwan. The one that alerts and then sends the missiles downrange."

"And how does that help us, if it's experimental?"

"I don't know. How would I know? I was told to get it, and I did. That's all I know."

Chen looked at him, and Jake felt like a mouse dancing in front of a snake. He said, "It's how they're going to defend the island. I've read the wargames. Their greatest defense is a thing called A2/AD. Anti-Access/Area Denial. If they can keep you from landing, they can win. If they can't, they lose, but they can't manually control systems across the island to initiate in time to prevent that from occurring. With multiple landings, and their hierarchical defense systems, it's just too slow. They need something faster. So they invented this."

Chen said, "And is it in play? Do they use it?"

"I don't really know. I'm just a contractor, but from what I've seen, yes, they do. They're waiting on an update for the system, but they're using it every single day in testing."

"And is this the update?"

"It is."

"Okay then, thank you. But before we end our relationship, we need to know how to affect the system."

"What do you mean?"

"How do we alter the system so it says something that isn't true?"

"You mean how to tell the system that it's not seeing an attack when it is?"

"Maybe. Or maybe have the system saying there is an attack when there's not one. Either way."

Jake said, "Uh . . . I don't know. I just brought the data.

That's what I do. I'm not involved in the end state. In fact, I don't want to hear the end state."

A hostess came over and said, "Would you guys like some food? I've noticed you've been sitting here, and you have to order at the bar. We don't have table service until happy hour."

Chen became a charming tourist, telling her, "We were just wondering about that. Thank you."

She walked away and Chen said, "We appreciate the data, but we're going to need you to implant it. We can't do that ourselves. We don't have the assets."

Jake said, "What the hell are you talking about? I'm not doing that. I give you the data, and you do with it what you will."

"No. You're coming with us. We need you to implant it."

"Implant it how?"

"Not for today's discussion. You *will* do it. Now go up to the counter and order us a few beers and some billabong grog. This doesn't have to be hard."

Jake said, "I can't go with you. I have to go back to work in two weeks."

"In two weeks, you won't have the contract for the defense of Taiwan. Go get us some food."

The man who'd rode with him on the train stood up, and Jake stared again at a scar on his forehead, tracking through his eyebrow and into his cheek.

Jake didn't want to know where that had come from.

The man said, "Let's get some food. While you can still eat."

# 59

We left the minivan behind, the team splitting out in designated pairs, leaving me a singleton. I went straight down the main road, ignoring all of the markets and kangaroo petting zoos, wanting to get in position before they entered.

I found a bench out front underneath a eucalyptus tree and waited, watching the flow of people around me, learning the rhythms of the village. Every area had one, even tourist places, and I had to find the secret to this location if I was forced to extract Jake Shu.

I heard Brett come on the net, saying, "Blood and Veep, inside. Nothing yet."

I smiled, because, like Jennifer, Brett refused to use his callsign unless it was on the radio. Knuckles had anointed Jennifer the callsign of Koko, based on a gorilla that could use sign language, and I'd given Brett the callsign of Blood because of a stupid-ass comment he'd made to me a few years ago after I'd had my pinky finger cut off. He'd said, "Put some monkey blood on it. That'll fix it," thinking he was being funny.

It had made me mad enough to give him a callsign that—as an African American—he just hated. Which was the point of a callsign.

I said, "Roger that. Koko, Knuckles, status?"

"We're in. Nothing sighted."

Veep came on, saying, "We have a crew of all Asians. I say again, we have a crew of all Asians. They're sitting at a table at the back of the bar. Pictures coming."

I thought, *Hell yeah. I'm not an idiot for tracking that phone.*

But I still could be one. Chinese people inside Australia were like buskers inside a New York subway, meaning they were everywhere. Not a reason to say we had won. But I knew we had. Jake Shu was here.

I came back, saying, "Good to go. No activity out front."

He sent his images, and I saw a table full of hard men, along with a guy completely out of his depth. A man looking for a way out. He was wearing jeans and a hipster T-shirt with the logo of Vampire Weekend and had a small gold loop in his ear. Like he was a pirate. But he wasn't a pirate, I knew, because that was what I was.

Even so, I sent back, The pirate with the earring is the target. That's Jake Shu.

I called Knuckles, saying, "Do we have any options here, or should we just trace?"

Knuckles said, "The bathroom is on the other side of the building, and there's a side exit door right next to it. It's away from the pub and looking pretty good. If you think that's the man."

"What do you think? We have the phone here, and we have him surrounded by a bunch of Yakuza-looking assholes. Are we wrong?"

"Yeah. Yakuza is from Japan."

I said, "Okay, okay, whatever. Is this the guy?"

Brett came on, saying, "This is Blood. I think it's him. He just passed a backpack across and the other guy pulled out a hard drive. Hard indicator it's Jake Shu."

I said, "Roger that. Let's take it slow. We have the man, let's start building the ability to take him down. Look for an opening for the beacon emplacement."

Veep came on, saying, "He's up and ordering food. Standing by the receiving station. He's isolated, besides one man next to him. He's twenty feet away from the table."

Knuckles said, "The toilets are on the far side. Completely away from where Veep and Brett are. I say we take him, right now."

Which was a little bit of surprise. Knuckles was a SEAL, and they routinely pulled shit out of their ass, thinking they were smarter than the laws of physics, but he was different. He liked prior planning and wanted to execute that plan—which was why he was my second in command. He rarely asked to flex on a mission if he didn't think it would work.

I said, "What are you telling me? Go for the ABS?"

He said, "Yes. Brett and I can stage in the toilet on the far side of the building. We can get him out the back side, off to the van, and out."

I thought for a few seconds, then said, "Are you sure?"

"Positive. The building is long, and they're on the other side. We're good."

"Veep, Veep, is he still isolated?"

"Yes. Still waiting on his order."

The information was coming in fast, forcing a decision on me. Twenty feet was enough time for the ABS to work. He'd be debilitated and running before he could get back to the table.

The easy thing would be to say just keep watching, building a pattern of life for a future interdiction, and that was probably smart. We didn't need to push it here, but we might not get another opportunity like this. We could take him without gunfire and killing, which is what we'd need to do if we hit the bed-down location—provided we could *find* the bed-down. Watching him walk away now might be like Tom Cruise in *Risky Business* waving a finger at Rebecca De Mornay. Getting nothing.

But compromising my team would be exponentially worse. There was definitely a Chinese element here, and attempting an interdiction invited showing our hand. If it went well, we'd be heroes. If it went bad, a second hit would be very hard, because they would know we were on the hunt.

And that was the choice.

I said, "Okay, okay, I have control. We are in Omega. Koko, Koko, are you on the net?"

Jennifer said, "Yes, I'm here."

As a female, she would present less of a threat. I knew she'd have a much better chance of closing on Jake than the knuckle-draggers of my team.

I said, "You put on the ABS, then disappear. Veep, you're security. Blood, Knuckles, you got him in the bathroom. You bring him down and take him out. I'm going for the van. I'll be out the side door for exfil. Acknowledge."

Jennifer said, "Moving now."

She heard Knuckles say, "We're set. He comes in here, and we'll get him out."

She entered the room and saw the target at the counter. She went next to him and raised her hand for the bartender. With her other, she removed what looked like a tube of ChapStick. The bartender asked her what she wanted, and she turned to the target, saying, "What did you get?"

He faced her, and for the first time, she had a clear view

of the person next to him. It was the man from the zoo. The one with the scar. His eyes widened in recognition and Jennifer sprang forward, slashing his face with the chemical from the tube. The bartender looked on in confusion, and the man turned back into the room, shouting something in Chinese.

Jennifer backpedaled to the far side of the bar, watching. The man shouted again, and then bent over, falling to his knees. He jumped up, grabbed his abdomen, let out a burst of flatulence, then began running toward the toilets.

She left the room, exiting the pub out the front door, walking fast to the side of the building, where she knew Pike was staging. She heard Veep come on the net, his voice incredulous. "Koko hit the wrong guy. I say again, Koko hit the wrong guy. He's headed to the bathroom."

Pike came back, saying, "What was that?"

"She hit the wrong guy. The target is running. The table is up."

Knuckles said, "What do I do?"

Pike came back. "Just watch him for a second. See what he does. Veep, Veep, what am I looking at?"

"They're leaving in a hurry. Throwing money on the table and about to run."

Pike said, "Going to the bathroom?"

"No. They look like they want to get the hell out of here."

"What happened?"

"No idea."

Jennifer said, "This is Koko. The guy with him was the one from the zoo. He recognized me. It was game time. I had to commit."

She heard back, "So I'm right. This is the anthill. Knuckles, status?"

Jennifer smiled. Instead of chastising her, he had come up with the sole reason why it mattered. Only Pike would find a silver lining from what she had just done.

"Nothing. He's shitting his pants in the toilet. Want me to interdict?"

Jennifer rounded the side of the building, saw the van, then Pike waving her forward. She heard him on the net say, "No. Let him go. Wait, can you get that Copperhead on him without him knowing?"

"Yeah, I think so, if we act like we're giving him medical attention."

"Do so, then exfil to the van. Veep and I will shadow the exit of the main group."

Knuckles said, "Roger that. I don't think I've ever seen so much work put into a beacon emplacement."

Jennifer reached the van and heard Veep say, "They're leaving now."

Pike leapt out, saying, "You really turned this operation into a shit sandwich."

She said, "Pike, it was either that or a knife. He *recognized* me."

Pike grinned and said, "I wasn't being mean. I just meant you literally turned this operation into a pile of shit."

He raced toward the front of the building to interdict the party just as Brett and Knuckles exited the side door. She got into the driver's seat while they spilled into the back.

Knuckles said, "Boy, you really turned this operation into a pile of shit."

Brett laughed, and Jennifer said, "Old joke. Where's Veep?"

"He linked up with Pike. What do you mean, 'old joke'? That was classic."

She put the van in drive, turned around, and spit out,

"Pike's already used it. So let it go. I don't want to hear about it ever again."

Brett said, "Whoa. Calm down. You're scaring the shit out of me."

She shook her head while they snickered, knowing the team would be telling jokes like this for a decade, then heard Pike come back, calm as the water on a lake, belying the damage.

"They're in line for the Sky Train. I can't do anything. They're gone."

# 60

Chen Ju-Long pushed Jake into the cable car, saying nothing. He waited until the door had closed and the car began rising into the air before saying, "What the hell was that?"

Jake said, "I have no idea! I didn't do that. You're the one who panicked."

Chen glanced at Zhi.

The car rose over the rainforest, going higher and higher, and Zhi pulled off her ceramic nail sleeve. She waved the finger in the air, then lightly touched his cheek, a razor against meat, drawing blood.

He recoiled into one of the other men and said, "I have no idea! That wasn't me!"

Chen said, "You'd better hope the data in this hard drive is worth your life."

He became obsequious, saying, "It is, it is. At least I think it is. I didn't create it! All I did was steal it."

Chen leaned back, watching the jungle fall away, and said, "How did they find us? Who have you contacted?"

Jake said, "Nobody! I don't know anybody here. I have no idea how they found us. In fact, I'm not sure they even did. You raced out of the place because your partner had a bowel movement."

Zhi snapped to him, putting the nail against his carotid artery. "He shouted that the woman there was the one that killed our men at the zoo. The ones sent to protect you and your information. You're lucky to be alive."

Jake slammed his head against the glass to get away from her nail blade, feeling the threat. Panting, he said, "How would I know what he said? He was shouting in Chinese. I'm not Chinese! I keep telling you guys that."

She raked his neck and he recoiled farther. She said, "You are Chinese now."

Jake looked at the other two men in the cabin for support. They stared back with dead eyes.

Chen saw the terror mounting in him and said, "Enough."

Zhi straightened up and Jake exhaled. Chen said, "Somehow they found us. Jake, stand up."

He did so, nervously flicking glances between the two of them.

Chen said, "Take off your clothes."

"What?"

Chen grew angry. "Take off your clothes! Now."

Jake glanced at the other two men, then at Zhi. He saw nothing but contempt. He began to slowly undress. When he was naked, wearing only his underwear, Chen said, "Search it."

The two other men went through the clothes, finding nothing.

Jake said, "It's not me. I've followed all of your instructions. It's not me."

Chen leaned back, thinking. He said, "I believe you're telling the truth, but they found us some way."

He pulled out his phone and stared at it for a moment, remembering how he had wanted to trap the man called Pike, using Clifford Delmonty's phone. He needed this handset as a conduit to his control, as it was built with Chinese encryption embedded. If he destroyed it, he would be reduced to talking in the clear, making mission decisions very difficult. But he understood, even given the technological advantages of encryption, it still used the cell network. Meaning it could be tracked.

He didn't know if it had been, but he had to suspect. Like a cruise ship on quarantine, the only way to stamp out the threat was to eliminate the chance of infection, good or bad.

He made his decision. "Everyone destroy your phones. Rip them apart to the microchip level."

Zhi said, "What?"

"They're tracking us somehow, and it might be through our phones."

She nodded and the gondola burst into a flurry of activity, everyone in it smashing their cell phones while Jake sat in his underwear, scared for his life.

The cable car continued on its path, all of them tossing the pieces of their phones out into the jungle.

Chen said, "Your hard drive. Can we be traced by that?"

Sitting in his tighty-whiteys, Jake said, "No. No way. It just holds data. There is nothing in that that transmits. Nothing. It's just a hard drive. Until it's plugged into a computer, it's nothing more than dead silicon."

Zhi said, "We can't toss that out the window. It's the whole mission."

Chen rubbed his face. "They found us somehow."

Zhi said, "It had to be the phones. They always leave a trail."

He nodded. "I hope you're right."

She said, "And you have one more phone. Not the operational one."

Incensed, he said, "What are you talking about?"

"Your child's phone. The emergency one. The one she uses to contact you. You should get rid of it as well."

He said, "I don't have another phone."

"Yes you do. I've seen it. You call every two days on it. You've left a trail because of it."

Growing angry, he said, "I don't need you looking at me twenty-four/seven. I use that phone to call my daughter. That's all it is. It isn't tainted by anything that's happened over here. There is no way they could find that handset."

She leaned back, saying, "If you want to believe that."

He thought about it, then pulled out the second phone, smashing it with his heel.

# 61

Paul leaned back from the computer screen, incredulous. There was no way the target he'd been tracking was this man. *No way*.

Since he'd lost any ability to leverage NSB assets, he'd gone his own way, using whatever means he had. He'd followed Fly Boy for days, taking picture after picture, and then had uploaded them into Google, doing a reverse image search.

He'd come up with nothing. Well, he'd come up with a slew of other possible identities, from a bit actor in a Korean soap opera to a millennial YouTube star. But nothing that was realistic.

He'd decided to track the man to his command, at least narrowing down his assigned unit. As a full colonel, it shouldn't have been too hard. He had to have a home base, which meant he'd have to at least check in once in a while. But Paul failed in that as well.

The man never reported to a regular unit. He spent all of his time working inside other government agencies, like the Mainland Affairs Council where Paul had first seen him. When he interacted with the military it was always some different unit, and he conducted strange interactions. He didn't appear to have any formal unit at all, but whenever he showed up, he was well known and treated like a DV—a distinguished visitor.

Like most of the men his age who had been conscripted in their youth, Paul was well versed in the military, and Fly Boy's ability to interface both with civilian government and disparate military units was an enigma. Especially since he couldn't put a name to the face.

Paul still wanted to believe the colonel wasn't a traitor, wanted to have faith in the uniform the man wore. But he'd had one final encounter with Fly Boy's outside protection, cementing the fact that the man was working something subversive.

Yesterday he'd followed Fly Boy to the high-speed rail terminal in Taipei, dressed yet again out of uniform, wearing khaki pants and a linen shirt. He'd watched him buy a ticket for a train headed south to Tainan, and Paul had followed, wondering what this trip was about.

The oldest inhabited spot in Taiwan, Tainan had been the original seat of government for centuries. Ruled at one time or another by the Chinese, Dutch, and Japanese, it was an eclectic city that melded the old with the new, and didn't have anything that should've interested Fly Boy. Well, there *was* one thing.

Tainan Air Force Base was located in the city, and as the country's southernmost military outpost—and thus the closest one to mainland China—it was home to the headquarters of the country's entire coastal defense, as well as the first base designated to house the new F-35 fighter jets.

Paul was sure that was Fly Boy's destination, but after the train arrived, he didn't travel there.

He'd exited the terminal and then taken a cab to Anping, the oldest section of the city. Set on the outskirts of town, right on the coast, with salt marshes running up to the original merchant ports, it had been the first area the sea traders used. Now it consisted of parks and markets, but as far as Paul knew, it should contain little of interest for Fly Boy—although Paul would be the first to admit that he was by no means an expert on the town.

The last time Paul had traveled to Tainan had been as a child. His grandfather had worked in the salt pits of the town during the Japanese occupation, and after he passed away, his mother had taken him there on a nostalgic journey that had ended with her embittered. Instead of fondly showing Paul his heritage, she had grown surly over memories Paul didn't understand, eventually cutting the visit short and returning to Taipei.

Since then, he had never been back, and the city had never been in his portfolio during his time in the NSB, leaving a glaring gap in his knowledge of the area. He was acutely aware of his inexperience, making his surveillance that much harder because he couldn't make any educated predictions on Fly Boy's movements. Complicating his efforts was the fact that he was a lone man. Had he wanted to surveil Fly Boy while still an active agent, he would have demanded a team of at least twenty.

Paul saw the brake lights of the target cab flash, then the target exit the vehicle on the outskirts of an open sports field. Paul had his driver do the same, getting out about fifty meters behind Fly Boy. He tracked the man down a pedestrian road clogged with people, eventually seeing him pass through a gate in a high brick wall, a large two-story whitewashed building behind it.

Paul approached the gate and saw a placard describing the original merchant house for Tait and Company, apparently the first international corporation allowed to operate in Taiwan. Just inside was a ticket booth with a small line of people, including Fly Boy.

Paul entered behind him. Fly Boy bought his ticket and left, following the signs for a self-guided tour. Paul fidgeted behind a family of four, wanting them to hurry the hell up. When they were finished, he hastily approached the counter and said, "One adult, please."

He glanced over his shoulder, seeing Fly Boy climb the steps to the second level. The counter clerk said, "The merchant house museum alone, or the museum and the Anping Tree House?"

Paul turned back, saying, "What's the tree house?"

Amazed, the ticket seller said, "Seriously? You haven't heard about the tree house?"

Not wanting to be remembered as someone who had traveled to the site without even knowing what it was, and unclear what Fly Boy was planning, he said, "Sorry, I misheard you. A ticket for both."

He paid and raced to the stairwell in the front of the building, taking the steps two at a time and passing the family in front of him. He entered a foyer detailing the history of the land around Anping. He ignored the displays, looking for Fly Boy. Following the arrows, he weaved through room after room, until eventually he'd descended to the first level and cleared the entire building. He found himself outside on a brick walkway, debating what to do.

Fly Boy hadn't been inside, at least not in the public areas. Paul considered retracing his steps more slowly, possibly entering the roped-off rooms and exploring the building more fully. Instead, he followed the signs for the tree house, walking to the rear of the building. He saw the limbs of an enormous banyan tree behind a ten-foot brick wall. He went through a gate, expecting to find some type of house high up in the branches. What he found instead was the opposite: an old brick warehouse that the tree had completely taken over, the banyan roots and limbs clinging to the brick like the hand of God had dripped wax all over the building.

The roof was gone, replaced by steel walkways that threaded through the branches to allow viewing of the rooms below, leaving him the choice of going up to the walkways or staying at ground level.

He entered the first room and caught a glimpse of Fly Boy through the broken brick in an adjacent chamber, ostensibly taking pictures of the tree's hostile takeover with his phone. Paul glanced up, seeing the walkway circle above Fly Boy's room, and rapidly exited, retracing his path to the steel stairway.

He reached the top of the stairwell, passing two men with buzz-cut hair, long on the top but shaved on the sides. Fixated on finding the overlook above Fly Boy, he failed to notice the interest they had in him.

He crossed over the open roof, the crumbling walls of the separate rooms seemingly being devoured by the tree. He reached a split at the corner of the building, the walkway heading left and right, the steel railing threading through the branches in a circle above the entire structure. He went right, finding a vantage point that allowed him to see down inside the room he'd marked earlier.

Fly Boy wasn't there.

He felt a tendril of panic, then saw the flash of Fly Boy's shirt through the branches, one room over. He let a couple pass, then crept along the walkway. He reached another vantage point and leaned over the rail, pretending as if he cared about the view. To the left and higher up in the scaffolding he saw one of the crew-cut men doing the same thing. Paul noticed the man was alone—something that stood out in a tourist attraction full of families. And he realized *he* stood out as well.

Something for him to keep in mind as a singleton on surveillance. He failed to realize the very point his subconscious was telling him, instead focusing on his own heat state.

He found Fly Boy and saw him walk to a darkened corner of the room, roots intertwined with brick. Fly Boy glanced left and right, then stepped over a rope line meant to prevent patrons from going deeper into the tree structure. He knelt down, reached his hand behind one of the giant banyan roots, and withdrew a package.

And Paul knew why he was here. *It's a dead drop.*

Fly Boy quickly crossed over the rope back to the path, then opened what looked like a large envelope. Paul watched him pull out an old-school flip phone and some sort of badge on a lanyard. Fly Boy shoved the items into the envelope and left the room, heading toward the entrance. Paul began following above him on the walkway, wanting to wait until he had exited the building before he descended the stairs. He caught someone out of the corner of his eye and looked up, seeing one of the buzz-cut men to his front, his eyes hard. He reversed and saw the other one behind him.

The first one said, "What is your interest here?"

Paul said, "Just sightseeing."

The man behind him closed the distance and said, "I think not."

The man to the front said, "Who do you work for?"

There was no way to get by them. With one to the front and one behind, he couldn't even keep his eyes on both of them at the same time. He did the only thing he could: He jumped over the railing into the branches of the banyan tree.

He snatched a limb with his hand and felt his shoulder wrench. He screamed, let go, and slammed into another limb on his rib cage, flipping upside down. He hammered the ground on his side, the wind knocked out of him.

He lay there for a moment in pain, gasping for air. He vaguely heard tourists shouting, then footsteps. A man knelt over him, saying, "Hey, are you all right?" He put a hand on Paul's shoulder, turned and shouted, "Someone get a doctor!"

Paul looked above him and saw the two buzz-cut men racing down the walkway toward the stairs.

He rolled over, groaned, and the tourist helping him said, "Don't move. Stay still."

Paul ignored him, standing up and shaking his head to clear it. He saw the buzz cuts skipping down the stairs, almost at ground level, and he began jogging toward the back of the building, the Good Samaritan shouting at him.

He exited onto an expanse of grass and ran up a bridge spanning a large canal leading to a viewing deck on a dyke. He darted across it, a hand on his injured ribs, seeing the two men break out of the building. He reached the far side, jumped over the railing, and rolled into the grass. He sprang upright and took off down the dyke on the opposite side of the canal, holding his side and wheezing in pain with every breath.

He glanced behind him and saw the two men looking over the railing, but making no attempt to follow him.

# 62

Reliving the events in his small apartment, feeling the uninvited adrenaline pulse, Paul cleared his mind of the fear and turned back to his computer, staring at the man on the screen. He still couldn't believe it. Once he had the name, it had been nothing to glean Fly Boy's entire biography through open source information, but he wanted to make sure the facial recognition was correct.

Paul ran the algorithm again, using a different picture, and the program spit out the same answer.

After the actions in Tainan yesterday, Paul had given up on physical surveillance. He had no idea who the men were that attacked him, but was fairly sure they weren't with the Triads. They looked too clean-cut. Too professional. Almost like they were working for a government. *Which* government remained to be seen.

The men at the tree house had made no further attempt to stop him, but that fact alone made him paranoid that others were out there, tracking him. He'd given up reacquiring Fly Boy, but the loss of the trace ate at him. Paul knew Fly Boy was in Tainan for something more than a dead drop. If it were just that, why do it so far south? Why not just access one in Taipei? He was sure that after Fly Boy serviced that drop, he'd used the phone and then the badge to do something else, but he'd never had a chance to find out.

Given the circumstances, Paul had fled the city, returning on the train to Taipei, highly alert to anyone showing the slightest bit of attention to him.

By the time he'd made it home the ribs on his right side were on fire, but he'd ignored the pain, returning to the computer energized by an idea he'd had on the ride back.

A standard Google reverse image search might not be any help in identifying Fly Boy, but there were other services that were much more refined. A few months before he'd been cast aside as a Ronin, the NSB had selected Paul to take a presentation from a company called BackRub that had developed a unique facial recognition program. Named Stargrazer, the company had created a webcrawler that scanned all social media platforms, culling images along with associated accounts. Twitter, Facebook, Line, Instagram, and others were all exploited—the vast majority without the owner's knowledge or approval.

At the end of the presentation, Paul had been astounded. Have a picture taken with a friend that *he* posts, and tags you in? You were probably in the Stargrazer database, along with the tag to your social media presence, which Stargrazer then culled for any images *you* posted and tagged, on and on in an endless quest to map everyone.

The second piece was a facial recognition program that could take a picture, compare it to the immense database, and come up with an identification. Because—outside of Amazonian tribes—everyone had a presence on the net, it would find a match. Have a shaky screen grab from a robbery surveillance video? Run it through Stargrazer and you'd end up with the Facebook page of the guy who did it.

At the time, Paul had been a little shaken by the presentation, incredulous of how much information the men had collected.

He'd demurred, thinking the system more resembled the People's Republic of China than it did his home country.

Now the company might prove useful. He'd been given a six-month trial account to test the system, and he'd never used it. He'd dug through his desk for the salesman's business card, which had his NSB login credentials. He'd found it, praying that the company hadn't realized he was no longer an active agent and deactivated his credentials.

He logged on, watched an hourglass spin, expecting to see an error message. Instead, to his surprise, he landed on the homepage for Stargrazer.

He loaded the pictures into the encrypted connection and hit send, waiting. Ten minutes later, he had his answer:

The man was Colonel Rae "Ryan" Won, officer in the Republic of China's Air Force. And not just any officer—he was the liaison between the military and a host of government agencies, which explained his lack of unit affiliation.

An ambitious up-and-coming rocket with an impeccable résumé, he was responsible for the interagency response to any Chinese incursion, to include the early-warning systems along the coast for hostile intent and advising the Mainland Affairs Council on engagement with the PRC during peacetime.

But yet again Paul thought there was no way this man was a spy. There were just too many different background checks involved in such a sensitive position. Won couldn't have passed them all and still remain.

He'd run the facial recognition search again, using pictures he'd gleaned of Fly Boy out of uniform, and the answer came back the same way.

He leaned back in his chair, wondering what he was going to do with the information. On the one hand, he didn't want to destroy a man's career based on some U.S. contractor's algorithm. But on the other hand, the man could represent the greatest penetration of the ROC in history.

He rubbed his face, not liking the choices he had to make after the death of his mentor. Charlie Chan would know what to do with this information. He had the channels and the means to prove it. But now he was gone.

Paul stared at the man on his screen, tapping his fingers on the desk, and his phone went off. A message from a friend on Line, a multiservice mobile application. He pulled up the video, saw a grainy image and a title saying, "The truth is out. Maggie Chou telling what will happen if the president is reelected."

The message was, Have you seen this?

Paul sent back, No. What is it?

You need to listen to it. It's going viral.

He played it, and, like his search for Colonel Won, he couldn't believe it was real. It was the cabinet minister from the Mainland Affairs Council talking about how the administration would prevent a war by reuniting with the mainland through economic efforts, working under the radar until such moves would be irreversible.

The current administration had been elected precisely because they were hard-liners on the PRC, flirting with outright declarations of independence and relentlessly supporting the protesters in Hong Kong. The incumbent president's main opposition was touting the exact opposite—growing closer to the PRC for the sake of economic stability.

*Why would the MAC ever consider such a thing?*

He heard shouting outside his window and saw young people in the street, yelling and chanting. He opened the window, grabbed a pair of binoculars, and focused on the crowd. He saw what appeared to be mainly students whipped up into a frenzy, but zooming in, he also saw marchers with tattoos marking them as members of the Bamboo Triad.

He thought one thing: *It's the trigger.*

# 63

Colonel Ryan Won saw the same video on Facebook, then on Twitter, followed by Line and other social media. He couldn't believe it. It was *everywhere*. Why had they sent his video out now? His contact in Tainan had told him he still had a mission, and while he didn't know yet exactly what that was, he knew it involved Taiwan's early-warning systems, and this most certainly would put him on the clock for survival. He wouldn't be able to accomplish his mission if his superiors suspected him.

He had a debilitating thought: *Maybe they're just playing me, wanting to give me confidence in their support. Wanting me to remain like a dog on a leash, waiting on a master that is never coming home.*

It wouldn't be the first time they'd tricked him. They'd done that the minute they sank their claws into him when he was a junior officer in pilot training.

Right after he'd been commissioned, he'd traveled to the United States on an exchange program and found himself living hand to mouth. His stipend didn't pay enough to even go to IHOP for pancakes, he had no friends in the course, and he felt like a stranger in a strange land, growing more and more lonely. He'd hated it.

His father was a general in the ROC Ministry of National Defense and had no time to coddle a boy who couldn't even survive a supposedly cushy exchange to America. There was no love lost between the two, and the PRC had picked up on the schism.

Brazenly, they'd approached him on U.S. soil. Very subtle at first, they just appeared as expat Taiwanese making connections in the United States. Only they weren't from Taiwan, as he would learn later.

He'd become friends, and in the "friendship" had given them some innocuous information about routine traffic patterns on the U.S. base. In return, they gave him the noose, blackmailing him with the bit of information he'd provided.

He'd returned home to a father who was less than impressed with his scores in the aviator course, and the hatred had simmered. His father talked all the time about how great the ROC was against the PRC, bragging about the sacrifice and demeaning Ryan and others of his age, and before Ryan knew it, he was providing information not because he had to, but because he wanted to. It was a way to prove he was better than his father.

Despite what his father constantly told him, he was in fact gifted, and he'd risen higher and higher in the ranks until he was the deepest asset the PRC had ever placed.

He watched the video one more time and thought, *Surely they wouldn't throw that away now, would they?*

He thought about running, but knew he'd have to activate his emergency extraction plan, and given the stakes, he didn't trust that mechanism at all right now. They might throw him to the wolves, his usefulness gone. The last place he needed to run was back into their arms.

*Maybe it is because of the man in Tainan.*

He'd received his forged access badge to the Ministry of National Defense's experimental artificial intelligence unit, run by the National Chung-Shan Institute of Science and Technology—the Taiwanese version of the United States' DARPA—but had been told he might have been followed, and to be very careful.

He had no idea if it was true, but the NCIST operations were some of the most sensitive in the entire military, and maybe he wasn't as highly placed as he thought. Maybe his compromise would mean the downfall of someone else.

Either way, the release of the video most certainly meant his downfall. The only question was time, and—given his placement and access—he'd at least earned some answers.

He pulled out the flip phone he'd been given and hit a speed dial number. The phone rang, finally going to voice mail for a restaurant telling him the hours. When he heard the beep, he said, "This is Ocelot. Call back."

He hung up, and before he could set the phone down, it rang again. He answered, saying, "Ocelot."

"This is Lion. Why are you calling?"

"Why did you release the video? I'm done here!"

He heard Lion's voice grow hard. "Calm down. We are executing a strategy. I had hoped to have the next phase in operation, but the timing couldn't be helped. The People's Liberation Army and Navy exercises in the strait are starting now, and they only last a week. I needed to set things in motion."

"What next phase? I want out, now."

"You aren't coming out yet. The next phase is coming. Did you get the access badges and make the introductions?"

"I got the badge, and yes, I met the man from NCIST at the airbase, but I was told to only spend minimal time there. I didn't get a full briefing."

"What? What do you mean?"

He said, "I thought you'd been told," and relayed what had happened at the tree house.

Lion said, "That is concerning. Who was the man?"

"I have no idea! Talk to the men who set up the drop. I didn't even see him. I thought it had gone fine. In fact, I wondered if you weren't setting me up with this badge and then the video."

Ryan heard nothing for a few seconds. He said, "You still there?"

Lion said, "Look, watch your back. I'll do what I can to protect you, but you're going to use that badge. We have a suite of software to install at the Tainan location."

"Software? How am I going to do that? I'm not a scientist."

"I'm bringing a man. He'll have it."

*What?*

This was getting out of control. He knew the location of the project on the airbase, and knew that it was being activated, but nothing more than that.

He said, "A man? You're smuggling a man into Taiwan, and you want me to escort him into the NCIST experiment in Tainan?"

"Yes. They're using that unit for a test with our exercises. Using the artificial intelligence to test reaction times for their counterstrike missile command when we start flying around and maneuvering forces. Correct?"

"Yeah, that's happening, but what does this man have to do with that? It's just a test."

"Trust me, it has everything to do with it. You continue what you're doing. I'll bring the man."

# 64

I crept up the iron rungs of the ladder, third man in the stack, watching Knuckles on the platform above me test the doorknob. He peered over the edge and shook his head, looking eerie in the green glow of my night vision goggles.

*Shit.* It wasn't a surprise, but I'd honestly hoped they'd have left the door unlocked. It would have made things infinitely easier.

I twisted my hand in the air like I was turning a lock, meaning, *Bolt lock?*

He shook his head again, telling me it was just the knob. A much easier task. That was a break on our side, because we needed to enter this house silently. With someone living on the floor below, I couldn't start the assault by smashing the doorknob with a Bam-Bam. This wasn't a hostage rescue—no innocent was in danger of dying inside by a lack of speed or violence. It was an extraction, and because of the threat of compromise from the couple renting the bottom floor, I wanted to maintain low visibility throughout. If we could find Jake Shu—or Pirate, as we called him now—I hoped to extract him quietly, without a gunfight like we'd done for Nicole.

Silence was the name of the game.

We knew from the reconnaissance earlier that there were two exits from the upper level, the one we were on—a fire-escape type ladder at the back of the building, and a nice wooden stairwell on the right side, but that one had an infrared camera above the doorjamb. As it had been hard enough to find this place, I wasn't going to compound the problems by assaulting up the stairwell in full view of the men inside.

After all of the high adventure in Kuranda, the only thing that had panned out was the emplacement of the Copperhead. Apparently our capture attempt in the pub had proven out my worst-case prediction—they had gotten away, and they now knew they were being hunted. Chen had turned off his "daughter phone" because, I was sure, he knew somehow we had tracked it. Which wasn't a pleasant thought, because any investigation would inevitably lead back to his daughter—and her roommate, Amena.

The only good news was the Copperhead beacon. Shitpants, as we called him now, had spent about thirty minutes in the toilet evacuating his bowels, then cleaning the mess he'd made. Eventually he'd left the pub, looking green and holding his stomach. As he was our only anchor, we'd followed. He'd loaded a car in the parking lot and had headed back to Cairns, giving us real-time geolocation as he moved. We gave him a little space on the road, then began tracking the beacon, leading us to this target house.

Once we'd pinpointed, we'd pulled back to our hotel to plan a bit, and then Jennifer and I had taken the lead, conducting a close target reconnaissance for assault, and I hadn't really liked what we'd found.

On a street corner, with a canal to the north protecting any approach from that direction, it was surrounded by a low concrete wall with an iron grate fence built into it, and had the appearance of a Dr. Seuss construction, with outside stairwells and ladders leading up to the second floor, foliage all over the place, and what looked like an underground garage or basement area. All in all, not a great target for a five-man team, and unlike the house in Manly, we weren't getting the golden egg here.

Jennifer and I had staged for a while in the parking lot of a school across the main north-south road, getting atmospherics of the neighborhood, and had been unpleasantly surprised to learn that the bottom floor was rented by a couple not associated with our target, which made things exponentially harder.

We'd returned to the hotel and I'd given the team the bad news: Our ability to smash through the place like rampaging bulls had been taken from us. Because of the risk of compromise from the lower-level renters, it was to be a clandestine entry and low-visibility operation. Which exponentially raised the risks for the team.

We'd decided to conduct the assault an hour before dawn, when hopefully everyone was bagged out, both upstairs and downstairs. I'd split the team into an entry force and a containment force. A three-man team of me, Knuckles, and Brett would breach through the rickety fire-escape ladder, while Jennifer and Veep would lock down the wooden stairwell on the other side. Jennifer and Veep would have suppressed long guns. The assault element would have the same slung over their backs, but the work would be done by Ruger MK III .22 caliber pistols. With a suppressor and subsonic ammunition, it was as quiet as I could get.

The intent was to invade like a virus, attacking each room while the other had no idea we were there. Once we got jackpot on Pirate, we'd make a determination on whether to continue the assault or exfil.

I clicked on the net, whispering, "Koko, Veep, we are at breach. About to make entry. Are you set?"

Jennifer, as the senior Operator, came back, "This is Koko. We're set. It's all quiet here. No pets."

My biggest fear in hiding them inside the jungle the owner of the rental called landscaping was the next-door neighbor having a dog. A pet going bananas would have been an abort.

"Roger that. Knuckles, you're cleared to breach."

I heard two clicks in my earpiece, a pause of about thirty seconds, then a whispered, "Breach, breach, breach." Brett began to scramble higher and I followed, cresting the platform and seeing both of them crouching inside a darkened hallway with faint light spilling out from the end, Knuckles with his weapon aimed at a doorknob.

I tucked in tight behind Brett and squeezed his shoulder. He reached forward, doing the same to Knuckles, and Knuckles swung open the door, racing inside as quietly as he could, Brett and I following.

It was a bedroom, but it was empty.

We stacked back on the door, getting set, then completed the squeezes again, flowing silently back into the hallway.

In a traditional assault, speed was of the essence, because once the explosive breach went off, everyone knew you were coming. Here, it was silence. The longer we could maintain our invisibility, the better.

We advanced slowly down the hall, the light becoming brighter, and Knuckles stopped at another door, this one on the right side of the hallway. He held up his finger, and we paused.

He pointed to his ear, then down the hallway, and I stopped breathing, focusing. I heard faint voices in the room beyond the hallway, the one with the light.

Someone was awake.

Knuckles looked back at me, and I motioned to breach the door. He turned the knob, swung it wide, and we flowed in, finding a man in bed. It was Shitpants. He heard us enter and snapped upright, snaking his hand under a pillow. Knuckles put two suppressed rounds into his head, the noise no greater than a cough. He fell back onto the bed and I kept a barrel on him while they cleared the rest of the room, Knuckles going to a closet and Veep into a bathroom. They came back out, and I pointed to the door.

Seated at the kitchen table, drinking coffee, Chen watched Jake trying to remain inconspicuous between him and Zhi. It was a losing battle.

Chen ignored him, saying to the others at the table, "Are we set with the boat?"

The man known as Bear said, "Yes. Your tickets aren't until tomorrow, but he'll take you today."

"What about the dive platform? Are they expecting us early?"

"I don't know. The boat driver seemed like doing this type of thing was habitual. People change their minds every day. Money talks."

Chen nodded and said, "You'll close out the accounts here. Call me when it's complete and you're safely leaving the country."

Bear laughed and said, "How am I going to do that? You made us destroy all of our phones."

"Buy new phones. Use the corporate account, not the personal ones you have from the MSS." Cheng pulled a card from his pocket and wrote something on the back, saying,

"This is where we're going to be in Taiwan. Meet me at that time."

Bear took the card, looked at it, then said, "You're inside this place? How?"

Chen smiled and said, "I'm an import/export powerhouse. I need to project such an image, and this location did so."

Bear chuckled and said, "I would love to have a cover such as yours. Living a life of luxury instead of houses like this."

Chen smiled and said, "Every effort is for the same goal."

Bear nodded, tapped his finger, then said, "How were we compromised? How did that happen? It wasn't me or my team. I know that. It had to be your man with the stomach pains. He came late, and I think he brought the team with him."

Chen shook his head and said, "He served me well in Sydney. He was on the team that eliminated the leak. He got away clean. It's not him."

"Then who? It had to be something. They found you in Sydney, and then they found *us* here. We had no contact in Sydney. None. How would they find us here? There is only one way, and it's on your team."

Zhi leaned forward and said, "Watch your tongue."

He held up his hands. "I'm just asking. For the mission." He pointed at Jake and said, "This piece of shit has cost the life of several men. Is he worth it?"

Jake realized they were talking about him but had no idea what they were saying. From the dismissive tone, he knew it wasn't good, giving him an unsettling fear. He had once been a promising software engineer who dabbled in foreign intrigue, selling secrets as a side job. Now he was nothing more than an American traitor, held in disdain by the very people he was serving, possibly to be killed by them.

It was a hard truth.

Chen glanced at him and said, "Only he will determine his worth. Maybe he will, maybe he won't. But I promise, if he doesn't, he'll be in the ground just like the men we lost."

Jake shrank back at Chen's gaze and Zhi stood up, saying, "Let's go. It's a fifteen-minute walk to the car, and that boat isn't waiting."

Chen stood as well, picking up his duffle.

He turned to Bear and said, "Don't mess around here. Get out. The men who are hunting us are good. Better than we've ever faced. Anyone that can track us like they did are worthy opponents."

Bear grinned. "I have no fear of them. You leave, and there is no threat. They aren't tracking me."

Chen's face hardened at the flippant attitude. He leaned over Bear, saying, "They have killed better men than you. Do *not* underestimate them."

The humor of Bear's statement evaporated like a breath in cold air. He nodded, asking, "What about your man down the hall? I'll take my team and vanish, but what about him?"

"Let him recover, and then send him on his way. I don't know what they gave him, but it wasn't deadly. He knows what to do."

Chen turned to Jake and, in English, said, "Let's go."

Jake shouldered his small duffle bag, glancing between the two of them. He said, "Where are we going?"

"Taiwan."

# 65

Knuckles crouched by the open door, staring hard down the hallway. He turned back to me and whispered, "I can see a kitchen island, but I can't see who's talking. The room opens up, but they're unsighted."

I said, "What's your take on how many?"

"With the picture from the pub, and Shitpants out of play, probably four, not including Pirate."

Four men. Not good odds given we'd cleared all the bedrooms behind us. They had to all be in the room, wide awake. With the element of surprise, we could probably drop them all, but not without a gunfight that would alert the renters below us. If they got off even one round, it would sound like an explosion in the house. And that was *if* all four were in the room, and not hiding somewhere else in an area we couldn't see.

I made the hard call. "It's an abort."

Brett flicked his head into the room with the body and said, "What about Shitpants? We're compromised either way now."

I said, "I know. Can't be helped. I'd rather be compromised clandestinely by the Chinese than the Australian authorities arresting us."

I took a knee near the doorjamb, seeing the light outside

and hearing the voices. I raised my barrel, picking up security and saying, "Search the room."

Knuckles pulled his barrel away. "Okay. Man, this sucks. Such a clean entry."

I said, "I know. Trust me, I know."

And then Jennifer came on the net, saying, "Pike, this is Koko. Front door just opened. Pirate is with two others, a man and a woman. They're headed out."

We heard the call and froze. I said, "Koko, this is Pike. We're committed inside. Can you interdict?"

I heard hesitation in her voice. "I can . . . but I can't subdue. I'll have to drop both of them to secure Pirate."

I looked at Knuckles, wanting some miracle to come out of his mouth, but he just shook his head, knowing there was no Hollywood ending here.

I said, "Drop them. We take Pirate and get the fuck out."

Jennifer heard the command clearly, but thought it was unwise. She said, "This is Koko. You want me to kill them in the yard?"

"Yes. We're going to clean up in here. We'll get out on foot. You take Pirate and exfil him with the van."

She looked up at the landing, seeing the taller man talking to another inside the door, the woman looking out as if searching for something.

"Pike, we're going to leave a couple of bodies on the ground next to the lower renters. Are you sure?"

She heard, "We're leaving bodies up here as well. Get it done, and we're on the Rock Star bird out of here with Pirate."

She said, "Roger all," then looked toward Veep, buried in

the foliage ten feet away, whispering off the net, "You get that?"

He shifted, allowing her to see where he was in the darkness. He whispered, "Got it. Targets?"

She couldn't see his face in the dark, but knew he was feeling the same adrenaline she was. She said, "I'll take the woman. You take the man. Let them get down the stairs. We hit them at the base, and then assault to Pirate. Roger?"

She saw him rise up, taking a sitting position in the bushes to allow him a sight picture, raising his rifle and resting his arms on his thighs, the elbows sinking into the flesh. He said, "Roger all. Your call for the send."

She did the same thing, seating her rifle into her shoulder, her legs crossed Indian style, her elbows on her thighs to give her a view through the bushes. She reached up and adjusted the throw lever of the scope, necking it down to two-power, then settled, her illuminated reticle centered on the woman's chest.

She whispered, "Veep, I have control. I'll take the first shot."

He came back, so low she barely heard it, "Roger all. Second target is acquired."

She watched them come down the stairs, waiting for them to reach the bottom, banishing from her mind that she was about to take a life. Controlling her respiration, she got into a rhythm, watching the reticle bounce slightly with each breath.

She watched the three of them descend, the woman in front, the two men behind. When the woman hit the third step from the bottom she whispered, "Stand by. Stand by."

Then she took up the slack on her trigger.

# 66

Jake waited for Chen to finish talking to the man called Bear, and the deadly woman took the delay to put her arm through his. Scaring the hell out of him.

She'd been doing it as a lark, but he knew it was also a threat. In fact, it was the ultimate threat. Disobey them and reap the results. He realized his life was no longer his own.

When Chen had said he was included in the delivery of the data he'd stolen, he'd thought it would be somewhere in Australia, believing he was going to instruct some Chinese computer geek on a laptop. He had no idea that he'd be literally flying out of the country. When Chen had mentioned Taiwan, it was one more stone emplaced in his growing conviction that he was a dead man. He regretted ever talking to the Chinese students on his college campus so long ago.

Jake was an intelligent man, and inherently understood that Chen and Zhi didn't care one whit about whether he lived or died. Helping the Chinese for a little bit of cash was one thing. Flying with them to a country he'd never even googled was something else. He needed to break free.

He knew if he went to Taiwan, he would be dead.

Chen finished talking to Bear and they began the walk down the stairs, each step sealing Jake's fate. He began sucking in oxygen in a pant, the panic reaching a crescendo.

The woman turned to him, saw the sweat on his brow and the shallow breathing, and said, "Don't worry, dear. We're not really going to dive with the great whites. It's just a boat trip to get you to safety."

The mention of the sharks only amped up his fear, to the point he felt like a cotton ball was surrounding his head, the sounds dampened from the outside as his ears began to ring.

They reached the bottom of the stairs, and Chen said, "We're going to walk to the car on the jogging path across the canal. If you see someone, remember to act natural."

He nodded, feeling like he was going to vomit. His face crossed into the light of a bulb above the stairwell and Chen said, "Are you okay?"

Zhi turned around at the words, and the pent-up fear Jake felt exploded out. He gave a banshee scream, throwing himself on top of Zhi and knocking her to the ground. They rolled in the grass and he leapt up, diving into the bushes, then running as fast as he could out of the yard to the canal. He heard a shout behind him but didn't dare look back.

He found the footbridge and was running like his life depended on reaching the far side.

Because it did.

He heard nothing but his feet slapping concrete, then a shout behind him. Soon, he heard their footsteps echoing off the concrete as well, gaining on him. He tried to increase his pace, his lungs burning in protest. Carrying forty pounds of hamburgers and donuts from a sedentary life, he began to weep, begging whatever gods existed to let him make it.

He was almost to the far side when he glanced back, and saw Zhi right behind him, closing fast. He shouted in fear and jumped over the railing into the canal, desperately trying to get clear. He landed in the marsh of the bank and began thrashing through the bushes, trying to hide in the dark, his noise doing nothing to help him.

She followed, launching herself over the railing and slamming into the muck right behind him. She stalked through the reeds like a jungle cat. He started to scramble up the bank, and she grabbed his leg, jerking him back down to the water. Frozen in fear, lying on his back, he held his hands in front of his face and said, "Don't! Please don't."

She slammed his head into the dirt, her eyes flashing in insane anger. She put her wicked nail on his neck and he heard, "Zhi!"

He looked up and saw Chen at the end of the bridge. Zhi hissed, then traced the nail on his cheek, drawing blood. She said, "You are lucky. The car is just up the hill. Next time I will kill you. And not quickly."

He nodded and she stood, saying, "Get up."

He did so, and then saw her eyes again, radiating a bloodlust. She *wanted* to kill him, for no other reason than that it would be fun.

Chen saw it as well, saying, "Get him up here. No more damage. We have a boat to catch."

I heard Jennifer's calls as the group descended the stairs. When she said, "I have control," I motioned to Knuckles and Brett, saying, "When they take the shot, we clear the rest of the house."

They nodded and we stacked on the door, waiting on the hit. I heard the call of stand by and raised my weapon, waiting on the shot like a stallion in a stall anticipating the gate.

It never came. Instead I heard a scream, then,

Koko: Jesus Christ! Veep, Veep, I have no shot.

Veep: I have a shot. I have a shot, but not on the female.

Koko: Take it. Take the shot.

I looked at Knuckles, incredulous of what I was hearing. We waited a beat, then heard Veep come on: "They're running. They're running. They're in the street."

Jennifer said, "I'm on them, I'm on them."

Snapping back into team leader mode, not knowing what was happening outside, but knowing for sure I didn't want to split the team into two different operations—especially since we still needed to eliminate the threat in the house to protect them—I clicked on and said, "Stand down. Stand down. We're clearing."

I flicked my head to Knuckles and he flowed out, Brett right behind him. We raced down the hallway, entering a kitchen area and seeing a family room to the left, a man standing next to an open door, looking out at the location of the scream.

He turned, and Brett put four rounds into his chest, the small caliber of the pistol not showing much damage, but he dropped with his eyes wide in shock. I turned into the room, seeing another man leap up, scrambling for something on the couch. I paused, tracked his movement, and squeezed the trigger twice, hitting his head. He flopped onto the floor, his skull cracked open like someone had used a clawhammer.

Knuckles continued on, clearing the final room, a kitchen closet. He came back out, shaking his head. I nodded and said, "Start SSE. We need to get out of here in under five minutes."

They went to work, and I called Jennifer. "Koko, Koko, status?"

"We're good, but the target is gone. We have no jackpot."

"What happened?"

Veep came on, saying, "Pirate freaked out. They reached the bottom of the stairs and he dove on top of the woman, then took off running. He cleared the edge of the yard in about a millisecond with the woman right behind him, and my target jumped to follow."

He paused, then said, "I held my shot."

I knew he was asking if he'd failed. Or owning up to failing, which was stupid, because he hadn't. I said, "No issues with the decision. We didn't need a firefight. Where's Pirate?"

"Pike, this is Koko. I followed to the road. They're across the canal. They're in the wind. I have no idea if Pirate is still on the run or under control."

With Knuckles and Brett still searching, I said, "Koko, Veep, collapse inside. We're leaving out of the back."

They came up the stairs, entered the room, and Veep said, "We really had no chance. When he went nuts—"

I held up my hand. "Stop." I turned to Jennifer and said, "What do you think?"

Veep believed I was looking for a scapegoat. Jennifer knew I was looking for solutions to the problem. He'd learn that eventually, but I didn't have the time to pat him on the back to make him feel good.

Jennifer said, "I honestly don't know. He's obviously hip deep in this, but I'm not sure it's because he wants to be. I tracked him all the way down the stairs, and it looked like he was having a panic attack. I was squeezing the trigger on the woman, and he literally freaked out, diving on her like he was jumping off the stage at a goth concert. He punched her in the head and then took off running like a scalded dog. It didn't even look like he had a destination. He just went nuts."

I nodded and said, "So we have a traitor who may not be a traitor?"

Jennifer thought for a minute, then said, "No. He's a traitor. I think he's a traitor who didn't know what that actually meant. He's scared because of what he has. What they want. That's what I think."

I nodded, saying, "I think you're right. What're the odds they found him?"

"Good. Really good. I'm sure he didn't get away. He was running blind, and they were right behind him. Panic can't compete with skill. They have him."

I nodded and said, "Maybe they'll come back here."

Veep said, "They were leaving for a reason. I don't think they were ever coming back here again. We need to find that location."

I heard the words and said, "I think you're *also* right. For once."

He smiled, taking the backhanded compliment, then said, "I think they were leaving the country."

I said, "How? They won't use the airlines because they know we're right on their ass, and they have to assume we're working with the Aussies as a Five Eyes country, monitoring all egress avenues."

Brett came down the hall, saying, "I have a brochure for a place called Quicksilver. It's a dive platform out on the Great Barrier Reef."

I said, "They're getting him out by boat? That makes no sense. It's like forty days to China."

Jennifer said, "It's a long way to China by boat, but it's a short jump to an airfield outside of Australia. They could go to New Zealand, or Indonesia. All they want to do is cut the tie with Australia because they know we're looking."

I said, "Shit. So we have no idea where to go next?"

Knuckles stood up from the body at the door and said,

"Maybe not." He held up a card and said, "This is an office in Taiwan."

Jennifer took it, then said, "This is a business card for that PLA front company the Taskforce found. Ju-Long Import/Export."

She flipped it over, then said, "It's got a handwritten date and time on here. Two days from now."

# 67

Jerry Tribble pretended to work at his computer station as Yuan Bo paced the floor behind him, berating another man in Chinese. Smartly, Yuan had all of the computer stations in the room against the wall, the screens facing back into the open space, preventing employees from doing something that couldn't be seen.

But Tribble was smart as well.

Upon his hiring, he'd been required to turn in his own laptop and cell phone in exchange for a "corporate" cell phone and laptop, both free of charge as if that was a perk of the job, but Tribble knew beyond a shadow of a doubt they were being tapped and tracked—which actually gave him an advantage. When he wanted to do something in the city outside of their view, he simply left the devices at home.

He took them along often enough to establish a pattern in his neighborhood, visiting places such as a noodle shop and café repeatedly, lulling the Chinese into a false sense of security that caused physical surveillance to cease, with them instead relying on the tracking of the devices.

He'd also been required to turn over his social media accounts passwords as a condition of the contract. The reason stated was that they needed to protect themselves from outside publicity and bad press, but he wasn't stupid. He knew it was another way to track him. He was sure his home desktop computer had become infected with all sorts of malware through his own social media, and they were now watching his every move to determine if he communicated with any unauthorized individuals—something he needed to do with his company.

He could have simply bought a new, stand-alone computer for communications with his home office, but he had no doubt they had thought of that and had his WiFi access tainted, or had even penetrated his apartment and searched it, planting things that would trigger in the event of an unauthorized communication. He couldn't trust the integrity of anything left behind while he was at work. So he'd gone a different route. A Trojan horse route.

The "company" computers in the lab were also monitored, but not with embedded malware. They were surveilled simply as a result of being on the network of the Twelfth Bureau, meaning that each stand-alone system could be manipulated—just like they had done to his own systems.

The Chinese were very good at their job, the entire lab fortified against outside intrusions, but they were naïve about the security from an insider threat. He thought it fitting that he would escape all of their hidden systems simply by using the computer he'd been assigned at his desk.

He'd implanted a very small chat program that piggybacked off of the VPN system the Twelfth Bureau used. He had no doubt that its version of a "virtual private network" was, in fact, not private at all, but the backbone was. They needed him to be able to talk securely to people all over the world, and had built the system for that purpose—as long as they could listen. All he needed to do was use their encryption and then cut them out of the loop.

It hadn't been hard.

He saw an avatar appear on the left side of his screen. A blonde woman wearing a bikini and beckoning him with a finger. He glanced behind once more, saw he was clear, and clicked on the avatar. A chat window appeared at the bottom of his screen.

He typed:

—What's up?

—Did you give access to the PRC for Stargrazer?

He leaned back, wondering why the question had come. He'd been trying to sell the Chinese on the system since he'd been in country. U.S. law enforcement had been a boon, but getting the Chinese on board would set him up for life, given their lack of concern over privacy.

He typed:

—No. Why?

—We just had a search for a guy in Taiwan. From Taiwan. It's an official member of the government. The access was from their version of the FBI. They used a guest trial account. Just wondering.

Guest account? He typed:

—What account?

—The one you gave to the National Security Bureau of Taiwan six months ago. They didn't buy the program, but have now accessed it. We thought it might be some contact of yours from mainland China inside Taiwan.

He read the text, drumming his fingers on the desk,

thinking. Given what he knew now, he believed they might be right, but just on the opposite side of the mirror.

—Why did you think it was the PRC? Instead of an actual member of the NSB?

—One, because the guy they searched is a high-ranking officer in the ROC Air Force. Why would they need to use our systems to find that? They'd already know. Two, it didn't come from their HQ. It was a local IP address in town on a civilian laptop. We thought it was some misdirection from you to the PRC, trying to make a sale.

He typed:

—No. But this might be the sale. Send me the information. Both the target and the login of the man who accessed the website.

—Will do.

Ten seconds later, he had a package on the VPN. He downloaded it onto a thumb drive, then closed out the chat. He turned around, saw Yuan, and waved him over.

Yuan approached and said, "What? Are you done with the second video?"

He said, "Yes, I am, and it's pretty good. Exactly what you wanted."

Yuan became excited. "It's pristine? You can't tell the alteration?"

"It's as good as I can get it. Look, the biggest problem for these things is the actual words or facial expressions inserted. If you create a video of a guy making facial tics he never does, it's easy to call it a fake. In this case, all I could do was insert your language. I don't speak Chinese, so I don't know if the president of Taiwan would have ever uttered the words. I don't know his mannerisms or his habitual verbal tics. If you did, then we're good."

"Let me have it."

"No."

"What?"

"No. I want to give it to the other man. The one paying the bills. It's my contract, and it's my product."

Yuan said, "This is *my* program. I pay your contract."

Tribble looked at him and said, "Not anymore. Not after that last meeting. Get him to the office."

Thirty minutes later, Han Ming came into Yuan's small office, looking aggravated. He said, "Why am I here? Why have you called? I have more important issues than some dispute with payment."

Yuan said, "He wanted to talk to you. He's finished the video."

"Good. And? Why did this require me to come here?"

Tribble said, "I'd like to talk to you alone."

Yuan said, "You might like a lot of things, but right now, just give us the video."

Tribble kept his eyes on Han, saying nothing.

Han said, "Give us a moment."

Yuan scoffed and said, "Why? Just make him give us the video."

Han looked at him, and it was enough. Yuan stormed out of the room, leaving the two alone.

Han said, "What's so important about this video?"

Tribble handed him a thumb drive, saying, "That video is good, and I've seen what's going on with the last one I sent.

The riots in Taiwan. The chaos in the streets. I see where this is going."

"You see nothing. You produce images like a YouTube star. You get paid to make videos and nothing more. Remember that."

"I get paid to help you with artificial intelligence. I have a program called Stargrazer. It's very, very good for facial recognition, but Yuan thinks he can do better with his own people."

Han said, "He's done pretty good against the Uyghurs. Nobody is complaining about his data collection."

"Mine is better. Maybe not for the Uyghurs, but for your other population. The one that uses social media."

"What's the point of this?"

"Taiwan is testing my program. Do you have someone inside Taiwan working for you? A high-ranking individual?"

Han narrowed his eyes and said, "Why do you ask?"

"Because the National Security Bureau used Stargrazer to find a man. I think he's yours."

# 68

Jake Shu watched the shore grow closer, then saw Chen coming across the deck of the boat toward him. Jake had specifically stayed on the deck, away from the cabin, to avoid both Chen and Zhi—but mostly Zhi.

Chen said, "Just like on the dive platform, you act normal. We're going to dock, leave this boat at the port, and immediately go to the airport. We'll get on a chartered plane and take off. If you cause any trouble between here and there, I won't kill you then. I'll wait until we're airborne, then throw you out over the ocean. Understand?"

Morose, Jake nodded, then said, "Where are we?"

"Port Moresby, Papua New Guinea. It's a five-hour flight to Taiwan. That may be the only sleep you get for a while, so I would advise you to make the most of it."

Jake was astounded at the level of effort they had put into this endeavor. It gave him a reptilian, prehistoric fear, because it meant that his data was something they wanted very, very badly.

He only hoped his life was considered as valuable.

After his capture in the canal he feared they were simply going to take him somewhere and put a bullet in his head. He'd been hustled to a rugby stadium, the lot empty save for a single car. He was shoved into the backseat, Zhi sliding in beside him and Chen getting behind the wheel.

They left the outskirts of Cairns behind, traveling up the coast, the surroundings becoming more and more rural. He had become convinced they were going to kill him here, in Australia.

He'd toyed with opening the door and jumping out at seventy kilometers an hour, taking his chances with the asphalt. He'd asked where they were going, and was told Port Douglas. He knew that was a lie. They'd told him earlier he was getting on a boat for a fake Great Barrier Reef dive tour from Cairns. Now he was sure they were simply going into the rainforest to bury his body.

His earlier panic rose again and he flung open the back door, causing Chen to jerk the wheel in surprise. He tried to leap from the vehicle and was yanked back inside by Zhi. She placed her nail against his neck, causing his bladder to release.

From the wheel, Chen shouted into the back, "What are you thinking?"

Chen turned on the child locks, preventing a repeat action, and Zhi said, "Let me kill him. He is more trouble than he is worth."

Chen said, "No. He is necessary. He is as much of the mission as his data."

Zhi said, "He just pissed himself. He's a coward."

Jake rolled his eyes from Zhi to the front of the car and Chen saw the debilitating panic. In English, Chen said, "Look, we are going to a boat in Port Douglas. We're going to get on it and travel to a dive platform. From there, our own boat will come get us. I'm not tricking you. I'm not going to kill you."

Jake remained still, feeling the nail on his carotid artery. Chen said, "Zhi?"

She removed her finger, allowing him to sit up.

Chen said, "Do you understand what I just told you?"

Jake nodded. Chen said, "The second boat is ours. The first is a commercial dive boat. It'll be full of people. You must act natural at all times. No more panicking. No more acting stupid. We are in a partnership here. You will be well paid. Do you understand?"

Jake said, "Yes. I understand."

"Good, because if you try to escape again . . . if I'm to lose you anyway . . . Zhi will cut your throat and throw you to the sharks."

Chen tossed a rag into the backseat and said, "Clean yourself up. You stink."

The rest of the ride went in silence, the sun finally cresting the horizon. They left the main highway, passing through the town of Port Douglas, ending up at a marina complex with shops, restaurants, and a giant trimaran boat next to a dock proclaiming "Quicksilver's Tours."

Chen parked in the designated lot and they boarded, along with seventy other patrons, Zhi glaring at him the whole time. Roughly an hour later the trimaran was docking on a double-decker Disney-like platform built over the reef. With swimming, snorkeling, dive instruction, overnight SCUBA trips, semisubmersible watercraft, bars, and a restaurant, it was a one-stop shop to see the Great Barrier Reef regardless of one's skill set in the water. There was something for everyone.

Except for Jake.

They ordered a bite to eat in the restaurant, killing time while Chen continually checked his phone.

Finally, he said, "They're here."

They went to the lower-level dock for the transfer vessels taking divers to the overnight ship excursions and boarded a boat manned by an all-Chinese crew. Jake took a seat on the outside deck, staying away from Chen, Zhi, and the crew. Three hours later, they were pulling into the marina at Port Moresby in Papua, New Guinea.

Chen went back into the cabin, exchanged some words with the captain, then motioned to Zhi and Jake. They exited the boat and walked up the gangway to a waiting car. Twenty minutes later they were in a private jet climbing to thirty thousand feet. As Jake watched the land fall away, he realized he was now completely alone. Nobody knew he had left Australia. Nobody would ever come looking for him, and he had lost the last anchor of escape. Boarding the plane had sealed his fate.

Sitting across from him, Chen tapped his knee, bringing his face away from the window.

"Things are reaching a culmination point. We won't have a lot of time in Taiwan. You need to get some rest."

"Culmination point? What do you mean?"

"I mean the entire reason I've kept you alive is about to come to fruition. And you need to be sharp to execute. We have about five hours. Get some sleep."

Jake nodded and reclined his seatback, but he knew rest would never come.

# 69

George Wolffe took a seat in a chair ringing the wall, leaving the more ostentatious ones tucked under the White House Situation Room table to the designated cabinet officials. Technically, he shouldn't have been in the room at all. It wasn't an Oversight Council briefing, but he'd been asked by President Hannister to attend anyway, as an observer.

He leaned back, taking in the others slowly filtering to the cheap seats, all staffers for the powerful men and women who had the proverbial "seat at the table." He wondered if any of them had an ounce of experience for what was about to be debated.

The topic of today's discussion was how to deal with the ongoing crisis in Taiwan, but he understood the subject matter itself didn't really concern the staffers. They were here solely to protect their bosses, and in the end, he was fairly sure the lack of expertise would matter little, because the information he had would dwarf what he was about to hear.

The men and women filing into the room thought they were about to debate the U.S. response to the ongoing crisis in Taiwan—which in Washington-speak meant how to properly thread the needle between U.S. support for the Republic of China in Taiwan while still placating the People's Republic of China in Beijing, a diplomatic game that had played out for decades. Unfortunately for them, Wolffe was now a believer that the events in Taiwan had a very strong chance of going kinetic, drawing the United States into an unintentional war, and all the diplomacy in the world wasn't going to prevent it.

But there was someone who might, if he could convince them.

He knew it would be hard, because Taiwan had been the boy who cried wolf for decades, and was now seen as just another simmering threat, like a volcano that spits lava every once in a while but never actually erupts.

Until it does.

Up until today, through multiple presidential administrations and sometimes confusing, conflicting signals, the United States' nebulous strategy for Taiwan had worked. Now, with China flexing its muscles in the South China Sea, building up its artificial islands and declaring the Nine-Dash Line as its sovereign territory, along with the president of China stating unequivocally that reuniting Taiwan with the "mother country" was goal number one, the situation was coming to a head. Something nobody in the room wanted to believe.

They wanted to think it was 1985, and this was just one more little flashpoint that would pass like a bad episode of heartburn after dinner. Not realizing that this time the symptoms could be reflecting a need for surgery—or death.

Wolffe was brought out of his thoughts by President Hannister entering the room, causing a flurry of people to stand up. The president went to the head of the table, saying, "Take a seat. Ian? Let's start."

The director of national intelligence, Ian McKellar, nodded and then gave a rundown of the latest developments. "We had hoped the protests would disappear, but with the release of the second video, it has only gotten worse. Today, for the first time, the police are involved, shooting water cannons and rubber bullets to disperse the crowds, and, like we saw in Hong Kong, the protestors are now saying those forces have been infiltrated by pro-PRC members and it's a Chinese plot."

On the screen was a picture of tens of thousands of protestors on the streets in front of the presidential palace.

President Hannister said, "Is it?"

McKellar asked, "Is it what, sir?"

"Are the Chinese involved here like they were in Hong Kong?"

McKellar paused, getting his thoughts in order. He said, "Yes, sir, they're most definitely involved, but we do not assess that they've infiltrated the police with jackboots like they did in Hong Kong."

"So how are they involved?"

"There is an underbelly of organized crime in Taiwan, and the PRC has been using them for years. We believe they're leveraging them to create the chaos, using social media and other means to exponentially increase the level of fear. Their preferred presidential candidate has already denounced the police and supported the protestors. We believe he's in the pocket of the PRC, and this is orchestrated. And the videos aren't helping."

The secretary of state, Amanda Croft, said, "I spoke to the foreign minister today. He's adamant the videos are fake. What's your take?"

McKellar said, "We believe the same, but it's really hard to prove. Both videos were taken inside the chambers of the Mainland Affairs Council. The first one filmed the minister of the council, and seemed to be surreptitiously taken, which is what caused the frenzy initially. It was like some secret truth coming out. The second was an actual video production, with the president speaking to the council. We've used our contacts, and, to a man or woman, all of them said the speech was just a pat on the back for something innocuous. They say the one just released is fake, but that may not matter. The truth is playing catch-up with the lies."

Alexander Palmer said, "How could they do that? How could they make a video that seems like it's real?"

The DNI said, "We've been fearing something like this since Russia interfered in our own elections. A person used to believe what he saw with his own eyes. Now that's no longer the case. It's called a deep fake video, manipulated through technology. The idea originated, believe it or not, with porn producers putting the face of a celebrity on an actor in a pornographic video. Those were very crude, and made not to trick anyone, but to make money. Everyone knew they were fake, but paid for the videos anyway. Since then, a more sinister application has come about, using the technology to manipulate popular sentiment by faking official statements. They've become better and better until it's almost impossible to determine if the video is real or altered."

President Hannister said, "What are we doing about it?"

"I had the NSA break down the code, and they found some anomalies that are inconsistent with a natural video. It's been manipulated. We're sure it's fake, but we can't prove it. It's just not something we're proficient in. It's not what we do. We took it to a private company called BackRub to see what they could make of it. This sort of thing is really in their wheelhouse and we've done some work with them in the past for artificial intelligence and facial recognition, but they refused to look at it."

Hannister leaned back and said, "What? Why would they refuse?"

McKellar said, "To be blunt, they took a contract with the People's Republic of China, helping them with their surveillance state, and because of it we broke our contract. It wasn't a good breakup. BackRub figured it could make more money in Asia than it could here because of our protections of privacy. When they made overtures to China we threatened to cancel their contract. BackRub basically said, 'Do what you want,' and went ahead. We broke the contract and now they won't lift a finger to help."

President Hannister's voice went cold, saying, "A United States company won't help us because they're helping the People's Republic of China?"

McKellar said, "Yes, sir. That's about it."

"Who is the CEO?"

"A wonder kid named Jerry Tribble. He's in China right now, which is the excuse they used to beg off, saying he was 'unavailable.'"

Hannister looked at Alexander Palmer and said, "I want all the information we have on that man and his company."

Unspoken was the reason why, but Wolffe was fairly sure the company was about to experience an unwanted colonoscopy. And he only hoped they used a baseball bat instead of a scope.

Palmer nodded, and the president returned to the issue at hand, saying, "So, you think the videos are fake, but why? How does that help China, other than seeding chaos? The Taiwanese people hate China, and those videos aren't making them look any better."

The DNI said, "We believe the PRC is trying to give the president's opponent in the election a leg up. We think they're twisting Taiwan on its head, giving the people there the belief that the incumbent is weak on China and the alternative is the hard-liner."

Hannister said, "How is that possible? The current president is as hard-line as they come. I'm constantly trying to keep her from declaring outright independence. And her opponent is from the Kuomintang party, whose entire platform is closer relations to China with a goal of economic unification under the 'one country, two systems' approach that's currently failing in Hong Kong."

The DNI nodded and said, "Yes, that's true, but in today's world, politics works in a twenty-four-hour cycle. All it takes is to stake a different stance, then say you never said what you said before, regardless of the evidence. That's what the KMT is doing, and it's effective. They're now the hard-liners—even as it's soft—and the president's party is now the secret appeasement party."

"So you think they're trying to sway the election? Get their man in?"

"Yes, sir. It's a gray war approach, like Russia and the Crimean Peninsula. They don't need to invade if they can get a government elected that allows them to just walk in."

President Hannister took that in, then said, "What can we do?"

McKellar said, "Not much at this point, outside of support. We can announce we believe the videos are fake, talk about election meddling, that sort of thing. We know for a fact that the Bamboo Triad is instigating the insurrection with money and social media presence, and they have a direct tie to China."

"Is that an attack point? Can we interdict them?"

"Not really. They're an organized crime outfit without

a center of gravity—but they do have a political party that's recognized in Taiwan. We can't stop them any more than the National Security Bureau, and believe me, they're working the issue. The problem for us is the same thing the NSB has—we can't give the impression we're affecting the election by imposing our will. Unlike China, Taiwan is a democracy. China can do what they do and dodge the blame, but we can't. We hit the Triads and we'll look like we're trying to affect the election by hammering a 'legitimate' political party. And, by the way, that party supports the KMT."

Palmer said, "Great. Just perfect."

Hannister said, "Okay, fine, then prove the videos are fake. Is there a way to tie the video to the Chinese? Is there something in the code that would allow that? Put this whole thing back on them about election meddling?"

"There is, if we can find a match. I mean, there's nothing in the video that will say 'made in China,' but if we could find another manipulated video with the same characteristics that also came out of China it would certainly boost our case."

"How do we do that? Does your team have a database for that sort of thing?"

"We do, but it's not nearly big enough. Truthfully, BackRub is on the leading edge. They've been doing this for years. It's not so much finding an anomaly, it's knowing what you're looking for, and they've worked in China. They would know what they were looking at. We're like a novice next to a birdwatcher here. That guy sees all the birds while all we see are the trees."

Hannister's face hardened at the words, and uncharacteristically, he cursed. "Fuck that. Go back to them.

Tell them to get on board or suffer the consequences, and if they want to know what that means, tell them I will crush them. I'm deadly serious. They get on board or they die. Is that clear?"

# 70

In his studio apartment on the fourth floor, Jerry Tribble surfed the web, going to pages that he knew the Chinese would expect him to visit. Because he also knew they were watching.

It was his day off, so he could do whatever he wanted, exploring the cultural sites of Beijing or other activities, but he spent his time on the computer, enjoying toying with the police state that believed they were his master. He went to a webpage called GreatFire.org—a dissident site that gave the Chinese state fits—solely to poke them in the eye, knowing they were tracking his every keystroke.

He surfed the site a little bit, just to make his overseers freak out, and the bikini woman appeared in the lower edge of his screen, beckoning him with a finger.

*What?*

His company wanted to talk, but not in an official way. They communicated on a daily basis, but all of those conversations were heard by the Chinese state, and both he and the Chinese knew that was the case. The avatar told him that his company wanted to talk outside of the eyes and ears of the PRC.

He knew it was too big of a risk to do so on his home computer. He was sure it was compromised. He watched the avatar, wanting to open the VPN, but didn't.

He shut off his system, then sat in the chair, thinking, afraid that someone monitoring his computer had seen the intrusion. There was nothing he could do about it now. If they'd noticed it, then they'd noticed it, but one thing was for sure—he couldn't talk from inside his apartment.

He grabbed a jacket and jogged down the stairs of his small building, passing families on their way up, the stairwell small enough that they had to press against the walls to pass each other.

He exited onto the streets of the Zhongguancun district and jogged to the office complex four blocks away. He entered the building, showed his credentials to the security man out front, and rode the elevator to the fourth floor.

The doors opened, and he used his RFID badge to access the office, looking at the camera as he did so. The control panel went green, and the doors opened. He knew there would be a record of his visit, and questions of why he'd shown up on his day off, but it couldn't be helped. The only way he could talk to his company securely was inside the very facility that was tracking him.

He'd thought it ingenious when he'd created it, but now regretted the setup.

He entered the glass enclosures of the laboratory, nodded at a man working the keyboards of a computer, and went to his own system. He sat down behind the keyboard, booted it up, then glanced behind him, seeing the solitary man.

He initiated the VPN and typed:

—Why are you trying to contact me outside of official channels? What is the urgent issue?

He waited, then saw:

—Do you have anything to do with the videos coming out of Taiwan?

And he felt the sweat build on his neck. He typed:

—Why would you ask that?

—Because the US government is asking us to help determine if the videos are fake, and we looked at them. They have your fingerprints on them. The same thing you did with the celebrity stuff. Same code. Is it you?

He leaned back in his chair. The only people who could make a match of the video code were in his own company, and because he was the best at video manipulation, the company had been asked to help determine if the video in question was manipulated. The irony was debilitating to him. *He'd* made the code, and now his *own company* was going to implicate him.

He tapped his fingers on the table, thinking. He couldn't tell them to ignore the request—not from the United States government. It would make him look guilty as hell. But he most certainly couldn't tell them to prove the video was fake. Not with his fingerprints on it. It would destroy his company.

He typed:

—What did you tell them?

He waited for the response, and then saw:

—We told them to pack sand. We no longer work for the US Government.

He sent back:

—Perfect. Let them figure it out on their own. Not our problem.

The avatar woman danced on the screen, then he saw:

—Is it not our problem? Did you do the video?

For the first time, he realized that his job as CEO held more implications than just his own paycheck. He typed:

—No, I did not. Just tell them we aren't helping.

He got back:

—Okay. Just checking in. There is significant pressure on this.

He sent:

—Fine. Screw the pressure. I think I have the contract in place for China. We're about to be bathing in gold. Ignore them. They should have thought about our help before they fired us.

A thumbs-up emoji appeared, and he closed out the VPN. He glanced behind his chair again, seeing the lone man still working on his computer.

# 71

Inside the White House Situation Room, President Hannister said, "What else can we do? How do we signal support for Taiwan without getting into a war with China?"

The secretary of defense said, "Well, we approved the sale of F-35s to Taiwan, but it's been held up by interagency deliberation on various logistics. We could expedite that as a show of support. It'll piss off China to no end, but it would certainly send a signal."

Hannister said, "Do it. What else?"

Amanda Croft said, "I'll harden the edge of our releases and answers, but we're really hamstrung by not having an embassy on the island. We have no way to directly impact anything there. We can talk from Beijing, but I would recommend against that, as it will only cause us problems."

"Problems how?"

"We can't outright say from inside China that we think the PRC is involved in manipulating the Taiwan election. I can do that from here, in a subtle manner, or from releases inside Taiwan from the American Institute in Taiwan—our de facto consulate in the country—but doing it from our post in China will upend a lot of diplomatic initiatives, to include the ongoing trade disputes."

Hannister nodded, thinking. He said, "Maybe that's the route we take. Economic pressure."

Amanda said, "We can't do that without proof of wrongdoing. Right now, it's just a whiff of smoke from the DNI. The crowds in Taiwan are protesting their own government *against* China appeasement. Blaming China at this point will make us look weak, like we're looking for a scapegoat. How will we sell that? Telling the world that China is fomenting protests attacking *them*? China will eat that up. They have the upper hand here, just like they do in Hong Kong."

Hannister took that in, then said, "Okay, okay. I hear you. Do what you said, but not from our embassy in China. It's looking like the video is the smoking gun here. Get me proof the video is fake, and who made it. If it's not China, then find out who it is."

The DNI nodded. "I can do that, but maybe not in the time we need. This thing is getting out of control, and it might be too little, too late proving the videos are fake."

Hannister rubbed his forehead, looked at the ceiling, then said, "What is the worst case here? If we do nothing?"

McKellar said, "The KMT guy wins the election and we lose influence. Our initiatives to expand consulate services through the AIT are gone, and China gets a leg up in the country. Worst, *worst* case is that they start enforcing the Nine-Dash Line with Taiwan acquiescence. Leaving us to concede the entire South China Sea to China."

The room grew quiet, and Hannister said, "That's not going to happen. Give me something to fight this. Jesus, people, give me *something*."

The men and women around the table simply looked at him, wanting to give an answer that they didn't have. He waited a beat, heard nothing, then stood, saying, "This meeting is over. Go to work."

The room started to break up, with people coalescing into groups and talking as they exited. Wolffe waited until he saw the president free from others. He went forward, breaking through the scrum. He came close enough for Alexander Palmer to stop his advance.

Palmer put a hand on his chest and said, "You have something to add?"

"Yeah. That worst case wasn't the worst case."

"What do you mean?"

"I mean you need to tell the principals to stay behind, because I think this isn't about an election. I think it's about taking over Taiwan."

Palmer stared into Wolffe's eyes, trying to find the political play, something Wolffe expected from him. Palmer's entire life was built on politics. He simply couldn't comprehend that someone would bring a problem that wasn't a political wedge to be used.

Wolffe said, "I need the Council, right now."

Palmer withdrew his hand and took a breath. "It's not going to happen tonight. Too much on our plate."

Wolffe leaned in and said, "Then tell the president that you had the keys to a war with China and decided your petty political bullshit was too important."

Palmer narrowed his eyes and Wolffe said, "Look, I'm talking to the president with or without the Council. You can act like you're in charge, or you can look like an asshole watching the bus drive by full of the people that are in charge. Your choice."

Palmer nodded slowly, the words sinking in. He finally said, "This had better be good."

Wolffe saw the tumbling behind the eyes and knew Palmer had made the political cost/benefit analysis, like every other puke who worked in the building. Wolffe understood that at the end of the day, no matter the political stripe, *nobody* wanted to be on the wrong side of national security. They all wanted the success, but not the pain of being responsible for the decision that enabled it.

Palmer turned to the room and said, "Could Defense, State, and the CIA stay behind?"

The people milling about heard the command, and Ian McKellar, the DNI, said, "You want me here as well?"

Which Wolffe knew was a nonstarter. McKellar was the highest intelligence official in the land, but he wasn't read on to Project Prometheus.

Palmer said, "No, Ian, we're good."

McKellar nodded slowly, knowing he was being cut out of something, but not questioning why.

Wolffe felt his pain.

The director of national intelligence position was created after 9/11, and as such it was much too political for something as sensitive as Project Prometheus. Wolffe personally thought the DNI job was a waste of time—nothing more than a political rat trap created to show the world that the United States understood the mistakes that had occurred leading to 9/11—but he genuinely liked McKellar. He was a good man, but that alone wouldn't let him in the door. His position had too many other interests to allow a look into Project Prometheus. It was, in intelligence parlance, close hold for a reason.

Palmer leaned into President Hannister's ear and whispered. The room cleared out, leaving the four members of the Oversight Council known as the principals.

When the final person left and the door closed, President Hannister said, "Okay, Wolffe, what's the lockdown for?"

Wolffe said, "Sir, I know you have a lot on your plate, but Pike is still on the hunt. You told me to turn him loose, and I did."

Hannister smiled and said, "Yes. As I remember, we have an Australian national in quarantine because of his actions. What's your point?"

Wolffe could see the stress on the man, and knew he needed to be precise. Whatever love the president held for Pike wasn't going to be enough to allow him to continue. To get approval for Omega actions, he needed to prove his case.

He said, "You told me once that Pike could save the F-35 program or save the world, and I think that has become true. But it's not the F-35 program. He might just save the world. He's in the air to Taiwan, but I need Omega authority to let him work."

Alexander Palmer said, "What? Why's he flying to Taiwan?"

Wolffe turned to him and said, "Because he missed Jake Shu. That traitor is on his way to Taiwan as well, and he's not going there to sell dumplings. I think China is going to attempt a takeover of Taiwan."

The secretary of defense said, "Oh, bullshit. This is just another one of China's blusters. They aren't going to cross the strait when they're spending all of their political capital building up islands in the South China Sea. That makes no sense."

Wolffe said, "It makes *perfect* sense. China builds up the islands to get us to focus on them, then they foment instability in Taiwan. Then, when we're all worried about 'freedom of navigation' operations, they invade. Fait accompli."

The SECDEF leaned back and said, "You miss one point. They can't invade without an army to do so. We'd see indications of that threat."

"They *have* the army. They're executing massive exercises right across the strait, practicing assaulting the island every day."

"They do that all the time—especially during a presidential election. It's what they've done for the last fifty years."

Wolffe sighed and said, "The boy who cried wolf. Ever heard of that story? Yeah, they're doing the same exercises we've seen for years, but have you ever thought that maybe—just maybe—those exercises were for a reason? Causing us to become complacent?"

Amanda Croft said, "That's like a hammer looking for a nail. Yeah, they have done them year after year, but why should we assume this year is different?"

The director of the CIA, Kerry Bostwick, said, "I agree. China knows that we can crush them if they attempt a unilateral assault without provocation. If they attempted to attack the ROC from a cold start, they know we'd defend them."

Wolffe said, "Would we? Really? After all of our adventures in the Middle East? Would we jump to get in a fight?"

Incensed, the SECDEF said, "Of course we would. We have a treaty."

Wolffe let a grim smile leak out, saying, "We *don't* have a treaty. We have a nebulous 'cooperation agreement.' We've spent the last three decades waffling. What if China thinks we won't press it? We didn't in Hong Kong."

"Hong Kong was a British protectorate that was given back to China. How were we supposed to engage there?"

Wolffe said, "I'll give you that. It's true, but why would China think any differently about Taiwan? While we're more concerned about Afghanistan or Iraq or other things? I mean, we've let them build up fighting platforms in the South China

Sea and done nothing. They've basically taken the Nine-Dash Line and made it real, and we've spent our time fighting in places with nothing but sand, not opposing them."

Bostwick started to protest, and President Hannister held up a hand, saying, "I agree with all you've said, but China has to know that if they conducted an invasion of Taiwan there would be unacceptable risks. And the rest of the world would be on Taiwan's side."

"Sir, Taiwan can't impose unacceptable risks when they're in turmoil. China is instigating these protests for a reason. Taiwan is consumed by the unrest. They're now using the military to put them down. They aren't looking at the threat across the strait, and because of that, I think China's going to attack."

The SECDEF said, "If they attack from a cold start, we'll intervene. They know that. I agree with what was said in the briefing by the DNI. They're going for the gray war victory, and we'll have to fight them on the gray war. There is no way that China will initiate a cold-start invasion."

Wolffe nodded and said, "I think you're right. But what if it wasn't a cold-start invasion?"

President Hannister said, "What's that mean? They can't invade the country invisibly."

Wolffe turned to the only man in the room who mattered and said, "What if Taiwan attacked China first?"

# 72

Entering the Chiang Kai-Shek memorial square just down the street from the presidential palace, Paul couldn't believe the numbers of protestors, amazed at their fury. It was something he watched on the news of other countries, not of his own. The air was full of smoke and the whiff of tear gas, with armored police vehicles ringing the park and police officers unsure of their orders, but still shouting into loudspeakers in an attempt to quell the unrest, the cacophony of noise overwhelming.

The protestors had come looking for a reason to fight, but were unsure of what they were fighting about, energized by nothing more than a few social media posts—and the Bamboo Triad. It was a tinderbox waiting on a match. The last thing he wanted was to be arrested along with the protestors, but it was looking like that would happen if he lingered.

He threaded through the crowd, hearing them chant hatred against the government and seeing multiple people holding up the videos that had been released on their tablets and phones. He had no ability to control the end state, but he *did* have the ability to control the why.

He tried to reach his surveillance position outside of the Mainland Affairs Council, where his target was located, but realized it was a waste of time. His target wouldn't show in this mess of chaos.

And then he did.

Paul saw Colonel Rae "Ryan" Won exit the building in civilian clothes, darting among the crowd, wanting to remain invisible. He flashed his credentials at the police barricade and slipped through, sticking close to the wall and moving away from the protestors.

Paul followed on the far side of the street, opposite the screaming demonstrators.

Ryan walked two blocks past the presidential palace to the main Taipei train station. He crossed the street and entered, Paul following close behind.

The interior was congested with people, the tension thick, most of the travelers wanting to just get home, but the protests making them fear their ability to do so. The government had threatened to shut down the rail system to prevent outsiders from traveling to Taipei for mischief, and Paul could feel the anxiety in the air, people rushing to their trains before such a thing happened.

Ryan walked away from the long-distance train platforms, going down a tunnel toward the city metro, and Paul stayed behind him. He stopped at a rack of lockers, pulled a scrap of paper out of his pocket, read the numbers, then punched in a code on a keypad. A locker on the top row opened.

Ryan went to it, withdrew a small satchel, then continued on.

Paul was intrigued.

His target stopped at a kiosk outside the metro terminal and bought a fare on the red line. Paul let him leave, then did the same. Because the metro worked on an RFID token system, where each fare was embedded with the cost for the length of the transit, Paul was forced to pay for the entire line, having no idea where Ryan would stop.

The kiosk spit out his token, and he went down the stairs, seeing Ryan at the front of the platform. Paul stood in the back of the crowd, watching Ryan's crew-cut head.

The train arrived and disgorged more protestors, all of them shouting and chanting about betrayal. The crowd let them pass and they boarded, Ryan taking a seat and Paul remaining near the door, holding a handrail.

Twenty minutes later, Paul saw Ryan stand up, the Taipei World Trade Center station approaching. Paul faded to the back of the crowd, allowing the doors to open, disgorging the passengers. Ryan exited, and Paul followed.

This section, the financial heart of Taipei, held no protestors. As with every other spontaneous uprising, the locality was a self-generating phenomenon, and apparently they'd decided to focus their attention on the government areas and the presidential palace.

Ryan broke out onto the street, Paul right behind him, the sun setting in the sky, the twilight allowing the lights of the buildings to begin to dominate.

Paul followed Ryan two blocks, until he reached a structure towering above everything around it, its architecture like that of a modern-day temple, with metal outcroppings every tenth floor or so, but stabbing into the sky higher than any temple had ever dreamed, almost as if it were trying to reach the stars above it.

Known as Taipei 101, it was, for a short time—until the Burj Khalifa opened in Dubai—the tallest building in the world.

*What is he doing here?*

Ryan entered the lobby and took an escalator to the second floor, weaving through an opulent mall full of storefronts that only the rich would dare step inside, Paul staying far enough behind to keep from being burned. He switched escalators, heading ever higher, the patrons in the mall not reflecting the chaos just down the road, all shopping for diamonds and outrageously expensive handbags as if the world wasn't coming apart next door.

Ryan reached a bank of elevators on the fourth floor and ignored them, moving down a hallway to a private one. He scanned a directory on the wall, running his finger down it, then tapped.

Standing near the bank of public elevators, Paul memorized the tap as best he could. Ryan reached into the satchel he'd taken from the train station and withdrew a badge, placing it on the controls for the elevator. The door opened, and he disappeared inside.

Paul waited a bit, then approached, tracing his own finger down the directory until he reached the business Ryan had tapped.

*Ju-Long Import/Export Limited.*

It was on the seventy-seventh floor, the space only accessed by this elevator. As such, the destination was out of reach of Paul's limited abilities, but it gave him something to work with.

Paul went back to the elevator banks overlooking the mall area—the ones used for the observation decks and other public spaces—bought a cup of coffee from a kiosk, and took a seat on a bench, waiting for Ryan to appear again. If Ryan had gone up that elevator, he might return the same way.

Paul failed to notice that he wasn't the only one doing the watching.

# 73

Jennifer leaned over the edge of the observation platform and said, "Okay, this is crazy—even for you."

Kneeling next to a backpack at my feet, I looked up, seeing the stars starting to blink in the night sky, the expanse of the Taipei cityscape spreading out into the distance. We were so far up in the air that any feelings of acrophobia were absent, like I was looking out the window of an airplane.

I said, "You got a better idea? We don't have time to mess around here, and you're good at this shit."

Miffed, she knelt next to me, opening the backpack and pulling out a harness. She stood, slipping her feet through the loops, then adjusted the webbing on her shoulders. She held her arms out like she was allowing a police search and said, "Why's it always me that has to climb?"

I stood and began checking her harness like a jumpmaster on a parachutist, trying to find a point of failure. I traced the webbing underneath her legs and said, "Because none of us knuckle-draggers are monkeys like you. And you're the only one who's used the Hollywood Rig and not died. No way am I going to give it a go."

She snapped her head to me and said, "Someone's died using this thing?"

What we called the Hollywood Rig was invented by a stuntman named Dar Robinson in—of course—Hollywood so he could leap off a building with the camera above him, not worrying about an airbag appearing in the scene below. It was basically a type of bungee jump, but instead of a thick rope, it used a very thin cable attached to a harness that wouldn't be seen by the camera, the clamps on the descender slowing the fall at a pace where it didn't break bones. We stole the idea because we also needed something that wouldn't be seen by a camera. The system didn't use a bulky rope or huge setup, having only a thin steel cable and a descender that could be clamped anywhere—all of it small enough to fit in a backpack the size of a book bag for a university student.

Jennifer had used it once on an operation in Singapore. At the time, I hadn't had the heart to tell her that—outside of testing—nobody on the teams had enough balls to deploy it operationally.

I said, "No, no. Nobody's died."

"Then why did you say that?"

I held up my hands. "Truth?"

Her eyes flashed and she said, "Yeah, damn it. What's the truth?"

"You're the only one who's used it on an operation. Everyone else is too chickenshit. It worked in Singapore, and it'll work here."

She couldn't believe the words that had come out of my mouth. She said, "You threw me off the roof of the Marina Bay Sands in Singapore knowing that nobody else had the guts to trust it?"

I said, "Guilty, but it worked in testing. *I* trusted it. Like I'm going to do now."

She shook her head, saying, "Seems like your trust is limited to using it with me in the harness. It's not your ass going into the wind."

She leaned over the edge again, getting a reference point on the overhang at the seventieth floor. "You're going to pay for this."

I grinned and said, "I know, I know."

We were on the outside observation deck of the ninety-first floor of Taipei 101, one of the tallest buildings in the world. The wind was strong enough to cause her hair to billow out. Honestly, the climb she was about to attempt wasn't something even *I* would want to do—but that was why I had Jennifer.

We'd been midway from Australia to Taiwan on the Rock Star bird when I got the word from Wolffe that we had Alpha authority in Taiwan, which meant the business card had panned out.

While we knew Ju-Long Import/Export LLC was a front company for the People's Liberation Army, they still had to do some legitimate business to maintain the façade, and the Taskforce had leveraged that weakness.

They'd found an American who had a current contract with them, then had stolen that man's identity, conducting a little social engineering with the company. In the end, it had been pretty simple: They'd called the company, said the CEO of the American firm was going to be in Taiwan on business and wanted to set up a meeting with Chen Ju-Long. They'd been told he was out of the country, but would return in two days.

Which matched what we'd found on the card.

What we didn't know at the time was that the damn office was on the seventy-seventh floor of one of the tallest buildings in the world.

We'd done the research on the nine-hour flight to Taipei and had learned that the building had been built with earthquakes and typhoons in mind, with blocks of floors used solely for stability and support separating the actual square footage occupied by renters.

We determined that there were three blocks of office spaces: the first—the low zone—from the fifth to the eighteenth floor, then the mid-zone from the twenty-second to the fifty-eighth, ending finally with the high zone at the upper level, each of the blocks separated by maintenance floors.

Of course, given our luck, Ju-Long Limited was in the high zone, with a private elevator that whisked approved visitors to the selected floor by use of a special badge. We didn't have the time to crack all of the systems to gain access to the elevator, and so had looked for another way to get inside his office.

On the plus side, as it turned out, most of the available space at the higher levels was empty, the builder still trying to find renters for the enormous price they were asking, meaning if we could get in we wouldn't have to worry about a bunch of different offices asking us who we were. The downside was we couldn't figure out a way to get that high in the building because of the private elevator. But we *could* by using another one.

The ninety-first floor was an outside observation deck, with the two floors below it being an indoor observation area and restaurants, all open to the public, essentially giving us the ability to get above the Ju-Long office. The seventieth floor was a maintenance and stability level with a ledge shaped to appear from the outside like the jutting outcroppings of a traditional Chinese temple. The ledge itself had a walkway not unlike the observation deck we were on, and had door accesses for the maintenance men to utilize the window cleaning scaffolding or perform other utility work.

Which was just perfect for Jennifer.

A gymnast in an earlier life, she was like a gecko when it came to climbing stuff, and the drop was only about 250 feet. Okay, that "only" was me. I'm sure it was something a little different to Jennifer.

On the flight over, looking at the blueprints Creed had sent, Knuckles had seen the same thing I had—we could drop her over the edge, get her down to the seventieth floor, let her break in to the maintenance level, then have her go back up to the seventy-seventh floor using the stairs.

Once she was there, she could break into Ju-Long Limited. The electronic security was focused on the access at the ground level, through the keypad on the elevator, and not on the floor space itself. It had nothing but normal locksets, and Jennifer could crack those easily.

She'd heard us discussing the mission as if she wasn't even there, and had brought out the obvious point—namely that if she got down to the seventieth floor and couldn't get in, she was going to have a hell of a time getting back up. But that's why she was paid the big bucks. We both knew she could climb plate glass with a little spit on her hands.

The entire mission was simply to access the Ju-Long office to see what she could find before he arrived tomorrow, using computer cloning devices, cameras, and good old-fashioned digging through file cabinets and desk drawers. It was a lot of work for such a potentially small payoff, but building a mission like this was always getting the little things to pay off, no matter the effort. Only in the movies were you handed the diabolical plot. The rest of the time, you had to work for it.

Jake Shu was doing something bad, and from what we'd seen with the protests since we landed, that ulterior motive was coming to a head sooner rather than later.

Jennifer held the cable against her chest and said, "What's going to happen if they come out here looking? What are you going to do?"

I grinned and said, "Drop you."

She scowled and I said, "Hey, we paid for the outdoor experience. They told us we had thirty minutes. Get over the edge. The clock is ticking."

There was a price of admission to take the observation elevator to the ninety-first floor, whereupon one could circle the building taking in the views. Usually, there would be a line of people wanting the experience, with a controller not letting a tourist out until someone else came back in, but two things were working for us: One, it wasn't a weekend, meaning there was naturally less interest from the public, and two, the current unrest in the city had depressed anyone wanting to do a tour of anything. Because of it, we were on our own, outside all by ourselves, the ticket guy two corners away and out of view.

Jennifer's ledge was twenty floors below, and we'd analyzed which side of the building to use. The rent was incredibly expensive in the building—especially at the high zone—and because of it, most of the floor space was unoccupied on the south side, with Ju-Long being the only tenant, while the north had several working offices. We'd analyzed the risk and decided that sliding down the building with a single office in operation was better than sliding down the north side that had several—even if the one Jennifer was going by was also our target.

I tested the belay system, seeing it was functioning, and glanced back to the edge of the corner we were on. I saw nobody and said, "Time to go."

Jennifer smiled. "You're *really* going to owe me for this."

I said, "I know . . . I *know*."

She crawled out over the edge, and my radio came alive from Brett. "This is Blood. We have a man going up in the special elevator."

Jennifer paused, and I said, "Okay? Why do we care? Jennifer is about to drop."

"Because he's got a man following him. The first guy had an access badge for the elevator. The second one did not."

I took that in and said, "We're executing. Probably just someone going up to the offices here."

Brett said, "Yeah, but he's being followed for a reason. And the guy tracking him is *also* being tracked."

Crouched on the ledge, Jennifer looked at me. I nodded to her and took a position on the descender. She shook her head, pointing at her earpiece, wanting to listen. Off the net, I whispered, "No time for that. Get over the side."

On the radio, I said, "Who's tracking who here?"

"I don't know, but the men tracking the guy who is following the man who went up are definitely thugs. Bad dudes."

I said, "Okay. Keep eyes-on. Jennifer is going over."

She scowled, then stood up on the edge, the sight alone scaring the hell out of me. Thank God it wasn't me doing the work.

She turned around, facing me, her eyes boring into mine, and then stepped off the ledge, the cable racing out of the spool. It hit a predetermined length and then slowed, the descender doing its work.

# 74

I looked over the side, seeing her two hundred feet below me, her feet on the wall. I said, "Koko, Koko, you okay?"

"Yes. Slack."

She was curt, which told me she was feeling the fear of the drop, and I completely understood. I worked the descender, giving her some cable and she said, "Stop. Stop. Stop."

I did so, and then she said, "I'm outside the window of Ju-Long Limited. I see Chen inside."

*Jesus Christ. He came home early. That's not going to work for a break-in.*

"Can he see you?"

"No. I'm on the outside edge of the window. He's inside with a guy I don't recognize. But if Chen Ju-Long is here, so is Jake Shu."

I took that in, then said, "The date on the card was for tomorrow. What's he doing there?"

As soon as the words were out of my mouth, I realized they were no help. Before she could respond, I said, "Okay, we can't conduct a B&E with them inside. I'm going to release you to the seventieth outcropping. Get inside the door and then get down. We'll have to reassess. On the bright side, at least we don't have to wonder if Chen's showing up."

She said, "Hang on. Hold me in place. They're getting up. It looks like the meeting is over."

I stopped my work on the descender, saying, "Get a photo. Can you get a photo?"

"Stand by."

I felt my phone buzz and looked at the picture, then said, "Blood, is that the guy you saw go in the elevator?"

He said, "Yep. That's the guy."

And we had our link. We didn't need to get inside the office now. We only needed to take that guy down.

On the net I said, "Jennifer, I'm dropping you to the seventieth floor. Don't worry about breaking into the office."

She said, "This is Koko. Roger all. What am I doing?"

"Get in the building through the access door, then find a way down to the bottom floor. We can't get in with Chen still there, and there's no telling how long he is going to stay."

She said, "Unsub is leaving. I say again, Unsub is leaving. Chen is there with the woman from the pub in Kuranda. And she's getting a little freaky."

"What's that mean?"

"I don't know. She's got a weird long fingernail and she's stroking Unsub's cheek like she wants to kill him. Unsub is freaking out. He's running to the door. He's out."

I didn't really know what to make of that assessment, but I knew one thing: Unsub was leaving.

I said, "Okay, get ready to drop. You good?"

"Yeah, I'm good. If I can't get the maintenance door open, am I still coming back up to you?"

"No. We'll have to figure that out. I'm headed down."

I heard, "What's that mean? Pike?"

And I cut the descender, dropping her another five floors. I looked over the edge, saw her on the outcropping next to the maintenance door, and said, "Koko, Koko, are you good?"

Breathing hard through the radio, she said, "I'm on the ledge, you asshole."

I grinned. "Okay. Good to go. Everyone on Unsub. I'm headed down."

Jennifer said, "Pike, don't you leave me here."

I said, "I'm not. I mean, I'm not for long. You can get through that door. Find a public elevator and meet me."

Before she could answer, I said, "Break, break, Blood, Veep, get a lock-on for Unsub when he exits."

Jennifer came on the net, cold as ice, saying, "You are literally dead to me."

I cut the cable from the descender, watching it snake over the edge, knowing it was Jennifer's only way back up. I packed up the descender and said, "Hide the cable. Work that door. It can't be hard. If you can't penetrate, I'll come back up to get you."

Knuckles came on. "What about the Unsub that's tracking our guy? He's still waiting on him out here."

Then Veep said, "And he's got company. He doesn't know it, but he's being tracked by four thugs. They keep circling around in this mall, and they definitely don't fit in. They're tracking him."

I went through the lobby of the observation deck restaurant, nodding at the access control guy and hoping he didn't ask where my date had gone, my backpack on my shoulder.

I cleared past him and said, "So we have someone else tracking our guy, and that guy is being tracked by others?"

"Yes. That's what I think is happening."

*What the hell? What is going on here?*

I reached the elevators and said, "Are you guys burned? Do either one of them know you're interested in the same thing?"

"No. We're clean. But that other guy is not, I promise."

I pushed the button for the lobby on the fourth floor and said, "Just track them all. Let's see what happens."

Jennifer came on. "I'm in the maintenance level. At the elevator."

I smiled. "Very good, Koko."

I went down twenty floors and the elevator stopped. It opened, and I was looking at one pissed-off commando.

Jennifer entered and said, "I ought to kick you in the balls for that."

Veep came on and said, "Unsub one is out. Unsub two is tracking him. Wolf pack is now tracking the entire show."

I punched the "door close" button and, off the net, said to Jennifer, "Yeah, you can kick my ass later. What do we do with this mess?"

She saw the conflict on my face and realized that any beatdown was going to have to wait. She went right back into problem-solving mode, which is something she was good at.

I saw her wheels turning, and waited. She said, "We know the guy in the room is attached to Chen, but we don't know who he is. He's the target. Whatever else is going on, we need to take him down. It'll just be a little harder."

"Or we could stake out the same elevator and wait on Chen Ju-Long. Jake's probably with him."

She thought a moment, then said, "Yeah, maybe, but we don't even know if Jake's with him, or whether Chen has an apartment here, or a host of other things. He might not leave for twenty-four hours. We *know* that guy was talking to Chen. It's the old 'bird in the hand' thing here. I say we focus on him. We can always come back and stake this place out."

Which is exactly what I was thinking. I relayed to the team to continue on Unsub One, and she gave me her little impish grin, then said, "That's not going to protect you from an ass-kicking, though."

I smiled back. "Plenty of time for that later. When we're alone."

The elevator dropped like a rock thrown into a well, so fast it made my stomach flip, the floors whipping by on the LED screen.

Knuckles said, "Unsub One is on the escalators down to ground level. Unsub Two is behind him. The wolf pack are following."

I said, "Unsub One is the target. I say again, Unsub One is the target."

Knuckles said, "What about Unsub Two and the wolf pack?"

I said, "Just track Unsub One. We're still coming down."

The elevators in the building were supposedly the fastest in the world, but when you had to go a hundred floors, it still seemed like forever.

We finally hit the lobby level on the fourth floor and began racing down the escalators. I said, "We're coming out. Give me a lock-on."

"On the north-south street, but Pike, I think this is going to get nasty. The wolf pack are tracking both of them, and they look like they came to play."

# 75

Paul saw Ryan exit the elevator, the appearance sending adrenaline through his body like an electric current. He jolted upright, then glanced around to see if anyone had noticed the reaction. He saw two twenty-somethings stare at him, but nothing else.

He paid them no mind. He'd seen their type before in places like this. Young men with no ability to afford the stores, but still wanting to show the elite class that they could explore the mall like any of the wealthy who came to shop.

He remained seated next to the public elevator bank, waiting on Ryan to pass. When he did, Paul began to follow, fixated on his crew-cut hair in the crowd, not noticing that the interest of the two men earlier hadn't waned.

Ryan went down the first set of escalators, rounding the corner for the next one, and Paul followed. On the turn, he glanced behind, and for the first time, he noticed the two men from earlier. He swiveled his head forward, his face showing no reaction, but he began to believe he was being tracked even as he was following Ryan.

Ryan rounded the escalator to the next floor and Paul stayed behind him. Using the natural choke point of the escalator, he identified two more men. He realized they were not average young malcontents wandering a mall with stores they couldn't afford.

They were Triad.

One more escalator switch later, and he was sure. By the time he reached the ground floor he knew the men above were tracking him, and it left him with a choice: Continue on with Ryan, or break free.

He decided that tracking Ryan might now be a risk—especially if the man himself was in contact with the Triad members following. It very well could be a setup designed to take him out.

He had no idea how the Bamboo Triad had identified him as a threat. Maybe they were just security for Ryan, or maybe it was his actions in Jiufen, but either way, he had no illusions about their capabilities. He had a dead asset for proof of that.

He decided the best course of action was to leave Ryan and get to a populated area. If they were working together, and they were simply security, that alone would cause them to break off.

He followed Ryan onto the street, and when he went right, toward the metro station, Paul went left, heading to a popular plaza known as the Xinyi shopping district. With three square blocks of the latest restaurants, stores, and nightlife interspersed among green spaces and pedestrian walkways, it would give him the protection he needed. Called the "Manhattan of Taipei," it was a natural deterrent for the men following. But he was sure when he broke away from Ryan, they would leave him alone.

He reached the lights of the shopping district two blocks away, seeing the crowds milling about, pretending that the chaos happening just down the road wasn't in fact ripping his country apart. He wondered if they realized that Taiwan was at a breaking point. If they thought that shopping and partying in this district would somehow protect them from the anarchy that was coming, but he knew they did not. Nobody his age in Taiwan did. China taking over the country by force was just a myth that the old people feared.

The human condition never wanted to believe that the worst has come. Whether Jews in Europe or Taiwan itself, it was easier just to believe the bad man wasn't coming.

Waiting to cross the street, Paul glanced behind him and saw the four Triad members. Unlike the people shopping, he knew who the bad man was, and he was here.

We reached the bottom floor, having a choice of going out the front door or leaving through the parking garage, and I got a call from Knuckles saying, "We're on them. This is a mess. We're following a team who are following a guy who is following a guy. Pike, we can't keep this up. There's no way to do this clean."

I said, "Okay, okay, I get it. Just stay on them for a minute. We'll make a call shortly. Where are you?"

"On the north-south street right out of the exit. I've got the eye. Blood and Veep are on Unsub One."

I said, "Front exit? Or the parking garage?"

"Front exit. Unsub One is headed to the metro."

I looked at Jennifer and said, "I'll be there shortly."

She started moving at a sprint and I followed close behind.

Knuckles said, "All elements, all elements, I have five-five. Unsub Two has broken free from Unsub One. He's headed my way. Who's got the eye on Unsub One?"

Brett said, "This is Blood. I have Unsub One headed south on Songzhi Road, toward the metro."

Jennifer and I broke out onto the street and I said, "Give me a status."

Knuckles said, "Unsub Two still headed north. The wolf pack is following."

Brett said, "Unsub One closing on the metro station, same road."

"Where are the bumpers? Veep, where are you?"

"I'm at the metro, waiting on pickup."

We started moving in the direction Brett gave and I said, "Knuckles, Knuckles, what's the wolf pack doing?"

"They're tracking him. Still on him."

*What the hell?* The fact that another man outside of our target was being tracked was disconcerting, and gave me pause. I said, "Are all of the wolf pack on him right now?"

Knuckles said, "He just entered a large shopping area, and yeah, he's got the assholes behind him."

I stopped walking, saying, "Meaning Unsub One is now alone?"

Brett said, "This is Blood. Unsub One is by himself."

*Perfect.* I tapped Jennifer's arm and started racing to the metro, saying, "Okay, Koko and I are headed to the station and Unsub One. Knuckles, break off of Unsub Two and follow. We'll give you a lock-on once we make contact. Blood, Veep, give me a track."

I heard, "Pike, Pike, this is Knuckles. These guys are looking like they want to take down Unsub Two. They're hunting him."

I slowed, hearing the tone of his voice over the radio. It wasn't just a situation report. He felt something. I said, "What's that mean? How do you know?"

"I can't give you an answer. I just *know*."

Jennifer looked at me, waiting on a decision, and I was torn. Something bigger was in play here. Why was someone trying to attack a man who was following our own target? Was he on our side?

Off the net, to Jennifer, I said, "What do you think?"

She paused, knowing I was asking because I wanted her opinion, and that that opinion held weight with me.

I waited a beat, then grew impatient. "Jennifer, what the fuck do you *think*? I have to make a call."

She looked up the street, where Unsub One was rapidly disappearing, then said, "Honestly? I think that guy is a bigger link than Unsub One. I think he was tracking a man who's associated with Chen Ju-Long for bad stuff. He's trying to solve the same problem we are, and Chen is trying to stop him."

"Meaning he's like us? He's a good guy? And Chen Ju-Long is trying to kill him? Here in Taiwan?"

She exhaled and said, "Yeah. That's what *I* think. He might be a white hat. But it's your call."

And that was the problem. She could give me an opinion all day long, but it was *my* decision, not hers, and she knew it. She understood the pressure, but honestly, she was pretty good at penetrating through the chaos, and her thought was exactly what I believed. *This* guy was tracking a bad guy, and he himself was being tracked by bad guys. He was following the same thread we were, only he didn't know he was about to be eaten by wolves. And we could stop it.

I got on the net and said, "Change of mission. Change of mission. It's now a PSD. Do not let any harm come to Unsub Two."

Knuckles said, "Come again? You want us to act as his personal security detail?"

I started jogging up the street in the opposite direction I

had been going, saying, "Yes. Veep, Blood, get your ass back here and into the fight."

Brett said, "Pike, you're leaving the very guy that was in Chen's office to track an unknown."

I could hear the incredulity in his voice, him understanding I was giving up the one thread we had to locate Jake Shu for something that was nothing more than a whisper.

I said, "Yeah, I get it, but we could use some help here in Taiwan, and I think that man can give it to us."

He came back, "Pike, are you sure about this?"

Truthfully, I wasn't sure at all. I looked at Jennifer, and she nodded. Meaning she believed, which was enough for me. I said, "Just do it. If he gets attacked, you interdict."

# 76

Paul crossed the street, entering the lights of the shopping district, thin tendrils of panic reaching the pit of his stomach. He immediately went to the first stairwell he could find and took them two at a time, then entered the indoor mall, speed-walking through an area selling clothes, then a mattress store. He found an escalator and went up one more level. He paused on the metal as he glided up, glancing behind him.

The men were still there, and still coming.

He felt the panic rise higher. Surely they wouldn't try anything here, would they?

But he didn't know that. He didn't know what they were being paid. The Triad may have said his death was the price of admittance into the group. The men behind him could be well prepared to kill him in full view of anyone, their lives forfeited to the Snow Leopard.

He hit the third floor, raced through a store onto an outside walkway overlooking a green space, and began sprinting, now trying to do nothing more than increase his separation, all thought of acting normal gone. He drew stares from his rush down the balcony, but no longer cared. He gave thought to leaping over it, like he had in Tainan, but didn't. There were no trees to break his fall this time. He'd just be doing their work for them when he impacted the pavement.

He passed outdoor seating for a restaurant, then reversed,

jerking open the door and seeing a sign proclaiming "Gordon Biersch" on a mirror behind the bar, the rest of the place an open floor plan full of patrons. The nearest tables jerked their heads to him at his rushed appearance, but he ignored them, racing to the hostess stand. He needed a place to hide, before the men entered the restaurant and regained sight of him. Somewhere to let them pass him by.

He said, "Where's the bathroom?"

The hostess looked at the sweat on his brow and said, "Out the front, through the next store. We don't have a bathroom here."

He snapped, "Where? Where is it?"

She backed up a step and said, "Go through the jewelry section of the next store and you'll see it on the left."

He thanked her, then followed her instructions, looking for the men behind him as he did so. They didn't appear. He slowed down, slinking through the department store adjacent to the restaurant, not wanting to draw attention to himself, glancing left and right like a bird looking for the cat.

He passed the jewelry section, saw a sign for the public bathrooms, and went left, threading through the aisles until he reached the hallway.

He went down the passage, seeing a sign for the women's restroom on the left, and the men's on the right. He peeked behind him and saw nothing. He went right, entering the bathroom and finding a man with his child. He nodded at the man, getting a strange look in return for the sweat coming through his shirt.

He realized he either looked like he'd run a marathon or he was a drug addict, but he could do nothing about that now.

Survival was his only thought. He entered a stall and locked the door. He sat on the toilet and let a breath out, feeling safe for the first time. He could stay here for hours—at least until the mall closed—but he intended to only remain long enough for the men to pass him by deeper into the labyrinth. It was a risk, but he viewed it better than taking the chance they would kill him in the open spaces of the mall. He pressed the chronograph on his watch, thinking, *Seven minutes, and then I'm gone.*

He heard the child flush his urinal, the father congratulating him for his abilities, then the fan of the hand dryer. Eventually, the door to the restroom opened and closed. Paul sat, waiting.

The door opened again, and he stared through a crack in the stall, seeing a younger man go to the sink, but Paul couldn't be sure if it was one of the men following him. The man didn't use the urinal, and didn't turn on the water. Paul held his breath.

The door opened again and another man entered, approaching the first one. Paul recognized him from Taipei 101. He flicked his head at Paul's stall, and Paul realized he'd now backed himself into a kill zone. His ruse had failed.

He began to pant with an open mouth, not wanting to make any noise. The door opened again, and a third man entered. Paul leaned forward, catching only glimpses through the crack, but it was enough to tell him they were working together. They advanced on his door, and he felt the adrenaline skyrocket, his body on a tripwire.

They banged on the stall.

He rose to a crouch, saying, "Hey, I'm in here."

In that instant, he realized he'd made a mistake. They didn't know if he was there, but he'd just confirmed it.

The door was kicked in, and he began to fight, the three men collapsing on him inside the stall. He hammered the first man in the head with an elbow, snatched the second around his head and rolled out onto the floor of the bathroom, breaking his neck as he did so.

He leapt up and saw a fourth man he hadn't identified through the crack. The man behind him leapt on his back, jerking his head and exposing his neck while the new man flicked open a blade.

He screamed, and then the door to the restroom slammed open, other men spilling in. He threw his elbow into the stomach of the man behind him, hearing the breath whoosh out, the arms holding him going slack. He slammed his hip back and rotated forward, flinging his attacker over his body and pounding him into the ground. He snapped upright, turning to the other man in the stall, his mind realizing he was dead.

There was no way to beat them all.

And the room exploded in a cyclone of violence.

He thrust a snap kick into the man in the stall, slamming his body against the tiles hard enough to crack his skull, heard what sounded like meat being slapped, then caught something in the corner of his eye flying across the room. A body hammered into the sink counter with the crunch of his spine loud in the enclosed space.

He whirled around, fists raised, and saw the fourth attacker on his knees, a black man with the shape of a fireplug snapping the Triad guy's elbow against the joint until it broke, the noise sounding like the crack of a dry limb.

The Triad man screamed, and the final intruder hammered him in the temple with a sledge of a fist, dropping him to the ground.

Paul took a fighting stance, unsure of what was happening.

The man who'd laid out his attacker, a tall, ropey Caucasian with long black hair, said, "We didn't come here to fight you. Let's go before someone else shows up."

Paul said, "Who are you?"

The black man said, "Do you really think that's the question right now? We're the ones who just saved your ass."

Panting, Paul nodded and said, "What do you want?"

The tall man said, "You. Follow us, if you want to live."

# 77

Chen Ju-Long waited for the bleeps and glitches of the encrypted call to connect, absently staring out the window of one of the tallest buildings in the world and seeing the landscape of Taipei spilling out below him. The biggest operation of his entire career was coming to a head, and he was feeling the pressure.

He saw movement, looked up, and waved a hand at Zhi. "Tell Bobcat he can leave the bathroom."

She nodded and left the room. After being rerouted from over a hundred mirrors around Asia, Chen finally heard the phone connect to his control, still in Australia.

"Is this Tiger?"

Chen said, "Yes. This is Tiger. Operation MANTIS is now in motion. I have a short window to turn it off. Do I have execute authority?"

"What is the risk of compromise?"

"Negligible. Ocelot just left the office. Bobcat is still here. As far as I can tell, they're both clean. They're meeting the day after tomorrow with the contact from NCIST to implant the malware."

"Is the contact a risk?"

"Only in so much as he believes Ocelot is cleared to access the platform. Bobcat works for the company that developed the algorithm, and Ocelot has the clearance through his work here in Taiwan and the badge we produced for him. If the contact suspects either is up to something nefarious, he becomes a risk, but right now, he's clean."

"There is another risk. Ocelot himself is not clean. He is under scrutiny by the National Security Bureau for reasons we don't understand. We believe we've tied off the knot, but I want you to make sure."

Taken aback, Chen said, "What? He just left my office. He didn't say a word about that."

"He doesn't know. We have other assets who determined his status. The threat is being eliminated by another team, but they aren't professional. I don't trust them."

"Who?"

"Triad. We want it to look like an internal matter, but I need you to ensure completion."

"Me? I can't make it look like an internal dispute. Why me?"

"Because we don't trust them. They are working for money, and might be running both sides of the fence. They are not Fifth Bureau. I'll send you a target package. If it alerts after tonight, it means they missed and he is your target. Do you understand?"

Chen saw Jake Shu enter the room, head bowed, Zhi behind him. He said, "Understood. But I'll need men. My mission in Taiwan was just supposed to be as an escort, not as a kinetic arm."

"We have two deep assets in Tainan. They are coming to Taipei tonight. They will contact you."

"Are they any good?"

"As good as you. And they know the target. They identified him when Ocelot gained his badge."

Chen pointed at a chair, telling Jake to sit. Into the phone he said, "So is MANTIS a go?"

"Yes. But we need to be able to control it. Can we do that?"

"Honestly, I have no idea. This is outside the scope of my abilities. Stand by."

He held the phone against his chest and turned to Jake, saying, "If you get this in the system, how will it be initiated? Is it on a timeline, or is it triggered?"

Jake said, "I don't have any idea what you mean. All I have is the data. I didn't build it. My job was just to bring it to you."

Chen bored into Jake's eyes and said, "But you're the computer expert. You aren't a simple drug mule. You *make* the drugs, correct? So you can manipulate this and make the system reflect something that isn't happening? Like you did with the F-35?"

"I . . . I suppose. But I didn't create this data, unlike the F-35."

Chen looked at Zhi and she went behind him, stroking his cheek with her nail. Jake's eyes flew open and he said, "I can do it. I can do it. I just need a powerful computer."

Chen smiled and said, "So you can manipulate this like you did in Japan, and then build a trigger? That can be accessed outside of the system?"

Jake's eyes went all over the room, looking for a way out. He said, "A trigger for what? I have no idea what you're asking."

"I'm asking if you can manipulate the data to do what we want. To make their systems think something is happening when it's not. Just like you did in Japan."

Chen saw the sweat break out on Jake's head, understanding that he was in much deeper than he ever wanted to be. He said, "I can't promise anything. I have to see the code, but I need real computing power. Not just a desktop system."

Chen looked at him for a moment, then returned to the phone, saying, "Okay, he can do it, and we can initiate via a remote trigger, but we need computing power. Can you give us that?"

He heard nothing for a second, then, "What do you mean?"

"I mean Bobcat needs to work on the data with the ability to manipulate it. He can't do it on an office computer."

Chen heard his control say something muffled in the background. He said, "Are you still there?"

"Yes. I'm still here. I'm talking to others. Stand by."

Chen waited, the clock in the room slowly ticking, the only sound in the office. Eventually, he heard, "We can get you the computing power. He will have to interface with the Twelfth Bureau in Beijing. Can you do that from your location?"

Chen looked at Jake and said, "Can you do this remotely? From a computer here? Send it to our facility and use their computing power?"

Jake nodded, saying, "If the pipe is wide, I can do it. Do you have a T1 connection here?"

Chen rolled his eyes and said, "I have no idea, but we're paying an enormous amount for the space in this tower, so I'd say yes."

Jake nodded, looking sick. He said, "Then I can do it, with remote access from the far end."

Chen started to say something into the phone when Jake waved his hand in the air. He paused. "What now? Can you do it or not?"

"I can, but I can't work with anyone in China. I don't speak Chinese. I need someone who speaks English."

"Why?"

"We need to work together. I can't code from here with someone there and not communicate."

Chen nodded, then returned to the phone, saying, "He can do it from here if we build a bridge. But he needs someone who speaks English. Is that possible?"

He heard, "Stand by," then silence. Two minutes later, his control was back, saying, "Yes. We have someone. In fact, this works better. We'll have him engineer the system with another American working for us on artificial intelligence. It'll separate us from the product. Can he do it from where you are?"

Chen looked at Jake cowering in the chair and said, "I think so. It'll depend on your man."

"My man is the best America has to offer. You set it up and he'll work the problem."

"Okay, but the MANTIS meeting is the day after tomorrow with the NCIST contact. Time is short. Is your man available now?"

"He will be. Let me work it. Is Bobcat up to the task?"

Chen leaned back in his chair, his eyes on Jake Shu. He said, "He had better be, or we have no more use for him."

Jake put his head in his hands, and Chen heard, "Good. We have one more issue, though."

Chen heard the change in Control's tenor, the words holding an ominous tone, making him wonder what was coming next.

He said, "Another issue? On top of everything else? What is it?"

"I told you that the Triads were eliminating the threat against Ocelot, and that is a good thing. But unfortunately, it leaves us with a loose end. The Bamboo Triad has outlived its usefulness. Its head, the Snow Leopard, needs to go. He is now a risk, and he is done."

Chen took a breath and then said, "Wait a minute. You

want me to initiate MANTIS using assets in China, eliminate the man hunting Ocelot, and *also* eliminate Leopard? Is that what you're saying?"

"Yes. That is *exactly* what I'm saying."

Chen said, "Sir, I'm not sure I can do all of that. Why Leopard? He's done nothing but help."

"He's a risk. We don't pick our missions. We just execute. We are the Fifth Bureau, and this is from the highest levels. Let him eliminate the threat to Ocelot, and then kill him. Is that a problem?"

Chen paused, thinking. He tried to alter the mission set, saying, "Not operationally. But it will put me in a bind for manpower."

"You have the men coming tonight. Check the target package, and if he's dead tomorrow morning, take Leopard off the board. Then initiate MANTIS. It's not that hard."

"What if the target against Ocelot is still breathing tomorrow?"

"Then do them both."

Incredulous, Chen said, "Sir, we have no cover here. I can't just start killing people. We'll last about twenty-four hours before we're rolled up."

Control's voice grew cold. "Twenty-four hours is all we need. Leopard is a risk, and Ocelot is in danger. MANTIS is going to happen, and you will make it so. Do you understand?"

Chen took a breath, looking at Zhi. She gave him her dead eyes back and he said, "I understand. I will make it happen."

# 78

Inside his small apartment, Jerry Tribble took a sip of his beer, then returned to watching an unauthorized Hulu video on his company-issued laptop, getting more satisfaction from beating the Chinese censors than from the recorded reality show.

The screen blanked out and he saw the blonde bikini avatar beckoning him with her finger, shimmering left and right to a music beat he couldn't hear.

*What the hell. This is getting annoying. They know better than to contact me here.*

She disappeared, the Hulu show resuming.

He knew as long as he didn't type anything on the system—transmit anything on his issued computer—he would remain clean. But he couldn't ignore the alert. Whatever they wanted to ask, they wanted it done in private. The only question now was how he was going to access his workstation at this time of night.

He leaned back, then checked his watch. It was closing in on 9 P.M. in Beijing, which meant it was not even six in the morning at his office.

*Who is calling me at the crack of dawn?*

It had to be something important.

He stood up, packing his work bag, trying to figure out how he would be able to penetrate his office complex at this time of night, when his corporate phone rang. He stared at it on the table, afraid to answer, wondering if the two were connected. It bleated and bleated, and he finally picked it up.

"Hello? Jerry?"

Jerry said nothing for a half-second, wanting to throw the phone into the street, sure that the contact on his computer had something to do with the call now. Wanting more than anything to leave Beijing.

He finally said, "This is Jerry. What's up? Why the late-night call?"

"We've had an issue come up, and you're the only one who can fix it. We need you to come into the office tonight."

He couldn't believe what he was hearing. *They* needed *him* to come in?

*Perfect.*

He said, "I'm on my way."

Twenty minutes later he was in Yuan Bo's small office, with Han Ming behind the desk, Yuan Bo sitting next to him.

Han said, "You remember that work you did for us with the videos?"

"Yes. Of course. We've been through this already."

"We have some more work for you. A little bit of artificial intelligence research, but it needs to be done swiftly."

Jerry glanced at Yuan, wary of the direction the conversation had taken. He said, "Who is the work for?"

"For me. Here, in China, but the data is from an American company. It is in Taiwan, but the American there does not have enough computing power. I need you to build a bridge to him and work with him to manipulate the data."

"What's the data? What am I supposed to do with it?"

"It's an artificial intelligence algorithm that's tracking our exercises here on the mainland. We want to manipulate what it sees, but we want to control when that manipulation occurs."

Incredulous, Jerry said, "Why would you want to do that? What's the purpose?"

Han held up a palm. "You don't need to know the why."

Jerry wasn't stupid. There was only one reason they would want to interfere with the data of the defense systems in Taiwan. And it wasn't a gag gift for someone's birthday, like he'd been told about the videos.

The thought made him queasy. He tried to beg off, saying, "But how am I supposed to help? I haven't even seen the data. This isn't like building a Lego toy set."

Han said, "I'm sure you can manage, but it would be better if the other man talked to you. This is a language I do not speak."

Han passed across a sheet of paper with a VPN address and said, "This is his contact information. We need you to start on it right now."

"Now? It's nearly ten o'clock at night."

"It is time-sensitive. He's waiting on your contact."

Jerry took the paper, saying, "And the payment?"

"Double what you received for the video."

Jerry stood and looked at his actual boss, Yuan Bo. "Now?"

Yuan nodded, and Jerry left the room, going to his workstation. He booted it up, then glanced surreptitiously behind him in the darkened room. He was the only one working. Through the window, he could see Yuan talking to Han, and realized this would be the only chance he had to contact his company.

He pulled up his secret embedded VPN app and sent a message, waiting on the bikini-clad woman to appear. She did so within seconds, and a chat window opened.

He typed:

—What is the urgency here? I had to come to the office at night.

He made no mention of the fact that he had been involuntarily recalled.

The screen bubbled for a minute, then he saw:

—Did you create those videos in Taiwan?

—Why would you ask that?

—We're being strong-armed by the US Gov. They're throwing around words like 'espionage' and 'treason'—because of our contracts with China. We took a look at the videos, and your fingerprints are all over them.

Jerry felt a hot flash race through his body, his forehead breaking out in sweat. He typed:

—I told you I had nothing to do with them. Why are you working with the US Gov?

—Because they are bringing the heat. No offense, but this company is bigger than just you. We have shareholders and a board and you are putting it all in jeopardy.

And Jerry realized that in coming to China he had relinquished his power as CEO. He was losing control.

—What is the next step?

—They want our evaluation. We haven't given it yet, but they're going to ask again. And they aren't going to ask nicely. They have the ability to put us out of business for good. Nobody will work with us if they give us a blacklist.

Jerry thought for a second, then typed:

—Hold off on that. Give them some technical reason to stall. I'm working on something here.

—What?

—I'm honestly not sure, but it might be something that makes the videos moot. If it works, the US Gov won't be worrying about our company.

—You better be right. Don't dig a deeper hole. I'll do what I can.

And that was the crux of his dilemma, but Jerry Tribble had no other choice. Han's money no longer mattered, and if it was a deeper hole, it wouldn't matter when those videos were analyzed. Jerry was now working to ensure Han's success for his own survival.

# 79

Chen Ju-Long took a sip of his tea inside the Huaxi Street market, the workers getting ready for another night. It was only noon, but the place was starting to bustle with people preparing. He watched them passing back and forth, bringing in propane, crates of drinks, and other goods, all of them desperately attempting to regain the glory of the market's past. But that was long gone, leaving in its place a sad reminder of what the snake market had once been.

The alley was littered with refuse and homeless people looking for a place to sleep outside the glare of the police. Chen spent most of his time waving off one or another asking for money while keeping watch on one specific door to a "massage" parlor at the end of the lane. The one that was owned by the Snow Leopard.

He kept his eye on it, waiting for his partner to return—or call for assistance—and saw neither. His phone on the table vibrated, breaking him out of his focus. He picked it up, thinking he would see something from Zhi inside, and saw a blocked number. He knew who was calling.

He picked it up and said, "This is Tiger."

"This is Control. We have a change of mission. The Triads are still on the threat to Ocelot. They missed him last night, but he checked into a hotel with a personal credit card.

They're on him now, so delay the mission against the Snow Leopard until that target is complete."

Incredulous, Chen said, "I *know* where he is. I directed the team you sent me from Tainan against the target this morning. What are you telling me? What do you mean, the Triads are still on him? I'm about to execute that target, and I'm now going to be fighting with other assets? *You* gave me the mission and I'm executing. Who's running the other side of this?"

He heard a cold voice come back. "The Snow Leopard, which is why you can't execute the mission against him. Let it play out, and then complete the mission."

"You're too late on that. I'm already executing."

"What?"

"I have the team against the Ocelot threat, and I have Zhi against the Leopard."

"Pull her out."

"I can't. I have no comms with her. She was searched when she went in. She's in there now."

He heard muffled shouting on the phone, his control giving orders to someone in the room, then the voice returned. "Get in there and turn her off."

Chen saw the door to the massage parlor fly open, then a man stumble out, his shirt red from a wound to his neck. Zhi appeared behind him, grabbed him by the collar, and jerked him back inside.

Chen knew how that would end. He said, "It's too late. Too late."

"Why is it too late? Call her off."

Zhi exited the doorway of the massage parlor, sucking her middle finger like it was a Popsicle, a thin trace of blood running down her cheek.

Chen sighed and said, "It's done. Leopard is dead."

He heard nothing from the phone. Zhi approached him, a look of pride on her face. He pointed to a chair, and she sat, expectantly waiting.

Control said, "Are you sure?"

Chen glanced at Zhi and saw the trickle of blood on her cheek. He pointed at his cheek, and she wiped her own clean. He didn't even bother to ask her. "Yes. He's dead."

There was a pause while Control determined the damage. He said, "Then nothing remains now but to protect Ocelot. MANTIS must go tomorrow."

Chen heard the phone disconnect and put his own away, saying to Zhi, "Any complications?"

Zhi gave him a smile full of teeth, the ring of her upper gums red from her makeshift Popsicle. She said, "No. They're all dead."

He closed his eyes, wondering about her mental state.

He said, "We have another target."

# 80

I opened the door to see Paul Kao glancing nervously to the left and right. I stood aside and said, "Come on in."

He entered and I said, "You look like you're still afraid of the boogeyman."

He grimaced. "You didn't really pick an inconspicuous place to stay. In the past, this hotel was ground zero for spies here in Taiwan."

I flicked my eyes to Jennifer and saw her return to the computer, her face turning a slight shade of red. I'd always left it up to her to pick our place to stay, and because she's a die-hard history buff, she'd settled on the Grand Hotel in Taipei.

Built like a temple palace, it was once the centerpiece for Chiang Kai-Shek's new government in the fifties, after he was forced to flee mainland China, and was originally used solely to house diplomats and distinguished visitors from abroad. Created as part of Chiang Kai-Shek's bid to win the information war against Mao Tse-Tung as to who made up the rightful government of China, in the fifties and sixties it had housed multiple world leaders, from President Eisenhower to the king of Saudi Arabia.

In the modern day, the hotel was bordering on a little shabby. Like an old crown jewel of Vegas that was now competing with the fancy new enterprises, it was struggling to maintain its status as *the* hotel—and losing. It held a sheen of the trappings of the past that was slowly fading, succumbing to the new world order of hotels built around the internet and USB ports, but was still pretty cool, given its history. Which is why Jennifer had picked it.

Spread over multiple acres, it offered tennis courts, swimming pools, saunas, and several restaurants. Situated on the Keelung River, and having been built in a time when the terrain of Taiwan was worth nothing more than the soil it sat on, it tried mightily to survive in the modern world—and succeeded in one respect.

While the new, modern hotels downtown could compete with the amenities they built inside the rooms, the Grand Hotel had a significant footprint. Unlike the half square block those establishments owned within the concrete jungle of Taipei, the Grand Hotel encompassed a large chunk of terrain, with sprawling grounds and an entrance that looked like something from a Disney movie, complete with a drive that circled around a staircase that spilled down the slope of a hill for a hundred meters. Built in a time before the internet, it still held a regal heritage.

I would give Jennifer a ribbing later, but it *was* pretty cool.

I closed the door and said, "Don't blame me. Jennifer likes a little history, and this place is full of it. We don't do Holiday Inns."

She glanced at me to see if I was serious, and I smiled. He misinterpreted my mirth and said, "You couldn't have picked a worse place for getting spied on. This room is probably rigged."

I pointed to our back balcony. "Then let's leave the room for the discussion, but from what you said last night, you'd have known who we were from the beginning, because it would have been the NSB doing the rigging."

After Knuckles and Brett had crushed the men chasing him, we'd hustled him into our vehicles and beat feet back to the hotel, with him giving us a limited history of who he was. He'd checked in under his own name with his own credit card—I mean, I'd save his life, but I wasn't going to pay his way—and he'd been given a room right next to ours.

He'd told us he was some supposed badass in the National Security Bureau who was now considered a "Ronin" because he'd been put out in the cold to run a super-secret mission, but on the drive back he wouldn't say what that was. He'd just thanked us, and then clammed up.

On the one hand, it sounded like complete bullshit, but on the other, I felt the words at a visceral level. Honestly, his story meant more to me than he knew, because I'd lived them once before—when I was what he called a Ronin. Either way, last night I didn't push it, because we had time and I needed to find out any updates from the Taskforce, getting them to locate links between the man we were hunting and the man Paul had followed.

It was always better for the interrogator to know more than the man being questioned, and the truth of the matter was we were all about to fall asleep on our feet, so I'd just called a pause. I'd told everyone to get some rest, then given Paul a time to show up at our room for a more detailed discussion.

And here he was.

He started walking to the balcony and then snapped his head to the television, a Taiwanese station showing the protests from the night before.

I said, "Yeah, it's getting bad out there."

He went to it, reading the scrolling banner at the bottom of the screen—which meant nothing to me, as it was in Chinese.

He said, "Holy Shit. The Snow Leopard is dead. Someone killed him."

I said, "Who?"

"He's the leader of the men who tried to assassinate me."

I pointed again to the balcony, and we walked out the sliding glass door, taking seats in hotel chairs. He said, "So, who are you?"

I said, "Not so fast. You go first."

"I told you who I am."

"That's not my question. Why were you in Taipei 101? Who were you following?"

He looked over the balcony at a large stone courtyard surrounded by concrete ceremonial lions, saying, "I appreciate what you did for me last night, but I can't say anything more."

"Why not? So saving your life isn't enough?"

He smiled and said, "No. China and the Triads work very hard to subvert our government. No offense, but I'm not blabbing to you just because you may have pretended to save my life."

I sat back in my chair, relieved. Honestly, up until this point, I wasn't sure *he* wasn't working for China and Chen Ju-Long.

Last night, after everyone had gone to bed, I'd contacted the Taskforce, and they'd proven about as useful as tits on a boar hog. They had no information about Paul Kao whatsoever, which wasn't that big of a surprise, since we spent all of our time hunting terrorists and not focusing on state systems, but it did leave me flying blind.

I was on my own—but, like Paul Kao himself, I'd been there before, in Australia. I was sort of growing used to it.

I said, "Okay, you just mentioned the Snow Leopard. Who were those men who attacked you? I assumed they were MSS, but from what my boys told me, they weren't that professional."

"They were Bamboo Triad. The MSS uses them here to penetrate our society. Basically, thugs and criminals. The Snow Leopard was their leader, and also the leader of a Chinese reunification political party."

I nodded and said, "So why on earth would you think I was working for China?"

He gave me a small grin, saying, "There is more than one way to compromise an individual, and it would be in the realm of the possible for China to set up last night precisely to co-opt me. No offense. I'm on my own in the wilderness of mirrors here."

I took that in, then decided to just lay it all bare. I believed him, and now I had to get him to believe me. "Yeah, well, I'm not working for China, trust me. The man inside Taipei 101 killed a friend of mine in Australia. A friend who has saved a lot of lives on the world stage, including mine, and for some reason, they decided to kill him."

I locked eyes with him and said, "I don't know what's going on here in Taiwan, but that man's going to pay for it."

His mouth parted at my words. He said, "The man who owns that company in Taipei 101 did this?"

I said, "Yes. He did."

"That's still just words. I have no proof of anything you've told me. I have nobody to trust, and certainly no reason to trust you."

He sat in the chair, waiting on me to speak, so I did, not in a way to brag, but just to let him know where I was coming from.

I leaned forward and said, "Look, you don't want to talk because you don't trust me, and I don't want to talk because I can't trust you, but make no mistake, that fucker is dead. I'm going to kill him."

Paul took that in, then leaned back and said, "You don't know what you're up against here. You Americans always assume you can win because you're *Americans*. This is a different world. You're fighting the entire Chinese government here. That man is probably the highest-ranking member of the Fifth Bureau for external operations. The head of a killing machine. You won't get a chance to eliminate him, and when you miss, he'll kill everyone you've ever talked to, and then kill the families of those men. I've seen it in real life. He is the devil. He *is* a killing machine."

I heard the words and felt a spasm of anger, thinking about Dunkin bleeding out in a cable car in Australia. Thinking about how some people believed they were above the law of combat because they were in a system of government that others feared. Thinking about how those assholes did what they did because they *believed* they were above it all. But they weren't.

At the end of the day, we are all flesh and blood. And I could carve that flesh and release the blood, no matter who they called a master.

I leaned forward and grabbed his collar, jerking him to my face and snarling, "*I* am the killing machine. *I* am the man you fear in the darkness late at night. I am worse than anything China can envision. And I'm going to kill Chen Ju-Long. With or without you."

Inside the room, Jennifer leapt up at my rage, running to the patio, but Paul showed no resistance. I released his collar and he sat back.

He considered my anger for a moment, then said, "So you think you stand a chance?"

I smiled. "Yes, I 'stand a chance,' trust me. So tell me what's going on with the guy who met Chen?"

He saw my eyes and made a decision. "The man I followed there is trying to subvert Taiwan's government. His name is Colonel Rae Ryan Won, of the Republic of China Air Force. He is a liaison to a plethora of different organizations, the linkage between the civilian world and the military. His father was a general and well regarded before he died, but I'm convinced Ryan produced some artificially altered videos which are causing my country to tear itself apart for no reason. I think he's working with the man in Taipei 101. And that man is working for the PRC."

I said, "You think those videos that are causing the riots are fake?"

He leaned forward and said, "I *know* they're fake. People have been trying to kill me for days, and they *did* kill my boss. This is the PRC trying to do the same thing they're doing to Hong Kong, and I'm a threat to them. They're going to generate unrest until the place is an inferno, and then come in here under the guise of 'just helping out.' Ryan is a bad man. Now, why are you on him? Why does the United States care about Taiwan? You've been slowly deserting us for decades."

I said, "Don't tie me to some diplomatic row over our two countries. I don't know enough about it. I have no idea about Taiwan."

I thought about his words and what I knew, saying, "But I believe you're right, only it's not just the videos. They're trying to cause massive unrest here to deflect the national defense of the country. I wasn't following Ryan. I was tracking Chen Ju-Long because he's the handler for an American traitor called

Jake Shu. *That's* who I'm looking for. I followed both of them here from Australia."

"What do you mean, deflect?"

"My friend who was killed by Chen Ju-Long was working in a company in Australia that has a contract with Taiwan for artificial intelligence. Before he died, he told me his thoughts, which at the time I thought was crazy. Now, not so much. I think this Jake Shu has a program of malware that he's going to insert into your defense systems. I think he's going to manipulate your ability to defend yourself. I hadn't figured out how he would be able to do it, since he's a nobody computer geek from America, but you just made the link. He's going to use Colonel Ryan for the penetration."

Astounded, Paul said, "You think that Colonel Ryan is going to leverage your traitor to debilitate our defenses? You think this isn't just Hong Kong disinformation for political gain?"

"I honestly don't know, but I do know the guy is heavily protected by Chinese assets, and they took an incredibly long, roundabout way to get here. They're protecting him for a reason, and I honestly don't know why. I *do* know that your Colonel Ryan is now my only link. Can we work together on this?"

Paul stood up, moving to the edge of the balcony. He finally said, "Yes, we can. I have a GPS tracker on Ryan's car. If he's going to link up with your Jake Shu, we'll know it."

He glanced over the edge of the balcony, then jumped back, saying, "Shit. The Triads have found me."

# 81

Confused by his fear, I stood up, saying, "What? Who's found you?"

"The men who were chasing me last night have found me. They're in the car down below in the parking lot. Which means they're also in the hotel."

He backed up from the rail and said, "I didn't think they knew who I was. I thought they were just protecting Ryan and chasing me because I was on him."

He turned in a circle. "Shit, if they know my name—if they tracked me here—they're the ones who killed my boss. I'm compromised."

I said, "But their leader is dead. You just told me that."

He said, "Maybe they think I did it."

From inside the room, Jennifer said, "Pike, you might want to come see this."

I entered the room, Paul right behind me. She backed up from the peephole of the door and said, "There's a maid out here arguing with two thug-looking guys. They want her to let them into Paul's room."

Paul leaned forward and said, "It's Triad. They get in and they'll find my computer. That can't happen. It has my clandestine communications with my boss."

"I thought you said your boss was dead."

Paul grimaced and said, "He is, and I want that computer.

It's my only proof that I'm working for the NSB. If this whole thing goes bad, it's my lifeline. My proof I'm not a real Ronin."

Jennifer went back to the peephole and said, "The maid looks like she's agreed. They're going in."

I said, "Jennifer, pack a go-bag. Our computers, tablets, a pair of socks, whatever else you can cram in there. Contact the team and tell them we're out of here. I don't want them to engage. I don't want them to be identified. Just let them know we've left."

She nodded and I turned to Paul, saying, "Can you fight?"

He smiled. "Oh, yeah. I can fight. What are you thinking?"

"Let them get in, go across the balcony, then kick their ass."

"Are you serious?"

"Only if you want that computer."

He started walking back to the balcony and Jennifer said, "She's unlocking the door."

We went back through to the balcony and then crossed over the thick wood railing that separated the rooms, crouching outside Paul's sliding door. I could see the men inside ripping through the room, looking for Paul. One went into the bathroom, leaving the other alone.

I whispered, "Wait here. This one is mine. You take the guy in the bathroom."

He nodded. "What are you going to do?"

"Get him out here. When that happens, you go in."

I didn't wait on an answer, sliding open the door and saying, "Hey, what the hell are you doing in my room?"

The shock on his face was priceless. He drew a gun, screamed something in Chinese, and ran toward me. I raised my hands and shouted, "Whoa, whoa, stop!"

He flew out onto the balcony, still running with the gun held in front, and I grabbed his arms, tripped his legs, then rotated, launching him over my back to the parking lot below. I heard him scream, the sound cut short by the impact.

I ran into the room and found that Paul could, in fact, fight. The second man was unconscious on the floor.

I said, "Grab your stuff. The car down below isn't going to be happy."

He started packing, and Jennifer came across the balcony, saying, "There's another set of guys outside the door."

I went to the peephole and saw two buzz-cut Chinese guys, neither looking like the tattooed young men we'd just taken out.

I said, "We have two more coming. Hurry up."

He shouldered a bag, went to the peephole, and said, "Oh my God."

He turned back and said, "We can't fight these two. They're deadly."

I saw real fear on his face. I heard a knock on the door. I whispered, "Who are they?"

"MSS assassins. They tried to kill me in Tainan. If they're here, the place is blanketed."

Jennifer said, "Over the balcony. We can climb down."

I said, "Not anymore. I just dropped a body over it. The Triad in the car will be waiting."

Astounded, she said, "You did what?"

They started banging on the door, no longer politely knocking. I said, "Back to our room."

We ran outside and scrambled over the railing to our balcony, hearing the Triad guys in the parking lot shouting at us. I heard the crack of a round, and the wooden railing splintered.

We raced inside our room and I pulled out my phone to call Knuckles, saying, "Well, this is a shit sandwich."

Paul went to the door, saw my phone, and said, "Don't call anyone. Don't do it. I promise they'll have more firepower than those two men. If we get in a fight here, we're dead."

I said, "Well, what do you want to do, die right here?"

He put his eye to the peephole and said, "No. Let them get in. There's one good thing about this hotel you've chosen."

"What's that?"

He turned back to me and said, "We can't go out the front, we can't go out the back, and we can't go out the balcony because I know for a fact they'll have all of that covered. But we *can* get out."

"How?"

He held a hand up, looking through the peephole. He whispered, "Stand by. They're working the lock."

He turned back and said, "They're in. Let's go."

"Go where? You just said we couldn't go anywhere."

He exited into the hallway, walking past the door to his room. Jennifer and I followed. I heard the men from the parking lot start shooting at the two who'd entered.

I said, "So they aren't working together. That's good news."

Paul began jogging down the hallway, saying, "Not that good. I promise they both have teams here."

He took a left into a narrow hallway, away from the main one leading to the elevators, and I said, "Where are we going?"

"Believe it or not, Chiang Kai-Shek built this place with an escape tunnel. He was petrified about getting caught and killed."

I looked at Jennifer and she said, "I read about it, but I didn't think we'd be using them. There's one on each wing of the hotel."

We reached a stairwell, went bounding down them two at a time, passing through to a basement level, then entered another narrow hallway, this one with no decorations on the walls, the paint a dull green with a steel door at the end. He said, "That's it."

The door had a large two-pronged handle on it like something from a Navy ship. I grabbed both ends, unlocked the mechanism, and swung it open, seeing a narrow concrete staircase leading down into the darkness, and to the left of it what looked like a kids' playground slide following the staircase into the blackness.

Paul said, "Close the door behind us."

Jennifer did so, and he jumped onto the top of the slide, put his pack in his lap, said, "Follow me," and slid away, disappearing into the darkness.

I helped Jennifer up onto the slide, put her pack on her lap, and pushed her, saying, "Have fun."

I clambered up, placed my pack in my lap, put on a Petzl headlamp, and pushed off with my hands. Initially, I was barely sliding, and then I hit a drop-off like a tube at a water park. I picked up speed, everything completely black except for my headlamp strobing against the walls like a horror movie, and I tucked my arms around my pack, protecting my head.

Twenty seconds later I flew off the end, plowing into Jennifer and knocking her to the ground.

I rolled over, stood up, grabbed her hand, and said, "Holy shit. Sorry about that. You okay?"

She stood and said, "Yeah, yeah, I'm good. Paul apparently knew to get clear of the landing. I couldn't see anything."

I shined my headlamp deeper and saw Paul eight feet away picking a padlock on a chain for another steel door.

He got it open and said, "Let's go. This is the side entrance to the palace grounds. We have to cross a parking lot to get there, but once inside, we're good."

He disappeared through the door. I turned my headlamp to Jennifer, seeing her hold her hand against her nose. I saw blood in the harsh glow of my light. Embarrassed, I said, "Did I do that?"

She grimaced at me, saying, "That's another karat on the ring."

# 82

Jake Shu heard his name called and sat up on the small cot, rubbing his eyes. He'd worked twenty-four hours straight since he'd arrived in Taiwan, using a small computer room to interface with an American called Jerry Tribble in Beijing. He'd dearly wanted to ask who that man was, but one look in Zhi's eyes and he knew it wouldn't have been smart. Not if he wanted to avoid her nail.

They'd locked him into a small room with a single desktop computer and a secure VPN. The next thing he knew, Jerry Tribble was contacting him from Beijing. He'd had his doubts that Jerry would be any help—other than an interface for computing power—but he'd turned out to be almost as good as Jake with the coding. They'd worked on the problem set straight through, manipulating the algorithm and building a back door to access the program. Eventually, upon completion, he'd been allowed to rest, but only in the small office.

He heard his name again, rubbed the sleep out of his eyes, and saw Chen Ju-Long in the doorway. Chen said, "Get up. It's time. Ocelot will be here soon."

He swung his feet over the small cot and said, "Who is Ocelot?"

"The man that's going to get you into the systems to implant what you've worked so hard on."

Jake began putting on his shoes, saying, "You haven't even told me what this is all about. Where are we going?"

"Ocelot will tell you."

Jake stopped tying his shoes. "That's not good enough anymore."

Chen entered the small room and shut the door. "I don't know what you thought was going to happen, but you're going to do this. After it's complete, you can fly home. If it's not complete, I'll kill you."

Jake saw the death in his eyes and felt the fear, causing him to cave in yet again. More worried about his own miserable life than the damage he was causing, he held up his hands and said, "Okay, okay. I'm in."

There was a knock on the door, then Zhi stuck her head in, saying, "Ocelot is here. Meeting is set for an hour and a half from now."

Chen nodded. "Follow me."

Jake exited the small room for the first time in thirty-four hours, seeing the same two buzz-cut Chinese men who'd guarded the office door. It didn't appear they'd moved since he'd first seen them, sitting in the same chairs and looking like robots. They reminded him of Thing One and Thing Two from *The Cat in the Hat*—neither showing any outward emotion, but both radiating mayhem by their mere presence.

In another chair was a man in a ROC Air Force uniform with the nametag "Won." Chen produced a badge from a briefcase, handed it to Jake and said, "This is Ocelot. He'll get you in. We'll be following for protection, but not close. Just do as Ocelot says."

He turned to the Air Force officer and held out a key fob. "You'll use this car. It's in the parking garage downstairs, first level, slot seventeen."

The officer said, "Why? I'll take my car."

"No, *I'll* take your car. I don't want it on camera or registered as entering the compound. We won't enter, but we'll be close enough to help."

Twenty minutes later Jake Shu was on the main highway heading south with Colonel Won. He said, "So, what's your name?"

"It's Ocelot to you, Bobcat."

It was the first time Jake had heard that he had a code name. He asked, "Bobcat? What's that?"

The colonel glanced at him and said, "Just do the mission. Nothing more. When we reach the gate, say nothing. If anyone asks, you're from Gollum Solutions, here to help them with their artificial intelligence. Nothing more, nothing less."

They spent the rest of the drive in silence, heading south out of New Taipei and into the countryside. Fifty minutes later they passed through the Longtan district, eventually stopping outside a concrete structure full of concertina wire and guard towers. Ocelot passed through the gate and Jake saw a sign proclaiming the National Chung-Shan Institute of Science and Technology.

Ocelot pulled into the visitor center, said "Wait here," and left the car. Jake glanced behind him for Chen Ju-Long or the car with Thing One and Thing Two, but saw nothing.

Ocelot returned with a pass, and they were allowed in. He circled the buildings until he found the one he was looking for, then parked. On the front walkway was an older man wearing a white lab coat.

Ocelot said, "That badge you were given will get you into the facility. Act like you know why you have it."

They walked up to the lab tech and Ocelot said something

in Chinese, then pointed to Jake and, in English, said, "This is the man from Gollum Solutions. He has the newest upgrades to your systems."

To Jake he said, "This is Hong Tao, the supervisor for the artificial intelligence systems experiment for the defense of Taiwan."

Unsure of what to do, Jake simply nodded. Hong said, "Shall we go in? I'm interested to see the new system you've brought."

He led them to the security post inside, where they were asked to show their access badges. Hong produced his, followed by Colonel Won, then Jake nervously presented the one he'd been given. It was scanned and then handed back, much to his relief.

Hong led them down a wide hallway to an elevator, where they rode up to the third floor. He used a different badge for an RFID reader outside a door, and then led them into what looked like a computer lab, with multiple men and women in white coats hunched over computer terminals. They glanced up at the opening of the door, but showed no interest, returning to their work.

Hong led them to a small room with a computer terminal, saying, "This is PRAYING MANTIS, our experimental AI system that Gollum has been providing solutions to input."

Colonel Won said, "Doesn't look like much."

Hong smiled. "This is just the input. The computing power is elsewhere."

Jake asked, "Can I begin the upgrade?"

"Please do."

Jake pulled out his portable hard drive and plugged it into the terminal's USB port, then began typing on the keyboard.

Feigning interest to distract from Jake Shu's infiltration of the system, Colonel Won turned to Hong and said, "How's this supposed to work?"

"Right now, it's just experimental, but basically, we have a large number of sensors out on the periphery that analyze various aspects of Chinese intent, ranging from sonar buoys to register large flotillas and underwater infiltrations to radar arrays for mobilization of land-based forces, but all of these are stovepiped to a greater or lesser degree. We wanted a way to synthesize the information, which is where PRAYING MANTIS comes in."

"So this program fuses those sensor feeds?"

"Yes, but it's more than that. It not only fuses the sensor feeds, but also analyzes all of the inputs and makes a determination if an attack is imminent. There are plenty of indicators that can be used, from deployment of potential naval forces to overflight of aircraft, but a single event is not enough to determine an attack. Putting them together can give us an edge on a response, but right now, each of those is analyzed individually, then fed into the system for further analysis using the other sensors. We just don't have the time for that. We're a hundred miles off the coast of China, and even an hour may be too late. PRAYING MANTIS uses machine learning to provide a much quicker analysis."

"So it spits out an 'attack' or 'no attack' solution?"

"Simplistically, yes, but eventually it'll be tied into actual shooting platforms. Right now, it's integrated into our new Yun Feng land attack cruise missiles on the Penghu island chain. We're using China's current mobilization exercises to develop more data on what a signature would be. In essence, they pretend to attack our Kinmen Islands every time we hold an election, and this time, we're watching to see what an indicator of an actual attack would be. As they practice maneuvers, PRAYING MANTIS learns what that looks like."

"You mean in the future it could actually launch an attack on its own? From a missile battery?"

"No. There would always be a man in the loop, but it will program the attack pattern for the missiles, meaning the man in the loop only needs to hit a button instead of determining the targets. It'll tell him where the threat is coming from."

"Where is that guy? Here? Is that where the decision is made?"

"Of course not. We're just scientists. The battery is controlled from Tainan, at the missile command on the airbase. In fact, we've run a few exercises with them, and so far, PRAYING MANTIS has proven very beneficial. By next year, we should be able to loop in the air command and our naval forces. It'll be seamless."

Jake looked up from his terminal and said, "I'm complete. The system is updated with the latest algorithm. You guys can test it out for a few weeks, then let us know if we need to tweak it again."

Hong said, "Thank you, but I'm sure that won't be necessary."

Colonel Won smiled and said, "I agree."

# 83

Sitting just down the street from a complex called the National Chung-Shan Institute of Science and Technology, I heard Jennifer come on the net, saying, "Fly Boy is on the move—leaving. He's got Pirate with him."

I glanced at Paul to make sure he was listening and said, "Both Fly Boy and Pirate? Confirm."

I used our original callsign for Jake Shu and had deferred to Paul's callsign for Colonel Ryan Won, because if anyone was listening, I wanted to ensure they had no idea who we were talking about.

"Yep. Both of them. Pirate looks a little green in the gills, but Fly Boy is all smiles. Whatever they did, Fly Boy thinks it was successful."

Which really made me rethink my decision from this morning. I'd considered taking them out once we left the main highway, but then for further intelligence had decided to see where they were headed. Now I knew, but I might have just allowed them to complete whatever nefarious mission they had planned.

It was the usual counterterrorist dilemma of develop or strike. I'd decided to develop, and now a strike might be too little, too late. But I knew that second-guessing was pointless.

After fleeing the Grand Hotel like a teenager caught in the bedroom with the farmer's daughter, we'd relocated to one of the more modern establishments downtown—this time without allowing Paul to use his credit card. I'd end up paying the bill, but I was fairly sure I could charge the U.S. government when it was all over.

We'd reconsolidated, with me pulling out my team from the Grand Hotel, and as the darkness grew, so did the protests. They had grown stronger during the day and a half we'd spent at the Grand, beginning as soon as the sun went down. We'd ignored the chanting while we planned for the next phase, which was following Colonel Ryan Won—AKA Fly Boy.

We'd waited until his GPS beacon had alerted, and then launched in a three-car surveillance effort, shocked to see that the protests from the night before now included property damage, with multiple buildings having had their windows shattered, glass and other debris littering the streets—although it seemed the majority of action was still centered away from us near the presidential palace and other government buildings.

I had Paul with me, Knuckles and Brett in another car, and Jennifer with Veep. Not unexpectedly, Fly Boy had returned to the Taipei 101 garage, and I'd set up a box around the place, with Veep and Jennifer acting as the trigger.

Sitting in our car, killing time while we waited on the call, I'd asked Paul what he thought about the protests.

"They're tearing the country apart, and they're supported by the Triads, paid for by China. I'm sure of it—and Fly Boy is the link."

"You don't think it'll just burn itself out?"

"I hope so—but it hasn't in Hong Kong. China is consolidating its grip there, and I'm sure they want to do the same here. I mean, any unrest is good for them. Best case, their preferred candidate wins the upcoming election. Worst case, they cause the government to fall. Either way, it's a win for them."

And then Jennifer had interrupted with the trigger. Fly Boy was leaving the garage, and he now had Pirate with him. I'd expected to see the beacon move before we actually had a visual, but that hadn't happened. Fly Boy had exited the garage in a different vehicle.

Thank God I hadn't relied on technology.

I said, "Give me a description."

"Late-model Hyundai SUV, black. I don't have the plates."

I said, "Good enough. Knuckles, Blood, you copy?"

"We got it. I see the vehicle. We have the eye."

And then my team had given chase, ignoring the beacon. The target had traveled an hour south, leaving the main highway and winding through the mountains on back roads, eventually ending up at some complex called the National Chung-Shan Institute of Science and Technology.

We'd pulled aside and let them enter. I'd repositioned everyone with bumper positions up and down the entrance road, because I was fairly sure there wasn't a back way out of the place. The complex was locked down like Fort Knox, so I knew they were coming out through the same gate they'd entered.

During our wait, Paul told me the facility was apparently a research arm of the ROC defense forces, used to develop missiles and other technology, not unlike our own U.S. Defense Advanced Research Projects Agency—or DARPA—which scared the hell out of me, given what I thought Jake Shu was doing.

Eventually, Jennifer had triggered again, confirming that both Fly Boy and Pirate were in the car. I had no idea what they'd done inside the facility, but I was sorely regretting not taking them down before they arrived.

Sometimes developing the situation is the way to go, sometimes it's the strike, but it was too late now.

She said, "Vehicle intending north. I say again, vehicle intending north, both packages inside."

Which was to me. I glanced at Paul and said, "We're on station. Knuckles, Blood, you copy?"

"Moving now."

Five seconds later the SUV passed us, headed back up the lonely road we were on. I put the car in gear and began to follow. We wound through the mountains outside the compound on the narrow blacktop, snaking through switchbacks every hundred meters as the road tried to get back down to the valley where it could run flat out. And it gave me an idea.

We had about seven minutes before this car reached the valley floor and the main highway. Seven minutes of switchbacks that I could use, while they were all alone.

I got on the net and said, "I'm going to PIT these guys. Knuckles, get on me now. Close the far end after I interdict."

Knuckles said, "I'm thirty seconds out. Give me the call."

Jennifer said, "This is Koko. Are you sure?"

"Yeah, I'm sure. You are the extract. I'm going to take him at the next turn. Knuckles and Blood are security. You're extract."

I heard Jennifer say, "Roger all," and knew she was now furiously trying to catch up.

The car wound around another mountain switchback, the road twisting back on itself as it descended to the valley floor, and I goosed my car, Paul saying, "What's a PIT?"

I saw the vehicle ahead of me and said, "It's basically where I crash the shit out of the car, forcing it to stop."

The vehicle reached another hairpin turn and slowed, giving me an advantage. I heard him say, "What? What do you mean, a crash?"

I sped up, sailing down the slope and hitting the curve at thirty miles an hour. I saw a look of fear from Jake Shu in the passenger seat as I pulled abreast of them. I swung the wheel right and kissed the left rear quarter panel of the SUV, causing its tires to break free from the pavement. I hit the gas while still steering to the right and their vehicle slid sideways for a moment, then spun around, hammering into a guardrail and stopping, its back end hanging over a cliff.

We sped past the wreck and I slammed on the brakes. I threw the car in park and jumped out just as another vehicle came from the other direction. I shouted, "Paul! Get on the target car!" then held my hands in the air as if I was flagging someone for an accident. Paul leapt out and began jogging to the car I'd wrecked. The vehicle stopped, and two men exited.

Two I'd seen before. The MSS assassins from the hotel.

They started shooting as soon as they set foot on the asphalt. I dove behind the back of my car, pulling my own weapon out and saying, "Paul! Threat!"

He flung himself to the ground and I started shooting back, not very accurately, but giving them a reason to duck. They flopped down behind the open doors of their car and Jake Shu entered my peripheral vision, running up the road with his hands in the air.

I shouted, "Jake! Jake! No!"

But it did no good. He was staggering like a drunk, his hands flopping back and forth, his eyes wide with fear. One of the men behind the Chinese vehicle raised up, saw him coming, and nailed him right between the eyes. He collapsed on the road like he'd fallen asleep while running, sliding forward on the pavement, his face grinding into the asphalt.

The man who'd fired realized he'd killed the wrong target and screamed in frustration. I saw his partner start sprinting from the other side of the car, trying to flank me on the hillside.

I raised my pistol, took a slow bead in my holosight, led him a fraction, and punched two bullets center mass. He staggered across the pavement and then fell into the hillside on the far side of the road, looking like a deer that had been shot and had kept moving until its body told him it was done.

I shouted, "Paul, Paul, get on Fly Boy!" and leapt up.

The second man put down a fusillade of lead at my appearance, and I dove back down behind the cover of my rental, the bullets puncturing steel and shattering glass. I heard an engine up the road, and Knuckles came around the corner, driving flat out. The man saw him coming and stood up, punching rounds through the windshield in an effort to get him to stop, but it did no good.

Knuckles ducked down below the wheel and slammed his car into the open door of the man's vehicle, hammering it hard enough to launch the man hiding behind it over the cliff.

I turned around, seeing Fly Boy leaping down the slope, Paul in pursuit. Down below me, on another switchback, I saw another car on the road.

Fly Boy reached it, the door was flung open, and Chen Ju-Long appeared. He looked at me, and I saw recognition. I snarled into the air, but there was nothing I could do to stop what was happening.

Fly Boy piled into the back, and the car executed an accelerated J-turn, snapping around like it was nailed into the road by the hood, and then began racing toward the valley.

I raised my weapon, wanting to shoot, but I knew it would do no good. Paul made his way back up the slope and stopped at Jake Shu's dead body.

I went to Knuckles's car, finding him and Brett outside, searching for the bad man in the bushes, but there wasn't anything left to harm us. He was dead from the impact.

Knuckles said, "Is this how it was supposed to end?"

I could tell he was pissed. My plan hadn't gone the way I'd thought it would, but that was water under the bridge now, and there was no reason to dwell on it. Instead, I gave it right back to him.

I said, "You mean you crashing your car into a guy we could have interrogated, launching his ass off a cliff?"

He grinned and said, "Well, I could have let him kill you."

I said, "Check your vehicle. Make sure it runs. We need to get out of here."

I got on the net and said, "Koko, Veep, exfil on the alternate route. We'll see you at the hotel."

Veep came back, "What happened?"

I said, "I'll tell you at the hotwash, but it isn't pretty."

I walked over to Paul. "He alive?"

"No. He's most definitely dead."

I sighed and said, "Fuck. What a debacle."

Paul said, "There *is* a silver lining."

"And what, pray tell, is that?"

"Chen Ju-Long is driving Colonel Won's car. And it still has the beacon."

# 84

Chen Ju-Long drove for about a mile and a half to the valley floor. Before he accessed the on-ramp of the north-south highway he pulled over, saying to Zhi, "Take the wheel. I have to make a call."

She did so, and he dialed his control, waiting on the encryption to synchronize. When it did, and the line cleared, he said, "This is Tiger. The implant was a success, but we have a problem."

"Problem? What happened?"

"The Americans from Australia appeared here in Taiwan. I was wrong about it being a coincidence before. It wasn't just an anomaly based off the killing of their friend. I don't know who they work for, but they are definitely tracking us."

"Can you evade them until we initiate MANTIS? After that, it won't matter what they do."

"That's the primary problem. They interdicted Ocelot and Bobcat's vehicle. Ocelot gives us the access we need to the bases here, but Bobcat built the program. He had the back door to execute. And he was killed."

"Killed? By the Americans?"

"Yes. They also killed the two men you sent from Tainan. They are skilled. Ocelot managed to escape, and he's with me now. We've broken the surveillance effort through the fight and by a change of vehicles, but we don't have a way to initiate now."

His control said, "This is very disappointing. Continue your mission. I'll call you back."

Chen hung up and said, "Go to Tainan." Zhi entered the highway and he turned around to Ocelot, saying, "What happened up there?"

Ocelot looked like he wanted to throw up, holding his head in his hands. "I don't really know. We were hit by a car, knocking us into the guardrail. Before I could even figure out what had happened, there was a gunfight between your men and the car that hit us. Bobcat freaked out and ran toward your men, trying to escape, I think."

"And the Americans killed him?"

Ocelot said nothing. More forcefully, Chen said, "And the Americans *killed* him? Talk to me."

Ocelot pulled his head out of his hands and said, "No. *Your* men killed him. He ran toward them seeking escape, and they shot him."

Chen slapped the dashboard in frustration. Zhi said, "They didn't know who he was. It isn't their fault."

"Yes it is. Continue to Tainan. Maybe Control can salvage this mess."

After two hours on the road his phone rang again. He saw the number and realized it wasn't his control. He answered, saying, "This is Tiger."

"This is Lion. I understand there is an issue with the execution of MANTIS."

"Yes, sir. We've lost the ability to initiate. Bobcat is dead. I don't have the back door. I have no way to execute now."

"I have one here, in Beijing."

"How?"

"The American here worked with Bobcat on the program. He has the access control. He can initiate. Let me know when you arrive at the airbase in Tainan. It has to happen today. The full mission profile of the PLA exercise begins soon. We need that signature to quell any fears that the algorithm is incorrect."

Traveling down the road, Chen wondered if they weren't pushing the issue. Wondered if they hadn't extended themselves too far. It had happened in the past, but it wasn't his job to question why.

He said, "Yes, sir. I'll let you know."

He heard some steel through the phone. "Tiger, make no mistake, Ocelot has to use his power to get the command to launch the missiles. Once we initiate, he needs to convince them that it isn't an exercise. Today is the day for victory. Tomorrow is too late. Do you understand?"

Chen said, "Yes, sir. I understand. I'll get it done."

We evacuated the target area, reconsolidating the surveillance effort at a roadside stand just outside the entrance to the valley highway. The team arrived one by one, coalescing around a picnic table under a gazebo.

Once everyone was accounted for, I said, "Okay, here's the deal. Jake Shu is dead, so we've probably short-circuited whatever China had planned. Mission accomplished. I'm about to call the Taskforce to give them a SITREP, but when I do, I'm going to tell them I'm not done."

Knuckles said, "What's that mean?"

"Chen Ju-Long killed Dunkin. Murdered him. I'm going to take him down. I realize that's outside our target set and the Taskforce charter, but I'm going to do it."

Veep glanced between us, looking at Brett, then Jennifer, clearly not liking where this was headed. He finally said, "Hey, Pike, I think we should get sanction for any further operations. I get the loss of life, but last year in Brazil was over the edge. Let's not do that again. I don't want to start a trend here. That's not us."

I turned to him and said, "That's why we're here talking. I want to know where you guys stand. You don't want to play, no harm, no foul. I'm not ordering anyone to do anything, and this isn't a Taskforce operation, but actions have consequences, and I'm going to be that consequence. If you want, you can go back to Taipei. I won't think any less of you."

Clearly uncomfortable, he said, "That's not what I meant. I mean, we do what we're ordered, and sometimes people die. We accomplished the mission, but we don't do revenge."

I saw Paul Kao on the outside edge of the group shuffle his feet, wanting to say something, but unsure if he should.

I said, "Veep, I understand where you're coming from. I honestly do, but that's not why I'm asking to execute. What I'm saying is that a Chinese intelligence organization killed Dunkin. The Taskforce cared about why, and we solved that riddle. I care about the death. He deserves our support. He's got a girlfriend in the United States who has no idea why he died. Yes, we stopped the Chinese, but they still murdered him, and there is not going to be any justice without us. Justice isn't revenge."

I looked at my team and said, "I'm going to deliver the justice. Chen Ju-Long will kill again somewhere in the world, and it will be some other innocent victim to project Chinese power. It might even be an American. We have the beacon trace of the car, and I'm going to find it. What I want to know is who will follow me. I'm not ordering. I'm asking."

Veep looked at Jennifer, asking her with his eyes what she thought. For the first time I realized she was someone the team relied on for an answer, and it gave me a small bit of pride. I should have been upset, because basically he was trying to split her from me, but I wasn't. She had earned that right. I would do what I was going to do, alone if necessary, but she would get a vote.

He said, "Jennifer, come on. You know this isn't right. We don't do assassinations. That's what the Chinese do."

She looked at me, and I saw the anguish of Dunkin's death. She still blamed herself. She took my hand in hers and squeezed it, then glanced at Paul, saying, "This isn't an assassination. Those men are trying to alter the life of an entire country. We stopped one small event here, but it won't stop the men like Chen Ju-Long from continuing. We don't have sanction here, but I'm willing to prevent it."

Veep said nothing, the tension thick, and Paul stepped forward, breaking it with his very presence.

Tentatively he said, "Can I speak?"

I said, "By all means."

He turned to Veep and said, "Look, this isn't a vendetta. I can't stop what's happening without you. The high command of the PRC are doing something bad. Can't we just prevent it? Without all this verbal dancing about vendettas?"

A little startled at his comments, I turned to him and said, "You don't think it's done? Jake Shu is dead. Whatever he was doing is gone."

"Maybe, but he just left the NCIST. You told me he was a computer guy, and that was the only reason he was in there. He's dead, but we don't even know if that matters. No, I don't think it's done. I think it's still going."

I glanced around at the team and said, "This isn't our

country, and there is no threat to the United States, but we can deliver some justice for Dunkin and maybe help Taiwan. I'll do it alone if I have to."

Knuckles said, "That took some time. Can we get our jihad on now?"

He hadn't said a word for the entire discussion, and I knew why. Leadership was a one-way road, and he was letting me work the problem. He understood the pressure I was under, but also knew the threat. He was the best of the Taskforce. And his vote meant something to the team.

Veep nodded, glanced away for a moment, and then said, "Okay. Let's get some."

I studied him for a moment, then said, "This is going to go bad. You know that, right? I can't have someone who isn't fully in, but I could really use your skill."

He said, "I'm in." He glanced at Jennifer, and she nodded to him. More forcefully, he said, "I'm in. Let's go."

I grinned and Jennifer leaned in, whispering, "Don't screw this up."

# 85

George Wolffe entered the foyer of the West Wing for the third time in a week, an absolute record. In the past, all Taskforce business was handled in the Old Executive Office Building, with him rarely stepping into the White House itself.

In truth, this was a double record, because it was closing in on midnight, and he had never, ever gone to the White House grounds outside of working hours. But Taiwan was turning into the biggest mess on the world stage, and he had the only men inside the inferno to give honest feedback. He really wished he'd never agreed to allow the Taskforce to focus on a state system. It wasn't what they did. Others did that, and they supposedly did it well, but now he was in the cauldron because others apparently didn't do it that well.

He stopped at the Secret Service desk to wait on his escort, and then his phone went off with the distinctive ring of an encrypted call. He saw his escort approaching and held up a finger, stepping back outside to the parking lot.

"This is Wolffe."

"Hey, sir, I didn't think I'd get you to answer the phone at this time of night."

"Pike? Yeah, well, I'm about to go into another one of *those* meetings about Taiwan. It's currently the crisis du jour, and since you're there, I'm here. What do you have?"

Pike said, "An Oversight Council meeting, or that bullshit National Security Council stuff?"

"National Security Council. Sorry."

"Why are you going?"

"Because you're the only thing playing in Taiwan, and it's turning to complete shit."

He heard Pike chuckle on the phone. He said, "Is that funny to you?"

"No. I understand what you're going through. What's funny is that you're now forced to have to defend me."

Wolffe felt the ancient instinct of fight or flight flood his veins. He wasn't sure he wanted to hear what was next.

In an even voice, he said, "What's happening? I'm about to see the president of the United States."

"Jake Shu is dead. That is tied off."

And the adrenaline flowed. Wolffe said, "You killed Jake Shu? Jesus, Pike, you had Omega authority for capture. Not kill."

"Yes, sir, but I didn't kill him. I tried a capture and was interdicted by the Chinese. *They* killed him."

Wolffe exhaled and said, "So the threat is gone?"

"No, it's not gone. He went to a place called the National Chung-Shan Institute of Science and Technology. It's like our DARPA. He was inside for an hour, and he was doing something bad."

"Bad? Bad how? What did he do?"

"Sir, I have no idea, but it's there now. It's like a virus waiting to be exploited. I need you to let them know they've been compromised."

Wolffe said, "Okay, okay. I'll get on it. But it won't happen quickly. We don't have any formal diplomatic ties to Taiwan anymore."

"Oh, bullshit. Are you telling me we don't have a CIA station chief in the country? Or we don't have a consulate? We have to have something here."

"Pike, what we have is a thing called the American Institute in Taiwan. It's a nonprofit, but it has a lot of State Department staff, without any formal U.S. linkage. The bottom line is we no longer have any diplomatic ties. The State Department gave up formal recognition of the Republic of China in 1979."

Pike said, "Well, someone had better get a formal connection, because the Chinese have done something here, and I don't know what it is."

Wolffe said, "Okay, okay, I'll bring it to the Council. Get your men back home. With Jake Shu dead, your mission is over."

He heard nothing for a moment. He said, "Pike?"

"Yeah, I'm still here, sir."

"Get on the Rock Star bird and come home."

"I can't do that, sir. Chen Ju-Long is still here. He's still working his mischief. I'm going to take him down."

"Pike, that isn't going to happen. It's not a U.S. threat. You got the bad guy. Get on the bird and come home. The rest of this is someone else's problem. Not the Taskforce. That's a direct order."

"Sir, I'm with a guy from the National Security Bureau. He's asked for my help. I'm asking *you* to let me give it."

"National Security Bureau? Who is he?"

"Just some guy we ran into who was tracking the same thread as us. We were on the American, he was on the Chinese. We met in the middle. He's solid."

"Then let him handle it. They have a much greater chance of success."

Pike said, "Sir . . . I would if I could, but he's been ostracized by the NSB. He needs our help."

Wolffe couldn't believe the words he was hearing. "Wait, what? You're running around with a guy that's been kicked out of NSB?"

"Yeah. Trust me, it's a little complicated."

"How am I supposed to brief that? Are you compromised?"

"No. We aren't compromised. At least not yet."

"What's that mean?"

"I'm going to track Chen Ju-Long and take him out, no matter what it takes. I just need your support."

"Pike, I can't give that. Get on board the aircraft and come home."

Pike said, "Okay, sir. No support. I understand. But remember this: You asked for some Pike magic, and I'm giving it right now. You can thank me later."

Wolffe said, "Pike! That's not going to happen." And then he realized Pike had hung up the phone.

He reentered the West Wing and signed the Secret Service access roster. His escort said, "Who were you talking to?"

"Nobody you want to know about. Trust me. Just get me inside."

# 86

Han Ming paced the floor of Yuan's small office for the next two hours, only pausing once to talk to a high-ranking member of the Chinese Communist Politburo, reassuring him that the mission was on track, even if he didn't feel the same confidence.

The mission itself was extremely close hold, with only two members of the Politburo and the president himself read onto the plan. None of the People's Liberation Army generals had a clue that a confrontation was coming even as they practiced for the invasion, and this was by design. They needed the PLA to react with genuine shock and disbelief at being attacked for no reason whatsoever—with the requisite reflections on numerous radio and satellite transmissions, all feeding into the Western intelligence systems to prove they were the aggrieved party. Such a thing couldn't be faked. It had to be real—and so it would be.

Finally, after nearly four hours of waiting, Tiger called him again.

"We're at the gate. It's surrounded by protestors. They're growing restless, shouting and beginning to throw water bottles and other objects."

Han rubbed his head, not believing that his counterplan for disruption of the political system of Taiwan was now possibly about to prevent the actual execution of the mission.

He said, "Can you get in?"

"We can try, but there is a good chance we'll get attacked."

"Can't you use Ocelot? Isn't he wearing a ROC uniform?"

"Yes, sir, but I'm not sure if that won't just inflame them."

"Drive through like you have a reason to be there. Get through the gate using his authority. We are out of time. The window for the assault is sundown. The exercises finish today. We can't roll over until tomorrow."

"Yes, sir. We're trying now."

"This is no fail. I'm initiating MANTIS. You have about fifteen minutes before that missile command begins to receive the feeds."

He hung up the phone and left the office, walking to Jerry Tribble's workstation. Jerry turned at his approach, and Han saw a haggard man. He'd been working for nearly thirty-six hours straight, and it showed.

Jerry said, "Can I go home now?"

"No. Not yet. I need you to initiate the program you worked on with Jake Shu."

"Me? I didn't have anything to do with that. All I did was help with some coding. It's not my program. It's his."

"Well, he's dead. So now it's yours."

Jerry's eyes grew wide and he said, "Dead? How? What is this thing?"

"Don't pretend innocence. Just initiate the program you built. Right now."

"I'm . . . I'm not sure that's something I should do."

Han leaned into his face and said, "There is a thing you Americans always love to talk about when you try to bend others to your will. The carrot and the stick. The carrot here is that I will make you rich. The stick is that I will kill you. You won't leave this building alive. Do you understand?"

He saw Jerry's face blanch, and said, "Do it. Now."

Jerry turned away and began working his keyboard.

After hanging up on George Wolffe, I looked at the team around the table and said, "Whelp, looks like we're pulling a Clark Griswold now. On our own vacation. Paul, are you tracking the vehicle?"

He went to his laptop and said, "Heading south on the main highway. My bet is he's going to Tainan, where I tracked him once before."

I said, "Okay, saddle up. They've got about a forty-five-minute head start. Let's go find him."

We loaded in the same vehicle teams we'd had before and began heading south on the main highway. It was about a four-hour trip, and the car, just like Paul had predicted, continued south, staying on the freeway.

Ryan's vehicle was driving just under the speed limit, not wanting to attract any attention. We, on the other hand, put the pedal to the metal, cutting their lead to about ten minutes by the time they entered Tainan. From there, the traffic and stoplights themselves let us catch up.

Paul and I trailed behind, not wanting to get compromised by Chen Ju-Long, and the target passed through the town until they were near the Tainan Airport—which was co-located with an ROC airbase. The vehicle ignored the entrance to the civilian side, continuing on until it was traveling toward the military base, and then was forced to slow because of the crowds.

Outside was chaos, with a large mob of people holding signs and throwing things at the front gate, all of them chanting slogans in Chinese.

I said, "What in the hell?"

Paul said, "They're working it down here too. It's getting worse. This is China's and the Triad's doing."

"Yeah, but why protest the airbase? What did they ever do? It's not like they make decisions for the parliament."

"I guess it's a symbol of the government. The only one down here, so they're protesting outside of it."

"Great."

I called Knuckles, saying, "You got eyes on the target? We aren't going to try to push through this."

"Yeah. He just went through the gate. The protestors banged on the hood a little bit, but let him go."

I turned to Paul and said, "What's the grid now?"

Paul said, "They made it inside. The vehicle is parked next to the 501st Missile Command."

I said, "What's that? What do they do?"

"They control the land attack cruise missiles on our forward-deployed islands, like Penghu and Kinmen."

*Shit*. So now I could develop or strike. Although I had no idea how I could possibly strike inside an ROC airbase surrounded by frothing lunatics.

# 87

Colonel Ryan led the way to the front entrance of the 501st Missile Battalion, seeing a sign that proclaimed the 501st as the vanguard of the Strategic Strike Counter Missile Group. He entered the hallway, stopping at a small security cubicle to show his credentials. He turned and pointed to Chen and Zhi, saying, "They are scientists from NCIST, working Project PRAYING MANTIS."

The guard let them pass.

Ryan led them down a hallway, past offices and restrooms, to a large room that resembled the bridge on the Star Trek *Enterprise,* complete with a ring of men and women in headsets staring at screens and a command chair in the center holding a lieutenant colonel.

Ryan approached and the man rose. Ryan said, "Good to see you again, Colonel Wang."

They shook hands, and Colonel Wang said, "To what do I owe the pleasure of the visit?"

"We just came from the NCIST. These scientists have upgraded the algorithm of the MANTIS system, and we wanted to make sure it took."

Wang smiled and said, "So it's to be another 'unannounced exercise'? Test my ability to react?"

Ryan laughed and said, "No, no. We just want to make

sure the patch took, and it's watching the PLA exercises. That's all."

"Good, because with the social unrest going on and those same massive exercises, now is not the time to conduct a drill. It could confuse things."

Chen said, "We at the NCIST completely agree. We just want to continue the experiments. See what the algorithm can pick up with the ongoing exercises. That's all."

Colonel Wang nodded and shouted across the room, "Fei, what is MANTIS showing us?"

A young man of about twenty-five, small, with a uniform that looked too large for his slight frame, turned from his screen and said, "Same as always. Exercises being conducted. MANTIS seems to know the difference."

Chen said, "Well, at least it's *learning* the difference. So the upgrade took? No interruption?"

Fei said nothing, staring at his screen. Chen looked at Colonel Wang and said, "Did he hear me?"

Colonel Wang said, "Fei, did you hear the scientist's question?"

Fei ignored him too, typing on his computer. Colonel Wang said, "Fei, what are you doing?"

Fei turned from the computer screen, his face white, a bead of sweat on his head. "MANTIS is projecting an attack," he said. "Right now. It's coming right now."

Colonel Wang said, "What?"

Fei returned to the screen, punched in a stream of commands, and turned back around. "MANTIS is saying they're coming. Less than two hours. It's an invasion."

Colonel Wang turned to Ryan and said, "I thought an exercise was stupid right now."

Ryan said, "It's not an exercise. That's not from us. That's PRAYING MANTIS giving its results."

They ran over to the computer screen and saw every single indicator of a massive assault—airborne aircraft, naval vessels, sonar buoys registering submarines, the works.

Colonel Wang said, "This has to be a mistake."

Ryan said, "PRAYING MANTIS doesn't make mistakes. It just reads what is out there. This is real. We need to launch the missiles. Short-circuit the attack. It's what MANTIS was made to do."

Now beginning to sweat himself, Colonel Wang said, "I need to call my command. See what they're seeing."

Ryan said, "They don't *have* MANTIS. Only you do. They're going to see a single indicator and decide it's not a threat. We have very little time here. You must launch."

Fei watched the argument, but remained silent. Colonel Wang said, "I'm calling my commander. I need more information."

Incensed, Ryan grabbed his arm and said, "This is exactly why MANTIS was created—to prevent the stovepiping and second-guessing. Look at that damn screen! We have no time for this. If we wait, we lose. We have to stop them from breaching our perimeter."

Colonel Wang jerked his arm away and said, "I'm not attacking the People's Republic of China because some computer said so."

He ran off to an office in the back, storming forward as if he was on fire. Ryan looked at Chen, and Chen flicked his head to Zhi.

She followed him.

To Fei, Ryan said, "What's MANTIS saying now?"

Looking sick, Fei said, "Same thing. They're building up for an assault. The Kinmen Islands are already being attacked." He turned from the computer screen and said, "Surely we can confirm that, right? If the Kinmen garrison is under assault, we'd know, right?"

"Not if they took them out quickly. There'd be nobody to talk on the radio."

The Kinmen island chain was the closest piece of ROC terrain to the coast of China. Consisting of fishing villages surrounded by tunnels, artillery batteries, and bunkers, it was the first line of defense against a Chinese invasion, and a necessary springboard for Chinese success.

Fei said, "Can't we call them?"

An enlisted member of the ROC, he inherently understood that a mistake here would be catastrophic, but also that his life was to follow orders.

Ryan said, "Let me go tell Colonel Wang."

He raced to the office, finding Colonel Wang on the floor, bleeding out from his neck, a secure phone handset dangling off of the desk. Zhi said, "He tried to call his higher command. That wouldn't work."

Ryan began to panic. "What have you done? I thought this was automatic! You murdered him!"

"I did, but it's really irrelevant. He would have been dead anyway in fourteen hours. And I'll murder you if you keep this up. Get out there and have them launch the missiles."

She showed him her bloodied nail and he staggered back to the door. She said, "Go launch the missiles."

He nodded and backpedaled out of the room, racing to Fei.

"Colonel Wang is still talking to the command, but Kinmen is definitely under assault. He told me to launch the missiles from Penghu. The ones working with MANTIS."

Fei said, "Launch?"

"Yes, damn it! Launch the missiles! We are under attack!"

Now fearful, Fei said, "Where is Colonel Wang? I can only launch on his command."

"He is on the phone to the Ministry of National Defense! He's trying to coordinate, but we have no time. I am your superior officer. Do as I say, now."

Fei nodded and turned to his computer screen. He put on his headset, gave some commands to the men to his left and right, and they all began punching in commands to their keyboards. Within five seconds, it was done.

# 88

A fisherman off the coast of Penghu Island hauled in his nets, the water calm and the weather balmy, the setting sun giving the sea a glow that he always enjoyed. He stacked the nets into a locker, his burly short arms strong from years of working at sea. He closed the locker, and then took a seat, just enjoying the twilight for a moment before he returned home.

He saw a flash of light from the coast of the island, and then four more. He sat up just as a Yun Feng hypersonic land attack cruise missile streaked over his boat, low enough to cause his craft to bend over in the water, the noise incredible. He leapt up, his boat still rocking, but the missile flew so fast it was lost to sight in a matter of seconds.

He had no idea what it was, but knew it couldn't be good.

George Wolffe entered the Situation Room of the White House to find chaos, the room broken up into small bands of men and women all trying to solve an intractable problem. Alexander Palmer saw him enter and came over, saying, "Things in Taiwan are growing a little tense. Are your men still there?"

George chuckled. He'd seen the CNN feed. He said, "Yeah, things a little 'tense.' And Pike is still there."

He didn't mention *why* Pike was still there.

Instead, he asked, "Did you prove the videos are fake? Do we have that shit Jerry Tribble on the hook with BackRub?"

"We do, but it's just him. BackRub ran the tests and have now disavowed him. We can't absolutely prove it was him, because anyone could have done the videos using his algorithms, but BackRub wants no part of it anymore. According to them, he never let anyone see his algorithms or the coding of his personal projects in the past, so the chance of someone else in China being responsible for it is pretty small."

"Then why don't you get that out there? Let the world know?"

Palmer shook his head and said, "Let the world know that an American firm created deep fake videos to alter an election in Taiwan? How in the hell can we do that? Putin will immediately start crowing, and the Chinese will bury us. We can't. That's just not going to happen. What we need to do is stop the protests, because we're about to be in a war."

"Why does it have to be an American? All you really need to do is prove they're fake. Tell them it was the Chinese. Why do we even have to mention Jerry Tribble? Or, hell, arrest his ass as a Chinese asset. Wouldn't that work?"

He nodded, saying, "Yeah, yeah, maybe you're on to something, but the problem right now are the protests in Taiwan. We can't overtly support the Taiwanese government without antagonizing China. All we can really do is offer platitudes about fair elections and warn China to stay away—even if we *know* they're involved. They've really got us in a bind, because it looks like China's preferred candidate is going to win the election now. But none of that is why I asked you to come tonight. What I want to know is if another shoe is about to drop. What's up with that traitor from Australia? Did Pike interdict him?"

George exhaled and said, "He did, sir. Jake Shu is dead."

Palmer's eyes went wide and he said, "What? The Taskforce killed an American citizen in Taiwan? Pike had no authority for lethal action. It was a capture mission. We didn't even know what he was doing there."

George held up his hands. "Hang on a second. Pike didn't kill him. The Chinese did, and we still don't know what he was doing, but it's apparently continuing. Pike is on the thread right now."

Palmer said, "What do you mean, 'continuing'? What was Shu working on?"

"We honestly don't know, but Pike thinks it's still going even after he was killed."

A man entered the Situation Room, saying, "I have an emergency action message from the NMCC."

Palmer turned around and said, "Bring it here."

The NMCC stood for the National Military Command Center. Buried in the basement of the Pentagon, it was the coordination mechanism between all strategic elements in an event of an attack on the United States. Focusing on missile launches and nuclear options, it was the means by which the United States could conduct a counterstrike should the worst happen, coordinating even as the missiles were inbound. As such, it continuously monitored any launch around the world from satellites in space and other sensors, a sole purpose of early warning. An EAM from them wasn't a good sign.

The man said, "We have a launch detected in the Taiwan Strait. Land attack cruise missiles."

Palmer said, "China just launched cruise missiles against Taiwan?"

"No, sir. Taiwan launched them against China. ETA on impact ten minutes."

★★★

The head of Pacific Command received the same emergency action message as the hapless members of the National Security Council, but unlike them, he had something he could do about it, with contingency plans in place. He took one look at the message and realized they were now about to be at war. He sent an immediate action alert to Carrier Strike Group 5, currently conducting freedom of navigation exercises in the South China Sea.

Aboard the USS *Ronald Reagan,* the commander received the same EAM as everyone else, but then had a follow-on message from the PACOM commander to steam directly to the Taiwan Strait. The commander saw that order and began moving the entire monolith of American power.

Comprised of an aircraft carrier, several antimissile frigates, destroyers, and a subsurface component of hunter-killer submarines, it was the most lethal force in the history of naval warfare.

And it was now turning toward Taiwan.

# 89

We remained outside the protests, waiting on the target car to exit, the tension within the crowd growing greater by the minute, with some eyeing us like we were against them. Like maybe we were secret police.

Paul said, "Maybe we should pull back a little bit, before these idiots decide we're the enemy."

I said, "Maybe so."

I got on the radio and said, "All elements, all elements, these guys are getting a little rowdy. I want to pull back from the front gate and expand the perimeter. Maintain contact for the exit, but don't let these idiots interfere."

Jennifer said, "This is Koko, we can stage right down the road, and can catch any vehicle coming from the south, but we'll leave a road in between. If he goes that way, we'll miss him."

I said, "Good enough. Knuckles, status?"

"I can do the same on the north, but we're going to have the same problem. There will be a road he can take in between my bumper location and the gate. It's small—more like an alley—but it's there."

"Not something I can prevent. It is what it is. We still have the beacon, so if we lose him out of the gate, we can locate him later."

And then my phone rang, with the encrypted ringtone of the Taskforce.

*What the hell?* I knew it was George Wolffe trying to get me to quit.

I answered officiously, "This is Pike."

"This is Wolffe. Where are you?"

Being a smart-ass, I said, "I'm in a hotel bar, spending my government per diem. Why do you ask?"

He came back hard. "Pike, Taiwan just launched a bunch of cruise missiles against China. They came from the Penghu archipelago, and the missile system is tied into an artificial intelligence experiment that Gollum Solutions was working. Jake Shu's company."

I sat up and said, "Holy shit. Dunkin was right. That bastard was going to cause a war."

"It looks that way. Are you still on the Chinese guy?"

"Yes. He's on an airbase at a Taiwanese missile command. I'm outside of it, waiting for him to appear again, but now I know why he went there."

"Wait, what? You've tracked him to a missile command?"

"Yes, sir. I wish I'd have killed him earlier. He's in there causing all of this havoc."

"Jesus Christ, Pike, that's it. You need to get inside that command, and I mean right now."

I heard the words, but didn't see I could help. I said, "What I should be doing is figuring out how to get my team out of here, because this is about to turn into a cauldron. Getting Chen Ju-Long now won't matter. The missiles are on the way."

I heard Wolffe's voice grow frantic. "Pike, we have a bunch of eggheads here who spend their entire life studying Taiwan and China. The missiles are called Yun Feng, and they're a test project. They're hypersonic land attack cruise missiles, and they have a self-destruct. They aren't fire and forget, like a bullet from a gun. You can turn them off."

"Then tell Taiwan to turn them off!"

"Pike, we don't have the time for that. We don't even have an embassy there. How long do you think it will take to even find the number of the command?"

I looked at Paul, getting no support, but thinking, *You have got to be shitting me.*

I said, "So I have ten minutes to penetrate this base, where I have no authority to be, going through a phalanx of protestors to do so, in order to convince a foreign power to blow up their own missiles because the attack they think is coming is fake?"

I heard, "Yes, Pike. That's the mission. The other one involves a lot of dead Americans and a Carrier Strike Group."

I thought about the options, then said, "And Chen Ju-Long? I'm going to have to kill him to do this. You're sanctioning that?"

I'm not even sure why I asked, because the mission was what it was. His death would be necessary to ensure success, but I wanted to know what George thought. Where was the new Taskforce line? Chen Ju-Long was a state asset, not a terrorist.

He paused, then said, "Pike . . . I can't authorize you to assassinate someone."

"But I can save the world, as long as I don't kill anyone. Is that what you're saying?"

And then George Wolffe became the leader I knew he was. "Go save the world, Pike. I'm not counting bodies at the end. Kill that asshole."

# 90

I pulled in the team to our little minivan outside of the protests, and when they were all seated, looking like we were headed to Walley World, I said, "Okay, this is a little heady, and we don't have a lot of time. Minutes actually. Taiwan has launched missiles into China because of Jake Shu and Chen Ju-Long, which is going to engender a response from China, and if you do the math, another response from the United States. The problem is it's all fake, except for the missiles flying."

I looked at Paul and said, "Just like the videos. Apparently, Jake Shu has made some program that says China is attacking Taiwan, but they aren't, and because of it, the military of Taiwan has launched cruise missiles into China. We have ten minutes before they impact. Probably eight minutes now. Our mission is to get them to self-destruct before they impact."

Veep went slack-jawed, saying, "Taiwan has attacked China? Seriously? If that's the case, we need to get the hell out of here, before it turns into Armageddon."

I smiled and said, "We *could* do that. Or we could stop the assault. They need the hit to reciprocate. We can stop that. Right now."

Knuckles said, "How are we going to do that? Have you seen the gate? We can't even get in."

I said, "Actually, I was thinking that *was* our way in."

Brett said, "I'm not sure I like the sound of this."

I said, "Yeah, you won't. The crowd is growing mean, and there are the riot police outside who are also getting antsy. They all want to see the bear."

Knuckles said, "Jesus Christ. You want us to cause a riot?"

"Yep. That's what I'm thinking. You get those men to charge the gate, and then the men on the gate will go nuts. It'll be chaos. We get through the gate and into the missile control system. But we need to do it now, because we're running out of time."

Brett said, "So I can cause a riot as a black man without getting blamed?"

I grinned. "Yeah. That's what I'm saying."

He grinned back and said, "Well, let's go get some, then."

We split up, Paul, Jennifer, and me on one side of the protestors, Knuckles, Brett, and Veep on the other. My team was the penetration team. Knuckles's team were the instigators. We closed in to the crowd and I could feel the anger. It was a mob, with the heat from each person feeding into the anger of the next, like a forest fire that turned into a hurricane of flame because of the fuel.

Jennifer said, "Pike, I'm not sure this is a good idea. These people are ready to really go off. Someone's going to get hurt."

I said, "Yeah, well, better some protestor getting clubbed than the fire that's about to come down on this entire country. You ready?"

She nodded, I glanced at Paul, saw he was good to go, and came on the net. "Knuckles, this is Pike. Are you set?"

Knuckles's team was outfitted with four water bottles each—a projectile that wouldn't hurt anyone, but *would* set off the military police. They were on a tripwire and it would take little to get them to respond—and the mob would feed off of them just like they were feeding off of each other.

He said, “Yeah, but I’m not sure this is going to work. We could end up getting our heads clubbed.”

“No other choice now. We’re down to six minutes. Execute.”

He said, “Roger that, but you’re really going to pay for this later. If I’m not in jail.”

I laughed and said, “I’ll get you out. I promise.”

Brett came on and said, “I’ve always wanted to do this. I mean, really. First one off.”

I saw something arc over the crowd, hit the shield of a military policeman, and explode in a spray of water. He sprang back at the offense, and then the rest of the team began launching their water bottles.

And that was all it took. The police came forward swinging batons and the crowd turned into a mob. Tear gas was deployed, the men behind the face shields showing true fear, and the mob overwhelmed them, storming the gates of the military base.

They spilled inside, having no idea what they intended to do, and we followed, dodging men clubbing people and protestors running amok.

Inside the chaos, to Paul, I said, “Where? Where do we go?”

He said, “This way,” and took off running. A military policeman chased him and came within striking distance before I interdicted him, slamming him to the ground.

I ripped off his helmet, said, “I’m sorry about this. You’ll understand later,” and punched him hard in the temple, knocking him out.

I leapt up and, on the radio, said, “Knuckles, Knuckles, where are you?”

“We’re in. I see you. Right behind you.”

I shouted at Paul, "Go, go!" and he took off running, Jennifer and me right behind him.

We reached a building proclaiming the 501st Missile Battalion just as a man came out front, holding a pistol. The protestors were running amok all over the place, and he waved the weapon in a manner that told me he would use it.

I said, "Paul, talk to him. Tell him to let us in."

The mob flowed around us like roaches looking for shelter, all wanting somewhere to go but having no idea why.

Paul talked to the guard in Chinese, and the guard talked back. I could tell it wasn't helpful. He waved his pistol at the protestors running all over the place, and I said, "Enough of this shit."

Jennifer said, "What are you going to do?"

"Show that asshole that force matters."

I walked up the steps to the battalion headquarters, and the man waved his gun in my face. I slapped it aside, locked up his wrist joint using the pistol he was holding, rotated around, and flipped him over my back, slamming him to the ground. I took away his pistol and said, "Paul, tell him we're not the bad guys here."

He said something to the man just as the crowd of protestors started coalescing on our position.

Jennifer said, "This is going bad."

I said, "Get inside. We're out of time."

She went in and I saw Knuckles and Brett run up. I said, "Where's Veep?"

Brett said, "Don't know. We lost him. Probably getting his ass beat. What are we doing?"

I said, "Protect this door. Don't let any of them in. I don't care what it takes, nobody penetrates here for the next five minutes."

The protestors were starting to destroy every building on the base, with Molotov cocktails being thrown, people being chased throughout the place, and the rage growing. It was starting to look like the beginning of the movie *Escape from New York*.

Brett said, "What's the force authorized?"

I said, "Hostile engagement. If they try to get in here, you stop it. If it means lethal force, you take it."

He pulled his pistol and said, "Okay. Get it done. We can't stay out here forever."

I released the man at my feet and he stood up, looking at us like we were crazy, which we most decidedly were. I said, "Paul, talk to him."

Paul said something in Chinese, and the man nodded, growing somewhat calm. I said, "Good. In fact, you're staying out here. Don't let someone die because of a language barrier."

To Knuckles, I said, "But don't let a language barrier prevent you from stopping an assault on this building."

He smiled, drew his weapon, and said, "Everybody speaks lethal force. There won't be a language barrier."

I said, "Good to go. Paul, where am I headed? Where is the command center?"

Paul talked to the guard, going back and forth with him. He turned to me and said, "Last room at the end of the hall. It's the control room."

I nodded and drew my weapon. "Jennifer, on me."

We sprinted down the hallway, ignoring the people poking their heads out of doors. When we reached the end, I looked at Jennifer and said, "Get ready to fight."

She raised her pistol at the high ready, and I pulled open the door. I entered first, scanning the room for threats, and then something like a baseball bat hit me in the right shoulder, slamming me to the ground.

I rolled over, realizing I had been shot and seeing Chen Ju-Long holding a pistol. Jennifer assaulted him, knocking the weapon out of his hands, and then his Chinese partner attacked her, stabbing out with a middle finger that had some sort of blade attached to the nail.

Jennifer whipped her hand up against her neck, and the blade punctured through her palm. She closed her fist around it and torqued the woman's wrist, bringing her to her knees, holding the hand with the blade still through her fist, the ceramic puncturing the back side of her palm.

I leapt up, getting back in the fight. Chen Ju-Long raised his fists as if this was some even contest he was about to win. With my left arm, I crouched down and scooped up my pistol. He attempted to do the same with the weapon Jennifer had knocked out of his hands, and I fired, missing him, but causing him to stop.

He looked at me and said, "You can't stop what's coming. I don't even know why you care. This is about China. Not the United States."

I said, "No. This is about Dunkin, you miserable piece of shit."

And broke the trigger again, sending him flying backwards, his head misshapen by the bullet.

I turned to Jennifer's fight, seeing her still tied to the woman by the blade through her palm. Jennifer jammed her weapon against the Chinese assassin's head and the woman screamed.

Jennifer pulled the trigger, dropping the assassin to the floor, the weight of her body pulling the blade out of Jennifer's hand.

I said, "You okay?"

She cradled her bloodied palm and said, "Yeah. Yeah, I'll live."

I rotated into the room and saw Fly Boy. I pointed my pistol. "Turn off those missiles. Right now."

He raised his hands and said, "I can't do that. I don't have the authority."

"Who does?"

"Nobody. Nobody does. They are on the way."

I saw a clock on the wall counting down, and it was at less than thirty seconds. I said, "Is that impact?"

"Yes."

"Turn it off. Self-destruct those missiles."

"No. China is attacking us. That is our first line of defense."

I took two steps to him, put my barrel in his face, and pulled the trigger, exploding his head and dropping him to the ground.

I turned into the room and saw the death had the intended effect, with everyone trembling at my capacity for violence. I said, "China is not attacking, but they will be soon if you let those missiles strike. Who can turn it off?"

The clock ticked into twenty seconds.

There were four Taiwanese sitting at computer terminals, looking at me like I was crazy. I went to the first man and put my barrel against his skull, saying, "You're all going to die today unless someone does what I ask. Fuck China. You'll be dead anyway."

A man on the other side leapt up. "I can do it. I can do it."

The clock ticked past ten seconds.

I said, "Do it. Right fucking now."

He sat back down and began typing, the others following his lead. I watched the clock go down to zero, and then impact.

I looked at Jennifer and said, "Probably a good time to get back to the Rock Star bird."

The man from the far side of the room said, "Self-destruct actuated. There was no impact."

He looked at me, then hung his head, saying, "I just destroyed our chances at defending Taiwan."

I exhaled and said, "Nope. You just saved your country."

# 91

Jennifer came back into the bar looking grim. I said, "What's up? Is Amena okay?"

"She is, but her roommate is not. Her father is dead, and she's headed back to China."

I said, "Well, we knew that."

Her eyes flashed and she said, "Yes, *we* knew that, but it doesn't make it any easier on Amena. She thinks she killed the guy by talking to you. And she's grown fond of her roommate. She feels guilty."

I said, "At the end of the day, she sort of *did* kill him."

I was sitting at a high-top table with the rest of the team. Jennifer took a seat on the barstool next to me and said, "Don't you *ever* tell her that. She followed your commands, and now her roommate's dad is dead. You can't let her think she's responsible for that."

I held up my hands. "Okay, okay. It'll be a natural event. He had a heart attack as far as I know."

She squinted at me, then said, "You have to take this parenting thing seriously. You can't treat her like your teammates. She looks up to you, and she's young. Impressionable."

I said, "I get it. I get it. Sorry."

Jennifer said, "Well, I hope so, because I told her she could come on the honeymoon. Which will happen as soon as we get home."

I said, "What?" and the table began laughing. Knuckles said, "Can I come too? Someone needs to record that shitshow."

I ignored him, saying to Jennifer, "Are you serious? I was just making a joke."

To my left, Knuckles said, "Not very funny."

I turned to him. "Sort of like the joke you did by leaving Jennifer and me in the wind? While we were fighting a bunch of Chinese assassins?"

"Wasn't me who gave that call. That was you."

Veep said, "Or maybe like sort of leaving me in the wind while you went to find a bunch of Chinese assassins."

Which made me smile. He had a lump on his cheek, and both of his eyes were black because he'd been tuned up by the military police after we'd entered the base, so I guess he had a point.

I said, "Okay, okay. We're not all perfect here."

Brett raised his glass and said, "A toast to that."

I said, "Do I really have to drink this?"

Knuckles said, "Oh yeah, you do. I'm sick of the pirate rum and Coke thing. I'm a bourbon man."

It had been two and a half days since our actions in Tainan, and things in Taiwan had calmed down considerably. The enormous attack against the island state hadn't occurred, and the protests had dwindled to nothing—mainly because the United States had shown through forensic evidence that the videos produced were deep fakes created by China.

What they hadn't said was that the man who'd produced them—an asshole named Jerry Tribble—was a U.S. citizen in league with the devil, but that was okay. After the attack had imploded, he'd fled Beijing and had landed at New York City's JFK Airport, where he was met by two federal agents with a host of questions.

I wish I'd been there, because the interrogation wouldn't have been as gentle as he received. Either way, he was done, because his company basically sold him down the river to protect themselves—and then the FBI had found forensic evidence that connected him to Jake Shu. He was going to burn in a bonfire.

We'd fled Tainan after the attack, getting out with the chaos of the ongoing protests, and had returned to our hotel, where I'd slept for ten hours straight after taking care of my wound. I had a through-and-through gunshot to my shoulder, which Brett had treated in the hotel, and I considered going to a hospital, because Brett might be a great medic, but he wasn't a doctor. But I hadn't, because Paul had worked some magic and brought a doctor to me.

I don't know what contacts he had, but somehow he'd managed to get an actual man of science to see me instead of some witch doctor from a temple waving incense. The bullet wound was clean, and hadn't impacted any bones or tendons, and because of it, I had to endure a ration of shit about being a crybaby—but I didn't mind. I'd seen gunshot wounds plenty of times, and if it was just flesh, I was very, very lucky. Jennifer's wound was much cleaner, a simple stab through the palm. She got a stitch or two and was good to go. I'd be wearing a sling for a while.

We'd spent a couple days hiding out, wondering if we were going to get arrested by the security establishment of Taiwan, and then Paul had showed up again, telling us he'd regained his status as a full-fledged member of the National Security Bureau.

To celebrate, he'd taken us back to the same shopping area where we'd rescued him. Originally he was intending to go to the specific restaurant where we'd found him, but as we walked, Knuckles had seen a bar on the way—an eclectic place that sold only whiskey, no rum.

He'd demanded we stop, and so we had, and he'd ordered us a round of bourbon—something called The Prisoner, made by a place called Bardstown Bourbon, from a region known as the bourbon capital of the world. I'd learned two things: One, Knuckles was really into bourbon, and two, even as I complained, it was pretty good stuff. And the name was about perfect for what we'd gotten away with.

We raised our glasses and I said, "What's the toast?"

Paul said, "To my country. May it remain peaceful."

I said, "I'll definitely drink to that."

After we'd stopped the attack, we'd fled the base on the run, heading back to Taipei, and I'd called George Wolffe in the Situation Room, telling him what we'd done. He couldn't believe it. In fact, he didn't believe it at first.

When the phone had connected, he'd said, "Get out. Get the team out now. We're going to war. Get on the Rock Star bird and get the hell out of there. I have to go. Things are a little crazy here."

I'd said, "Hey, sir, calm down. The missiles didn't impact."

"We saw the impact from satellites. China is about to go nuts. We have a carrier strike group launching."

I said, "You need to stop that. The missiles didn't impact. What you saw was the self-destruct. There is no damage to China, other than a debris field of missile parts."

He said, "What?"

"We were able to stop it. China has no pretext to launch a war now. All they have is four missiles that blew themselves up over open terrain. You really need to get that to the National Command Authority, because if that carrier group postures, it could be the trigger they were looking for."

"Are you positive about this? I mean, absolutely sure?"

"Yes."

He said, "I gotta go." And hung up. Ten minutes later, he called me back, now much calmer, saying, "Well, well, well, looks like you guys saved the world."

Driving back to the hotel, Paul behind the wheel, I'd said, "My stock in trade. All it took was a bullet to my shoulder."

He'd grown serious at that point. "Are you okay? Anybody else hurt?"

I said, "I'm not okay, but I'm not on death's door. Jennifer got dinged up a little too, but we're going to be fine. We might need some help to get out of here, though. I have no idea how Taiwan is going to look at our actions."

"What do you mean?"

"I had to . . . go a little extreme."

"What's that mean?"

"It means I had to kill some people. One of them was a colonel in the ROC Air Force, but he was a traitor just like Jake Shu. The NSB guy I told you about was with me the entire way. He can back it up."

"I thought he was disavowed?"

"He might be, but he's a good dude. We need to protect him as well."

Wolffe sighed, then said, "Don't worry about any of that. With what we've done for Taiwan, we could make him the next president. They owe us big time. Just lay low for a couple of days, and then leave. You're protected."

I'd said, "Because you say so?"

I could almost see the smile through the phone when he

answered. “No. Because the president of the United States says so. Trust me, you’re good.”

Two days later, I was drinking bourbon with the man who’d saved his country. We clinked glasses, took a sip, and I said, “So you’re back in the game now, huh?”

Paul said, “Yes. My computer was my passport. The proof was on it from my messages back and forth between me and my boss. The entire file about Colonel Ryan was on there. I’m no longer a Ronin. They’re even talking about giving me a medal.”

I knew that the United States had something to do with that decision, but said nothing. Brett said, “You certainly deserve it. No doubt. What about the mole you talked about before? Did they find him?”

Paul grew cold, saying, “No. They have not. He is still inside, somewhere. The game will continue, with China still fighting us.”

I said, “But at least they failed this time. It looks like the election is back on track.”

“Yes. The expertise of the United States with those videos not only helped us, but others under China’s boot as well. Nobody believes them anymore.”

He took a sip, then coughed, a deep, rattling thing.

I said, “You okay?”

He smiled and said, “Not enough rest. I caught some kind of cold and I can’t shake it.”

# Acknowledgments

This has been one of the weirdest writing years I've had since I decided to give writing a try. I had originally planned on setting the manuscript a year after the elections in Taiwan—January of 2021—keeping the timeline intact with the release date. Then a little bug called coronavirus destroyed that notion. As I was locked in my house, like everyone else, I just couldn't figure out a way for Pike and the team to go globetrotting around during a pandemic. Nothing I'd researched matched anymore. How would Pike conduct surveillance when the streets were essentially empty? How would the team fly between countries when there were no aircraft in the sky? In the end, I decided to simply set the novel in the fall of 2019, when I did the actual research—before the pandemic—and right before the actual elections in Taiwan.

The story itself began brewing long before our COVID trials, with little bits of information pricking me that eventually coalesced into a plot. I would be remiss if I didn't mention the biggest thing poking at me was my wife, the Deputy Commander of Everything. She has about fourteen diving qualifications and has been wanting me to set a book in Australia so she could dive the Great Barrier Reef. As much as I would have liked to set a story Down Under, I needed more than the reef for a manuscript. That something came a few years ago and planted a seed in my head.

While conducting research in Lesotho, Africa, for *Operator Down,* I traveled to the country's government center, which was brand new with some areas still under construction. On the still-under-construction walls were instructions for the workers—what I assumed were the usual, "wear a hardhat" type stuff, but it was written in Chinese. I asked my guide why there were Chinese instructions when we were in Africa. She said China was footing the bill for the complete reconstruction of Lesotho's government center. When I asked why, she said, "No reason. They just want to help."

From my own research into Lesotho—in fact, the premise of *Operator Down*—I knew that it was rich in rare earth minerals and diamonds, and I found the explanation hard to believe. Inherently, I knew China wanted something in exchange—they just weren't saying it out loud. Yet. It was my first real-world exposure to China's Belt and Road Initiative, whereby China seeds its tentacles through the world ostensibly out of goodwill, but in reality to control. At the time, it was a side note, because *Operator Down* had nothing to do with China, so I let it go. And then China just kept appearing.

*American Traitor* was driven by four disparate factors:

1. In 2019, the Japanese lost an F-35 Joint Strike Fighter off of the Sea of Japan, in an accident that was decidedly strange. How on earth does a pilot, flying the most advanced fighter on earth, drive it into the ocean at 600 knots? I started digging into that and was surprised to find that components for the F-35 are built all over the world—to include a production facility in Australia. The DCOE had something in her favor.

2. The battle for artificial-intelligence research is reaching a crescendo, with China trying to steal everything the United States invents while simultaneously pouring billions into its own research—some done by our own American

companies—and also using that technology to turn its country into a surveillance state. Deep Fakes are a real thing, and in the fight to prove a fake versus the fight to develop one, the "proving" side of the house is lagging. It has become a disinformation tool that will literally make the phrase, "Believe it when you see it" irrelevant.

3. China is expanding the Belt and Road Initiative throughout the world, using both hard power and soft power. Hard power includes building up rock atolls in the South China Sea along what they call the "nine-dash line," basically claiming that those bits of rock are now the forward line of Chinese sovereignty located on the other side of the sea. Nobody—including the United Nations—believes it's legal, so China uses soft power, which, in a word, is economic. Someone in the NBA supports Hong Kong in its fight for democracy against China and China stops the NBA from playing inside the country—a multimillion-dollar loss. What happens? LeBron James chastises the people complaining because it's hurting the NBA. Disney wants to sell the movie *Abominable* in China? In order to do so, one of the maps in that animated picture must portray the nine-dash line, instead of the boundaries the entire world recognizes. It's insidious, but real.

4. China's president, at what is analogous to the U.S. State of the Union, said that he would not pass down the "Taiwan question" to another generation. It has to be solved, which is easy to read as "Solved in our favor." He is hell-bent on the reunification of Taiwan with the mainland, just as he was with Hong Kong.

With all of that as grist for the mill, I started researching, and what I found astonished me. Australia has awakened to the threat, but not before it's basically been infiltrated from the grass roots with Chinese interference. One of the books I read, called *Silent Invasion,* was written by an Australian scholar about the insidious Chinese infiltration of all facets of the Australian government and economy. When it came time to publish, the Chinese brought enormous pressure to bear on the publisher, and they declined to put the book out. Several other publishers followed suit, refusing to publish. Nobody wanted to upset the apple cart of Chinese investments. Not long after it was written, one of the largest ports in Australia—Darwin—was sold to the Chinese. That was a wakeup call, and the book was released afterward. Then, a man of Chinese descent was running for parliament, and blurted out that he'd been paid to do so on behalf of China. He ended up dead shortly after. Bo "Nick" Zhao is a real person, and he really died. Nobody can prove that he was killed by the Chinese, but it was decidedly strange that he said he was being paid by China to infiltrate parliament, and then ended up dead. Not to make light of the tragedy, but that sort of thing was working in the DCOE's favor. I was focused on Taiwan—but Australia had so much intrigue going on, we *had* to go there. And so the DCOE got to dive the reef.

We traveled to both Australia and Taiwan, and there were many interesting spots I wanted to include in this novel but was overwhelmed by the scope. Both countries are incredible places to visit—if the pandemic ever leaves and you get the chance, put it on your bucket list. I had a sweet leg up from my friend Tami, an old Army buddy I've written about before for her help with Jennifer's character. She's one generation removed from Taiwan and had visited before, and recommended some sights like the Shilin night market, Taipei 101, and other spots in the country. She knew who I was, what I write, and immediately homed in on what I would want.

In that vein, I'm forever indebted to a man you've probably read about, if you've come this far in the book. Yu-Feng "Paul" Kao is a real person—but not a secret agent. My twin brother worked on a contract in Taiwan years ago, and he told me that he had "contacts" in Taiwan if I needed some help. Usually, when friends or family gets involved in these trips, it ends counterproductively, whereby I want to do research and the "contacts" want to go party with the American Friend, leaving me wasting time at whatever event they think is cool. In this case, it worked out perfectly. Paul showed us all the intricacies of Taiwan, from the temples to the red-light district, explaining everything along the way. He was so helpful that I named the character after him.

As for Australia, that was all the DCOE. She read a synopsis of *American Traitor,* saw what I needed to do, and then began working how to get us up to the East Coast for a dive. Which is where Kuranda entered the book. I wanted to include a dive scene in the plot, maybe fighting off a great white, but I couldn't manage it. Hell, I couldn't manage a crocodile scene from another place we went—because I was kicking myself for using piranhas in *Hunter Killer.* I didn't want to have two scenes that were so similar. In between, the DCOE set up everything from Sydney to Cairns. I would add Brisbane to that list, but the truth is the only reason Brisbane made the book at all was that our plane broke down on takeoff—literally—causing us to spend the night there. I'll give her credit, though, because while I just wanted to sleep after a ten-hour flight from Taiwan, and about five additional hours sitting in the Brisbane airport, she wanted to see what was there—since we were stuck anyway. She found the river walk in the book, and we had a beer at the same table where

Control drinks coffee. Which is why she's the DCOE and I love her . . .

I have to thank my awesome team at Morrow. Even with the pandemic at its height, right at the end of a book tour while trying to produce another one, they worked tirelessly to take Pike Logan and the Taskforce Team to the next level, all of it in the middle of the worst catastrophe the United States has seen in my lifetime. I'm indebted to my editor, David Highfill, for continuing to enhance my work while simultaneously trying to survive in New York City. Selfishly, I had hoped the pandemic would give him pause from my manuscript, but it did not. As always, it required more work, but the book is much better in the end. My marketing team, led by Tavia Kowalchuk, is top-notch and always using dynamic means to reach new markets—especially now—and Danielle Bartlett, my publicist, who keeps me on my toes with more interview requests than I can possibly meet. Yes, I hate Zoom now. And, of course, the sales team who makes sure my books are available all over the country. They are doing phenomenal work under dire circumstances and I'm so thankful.

If you prefer Pike Logan on an audiobook, I'm sure you're familiar with Rich Orlow, who has been narrator of almost every book I've written. The audience loves him and he continues to bring Pike alive in the most appealing way. Thanks so much.

Finally, to my agent, John Talbot, thanks very much for sticking with me and staying on top of it all. You've been here from the beginning and it's been a journey, to say the least.

HAVE YOU READ *HUNTER KILLER*?

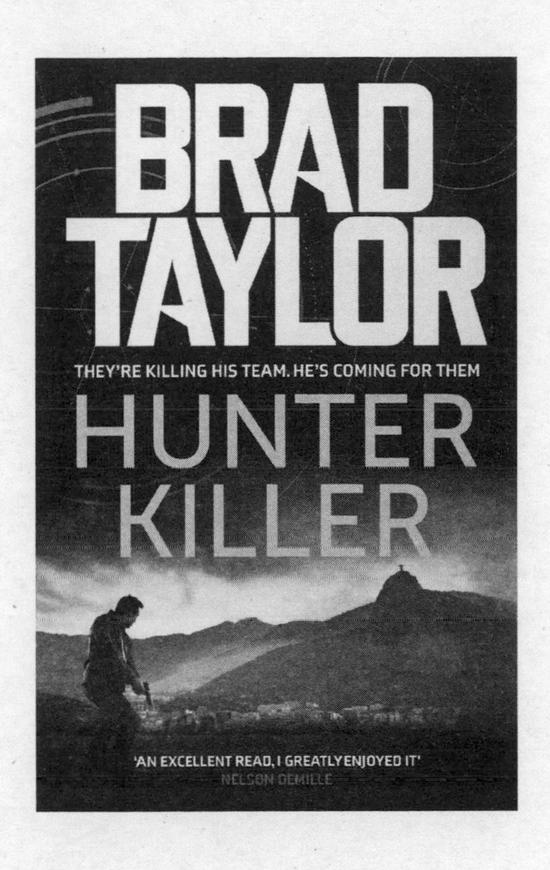


THEY'RE KILLING HIS TEAM.
HE'S COMING FOR THEM.
HAVE PIKE LOGAN AND THE
TASKFORCE MET THEIR MATCH?